I0554053

Let It Be

B.K. Wright

Let It Be

Beau to Beau Books
E-mail: info@beautobeau.com
Website: http://www.beautobeau.com
ISBN: 978-1-6184-5189-7
Printed in the United States of America

History is written by the victors. That which society does not want known is omitted. Such is the history of Male Love, which has been revered and prevalent in societies from the earliest times of record. Beau to Beau fictional stories of Male Love are written with sincerity and passion, to hopefully inspire gay men to enjoy their lives to the fullest, without shame, which is deservedly theirs to be realized. Shame is not the gay man's to be borne. Shame is the lot of the ignorant!

Among the Greeks, Male Love did more than dare speak its name; it fairly shouted it from the rooftops. It was one of the fundamental traditions of Greek life, one practiced and enjoyed to the fullest. Indeed, it was a social must which no poet, no philosopher, no artist disdained to explore. It was discussed in public as a matter of course and included in the reflections of the greatest minds.

Table of Contents

Along Came Two

David's life is very fulfilling. He has a great career, good friends, and now he has a son. When he takes his son Trey on a much deserved vacation, he meets someone who he thinks may be the one for him. Both fathers, the two men have no idea if or how they can possibly be together or if they can some day become "one big happy family."

One

Vacation for Two

Holding his son's hand, David hurried toward the gate when their flight number was called. "I love you, Daddy," Trey said, as he looked up into the eyes of the man he worshipped. These four little words, David thought, were the sincerest and the sweetest words he had ever heard. For years, David had dreamed of being a father and finally, one week before his fortieth birthday, this dream had been realized. His fortieth year, the year which is dreaded by so many, had been the happiest year of David's life. He sometimes wished he had a partner to share his life with, but for now Trey was all he needed.

For the next two weeks he and Trey were going to do something that neither had done. They were going on a cruise. David had decided to spare no expense on his and Trey's first vacation as father and son. Trey was going to experience the very best that David could give him.

Trey had never flown before, but he did know the difference between the first class section on an airplane and the coach section. "Right here, son," David said as he stopped Trey from getting too far ahead of him.

"Oh, boy, we're in first class, Daddy?"

"That's right, son, first class."

David hoped he never got used to being called Dad or Daddy. He wanted to feel that wonderful feeling he felt when Trey called him Daddy for the rest of his life. They settled into their very comfortable leather seats, and David helped Trey recline his seat just as he had his own. Trey was staring out the window, watching everything with great wonderment, as only a child can. David could see over Trey out the window also, but was more excited to be watching Trey. Life's treasures looked so much brighter, much more spectacular, through the eyes of a child.

So many emotions were coursing through David right now that he couldn't speak, but words were not important now. Being with Trey on this once-in-a-lifetime adventure was what was important now. From their home just outside of Denver, it had been a relatively short drive to the airport, but they were in for a long flight to Atlanta where they would board their connecting flight to Miami, and from there they would begin their cruise. "Look, Daddy," Trey would say at every new site he viewed from his coveted window seat. David would smile and look, but he was mostly looking at Trey. Trey was his life. Trey was his son, and having a son or daughter was the one part of his life he had almost convinced himself would remain unfilled.

David had been told by many that adoption was not an option for a gay man, that no agency would ever approve him. He was just glad that he hadn't listened to all the negative comments, but had persevered in spite of them. Trey had needed a home and someone to love and care for him. David felt that he was the one who had truly been blessed, however. It had been Trey who had transformed David's house into a home filled with love. After this past year with Trey, David could barely remember his life without him.

It was cloudy when the back wheels of the plane arose from the runway and they were airborne, but as the plane ascended through and above the clouds, Trey was wide-eyed. "The clouds are below us, and the sky is as blue as I've ever seen it, Daddy."

David smiled and said, "It sure is, son, it sure is."

As the plane reached its cruising altitude and there wasn't much to see outside his window, Trey settled back in his seat just as they were being served breakfast. He thought this was paradise. He loved eating breakfast on the plane, and hadn't felt sick during any part of the trip so far. David had brought along motion sickness tablets just in case, but so far Trey was fine. David had hoped for a smooth flight, without turbulence, so that this would be an enjoyable one for Trey.

Surprised that Trey hadn't become at least a little bored on the long flight to Atlanta, David was happy to color with him in his coloring books, and he was even happier when Trey offered to read a book to him. Trey was in the first grade this year and loved to learn. Every night they would read at least one book. Watching Trey progress in his schoolwork was more satisfying to David than it was to Trey, David was pretty sure of that.

When the pilot announced their descent into Atlanta, David helped Trey adjust his seat, and buckled his seatbelt for him. The plane flew downward through the clouds this time, which fascinated Trey, and once they had emerged through the clouds, they could see the city of Atlanta below them awaiting their visit. "Are we here, Daddy?" Trey was wide-eyed with anticipatory excitement.

"Not yet, buddy. We change planes here, and board another one to Miami."

They packed their carry-on bags and made their way into the airport. They had just enough time to use the restroom, get something to drink, and relax for about twenty minutes. When they heard their flight number called once again, they picked up their bags and boarded the plane. "We're big time travelers now, aren't we Dad?"

"We sure are." David marveled at everything Trey said. He couldn't get enough of him. They were in first class once again, and Trey made himself at home. He knew the drill now, and felt proud to be with his Daddy. Trey loved David more than David could possibly know. David was Trey's dream come true.

The plane ascended once again, and before they knew it they were landing again, this time in Miami, and waiting in line to board the cruise ship from Miami. Trey had never seen the ocean before, and now he was going to be a part of it. He also had never seen a ship this big before. He had toy ships at home, but this ship was huge. "Look how big it is, Daddy."

This was David's first cruise, too, and he was as impressed as Trey. "I see, Trey. It's bigger than I thought, that's for sure."

"It's bigger than I thought, too, Daddy."

David smiled at Trey's imitation of his own comment.

They boarded the magnificent ocean liner to be greeted by a welcoming crew unlike anything Trey had seen on television. This wasn't just any ship; this was the Disney Dream, the very majestic third ship in the Disney Cruise Line fleet. David had gone all out for Trey's Disney cruise, and had booked the Walter E. Disney Suite, one of the very exclusive Concierge Royal Suites, located on Deck 12.

David's and Trey's vacation cruise began with the best that Disney had to offer. It began with a priority check-in at a dedicated very exclusive check-in station. They were met immediately following check-in by the concierge team at a private welcome reception. Trey's eyes were wide as he took in everything that was happening all around him. David couldn't take his eyes off Trey. Seeing everything, or anything for that matter, through the eyes of a child is a treasure more precious than gold and David knew that he was truly blessed.

David and Trey were escorted to their suite by a very bubbly young lady who presented Trey with his favorite stuffed Disney characters. "How did you know these were my favorites?" Trey asked in wonderment.

The lady just smiled and winked at Trey. David had listed Trey's favorite Disney characters on their check-in form. The lady talked mostly to Trey on the way to their suite, as she boasted about all the fun activities offered on the cruise.

When she opened the door to their suite, Trey's eyes once again were wide with amazement as he held tightly to David's hand. David tightened his grip on Trey's little hand to help him feel more at ease. David thought Trey might be feeling a little overwhelmed by this amazing experience. The lady showed them around their suite, and then politely excused herself.

"Is this just for us, Daddy?" Trey's big eyes seemed to penetrate David's blue ones.

"This is just for you and me, Trey. Let's look around."

Trey held David's hand as they looked around. The bedroom was huge. There were two bathrooms, a dining area, a separate media library, living area, rain shower as well as whirlpool tub, pull-down beds, and walk-in closets. "This is like a house, isn't it, Daddy?"

"It sure is, Trey, it sure is." David knew now why he had been saving his money all these years. He had been saving it for Trey. David was particularly impressed by the fine artwork that graced the walls of the suite, and the Art Deco décor throughout was magnificent. Elegance surrounded them throughout the entire suite.

Their luggage was waiting for them in their suite when they arrived, and they busied themselves unpacking before seeing the rest of the ship. David thought that Trey needed a little quiet time after having had so much stimulation from the time of his early morning awakening. They talked about the day as they unpacked, and David realized that he was more tired than Trey. Trey probably could have gone another twelve hours without resting. "Let's go look around, Trey." Trey hurried to take David's hand, and the two of them left the suite.

They ventured into the concierge lounge which was located among the other concierge suites. It was exquisitely decorated in a stylish, modern way, with a giant assortment of food and beverages provided solely for their enjoyment. "Is it okay if I eat something?" Trey asked sheepishly.

"Of course you can, son. I'm a little hungry myself." David and Trey helped themselves to a small plate of assorted delectables and while Trey drank his juice, David helped himself to a cocktail.

They ate in silence, both hungrier than they had thought they were, and when finished Trey asked, "Where is everybody?"

David set down his plate and said to his precious son, "Let's go see, shall we?"

They made their way to the ship's deck where many had gathered as the ship's captain was announcing its imminent departure. "I think we found everyone Trey, or almost everyone." Once again, those big brown eyes opened wide as Trey looked around at the crowd that had gathered for the ship's big adventure on the open water. They found a place to watch as the ship made its way out to sea. David was just as amazed as Trey. He felt so alive here with his son. The sea was beautiful, and David looked forward to a relaxing and exciting vacation with his son, a boy who was definitely deserving of fun.

David knew that Trey had lived with his grandmother from the time of his birth until his grandmother's death when Trey was four. For six months following her death, Trey had lived with a foster family. David had heard of Trey through one of his patients, who had told David that the little boy was very sad and that his foster parents were too busy to spend much time with him. Fortunately, Trey wasn't in foster care for long. David had fallen in love with the boy from the first time he saw him, and now they were a family. Trey hadn't spoken of his grandmother to David, and David wasn't sure if the little boy really remembered her. One day David planned to talk to him to assure Trey that his grandmother had loved him a lot, and that it was not by choice that she had left him. This past year, however, had been devoted to making sure that Trey felt safe and loved. They had been through a lot this past year, both David and Trey, and this vacation was a culmination of both their trials and their triumphs.

As the ship reached the open water, Trey, still holding tightly to David's hand, looked up and gasped. "Daddy," he exclaimed, as he pointed. David looked up to see what had claimed Trey's attention. David could not believe his eyes.

There above them was the water coaster David had seen pictures of in the brochure. Trey and David both loved the water. David had an indoor pool installed in the sunroom of his house when he adopted Trey. "Look," Trey exclaimed again, as he continued to point and watch one of the water tubes as it carried two passengers along their amazing journey through the enclosed slide.

One of the crew members noticed the excited look on Trey's face, and stopped to tell them about this magnificent adventure ride. He stooped down until he was at Trey's eye level, and began to describe the ride as if he were telling him a story. "This elevated water coaster is the first of its kind at sea and travels seven hundred sixty-five feet, with a four deck drop. Its name is the AquaDuck, and it is an extraordinary elevated coaster that circles the entirety of the ship."

Trey was so engrossed in this man's story and watching the two travelers making their way through it that he didn't notice that David was impressed with this man also. The man, about David's age, had his arm loosely around Trey's waist. David thought that the man's legs must be killing him, but he still continued to remain at eye level of Trey to tell him the rest of the story. "The guests enter this amazing journey on Deck 12, Aft from where they are propelled at high speeds through an acrylic tube, journeying up, down, around, and at one point they circle off the side of the ship over the ocean." The man pointed to where the half circle was at the other end of the ship. "Wow," was Trey's response. "Then this fantastic journey through this amazing ride takes the guests through the Forward Funnel, then makes a four deck drop into a lazy river." The man placed extra emphasis on just the right words so that Trey could almost feel the ride even though he wasn't on it, yet. "When you're way up there, you can see the ocean, and also the ship right here where we're standing, but it will be below you. Does that sound like fun?"

"Oh, yes. Daddy, can we go?"

"You bet, buddy, let's go right now," David replied, looking forward to the ride himself.

When the man stood up, David said, "Thank you for that. I'm David." The man shook David's hand and introduced himself. "I'm Kurt."

For a moment the two men stared at each other, neither wanting the moment to end. David wondered if he saw something in Kurt's eyes, other than kindness. David felt a tingle that he hadn't felt in a long time. Very impressed with his taking the time to tell Trey this amazing story, David wanted to know more about Kurt.

"Would you like to go on the ride with my daughter and me?" Kurt asked. Neither man saw a ring on the other's finger, and each more than a little curious about the other.

"Can you get away from your work, Kurt?"

"Oh, I'm not a crew member, just a passenger. I'm here with my daughter, Cheyenne."

David felt embarrassed, and even more impressed that a fellow passenger would take the time to share as much as he had with a boy he didn't know. "Oh, I'm sorry. I thought you were a crew member because you took the time to describe this fabulous ride so vividly."

"Well, thank you very much. I've learned to tell stories because of Cheyenne. She loves to hear them."

David and Kurt were still holding the other's hand, not feeling uncomfortable at all. When they finally let go of the other's hand, they continued to look into each other's eyes. To Kurt, David's eyes looked like small replicas of the ocean that was all around them. To David, Kurt's eyes reminded him of the beauty of the wheat at the time of the summer harvest on the farm in eastern Colorado where he had grown up. These eyes were a medium shade of brown, not too light, not too dark, but just right. They complemented Kurt's dark brown skin color, just as David's eyes complemented the paleness of his skin.

"Come with me. I'll get Cheyenne. She's with her nanny."

David and Trey followed Kurt to his suite which was, coincidentally, very close to theirs. David laughed when they arrived at Kurt's door. Kurt looked puzzled. Then David explained that his and Trey's suite was very close, the Walter E. Disney Suite, and here they were at the Roy O. Disney Suite. Kurt laughed at this, too. Kurt opened the door to the suite, and they all stepped inside.

"Daddy, this is like ours almost," Trey pointed out.

"Yes, it is. How about that?"

Trey looked around with the same wide eyed look that he had when they had walked into their own suite.

Cheyenne came running when she heard Kurt's voice, and he scooped her up in his arms. "Daddy, Daddy."

Kurt kissed her on the cheek. "Cheyenne, this is Trey and his daddy, David."

Shyly, she said hello, and then buried her face in Kurt's shoulder. She was tall, like Kurt, and David thought she was close to Trey's age, though Trey was tall for his age of five and a half.

"Hi, Cheyenne, I'm Trey, and this is my daddy, David."

Cheyenne turned her head to look at this boy who was not at all shy. Trey went on, hoping to impress his new friend. "I'm five and a half. How old are you, Cheyenne?"

Cheyenne held up four fingers in response, and Kurt added that she would be five in six months.

"Cheyenne's in pre-Kindergarten," Kurt added.

"I'm in the first grade," Trey boasted proudly. "I can read," he added, hoping to impress her.

"I thought Trey and David might want to try out the big water slide, and I thought we would go too."

"Okay. Daddy promised we would." Cheyenne hugged her daddy tightly after she shared this news with Trey.

"We'll go get on our swimsuits and meet you in the lounge," David offered, and he and Trey left Kurt and Cheyenne to change, too.

"I like them, Daddy." Trey's first words once the two of them were back inside their suite echoed David's.

"I do, too, Trey."

They changed quickly. Trey couldn't wait to try the waterslide, and David couldn't wait to see Kurt again.

David and Trey arrived at the concierge lounge just as Kurt and Cheyenne did, and the four of them made their way to the entrance of the waterslide. The four of them shared a raft, with Trey in front, then Cheyenne, Kurt, and David. They held tightly to the hand rails, but they couldn't help but lean backward as they rounded corners and were thrust upward by the rapidly moving water. When Kurt leaned backward into David, both men felt sensations that neither had known for quite awhile. When the ride took them out over the ocean, all four travelers marveled at the site of the open water below them. It was as if they had defied gravity and were suspended only by the water.

Trey and Cheyenne squealed with delight as the raft made its four deck drop before floating into the lazy river. David and Kurt didn't squeal, but did feel as if their stomachs had been thrust upward into their chests.

"Can we go again?" Cheyenne and Trey asked in unison.

Kurt looked at David, and David looked at Kurt. "One more time and then we'll take it easy for awhile," Kurt spoke up, and David quickly agreed.

David said quietly to Kurt, "One more time might be all this soon-to-be forty-year-old can take."

Kurt laughed, and added, "Try forty-five."

They smiled at each other, and followed Trey and Cheyenne back to the entrance to the slide. David would have guessed Kurt to be younger than he, but now knew that David was the younger one.

When they had enjoyed the slide a second time, David and Kurt were tired, but Trey and Cheyenne were two balls of energy. When David and Trey walked Kurt and Cheyenne to their suite, Cheyenne's nanny was preparing for a popcorn and movie night, which Cheyenne loved. "Can Trey stay for popcorn and movie night, Daddy?"

"Sure, honey."

Kurt really preferred a quiet night with a couple of drinks. David could sense that Kurt was tired, or perhaps weary, and offered him a drink and conversation in his and Trey's suite while the kids enjoyed their evening. Kurt gladly accepted.

David spoke to Trey privately to be sure that he was okay with the evening's plans. David had promised himself and Trey that he would always tell Trey the truth, and would never make decisions without him that affected him. Trey, the ever easygoing child, graciously agreed to the plan. "I'm not ready to go to bed yet, Daddy. This will be fun." David and Kurt wouldn't be far away, so neither was worried.

David poured a drink for Kurt and one for himself, and then seated himself on the sofa not far from Kurt. "I'm beat," David remarked, as he leaned back on the sofa.

"It's tough being a single parent, isn't it?" added Kurt, and then immediately regretted it. "I'm sorry, David, I'm being presumptuous. It's just that I didn't see a ring on your finger, so I assumed." He turned to face David, and David turned to him.

"Don't be sorry, Kurt. You're absolutely right. I am a single father. I adopted Trey about a year ago." David wasn't sure if he should have added this last part. He knew it was a statement just begging for questions.

Kurt didn't ask any, though. "I'm a single dad, too. Cheyenne was my sister's daughter, and when she and her husband were killed in a car accident two months after Cheyenne's birth, I became her guardian as stated in their will, and have since adopted her. She doesn't remember her parents, which may be for the best, but I have their wedding photo and one day I will explain it all to her. I fear that day isn't far off because Cheyenne has been hinting some about who her mommy is."

David found Kurt very easy to talk to, and their self-disclosures made them seem more vulnerable to each other. David had missed intimacy in his life, but wasn't sure if he was ready for it, and didn't know if Kurt was either.

Kurt continued to talk about Cheyenne, and David listened attentively. "Cheyenne has asked me why her skin is so much darker than mine, and I told her that her daddy was African-American, which was no big issue with her or me. She just wondered, and I feel very strongly about always telling her the truth."

Kurt finished his drink, and went to the bar to pour himself a second. He motioned for David's glass for a refill, and David gave it gladly. "So, David, where do you and Trey call home?"

"Denver, beautiful Denver."

Kurt handed David his glass, and sat down beside him. Kurt looked at him in disbelief. "We're neighbors, David. Cheyenne and I live in Colorado Springs. I'm a business consultant."

David was just as surprised. "What a coincidence. I'm a physician's assistant." Kurt smiled.

"I'm very lucky to have found Cheyenne a good nanny. She's a college student, and free room and board plus a paycheck is a student's dream. She's been with us since I became Cheyenne's dad, and she's the best. She loves Cheyenne. My job requires some air travel, so I appreciate her greatly."

David wondered if maybe Kurt and his nanny were more than friends, but she appeared to be quite a bit younger than Kurt.

Neither said anything for awhile, but each was thinking much the same thing. They had so much in common, and each was definitely attracted to the other. It was David who asked the first question. "Are you involved with anyone, Kurt?" David wished he had said "woman", "any woman."

"No, I, um, haven't really had the time, with work and Cheyenne. How about you?"

David thought for a minute. He had to know. "I haven't really thought about investing in a relationship for a couple of years. This past year with Trey has gone by so quickly, and before that it was touch and go before the adoption was final."

Very intuitive, Kurt wondered if David was trying to tell him something. "Is it difficult to adopt, as a single man, I mean? It was a little different with Cheyenne, you know."

David stood up and looked out across the verandah at the ocean. It stretched as far as he could see, an open entity, hiding no secrets. Was this a living photograph of the way he should be, and wanted to be, open, with no secrets? Lost in his own thoughts, David hadn't heard Kurt's voice. Kurt hoped he hadn't offended David. Kurt stood up and walked toward David. David's arms were folded.

Kurt surprised him when he stood in front of him and placed his arms on David's arms. He looked David directly in the eyes, and asked, "Or is it difficult to adopt as a gay man?"

David had no idea how to respond. Was Kurt mocking him, or was Kurt disclosing something to him? By the stunned look on David's face, Kurt could see clearly now what he had thought he had seen, and definitely what he had wanted to see.

Holding David's arms which were still folded, Kurt leaned in and lightly brushed David's lips with his own. Then he backed up and looked at David. David's eyes were closed and his mouth was open slightly, expecting and desiring more. Kurt unfolded David's arms and held them in his own. Then he leaned in again and kissed David again. David didn't hesitate to kiss him back, and soon they were embracing each other, enjoying the taste and feel of the other's lips.

It was David who finally broke the kiss. He held Kurt tightly, and answered his question. "Yes, Kurt, I meant that it is difficult to adopt as a gay man, but it was worth all that I had to go through to adopt Trey. He's my life."

Kurt knew exactly how it felt to be a gay father. He was one. He also knew how lonely it could be, with very little social support. Kurt kissed David on the cheek, and then leaned back to look into David's eyes. "Do you think there might be a little room in your life for two more?" David's heart was beating just as fast as Kurt's at these words.

David embraced Kurt as he answered, "Definitely, yes." David's mouth found Kurt's, forcing it open, and kissed his open mouth eagerly, forcefully, as Kurt was kissing him, too. Neither had been kissed like this in a very long time, and neither wanted to stop.

After several minutes, though, they broke the kiss, and poured themselves just one more drink. They sat on the sofa together again, but this time they weren't talking. This time they were holding each other, kissing each other, lightly on the cheek, then forcefully with open mouths. Each could feel the other's hunger for love, a hunger for each other. Kurt wanted David, and David wanted Kurt. They broke their full mouth kiss, which left each gasping for air as they held tightly to the other.

"We should stop, for now," Kurt said breathily into David's ear.

"I know," David agreed. Neither wanted to stop, though both knew they should. David and Kurt held each other for a long time. It had been far too long, they were both thinking.

"David, it can't end this way. There has to be a way." Kurt was serious now, and looking directly at David.

"It's not the end, Kurt. This is the beginning."

Kurt's heart was beating fast, as was David's. "Let's go check on the kids, it's getting late."

David agreed with Kurt, and they walked past the lounge to Kurt's suite.

The movie had just ended, and Cheyenne had fallen asleep. Trey followed sleepily behind David, as they left Kurt's suite. "Let's have brunch, guys, around 11:00 tomorrow, okay?" Kurt offered, as David and Trey were leaving.

"We'll be there," David replied, and he and Trey returned to their suite.

Trey fell asleep immediately, but David couldn't sleep. He thought about Kurt, and all they had talked about. David hadn't realized how much he missed being in a relationship until he met Kurt. But could he be in a relationship without cheating Trey? David was feeling so many emotions all at once. I need to get to sleep, he thought.

Not far from him, a sleepless Kurt was struggling with the same emotions.

Trey awoke around 9:00 the next morning, and immediately woke David. "Daddy, time to get up, rise and shine." Full of energy as usual, Trey was happily telling David about last night, watching a movie and eating popcorn with Cheyenne and her nanny. David knew he hadn't gotten to sleep before 4:00 a.m., and was struggling to wake up. He half listened and half slept as Trey chattered on. "I like Cheyenne. I'm older, so I have to teach her stuff."

At least, David thought, the kids like each other, and in blended families that was a huge battle won, or at least that's what he had been told. About an hour later David made himself a very strong cup of coffee, and Trey drank some juice. "Is it time to go yet, Daddy?"

"Not quite, buddy. Let's shower first, and then we'll get ready."

David let Trey shower first, while he drank the rest of his coffee. Boy, I'm beat, he thought. Trey watched cartoons while David showered.

The hot water felt good as it rained down over David's body. As he showered, he daydreamed that it was Kurt's hands touching his body everywhere. He dreamed that it was Kurt's hands that would relieve his erection. He leaned against the shower wall and closed his eyes. He massaged his balls and stimulated that area beneath that begged for attention, wishing that Kurt's mouth was doing this. As he stroked his erection, he thought of how long it had been since he had felt the touch and kiss of a lover. He dreamed that Kurt was stroking and sucking him, until he came with an intensity that hadn't occurred in a very long time. He was suddenly aware that the moaning sounds he heard were coming from him, and hoped that Trey hadn't heard. He turned off the water, and could hear Trey laughing at his favorite cartoons, so was sure that he hadn't heard the sounds from the shower. David hadn't felt this way about someone in so long he had almost forgotten what it was like. He missed it, this feeling. He realized now that there were a lot of feelings he missed.

David dressed, and at 11:00 a.m. he and Trey were knocking on Kurt's and Cheyenne's door. Cheyenne opened the door, wide-eyed and ready for a day of fun. Trey entered first, and Cheyenne took his hand and led him to where she was putting a puzzle together.

David followed Trey into the suite just as Kurt was emerging from the bedroom. They looked at each other with the same sleepy look. They each knew why the other hadn't slept much last night. Kurt smiled at David. "Ready for a day of fun?"

David yawned. "Oh, yes, can't you tell?"

The five of them headed out for a fun breakfast.

"We want Mickey Mouse pancakes, Daddy," Cheyenne stated emphatically.

"Okay, honey, we're almost there."

They walked into a noisy, very child friendly restaurant, where children were happily talking about the day ahead, and parents were guzzling cup after cup of strong coffee. Once Kurt and David had finally gotten enough caffeine in them to be alert, they felt like having fun too. "What's next, kids?" Kurt addressed his question to both Trey and Cheyenne. David liked the sound of the word "kids."

"We want to go to Donald's Pool, Daddy." The nanny had told Trey and Cheyenne all about the wonderful fun things to do on the ship.

"That sounds great," Kurt answered.

"Let's go get changed," the nanny offered, as she walked ahead with the children.

The five of them met again after changing, and headed to Donald's Pool. It was sweet, Kurt had to admit, with its drawing of a smiling Donald Duck on the bottom of the pool. While Cheyenne and Trey splashed around happily with Cheyenne's nanny, Kurt and David emerged themselves in the shallowest part where they could sit on the bottom of the pool. The water came up to their waists, and they were both enjoying relaxing, after having had very little sleep. They were staring up at the wispy clouds floating by, and with their heads resting on the side of the pool they struggled to stay awake. With their arms resting on the side of the pool, there were at least two feet between them, but they were still close enough to talk.

Kurt was the first to mention the events of last night. "I thought about you last night," he admitted. Both continued to stare up at the clouds. "That's why I look so tired. I think I had about four hours of sleep."

David could see Kurt with his peripheral vision, just as Kurt could see him. "Same here, Kurt. I thought of you this morning, too, in the shower. It's been a long time."

Kurt knew exactly what David had meant. It had been a long time for him too. "I guess there was a part of me that I tried to ignore. I just wanted to give Cheyenne the security she deserved," admitted Kurt.

"I know, Kurt, I know. I felt the same about Trey, and still do. But, I guess I need more." David knew that he had to have a fulfilling life if he were to be a good father to Trey, but a relationship required time and he didn't seem to have any extra time for anything lately.

"Our kids get along well together," Kurt added.

"That's true, but would they if they were together more often?" David had to ask. He needed to know if Kurt were interested in a long-term relationship, or simply a shipboard fling.

"I don't know, David. I don't know." Kurt was being honest. "I wouldn't mind finding out, though."

They looked at each other. They wanted each other, that was certain. "Sara offered to take Trey and Cheyenne to a live Disney show tonight. I think she may have seen something between us yesterday." Kurt had been hesitant to share this information with David, until now.

"That sounds great, Kurt," David said in response.

"Sara probably has already asked Trey. She was going to as soon as she could."

There was no mistaking the look in David's and Kurt's eyes when they looked at each other.

David hadn't seen Trey approaching until Trey splashed water in his face. He talked fast, telling David about Sara's plan. "Can I go, Daddy?"

David hugged him tight. "Of course you can, Trey. Of course you can."

Trey scurried off to play, and left David and Kurt alone again. Kurt told David that the kids would be with Sara from dinner until at least midnight. That left plenty of time for Kurt and David to be alone. They enjoyed the afternoon with the kids, trying out some of the fun activities.

Kurt, Sara, and Cheyenne arrived at David's and Trey's suite in time for the big night, and when Trey and Cheyenne left with Sara, Kurt closed the door behind them. He and David were alone. Kurt stood leaning against the door looking at David. David was seated on the sofa, looking at Kurt. Neither could move.

David finally broke the silence. "I ordered a couple of light meals for us," he said, as he motioned toward the table. "I think I'm ready for a little 'grown-up' food for a change."

Kurt felt better. The "grown-up" food comment seemed to have broken the ice. David and Kurt seated themselves at the little table and enjoyed wine with their meals. "I love Cheyenne, and I know you love Trey, but it is a welcome change to have a little quiet time. Thanks, David."

David smiled at Kurt, and they began talking again, both feeling better about being alone together again.

They finished their wine on the verandah, enjoying the feel of the ocean breeze as it lightly brushed their skin. It may have been the wine or the ocean breeze, or perhaps because they were both very relaxed from the wine and being tired already that made it easy for Kurt and David to talk openly with each other, about their lives as fathers as well as their lives before becoming fathers. Both men admitted that neither had thought that fatherhood was a possibility for him, and both had felt truly blessed that fatherhood had become a reality for them.

David explained to Kurt that before Trey his life had been centered around work, and the very few relationships that hadn't lasted. Kurt confessed that before Cheyenne his life had seemed an endless cycle of business trips and business meetings. He further confessed to David that he had had a couple of yearlong relationships, but had been faulted for choosing work over his partners. You stupid fool, Kurt thought. Now David definitely won't want to get involved if he thinks he'd come second to your work. Kurt's vulnerability in his honesty was heartwarming to David.

Kurt was waiting for David to say something after his last comment. David set his and Kurt's empty wine glasses on the table with the bottle of wine. He stood up and walked around the table to where

Kurt was seated. He leaned down and kissed Kurt's awaiting wine flavored lips. "Come here," he said, as he took Kurt's hand in his. Kurt followed David back inside the suite.

David led Kurt into the bedroom and closed the door. David stood directly in front of Kurt, and took his hands in his. "I would never ask you to choose between your career and Cheyenne, or a relationship, Kurt. If I did that, I would be asking you to compromise a part of you, which would in turn compromise your further growth as a person. No one should feel good about discouraging another's goals and dreams, Kurt, no one." Kurt couldn't say anything. He didn't know what to say.

Continuing to hold Kurt's hands, David leaned in and kissed Kurt's eagerly awaiting lips. The last time their lips had met seemed so long ago. The wine tasted sweet on Kurt's lips as David enjoyed the feel and taste of them. He embraced Kurt as he continued to kiss him, letting his tongue linger before entering Kurt's awaiting mouth. Kurt discovered the pleasure of David's smooth skin as he quickly pulled David's shirt up and off. David stood like a statue as Kurt caressed every inch of his upper body. David's head was tilted back as Kurt's hands found David's nipples. Kurt encircled each nipple, not allowing them to be touched until they were fully erect. To steady himself, David was holding onto Kurt's jeans by placing his hands half in and half out of them in the front. He could feel the top of Kurt's erection desperately trying to find freedom from its captivity within Kurt's jeans. When Kurt allowed his fingers to move inward and over David's erect nipples, David could hear himself moan. His own erection was full. He ran his hands alone either side of Kurt's erection, causing Kurt to gasp. It had been too long for both of them. "David," Kurt said breathily as David slid Kurt's zipper downward along its path. They were both on fire.

David looked at Kurt as he slid his hands inside Kurt's jeans, caressing his buttocks as he undressed Kurt from the waist down. David caressed Kurt's legs from bottom to top, slid his hand between them, and when he reached Kurt's balls, he massaged him deeply until Kurt was holding onto David to keep from falling. Kurt's knees were weak, and as David's probing hand squeezed his balls and held Kurt's erection before sliding his hand along the shaft of his penis, Kurt held even tighter to David. Kurt spread his legs to allow David full access to whatever part of his body he desired. When he was able to regain some composure, Kurt freed David's own entrapped throbbing entity practically bursting its way out.

At Kurt's slightest touch, David gasped. Kurt stroked David's inner thighs, letting his hand slide over that special area between, making David hornier than he could remember being. Kurt gave David's balls and erection the attention they deserved, forcing David's legs apart, and reaching all the way to where David's buttocks were parted just slightly. It was David who was holding onto Kurt now. David leaned on Kurt, spreading his legs wide to encourage further attention. Kurt gave David what his body was aching for. He massaged, squeezed, and probed over and over.

Kurt gently backed David to the bed, and as he fell backward, David lay on the bed, his knees bent, his legs spread wide. Kurt pulled his shirt up over his head and stood naked before David. David looked at Kurt's naked body. He was gorgeous. His chest was covered with black and gray hair from his neck to his balls, as were his legs and arms.

David rose up to sit directly in front of the standing Kurt. He looked up into Kurt's eyes. Then he ran his hands along Kurt's chest from his neck to just below his waist where Kurt's erection was standing proudly. "You're beautiful, Kurt," David said, as he continued to look into his eyes. Kurt closed his eyes when David lovingly took one of his balls into his mouth. David continued to watch Kurt's face, as he treated the other ball to the same stimulation.

David slid his hands between Kurt's legs and slowly made his way to Kurt's buttocks, holding one in each hand. As he massaged Kurt's buttocks and the area between his legs, David slid his tongue along the shaft of Kurt's erection from his balls to the tantalizing tip. He swirled his tongue around Kurt's penis as he welcomed it into his mouth until he had taken it all. He had forgotten how much he loved the taste of this mouthwatering delight, and realized how much he missed it. Very slowly, David swirled his tongue around Kurt's erect penis as he made his way back to the top, and then back down again. He heard Kurt moan, and realized how much he had missed pleasing a man, and ultimately bringing him to orgasm. David scooted himself back onto the bed, and pulled Kurt toward him by the buttocks until Kurt fell onto the bed. With his dick still inside David's mouth, Kurt lay over David and rested on his arms and his knees. In this position, with David's hands and mouth stimulating him beyond all concentration, Kurt could only moan. David had full control of the situation. David expertly increased the intensity of his sucking until Kurt was moaning louder. Just when David could feel Kurt's climax nearing, he would slow his sucking just enough to prolong the sensation. Kurt thought he was going to lose his mind.

David was an expert at this. After nearing climax three times, and each time being stopped by David's expert oral abilities, Kurt had to climax the next time, he just had to. As David increased his intensity this time, and by holding Kurt's buttocks firmly, Kurt's head was on the bed. He had no energy to lift it. All of his energy and concentration was on his climax which he couldn't let David stop this time. "David, don't stop, please, oh," Kurt moaned, and then gasped as David didn't stop this time, but increased his intensity more than Kurt had thought possible. He could barely utter the words, "David, I can't stop, it's now." He couldn't stop, and David didn't want him to stop. With his mouth, he pulled and squeezed Kurt's dick as Kurt experienced what he thought was the orgasm of all orgasms. He came for a longer time that he could remember. His heart was pounding, he was gasping for air, and only a few utterances came from his mouth. David held Kurt's penis firmly within his mouth until it had been completely relieved of its tasty delights. He felt it slip out as Kurt lowered himself on David until they were face to face.

He kissed David on the mouth, and then spoke directly into his ear. "How can I pleasure you? What do you like the best?" Kurt was kissing David's neck, making his way down to David's nipples that were hard and begging to be sucked. Kurt's sucking made David's hard dick throb. He moaned loudly, and Kurt wanted David to feel all the pleasures that David has just given him.

As Kurt nibbled and sucked David's nipples, he spread David's buttocks so that David's penis could slide between them. "Mm, I like that, Kurt."

Kurt was hoping that meant that David wanted to enter him, because Kurt wanted to be entered by David. "You like that, David? You want more of that?"

David began trying to enter Kurt in response. "Yes, yes," he said, to assure Kurt. Kurt opened himself to David, and as he slid himself slowly onto David's erection, both men moaned in unison.

This is what David had missed, and this is the kind of love that he had been aching for. This was mature lovemaking, pleasing each other, caring for the other's pleasure more than their own. This he hadn't experienced until now, as a middle-aged man, with a middle-aged lover. David was thrusting upward as Kurt was squeezing more and more each time he lowered himself onto David's penis. They were holding each other as they continued. David wanted Kurt to reach ecstasy once again, and with one quick movement rolled Kurt onto his back, spread his legs wide, and entered him with a force that Kurt hadn't expected. He gasped, and David knew he had entered Kurt more deeply than he had been entered before. Over and over, David entered Kurt deeply with forceful thrusts until Kurt was biting his lip to keep from screaming. David could feel his own climax nearing, but continued his thrusts, going deeper, until his own explosion took him by surprise. He held onto Kurt and Kurt held onto him. Each hadn't expected this night to bring such passion. They cared for each other. There was no mistaking that.

David lay on top of Kurt, and each could feel the other's heartbeat as they tried to catch their breath. Kurt placed his arms above David's head and laid his head over David's shoulder. Neither man wanted to let go of the other. Neither man had expected such passion tonight. Each had felt a strong attraction to the other, but had expected more of a sexual release than a strengthening bond.

"Oh, David," Kurt said, once he had caught his breath.

"I know, Kurt, I know," David replied.

David did know. Kurt leaned up to turn his head toward David, and stated, "oh, no!"

David looked at him. "What is it, Kurt?"

Kurt pointed at the clock. "It's almost midnight, David. I promised Cheyenne I would be back by midnight."

They dressed quickly and headed for the door. They stopped at the door before heading out. David and Kurt embraced, and kissed a kiss that was not a goodbye kiss, but rather a kiss that held great promise for the future. "This is our beginning, right David?"

"Yes, Kurt, this is our beginning."

The next two days were spent enjoying the many amenities this wonderful cruise had to offer. The four of them, sometimes five when Sara accompanied them, enjoyed the pools, the live Disney shows, the scrumptious food, and evenings enjoying the ocean breeze on the verandah. They fit well together, like a family. Sara noticed, even if the kids were too busy having fun to think about things like that.

Two
Tough Decisions

Kurt, Cheyenne, and Sara were scheduled to return to Colorado Springs a week prior to David's and Trey's departure. They had booked a one week cruise, unlike David and Trey who had been booked for a two week cruise. They had been having so much fun that neither David nor Kurt had mentioned the length of their cruise. Sara pointed this out to Kurt the night before their scheduled departure.

Kurt looked stunned when she brought this to his attention. "I hadn't even thought about that, Sara." He immediately thought of the kids. Then he thought of David. Then he felt sick to his stomach.

Sara took Kurt's hand and immediately led him to the sofa. "Lie down, Kurt. You look white." He broke out in a cold sweat, as he tried to even his breathing.

"I'm okay, Sara. I guess I just had one of my anxiety attacks."

"Stay here, okay," Sara said, and hurried to get David. She knew that David was a physician's assistant, and she also knew that she had no idea what to do.

Sara took Cheyenne and the two of them hurried to get David. "I'll watch the kids, David. Kurt is a little sick. Could you check on him?"

Trey and Cheyenne were already playing, but David saw the fear in Sara's eyes. He was out the door and at Kurt's side in seconds. He was wet with sweat, and breathing fast. "Hey, buddy, you don't look so good." David knelt beside him, and checked his pulse. It was racing. "Do you take any medication, Kurt, that maybe you need now?"

"In the bedroom, David. I have panic attacks." Kurt hated to admit his shortcomings, and closed his eyes, turning toward the inner part of the sofa. David hurried to the bedroom to find Kurt's anti-anxiety medication. There were Klonopin Redi-Tabs, and David broke one off and hurried back to Kurt. "You have Klonopin, right Kurt?"

"Yes."

"Let's take one, okay?"

Kurt didn't move, but David forcibly rolled him onto his back. "Kurt, it's okay. Really, it's no problem. Will you take one for me, please?" David's manner quickly converted to "doctor mode." Kurt opened his eyes and saw a blurry looking David studying him concernedly. Kurt tried to take a deep breath, but could only take shallow ones. David softened his voice, and calmed his own actions. He didn't want Kurt to know how scared he was. He gently placed a hand on Kurt's cheek. "Close you eyes, Kurt, and rest. Let your body relax as much as you can, baby. Let me do everything."

Kurt closed his eyes, and David slipped the tablet inside Kurt's mouth and under his tongue. He held Kurt's tongue down until he felt certain that at least most of the tablet had been absorbed into his bloodstream. He caressed Kurt's cheek until the tablet had dissolved. Kurt started to shiver, and David took the spread off the bed and wrapped it around Kurt. He sat on the sofa beside Kurt and held him. He didn't know if the tablet would make him sleep, or just calm his nerves. He looked at David. He wasn't blurry any longer.

David kissed him on the cheek, and scooted onto the floor so that he was face to face with Kurt. "Do you feel that you need to sleep now, Kurt?"

"No, I'm fine. I just feel like I've run a fast race." Kurt closed his eyes again. "I'm so embarrassed, David, and I'm sorry."

David caressed his cheek. "Baby, there's no need to be sorry or embarrassed. I'm here for you. I want to be here for you." Kurt rested for awhile, relaxing with the touch of David's hand on his cheek.

Kurt opened his eyes once again, and looked around. "What is it, Kurt? Can I get you something?" Kurt started to sit up, but David was on the sofa in a second holding him back down. "Not yet, Kurt. You need to rest awhile longer."

"Where's Cheyenne, David?"

"Sara and Cheyenne are with Trey in our suite, Kurt. Cheyenne is fine."

Kurt relaxed again, comforted by David's words. David sat on the floor once again, and talked directly to Kurt.

"Kurt, can you tell me what caused your anxiety attack?"

Kurt hated to answer that. He had always considered this a weakness. "I have had them since my sister died. They occur when I sense that something is going to be taken from me." It had taken him several years to admit that he had panic attacks. David was in the medical field, so Kurt thought that he would understand.

"It's good that you know this, Kurt. It's not uncommon at all to experience anxiety and panic attacks, especially after losing someone close to you." David did understand. Kurt knew that he would. "What did you sense was going to be taken from you today, Kurt?"

David was direct, that was for sure, thought Kurt. Not at all expecting this question, and definitely not prepared to answer it, Kurt hesitated before speaking. David brushed the hair back from Kurt's forehead, and kissed him gently. He reached underneath the spread so that he could massage Kurt's back. "We've already shared too much to turn back now, Kurt."

David held Kurt's hands underneath the spread. Kurt opened his eyes. "Sara reminded me that we leave for home tomorrow. We are scheduled to return to Colorado tomorrow, and you and Trey have another week here. I hadn't thought about it until Sara mentioned it. Cheyenne and Trey are having so much fun together. I can't let her lose someone else, and I don't want to be without you."

David had no idea. He hadn't thought about it either. "Kurt, I had no idea. But there's a simple solution. Trey and I don't have to stay here another week. You and I live close enough to each other that I can drive Trey to Colorado Springs to see Cheyenne, or she can come with us to spend time with Trey. "Do you return to work right away?"

"Unfortunately, I do."

"It's okay, Kurt. We'll work it out. You'll see. I don't think Trey wants to stay here without Cheyenne, and I definitely don't want to stay here without you."

Kurt looked at David. His words were genuine. Kurt felt better, but tired. "If you like, we can make very definite arrangements for seeing each other, and for the kids to spend time together. Would that help, Kurt?" David knew that reassurance and a definite schedule were extremely important to people with anxiety. Kurt agreed that it would. He felt so weak, and David seemed so strong.

Kurt's phone rang then, and David answered it. Sara offered to take the kids to see a magic show, and also offered to stay at David's tonight with Cheyenne and Trey. Kurt agreed, and Sara told David that they would be back at Kurt's first thing in the morning. She knew that they still needed to pack so they would be ready when the boat docked.

David helped Kurt to the bed, and lay down beside him. "Let's get a good night's sleep, okay? Everything will be fine, Kurt. You'll see." Kurt finally allowed his body the rest it had been craving for a very long time.

David lay on the bed wide awake, holding Kurt as he slept. He was thrilled that Kurt wanted a relationship just as he did. He thought of ways they could make a relationship work. David was busy, Kurt was busy, and they both wanted to give Cheyenne and Trey all the time that they could. He had realized, however, just how much he missed and needed a lover and companion in his life. Am I fooling myself, wanting it all, he wondered?

David fell asleep around midnight, and Kurt was still sleeping when he awoke at 7:00 a.m. He hated to wake Kurt, but knew he had to if they were to be ready to leave at 9:00 a.m. He kissed Kurt lightly on the cheek. "Kurt, it's time to get up." Kurt barely stirred, but snuggled closer to David. David spoke softly into Kurt's ear. "Honey, it's time to go home now. We're all going back to Colorado today, remember?" Kurt awoke suddenly.

David explained to him that he had already been on-line and changed his and Trey's plane tickets to match Kurt's, and that he had been pleasantly surprised that all of them had first class tickets. "We must think alike, Kurt."

Kurt just smiled. He was so grateful to David for cutting short his vacation, and also for accepting him for the imperfect person that he was.

"I haven't told Trey yet, but I think he will be happy to be traveling with Cheyenne. She's like a little sister to him now."

Trey didn't mind at all. He loved Cheyenne. At his age a vacation didn't have to be a certain length of time. Having fun was all that mattered. The only question that Trey had for David as they packed was if he could sit next to Cheyenne on the airplane. David smiled, and tried not to laugh. He and Kurt worried much too much about upsetting Cheyenne and Trey.

David and Trey arrived at Kurt's and Cheyenne's just as they were finishing packing. "We get to sit together in first class, Cheyenne," Trey couldn't wait to tell her. Sara urged the kids to help her finish packing, so that David could talk to Kurt in private if he liked. David took the hint. Kurt looked good.

"You doing okay, buddy?"

"I am, David, I am."

"We'll have plenty of time on the plane to decide how to join our families," David said with a smile. Kurt just smiled. He wasn't at all sure how, or even if, things would work out.

The five of them waved goodbye to the wonderful concierge staff as they left the ship. A car was waiting to take them to the airport, where they were comfortably seated on the plane in first class seats. They would have a brief layover in Chicago, but by dinnertime would be back home again in Colorado. Kurt and David were seated in front of Cheyenne and Trey, with Sara across from the kids.

Once the plane had reached cruising altitude, Kurt and David began to discuss the reality of their situation. "I'm gone a lot, David, sometimes from Monday through Friday."

"I'm not going to ask you to stop doing what you like, Kurt."

"That's just it, David. I want to be with Cheyenne more than I want to travel on business. I'm so tired when I return that I'm not much of a dad to her." Kurt explained to David how his business worked, and how he assisted his clients in growing their businesses. David listened intently, but was trying to think of a way that Kurt's business could work via the Internet. "I tried that for awhile, but most of my clients are older and prefer face-to-face contact," Kurt said resignedly. David was silent, and Kurt was, too. Kurt had been through this many times before, and his business always ended his personal relationships.

Kurt further explained that he had had it all set up via the Web, and was very computer savvy, but his most successful and most affluent clients wouldn't budge. He had had a few clients whose businesses were just getting started, and had since become quite successful, but he had had to let them go to keep his older clients happy. "I have to think of Cheyenne, David, and her future."

David understood completely. He wanted to give Trey the best of everything, especially education. "When you did work with young entrepreneurs, did you enjoy it, Kurt?"

Kurt's face brightened, and he was filled with enthusiasm. "More than I can say, David. I felt that I was actually doing something meaningful. I was mentoring them, and they trusted me. Yes, David, I enjoyed it." He looked at David as he said this.

David patted Kurt's hand. He would have loved to hold his hand, but it wasn't time yet. That would no doubt confuse Cheyenne and Trey. David was thinking. He was thinking about the look in Kurt's eyes when he talked about working with young entrepreneurs. It was a look of childlike exuberance.

Once they had reached cruising altitude on the flight from Chicago to Denver, David turned to Kurt. "Kurt, I have an idea, for us and for the kids." Kurt turned to face David. He looked so very tired. His job had taken a lot out of him over the years. "Look, Kurt, I know this is new to both of us in many ways, this relationship we're beginning. But you must admit, we have very strong feelings for each other, and we enjoy each other's company." David smiled at Kurt, and Kurt half smiled back. He had no idea what David was thinking. "Why don't you give yourself a break, and do what truly makes you happy. If you like to mentor young upstarts, then do it. Being single until a year ago, I've saved a lot of money, and I have only Trey to spend it on."

Kurt immediately thought that David was going to offer him a loan, and stopped him short. David continued, undaunted. "Hear me out, Kurt. If one of us sells our house, and we all live together, we'll have plenty of money for you to start your own business. Or, we can both sell, and build or buy a different house so that neither would feel as if he were encroaching on the other's turf." Kurt thought it made sense, from a business perspective, but when real feelings were involved, that was different.

Kurt couldn't help but play devil's advocate. "What if things don't work out, David, between you and me?" Kurt didn't want to ask this, but had to know if David had thought about it too. They weren't in their twenties.

"That's a chance we would have to take, Kurt, like anyone else. There are no guarantees, but you and I both know what it takes to make a relationship work, and we both know what it takes to kill a relationship. We have maturity on our side, and that's half the battle, in my opinion."

David had thought about the "what if", but Kurt was still hesitant. "I'm scared, David."

"That's good, Kurt. So am I. That's one more commonality between us."

"Where would we live, David, in Denver or Colorado Springs?"

David thought about this. "If you're asking my opinion, Kurt, I would suggest Colorado Springs. It's not as large, and it's a beautiful city. We would have an excuse to visit the big city that way, when we wanted a change."

Kurt was truly touched. David could definitely find a job in Colorado Springs, but was offering to give up his position in Denver just for him. David knew that changing cities would be more difficult for Kurt, if his anxiety was as big an issue as David thought it was. Relocating could increase the frequency, and also the intensity, of Kurt's panic attacks. "That would probably be best for the kids, living in a smaller city," Kurt offered.

"I think so," David agreed.

"But what if we find out that we can't live together, and what if the kids start to fight, and what if you don't find a job right away and want to move back to Denver?"

Kurt rattled these "what ifs" off so fast that David couldn't keep up. "Slow down, buddy. We're not a couple of kids. We can work out our differences. I like to think we've matured at least some from when we were in our twenties. Kids fight and make up all the time. We'll take life the only way anyone can, really, one day at a time." Kurt took a deep breath. David winked at him, and Kurt smiled.

When the plane touched down in Denver, David told Trey that they were going to have lunch at their house and then drive to where Cheyenne and Kurt live. Trey was so excited. He had no idea that they lived in the same state, and not that far from each other.

Cheyenne squealed with delight when told of the plan. "I have a big house and a big yard, and lots of toys," she proudly informed Trey.

David looked at Kurt sitting in the front seat with him. Kurt looked back and smiled. Kurt always took life so seriously. The kids would be fine.

David's house was in a very nice neighborhood, with mature trees, and of very quaint architecture. Kurt caught himself thinking about the house's marketability which he felt would be very good. David showed Kurt the house while Trey took Cheyenne's hand and motioned for Sara to follow him to his room. David ordered pizzas delivered and while they waited for its arrival, he and Kurt packed more of David's and Trey's things to take with them to Colorado Springs. David and Trey didn't get out of the city much, and David was looking forward to showing Trey and Cheyenne some of the sites. He also planned to contact a realtor, and look for a job in Colorado Springs.

After lunch, David went with Trey to his room to explain the plan to spend the week with Cheyenne and Kurt. He was excited, and started to rush out the door to tell Cheyenne. David stopped him, though, and explained to him that Kurt was talking to Cheyenne about the plan just then. Trey hurried and packed the toys that he wanted to take with him, and very soon Cheyenne came running in to tell Trey the good news. The two of them ran outside to play in the backyard until they left.

Kurt followed David to his bedroom. David closed the door behind them, and turned to face Kurt. He kissed Kurt and wrapped his arms around him. Kurt kissed David just as lovingly and hungrily, and reached between David's legs. He couldn't seem to pull his hand away. He didn't want to. He wanted to feel David's naked body against his own again. "I want you David." "Tonight, my love," David responded, squeezing Kurt's ass. They kissed each other with a passion neither could deny, and then forced themselves to stop before they wouldn't be able to stop, which wasn't far away.

They finished packing David and Trey, locked the house, and Sara escorted the kids to the car, as David and Kurt followed behind. They didn't mind the drive, after being in the air for so long. It felt good to be on the ground.

They were at Kurt's and Cheyenne's before they knew it. Unlike David and Trey who lived in the heart of Denver, Kurt and Cheyenne lived just outside of Colorado Springs, on a two acre lot. The house was huge, and David knew that Trey would never tire of the back yard. It was big, with a play house, sports court, and an indoor/outdoor swimming pool. Trey's eyes were big when Sara and Cheyenne showed him the back yard.

David loved Kurt's house. They immediately noticed that they had similar decorative tastes. The house was of modern architecture, but the inside contained mostly antique furniture and classic artwork. David felt right at home. Kurt kept a much tidier home that David, but he did have Sara to help.

Kurt led David through the house. The basement was completely finished, and was a museum of past pinball games and other memories of the "old days." On the main floor there was a very spacious eat-in kitchen, equally spacious dining area, living room, and not one, but two family rooms, one on either end. Kurt led David to the upper level where he was surprised to be shown two large master bedrooms, and two regular sized bedrooms with a bath between them. A beautiful bath and separate sitting area completed each master bedroom. David was impressed. Kurt hoped he would be, and would feel at home here. "Your home is beautiful, Kurt."

Kurt explained that it was his sister's and her husband's. "I lived in a much, much smaller house in town, but I thought it would be best for Cheyenne to live out here."

It was clear to David that Kurt was a very thoughtful and caring man, though he didn't think that Kurt realized it. It's not uncommon that we see in others what they will probably never see in themselves, thought David. "My sister and her husband wanted Cheyenne to have everything they could possibly give her," Kurt commented. David could see in Kurt's eyes that Kurt wanted the same for Cheyenne that his sister had wanted for her. David patted Kurt on the back.

Kurt showed David to Cheyenne's room, and explained that Sara's room connected to Cheyenne's by the shared bathroom. These rooms were large, too. "Sara doesn't stay here all the time. She has classes at the University of Colorado in Colorado Springs, but she is here most of the time, and definitely all the time when I'm away on business." Kurt's mood changed suddenly when he spoke of being away on business. David noticed the sadness in his eyes when he spoke. Kurt showed David to the master at the opposite end of the floor from his own, and asked if this would be okay for him and Trey. "It's better than okay, Kurt." David winked as he said this, in reassurance.

Trey and Cheyenne came running in at that moment, rushing over to David to lead him outside. Cheyenne was exuberant. She loved showing off her back yard and all of its treasures. The pool was unique in its ability to transform itself from a sunny delight to a cozy homey entertainment, as it could go from outside to inside as easily as day drifted into night. David thought it was beautiful out here. With the Rocky Mountains in the distance, through the lens of a camera this would be the perfect setting for an Ansel Adams photograph. The lawn had been manicured to perfection, the grass green and lush.

It was evening now, and they were all looking forward to a good night's sleep. Cheyenne wanted to show Trey how she and Sara played "campout" in the basement. They would put up a tent, Sara would make s'mores, and they would sleep in sleeping bags inside the tent. Kurt and David both agreed with Cheyenne's idea. The two men needed to be with each other tonight, if only to hold each other for awhile. With the kids two floors below them, David quickly took a shower, and then walked down the hall to join Kurt in his room. Kurt was stepping out of the shower as David walked in. Wearing nothing but a towel, Kurt walked over to wear David was standing just inside the door, and locked it behind him. Kurt's hair was wet, and droplets of water sprinkled throughout the thick hair on his body and made his skin glisten underneath its coat of hair that felt as soft as down. David was barely dressed himself, with shirt untucked over unzipped jeans, just decent enough for the walk down the hall to Kurt's room.

Kurt unbuttoned the few buttons necessary to remove David's shirt, and their hands once again enjoyed the feel of the other's skin. With one swift motion, David untied the towel that prevented Kurt's beautiful body to be seen in its entirety, and watched as the towel fell to the floor. Kurt wanted him. David knew it and Kurt knew it, and both could see it. Kurt eased David's unzipped jeans over his luscious buttocks and followed them with his hands along David's legs until they lay on the floor. Then he gently removed David's feet from the jeans that lay at his feet, one by one, doing so in a way that left David's legs wide apart. Then Kurt's hands made their way upward along David's legs, lingering at his inner thighs to taste the erection that was eagerly awaiting Kurt's arrival. Kurt's touch along his inner thighs caused David to gasp and close his eyes in ecstasy, and Kurt's mouth on David's erection was dizzying. As Kurt's hands slid between David's legs, paying a teasing amount of attention to that special area between, they held David's buttocks firmly as Kurt welcomed the whole of David's erection into his mouth. David steadied himself by sliding his hands through Kurt's hair, but found that the feel of this luscious blackness aroused him even more. Kurt's hands made their back to that sensitive area between David's legs where they stimulated him beyond belief. David would have fallen backward onto the bed if Kurt hadn't been holding his erection firmly in his mouth. Kurt could see David's legs were becoming unsteady, and removed his mouth from David's penis to be replaced by his hand as he guided David backward onto the bed, never stopping his motions, both seductively masturbating him as well as enjoying the feel of those delicacies between David's legs. David lay on the bed with Kurt leaning over him fully controlling the pleasure that David was enjoying.

As David opened his mouth to speak, Kurt prevented him by kissing his open mouth hungrily, taking David's tongue into his mouth just as he had David's erection. David had neither the strength nor the will to move. The pleasure Kurt was providing was too great. David held Kurt in as tight an embrace as he could as he tried desperately to reach Kurt's penis. He wanted it in his mouth. Kurt wanted to enter David, just as David had entered him that night on the cruise ship. He wanted David to know the pleasure that he had known. He let his fingers glide along the path that separated David's buttocks. David closed his eyes. Kurt kissed David on the mouth. "I want you to feel me deep inside you, David," Kurt said breathily into David's ear. David didn't respond, but continued to kiss Kurt and pulled him closer to him. Reaching down, David held Kurt's hard penis firmly in his grip. Kurt moaned. David's touch had been electrifying to Kurt the first time he had felt it, and it was even more so now. Kurt's mouth rested on David's. He cupped David's balls as David continued to stroke Kurt's penis. Kurt felt as if time stood still. He could feel nothing but David's touch.

As Kurt's body went limp under David's magical touch, David rolled Kurt onto his back and forced his mouth open with his own. David squeezed Kurt's balls and deeply massaged underneath. Kurt moaned and broke the kiss as the tried to breathe. David continued his squeezing and massaging, watching Kurt's face, enjoying the look of ecstasy which was clearly visible. David was separating Kurt's buttocks and entering him just slightly with the tip of one finger which Kurt tried to force into further entry. Just when Kurt thought he couldn't take any more, David swirled his tongue around the head of Kurt's penis and let it slowly slide its way inward as his finger entered Kurt. Kurt, completely lost in his own pleasure now, bent his knees, offering himself to David completely. Kurt didn't say a word, couldn't say a word, but could feel only that part of him that was being stimulated by David's mouth and David's touch. David abandoned Kurt's penis for that space now being massaged by his hand and replaced it with his tongue. Applying increasing pressure, a low moan left Kurt's lips. David spread Kurt's buttocks even further now, allowing two fingers to enter deeply between. Kurt wanted more, and tried desperately to squeeze around David's fingers, but David was forcing him to wait. Kurt was on fire, and was helpless under David's touch. Powerless under David's touch, Kurt was like a rag doll as David positioned him for the climax of a lifetime.

With Kurt's knees already bent, David flipped him over so that Kurt's knees were underneath him and his spread buttocks eagerly awaiting entry between. David reached between Kurt's legs and slowly masturbated him, as Kurt moaned. David allowed his penis to glide slowly between Kurt's buttocks, stopping at the entrance that Kurt was begging David to fill. Kurt was moaning and doing what he could to force the entry of David's erection into his empty space begging to be filled. David entered Kurt slowly as he also masturbated him. Kurt didn't even try to maintain composure. He moaned and gyrated as he enjoyed every minute of this amazing pleasure that David was providing. David had gotten so aroused watching Kurt that he had to slow things down to prevent his own climax from coming too soon. He wanted this to last as long as it possibly could. Kurt squeezed David's penis with all the strength he had. The feel of David deep inside him was overwhelming. As David went even deeper, Kurt once again lost all control. David masturbated Kurt faster and faster, and entered him deeper and deeper, until they came at the same time. Both men moaned loudly, and called each other's name.

When their climaxes were finally complete, David pulled Kurt's legs out from underneath him, and lay on top of Kurt, his penis remaining deeply inside of Kurt. Their hearts were beating rapidly as they enjoyed the feel of the other. When they were able to breathe once again, Kurt said, "David", and David's response was, "I know, Kurt, I know."

They turned onto their sides and held each other, their arms and legs intertwined. They kissed each other with long lingering kisses until their bodies were begging for sleep. They slept in each other's arms until morning.

It was David who awoke to the sound of youthful voices. He lay still, just listening for a moment. He should have gone back to his room last night. Kurt and he should have somehow explained this to Trey and Cheyenne, though he didn't know how they would. When David heard Sara call the kids for breakfast, he breathed a sigh of relief. He kissed Kurt on the cheek and tried to wake him. "Kurt, time to get up."

Kurt didn't even stir.

"Kurt, the kids were just up here."

At that, Kurt awoke. "Oh, I knew this would happen. Did they wonder why the door was locked?"

David assured him that they hadn't attempted to open the door, and Sara quickly called them back downstairs for breakfast.

"Okay, thanks David. We'd better get down there." They dressed quickly, and headed down the stairs.

"Daddy, I opened your door and you weren't there. Were you in the shower?"

At this question from Trey, David stiffened. He had promised never to lie to Trey and to always tell him the truth, no matter what. "No, Trey, I was in Kurt's room helping him with something," David half lied.

Trey didn't seem to care, as he was busy shoveling a big bite of chocolate chip pancakes into his mouth. He looked happy, thought

David. Trey and Cheyenne chattered happily about their fun night in their make-believe campout with Sara.

"We should have a Sara, Daddy," Trey stated emphatically.

David realized their talk was going to be soon.

"Cheyenne doesn't go back to school for a whole week. Can we stay here?" Trey asked.

"We'll be here all week, Trey," David replied, adding nothing more.

Kurt had gone into his office off of the living room to check his business messages for the day. No one heard him come out and go back upstairs to his room. Cheyenne was busy telling Trey what they could do all week, and Trey was listening attentively.

Three

Kurt

Sara was the only one who had heard the door to Kurt's bedroom close. She had assumed somewhat of a motherly role to both Kurt and Cheyenne, even though she was much younger than Kurt. She excused herself and went upstairs to check on Kurt. She knocked, but there was no answer. She entered slowly and heard the shower running. Walking toward the bathroom, she stopped outside the half open door, and asked, "Are you okay, Kurt?" No answer. "Kurt?" "I'm okay, Sara. Close the bedroom door on your way out, please." Kurt was in the whirlpool, but had turned on the shower so no one would hear him.

Sara thought Kurt's voice was shaky. She quickly headed down the stairs, and asked David to come into Kurt's office with her. She explained to him what she had heard, and how troubled Kurt had been about his business. They both agreed that David would best be able to talk to him. She explained to David how bad Kurt could get when he was down, and hoped that he would give up his business entirely. "His clients think he should be available for them twenty-four hours a day, seven days a week, all year long, and Kurt just can't take it anymore, David." David hadn't realized how bad it was, but was happy that Sara had confided in him. "I'll take the kids today, and Cheyenne can show Trey all of her favorite places," Sara very kindly offered.

David thanked her, talked to Trey about the day, and upon Trey's enthusiastic agreement to the plan, hurried up the stairs to Kurt's room. He closed and locked the door behind him. Outside the bathroom door, David spoke lovingly, yet sternly to Kurt. "Kurt, come on out now. We need to talk, just you and me."

Kurt didn't budge. "I'm taking a bath, David."

David walked inside the bathroom. He reached inside the shower and turned off the water. "Then why is the shower on, and why are you fully dressed sitting inside the whirlpool?" David walked toward him and sat on the side of the tub. "What is it, Kurt?" David's tone softened, and he spoke as a doctor to a patient. Kurt was shivering, just as he had when his panic attack hit on the cruise ship. David offered his hand. "Come on, buddy, let's come out of the tub." Kurt was shaking now, the beads of sweat beginning to form on his forehead. David stepped into the tub and helped Kurt to his feet. He was too big to carry, or David would have lifted him up and out of the tub. David held Kurt's arms still at his sides and held him with both arms. "Can you walk, buddy? Just a few steps and we'll get you all warmed up again, okay?"

Kurt was in full panic mode now, but with David's help managed to shuffle to the bed where David tucked him into bed.

"Where do you keep your tablets, Kurt?"

Kurt looked confused.

David looked in the bedside stand, with no luck. "Kurt, tell me where they are now."

Kurt stuttered the words, "top drawer", and David hurried to the dresser and opened the top drawer. Good, they were there.

David climbed into the bed and underneath the blankets with Kurt. He held him tightly in his arms and looked at his worried face. "Under the tongue, baby, just like last time," David said, as he was placing the tablet and holding Kurt's tongue in place as it dissolved. Kurt's eyes were wide with terror. David stroked his face, and closed his mouth. Then he held Kurt's face in his hands and kissed him lightly on the lips. "It's okay, Kurt. I promise you that. We can face anything, you and me. Sara took the kids for the day, and you and I are going to talk everything out."

David continued to hold Kurt in a vice-like grip, his hands firmly on Kurt's face. Kurt's eyes closed, and his heart stopped racing. His body relaxed. David continued to assure him that everything would be fine. Kurt tried to focus on David's face, but couldn't. "Close your eyes, Kurt. We'll talk in a little while." Kurt pulled David down to him. "I'm not going anywhere, baby," David assured him. Kurt drifted into a semi sleeping state. He mumbled incoherently, though David did his best to try to understand what he was saying. Kurt was also trying to free himself from David's tight grasp, as if he were fighting to break the chains that bound him to something or someone.

After about an hour Kurt opened his eyes. David looked at him. Kurt could see him clearly now. "You okay, buddy? You seemed to be dreaming."

"I'm okay, David, I'm okay." Like every attack, immediately afterward he felt as if he had run ten miles in as many minutes.

"What's up, Kurt? Last I knew you were in your office, and then for some reason you fell apart." David hated to be so blunt, but had learned from seeing patients that sometimes he had to be tough with them.

"I'm fine, David. I've just got a lot on my mind," Kurt said, just wanting to get away from David and think things through.

"Look, buddy, I don't want to just share your bed, I want to share your life. I want all of you, Kurt, not just your scrumptious body." David winked at Kurt, and Kurt closed his eyes. When he opened them, David was looking at him.

"David, when I checked my messages, my biggest client who lives on the East Coast informed me that he was pulling his account. He said that he had been on the same cruise that we were on, and evidently saw us in an embrace. Anyway, he said that it wasn't good for his image to be represented by… 'a fag'." Kurt placed such emphasis on the word fag that David almost laughed. But it wasn't funny to Kurt. "His business was half of my business, David, and his colleagues will follow suit, I'm sure. He's very powerful. Then my business will be approximately ten percent of what it is, or was."

David understood all too well how hard it was to be gay in a "good old boys" world. He had never told anyone in the medical world that he was gay. He was sure that some knew or suspected, but he had never told anyone.

"I'm sorry, Kurt, I really am. I do know what it is like to be gay in a world that doesn't accept it entirely." Kurt was thankful for David. David did understand. "But isn't your business the one thing you had wanted to change, Kurt? I can see how much energy it sucks out of you. You look exhausted, Kurt."

"I am exhausted, David. I just want to do what's best for Cheyenne, and give her everything she deserves." Kurt couldn't see that Cheyenne needed him much more than she needed his money.

David saw it. David knew it. "What's best for Cheyenne is a father who isn't sick with worry all the time. She wants you, Kurt, not your money. I think that deep down inside, you know that."

Kurt looked away trying to avoid David's piercing eyes. "You're obviously a good business man, Kurt, to have assisted others in cultivating their own success. Is there some specific type of business that you would like to see become successful, for yourself?"

"Not really, David. I like teaching others, sharing what I have learned."

David loved Kurt's selflessness. He was as selfless in business as he was in bed. David thought about what Kurt had just said. He could teach business classes in the local schools, but he was pretty sure that Kurt liked the one-to-one approach.

"Kurt, you said there was about ten percent of your business that would remain with you. What types of businesses comprise that ten percent?"

Kurt explained to David that there was a gay couple in Chicago who had started a cake decorating business and were quite successful, and very good. David noticed that Kurt's face lit up when he spoke of this. "They call themselves the 'cake artists', and they are exactly that. They are wonderful, David. You should see their cakes. There is one other couple, also in Chicago, who formed their own auditing business. They are a lesbian couple who were referred by the cake decorators. I really enjoy seeing both couples."

David kissed Kurt then, a lover's kiss, and Kurt was kissing him back. When they could finally pull their hungry mouths off of each other, David looked at Kurt and waited for his eyes to open. He looked at David, wanting him even more than he had last night. "I think you've just stumbled upon your true calling, Kurt." Kurt looked confused. "Your face lit up and there was a definite look of pride in your eyes when you spoke of the two gay couples, Kurt. As you and I both know, it's extremely difficult to be gay in the business world, no matter what the business. Perhaps focusing solely on the gay community and assisting gay businesses to get their start would be very rewarding. Not only would you be helping others build their businesses, but you would be helping those who find it extremely difficult to obtain needed assistance."

Kurt seemed happy with this suggestion, and told David that there were others in Chicago who had sought his assistance, but that he had always been too busy.

"Well, now you can realize your dream, Kurt. Think about it."

Kurt was thinking about it, and when he looked at David again, he knew that he loved him, had loved him for awhile. "I did enjoy helping those guys, you know. They always wanted Cheyenne to come with me when I went to Chicago. In fact, they insisted on it, and always doted on her, even when she was a baby." He closed his eyes again.

David was watching him the entire time, watching him closely for signs of stress or distress to return. He didn't see any yet.

Kurt had dozed off and David was almost asleep on top of him when he suddenly felt Kurt's heart beating so fast he thought it might jump out of his chest. Kurt's eyes were fluttering as he slept. He was having a nightmare. David didn't waste any time in waking him. "Wake up, Kurt." David was rubbing his cheeks.

Kurt was in such a deep sleep, though, that he didn't wake up very easily or very rapidly. Instead, he began to thrash about, trying to break free of David's hold. David held his arms to his sides and spoke sternly by his ear. "Kurt, wake up, now. It's David. You're dreaming, but let's wake up now, okay?"

"No, no!" Kurt was practically screaming now. David spoke calmly now.

"Kurt, wake up," he spoke directly into his ear. You're okay, Kurt, let's wake up."

Kurt stilled his movements. David once again rubbed one cheek while speaking into Kurt's ear. "Slow your breathing, baby. You're okay. Wake up now." Finally, Kurt was once again awake. "Tell me your dream, Kurt." Kurt's heart was racing. David hoped that Kurt's career adjustment would have a positive effect on his panic attacks.

David reached for Kurt's tablets and broke one in half. "Here, Kurt. Let's take half a one, just half." David had it under Kurt's tongue before he could argue about it.

This seemed to calm Kurt, but not make him sleep. He seemed to be thinking more clearly. "I was dreaming about Cheyenne's visits to Chicago, and then I thought about how she might reject me someday because I'm gay," Kurt admitted.

"It's okay to be concerned, Kurt. You love Cheyenne. The more diversity she is exposed to as she is growing up, the greater her chances of accepting others just as they are. Trust me, Kurt. Cheyenne will be a wonderful woman. I'm sure she can see that yours and her skin color are very different, but that you love each other regardless. It's our differences, not our similarities, which make us unique, Kurt, and uniqueness breeds acceptance."

David was making too much sense, but Kurt knew he was right. "She is a good kid, my Cheyenne," Kurt smiled as he said.

"She is, Kurt, she is, and that is because of you." David lightly touched Kurt's nose as he said this. Kurt just thought about his lack of income until he could build his new business. "I can see you thinking, Kurt. Talk to me. Let's not keep those worries inside."

"I'm not going to have the money I did for quite awhile, David," Kurt admitted, and felt better for doing so.

"Well, my love, as of today my house is on the market and that, combined with my income, will be more than enough for all of us. I'm sure the house will sell quickly." Kurt looked surprised, and confused. "Remember what I said, Kurt. I plan to be a part of your life, your whole life, not just your lover, although I do love being your lover." Kurt was almost embarrassed at David's words when he was trying to be serious.

David kissed Kurt then, a long lover's kiss that Kurt could never resist. David could stay in bed with Kurt for the rest of his life. He had never cared for a man as much as he cared for Kurt. "As much as I would love to stay here forever, Kurt, you and I both know that we've got a few things to do before the kids get back."

Kurt knew that David was right, but didn't want to think about anything right now. "I know, David."

Kurt showed David his website and how he communicated with his clients. "The couple in Chicago and I communicate a lot with the help of this little gadget." Kurt showed David how he talked to them through his computer rather than the phone, and how they sent each other text messages. He introduced David to the couple. They were thrilled to have another couple to talk to. David agreed that their cake designs were gorgeous. Kurt felt comfortable with this couple and explained to them, while holding tightly to David's hand, what had happened and also of the way he planned to restructure his business. They stopped what they were doing and offered their suggestions. Kurt felt better already. They were the only business clients that Kurt had told he was gay. They gave him the names and numbers of two of their friends who were in the first stages of a great business. "We knew you were very busy, Kurt, and didn't want to impose," they admitted. Kurt looked at David, and David winked at him. They promised to send a list of businesses and individuals that would love to have his assistance. "We're behind you one hundred percent, Kurt. We're also thrilled about your non-business success." They kissed each other as they said this, and Kurt felt his cheeks become hot. Kurt thanked them, and then settled in at his desk to set up some new accounts.

David left Kurt alone and called the realtor to get going on his house, and also called Cheyenne's school to obtain the necessary information to enroll Trey. Then he checked on-line for P.A. openings in

Colorado Springs and found three. He called and set up interviews for later in the week. He wanted to make sure Kurt and Trey were taken care of before thinking about his own change.

Kurt was still working when David walked into his office. He had made the contacts suggested by his clients in Chicago, and both parties had been very receptive. One had signed on with Kurt immediately, and Kurt was busy setting up their account and e-mailing necessary paperwork. David was happy for Kurt. His mood had brightened.

Kurt motioned David into his office. He walked over and kissed David which David eagerly returned. Their kisses were always a turn-on for each other, and both fought the urge to rip the other's clothes off and take each other right there in Kurt's office. Kurt broke the kiss and held David close to him. "Thank you," he whispered in David's ear.

David responded by sliding his hands down along Kurt's back and gently squeezed his ass. "When do you think you can take a break?" David whispered.

With David's hands on his ass, Kurt knew it couldn't be too soon. "Give me an hour, okay?"

David held Kurt's head in his hands and kissed his mouth, forcing it open with his own. "I'll be waiting for you," he said as he broke the kiss as suddenly and with the same force as he had when starting it. Kurt had to steady himself after David's erotic kiss and words.

David closed the door behind him and walked up the stairs. He took a hot shower in his own room, and unpacked his things, though he and Kurt needed to discuss sleeping arrangements. He didn't want to sleep alone any longer. He wanted to go to sleep and wake up with Kurt in his arms every night and every morning. He and Kurt needed to talk to Trey and Cheyenne about this, though neither knew exactly how. Telling them that he and Kurt cared for each other a lot and then answering any questions that they may ask, without bombarding them with any excess information, was best. That was what David had overheard other parents say, anyway, when they had been discussing various issues while waiting to pick up their children from school. He hadn't spent much time with Trey since their return from the cruise, but as long as Trey was happy, David was happy.

David walked down the hall to Kurt's room. He cleaned up some and finished unpacking for Kurt. He was putting away some of Kurt's things when he noticed the picture of Kurt's sister and her husband in the top drawer. His sister was holding Cheyenne who was just a few weeks old at the time. They looked happy. The photograph, however, made David feel a little sad. He had often wished he had been with Trey from the time of his birth, and this picture reminded him, once again, of what he had missed. Snap out of it, David. You have Trey now, and that's what's important, he told himself. He placed the picture back where he had found it, and stood for a moment thinking of Kurt. His passion for life and compassion for others were the reasons for David's strong attraction to him. That attraction quickly became physical whenever he thought of Kurt, like right now. Thinking of his selflessness was causing David to become extremely aroused.

David quickly undressed, as Kurt would be coming up the stairs any time now, and got into bed. He could hear Kurt's footsteps on the stairs, and then his hand on the doorknob. Kurt walked in and looked at David lying in his bed. "Mm, I like what I see," he said, as he locked the door behind him.

"Well, what do you think of this?" David teased, and threw the covers off of his completely naked body. He folded his arms behind his head, and spread his legs wide. He was, without a doubt, more than ready for Kurt. His full erection was pulsating and he licked his lips seductively as he watched Kurt's expression.

Shock and excitement were both registered on Kurt's face. Kurt stared at David's body. He loved David's body. He especially loved his and David's bodies together in as many ways as were possible.

Kurt was out of his clothes in seconds, his erection fully available for David's enjoyment. He climbed onto the bed and onto David, straddling him, and holding his hands as they lay behind David's head. He pressed his lips to David's, forcing his mouth open and kissing him hungrily. David was kissing back, finding this captive role extremely arousing. Kurt positioned himself so that his and David's bodies were meshed for maximal arousal. His erect nipples were kissing David's equally erect ones, his lusciously hairy chest was caressing David's smooth one, their bodies fit together so that their erections could feel the other, and Kurt's legs were moving off and then back onto David's which was arousing both men more than either had anticipated.

Kurt kissed David slowly and lightly, and then would force his mouth open with his own and tease David's tongue into its awaiting lover. The feel of Kurt's nakedness on his own was almost overpowering to David. Kurt was feeling just as aroused, as he held David's body underneath his own and was enjoying the feel of David's erection against his own. Kurt wanted to enter David and feel David squeeze his throbbing penis until he exploded deep within him. Kurt released David's tongue from its loving home and coaxed his lips off David's. He looked at David's face.

When he opened his eyes, Kurt asked, "How do you want me, David?"

David hadn't been asked this before. He thought it was part of Kurt's seduction. "Any way I can have you, baby," David replied.

Kurt let his engorged penis slide between David's spread buttocks and rest at that opening Kurt knew that once entered would bring David unimaginable pleasure. "I want to bring you pleasure like I know I can, David."

David was aroused even more. He knew that Kurt loved him, and he knew that he loved Kurt. "I know how to give you the pleasure you deserve. Let me show you, David."

Feeling Kurt's dick eager to enter him was exciting to David. This was Kurt loving him. Kurt was stimulating him with the most sensual oil he had ever felt. David bent his legs so that Kurt could give him even more. Kurt was watching David's face and could see that he was aroused. When Kurt combined this stimulation with a massage of that erogenous place beneath David's balls, David moaned and spread his legs as far apart as he could. Kurt's massage intensified, and so did David's moans.

When Kurt was sure that David was ready, he entered him slowly with an oil stimulated dick that knew exactly where it was going. As Kurt's dick slid into David's tightness, Kurt slid his body back on top of David's until they were once again face to face. When he had entered him fully, Kurt kissed David lightly on the lips, and then slid his tongue along David's lips. David held Kurt tightly as he entered him again and again, slowly each time enjoying the feel of David tightening around him. After David had moaned with pleasure more than once, Kurt entered him fully and David gasped with pleasure. "I love you, David," Kurt said with a conviction that caused David to open his eyes in surprise. Kurt's selflessness had once again shown itself with intense clarity. "Oh, baby, I love you so much," David said in response.

They both had known of the other's love for some time, and now this love had been verbalized, making it more real somehow. David reached down and grabbed Kurt's ass, pushing it back and pulling it forward, loving the feel of Kurt's most intimate self enter him again and again. Kurt was powerless under David's control, and powerless under the control of his own orgasm which came with such force that it made him moan and gasp in the same breath. David loved the feel of Kurt inside him more than he had ever thought possible. As Kurt's lifeless penis slid out of its new home, Kurt slid downward on David's body and began to welcome his erection into his mouth.

To Kurt's surprise, David rolled him over and was behind him before Kurt knew what had happened. "I know what you like, baby, and I know how you like it," David said, and he too enjoyed the feel of the stimulating oil on his dick and almost came before he had even entered Kurt once. Kurt was pushing back against David's pelvis wanting more and more inside him, and squeezing around this thick engorged lover that was filling him so completely. David was giving Kurt what he knew he wanted. With hard thrusts, he was going deeper and deeper, until Kurt was solely at his mercy. Kurt surrendered his entire being to David, as his upper body lay on the bed, with David's hands firmly on Kurt's thighs pulling his body toward him with every thrust. Kurt moaned each time David's satisfying erect penis reached deeply inside him as far as it could. David was trying to keep from climaxing, but the sight of Kurt's gorgeous ass swallowing his erection entirely was finally too erotic for him to sustain his erection. After thrusting so hard and so deep inside him that Kurt cried out in both ecstasy and surprise, David's entire body shuddered as he came harder and deeper into Kurt than he ever had.

Kurt's complete surrender to David was so powerful that David's knees were weak as his explosion neared its completion. He laid Kurt's widespread legs on the bed and lay on top of him, his penis still snug in its always welcoming home. David placed his hands on Kurt's and kissed his cheek. "I love you so much, Kurt."

When Kurt could finally breathe again, he said, "Mm, I love you, baby." They lay in this position for as long as they could, until they felt that they probably should get dressed in anticipation of the kids' return home. They held each other, and enjoyed the taste and feel of each other's lips.

"You know we should get up, right?" David asked, and then kissed Kurt again so he couldn't respond.

"Mm, do we have to?" With one last hug, they forced themselves to get up and get dressed.

It was mid afternoon when they walked down the stairs to the kitchen. "Hungry?" David asked.

"A little, I guess. I thought maybe we could all go out tonight, unless the kids have eaten too much already," Kurt added. Then that familiar panic look came into his eyes. David quickly went to him and led him to a chair.

David pulled out a chair and faced him. He took Kurt's hands in his, and spoke directly. "Okay, now, what just went through your mind?"

Kurt looked pale. David bent him at the waist and held him with his head almost to his knees. David was determined to prevent a panic attack. He knew Kurt could handle this. David rubbed his back in slow smooth strokes. "It just hit me that people might think we're a couple."

"That's okay, Kurt. Most people are too caught up in their own lives to give too much thought to others. Some may talk, but we just have to ignore it. Sometimes what we think we see isn't what is truly being shown. Sometimes a look or glance is just a look or a glance." There is a quote by a famous writer that speaks to this, Kurt. "Be who you are and say what you feel because those who matter don't mind, and those who mind don't matter." Feeling better, Kurt sat up, and asked, "Who said that?" David grinned as he answered his own question. "Dr. Suess said that, Kurt."

Kurt felt better both physically and emotionally, but he always did when he was with David. He wondered how he had ever lived before David, and also wondered if he really had lived until David. They heard the car in the drive just then. David suggested that Kurt might want to splash some water on his face, and it was then that Kurt realized he had been sweating. He had had a panic attack but had come out of it without medication, and that was a first for him.

He hurried upstairs just as the kids were coming in the door. Trey and Cheyenne were full of stories about their day, talking constantly. Sara looked tired, but was very good with the kids and happy that Cheyenne had a new friend and probable stepbrother. Kurt came down the stairs and scooped Cheyenne up like a doll.

She squealed, and said, "Put me down, Daddy. I'm not a baby."

Kurt set her down and put his arm around Trey. "How was your day, buddy?"

"Fine," he said sheepishly. He went over and made himself comfortable on David's lap.

Sara had excused herself and gone to her room. David and Kurt knew she was tired, and decided to have their own basement campout tonight, just the four of them. After all, they were a family now. They just needed to tell the kids.

Four

Two to Four

Trey and Cheyenne loved the idea of a campout with their dads. Kurt went upstairs to tell Sara, but she was sound asleep. David ordered pizza and once it arrived, the four of them set out for the perfect basement campout. Trey and Cheyenne explained to Kurt and David how to play "basement campout", and after they ate their pizza David and Kurt snuggled with their children inside the tent.

David looked at Kurt for a sign that he was ready to tell the kids about the love that had blossomed between them, and Kurt nodded. David hoped that Kurt was strong enough for this. At least he was lying down. David knew that this was important for Cheyenne, and when it came to Cheyenne, Kurt would find the strength somehow.

Kurt began the conversation. "You two like each other a lot, don't you?" He looked at both Cheyenne and Trey.

"Uh, huh," Trey spoke with authority.

Cheyenne just shook her head in agreement.

So far, so good, thought David.

Kurt looked at David to continue. "Well, how would you two like to live together, all the time?"

Trey looked confused. Then he looked horrified. Then he ran out of the tent, tears streaming down his face.

Oh God, what have I done, thought David, as he ran after him. He caught up with him in the kitchen. "Hey buddy, let's talk." He led Trey over to a chair and set him on his lap. "I'm sorry, Trey. I should have talked to you alone about this first, just you and me. I'm new at this family stuff, too, buddy."

Trey looked at him, the tears still pouring down his face. "You don't want me anymore, but why? And how do you know that they won't get rid of me?" Trey choked out these words with his shaky voice.

David felt like the worst parent that had ever lived. He held Trey, forcing him to look at him. Wiping the tears from Trey's face, David spoke calmly and reassuringly. "No, no, baby. You and I will always be together, always. What I meant was that you and I and Kurt and Cheyenne all live together, and become a bigger family. You and I are forever, Trey, just like I promised." He held Trey and rocked him like a baby. "I'm so sorry, baby. I'm so sorry."

Trey's crying stopped and he calmed with David's rocking. "I'm sorry we haven't been spending much time together, just you and me. I love you, Trey, and that's forever, too." David kissed him on the forehead and wiped the tears from his face.

Trey hugged him, and said, "I love you, too, Daddy."

David would do anything for Trey. He hugged him and rocked him, and kissed his tears away.

"I thought we were a family, Daddy."

"Oh, baby, we are a family. I really like being with Kurt, talking with him about work and things. He asked if you and I would be a part of his and Cheyenne's lives." David hoped he wasn't doing as bad a job explaining this as he thought he was.

"Oh, okay. I like Cheyenne, and Kurt's real nice to me too. Can Sara come too?"

"Yes, honey, Sara helped Kurt with Cheyenne since he traveled a lot on business, but he won't be traveling as much anymore. Sara will still be with us though." He explained to Trey as best he could Sara's role in Cheyenne's and Kurt's lives.

Trey hadn't asked anything further specifically about his and Kurt's relationship and David thought it best that he wait until Trey asked very specific questions before offering unnecessary explanations. David felt as if he had no idea what he was doing as a parent. But according to the parents of Trey's classmates, this feeling was very normal and would be with him for a very long time.

Trey did ask some about David's and Kurt's relationship. "Daddy, will you be working for Cheyenne's daddy?"

Still leaning against his chest, David held Trey and stroked his hair. "No, buddy, I will continue the work that I've been doing, and Kurt will continue doing his job." Just answer the questions, David, he kept telling himself.

"Daddy?"

Oh, no, hold on, David, another question. "Yes, Trey?"

"Can we go back to the campout now?"

What a relief, he thought. He picked Trey up and carried him back down the stairs.

Cheyenne was thrilled to see Trey again, and squeezed him as hard as her little arms would allow. She was echoing the good news that Kurt had told her while Trey and David were talking.

Kurt looked at David and both of them looked tired. They realized then that they should have spoken to the kids one-on-one. They just smiled and shook their heads, having realized that parenting, although rewarding, was by no means easy.

Cheyenne was chattering away about how much fun they would all have. Fun was her main goal right now. Trey, however, still had a few unanswered questions. "Where are we going to live?" he asked.

Kurt spoke up before David could respond. Kurt could see the distress on Trey's face. Kurt looked at David as he spoke. "Well, Trey, where would you like to live - here or Denver, or maybe somewhere else?" David just winked at Kurt in gratitude.

Trey thought about it. "Denver, in our house, and you and Cheyenne can move in with us and Cheyenne can go to my school and I'll walk her to school every day."

Trey announced his plan as if he were announcing a major news event. Giving Trey the power to choose was a good idea that Kurt had, thought David. It allowed Trey to feel as if he had some control over the situation. David knew that Kurt and he would be better parents together than they were alone. Their parenting seemed to complement each other's. He wondered, though, what toll the move to Denver would take on Kurt. Perhaps Kurt would feel better about the two of them as a couple, though, since Denver was a much larger and much more diverse city.

"Denver it is," announced Kurt, as he shook Trey's hand. "Good choice, buddy."

Trey beamed and sat next to Cheyenne, proudly proclaiming the fun activities there were to be had in Denver. David gave Kurt a questioning look, and Kurt returned a reassuring one. Kurt drew emotional strength from David, just as David drew parental strength from Kurt. The rest of the evening was spent enjoying the basement campout, and becoming a new family.

Sara awoke in the middle of the night and walked quietly down to the basement. When she saw the four of them all together she knew they would be a great family. She went back up the stairs to her room.

Kurt and David awoke early the next morning and reached out to each other and held hands. They turned on their sides, the kids between them, and looked at each other. They were meant for each other, and meant to be a family. David mouthed the words, "I love you", and Kurt returned the same mouthed words. After the long day yesterday they thought the kids would probably sleep late, so they eased out of their sleeping bags and quietly walked upstairs to begin reworking their plans.

David called the realtor to take his house off the market and to place Kurt's on the market. The realtor looked up Kurt's house and felt certain that it would sell within days. In fact, the realtor thought she may have a few clients who would be interested already. Alone in the kitchen, David and Kurt had the chance to discuss last night's events. As they drank a cup of coffee, they held hands. "What was I thinking, Kurt, blurting things out like that without talking to Trey first?"

"Oh, David, don't be so hard on yourself," Kurt assured him. "The way I see it, you and I are both good parents, but together we are going to be great parents." Kurt's words were reassuring to David. He knew Kurt was right. They were going to be great together, as parents and as lovers.

"Are you sure you're okay with moving, Kurt?" David was very concerned about this. "Won't the change be very difficult for you, Kurt, make you more anxious?"

Kurt ran his hand through his hair, and looked into his coffee. "No, David, I don't think it will. I think I need a change. It will be like leaving my old business behind me and moving to my new business, figuratively speaking of course. And, if we're going to be a family, we need to start thinking like one. Financially it will be a good move because you are already established in your job, David." David did know all of this, but would have done anything to make life easier for Kurt. "Who knows, I might find some clients in Denver," Kurt added.

Neither knew what their future would bring as a family or as a couple. They didn't know if they would make it. What they did know, though, was that they loved each other, loved each other's kids, and wanted to be together.

"We'll make it Kurt, we will," David reassured him.

"You bet we will," Kurt responded, and leaned across the table to kiss David.

Sara walked in on them in mid kiss which embarrassed them much more than it did her. She cleared her throat, and Kurt sat back down in his chair. "Oh, you two, I have a lot of gay friends." Then she walked over to them and placed a hand on each of their backs. "I'm very happy for both of you. I knew you cared about each other even before you knew it." She laughed smugly at this last part.

They smiled at her and then at each other. "I'm sure you did, Sara," Kurt added. They asked her to sit with them, and Kurt explained about last night and that their plans had changed. Kurt was afraid he would lose her. Cheyenne loved her, and Trey had grown to love her too. "Oh, no, Kurt. This will make it easier for me." Kurt looked confused. She explained that she was at the point in her studies that she would need to drive to Denver two nights a week, and didn't know how she would do that with Kurt out of town as much as his business required him to be. He explained about that too. The subtle change of tone in his voice didn't go unnoticed by either David or Sara. David hoped that Kurt's new business structure would help him to forget about the business he had lost. Sara assured Kurt and David that she would be there for them.

David offered Sara the attic apartment rent-free if she wanted to live with them. He told her that he had lived in the apartment before he had bought the house. "It has plenty of room and is very nice, Sara. The former owners were great landlords." He told her that it had a separate outside entrance as well as an open stairway leading to the upper floor of the house where the bedrooms were located. "We can drive up to Denver today if you like, so you can see it. I think the sooner Trey gets back to his home, the better he will feel. He needs to be surrounded by the familiar right now."

Sara graciously accepted David's offer, and assured him and Kurt that she would always be there for the kids. Not having to travel far to take classes and having a free place to live was more than any college student could ever dream of. She headed off to begin packing Cheyenne's clothes and toys.

The remainder of the week was a blur of boxes and bags, moving and mayhem. Kurt's house sold immediately, with the new owners demanding immediate occupancy. David and Kurt both knew that moving quickly was best for everyone, but it was nonetheless exhausting. David was secretly happy to be in his house in Denver. It had approximately the same square footage as Kurt's, but was built more upward than outward like Kurt's.

Five

David's House

Kurt's office was in a small alcove off the dining room from where he could easily see the kitchen through one doorway and the living room from the other doorway. There were no doors to his office, but arched doorways. Kurt loved his office. He felt snug and secure there, and not cut off from the other activities in the house. The kids could see him, too, which was a comfort for them.

There were two bedrooms upstairs separated by a bath, which was perfect for the kids. The open staircase that led to Sara's attic apartment was fun for the kids to explore, and Sara didn't mind at all. She insisted on having Cheyenne's toy box in her apartment so that the kids could play while she was studying.

At the far end of the main floor was the master bedroom that David had surprised Kurt with by decorating it much like his old bedroom, so that it now reflected both of their tastes.

While Kurt was closing on his house in Colorado Springs, David had moved some of his own furniture to the basement so that Kurt wouldn't feel that he was an outsider. He had repainted much of the house, replaced window dressings, and had placed many of Kurt's personal effects in the house. This was David's and Kurt's place now, and the two of them plus the children were a family. He had insisted that Kurt make all the decisions pertaining to his office, and had redone it to Kurt's specifications while he was still in Colorado Springs. While the kids "helped" Sara move into her new apartment, David had unpacked as fast as he could in preparation for Kurt's homecoming.

When Kurt walked into the house, he didn't know what to say. David watched as Kurt walked through the house looking at everything, the smell of fresh paint vaguely evident. The kids were with Sara in her apartment, so David ushered Kurt into their new bedroom. Kurt's bed was there and took up over half the room, the aroma of fresh paint was evident here too, and David had redecorated it to reflect both of their tastes which complemented the other just as David and Kurt complemented each other in so many ways. Kurt set down the last of the suitcases he had brought with him and threw his arms around David, kissing him with quick kisses at first, then finding his mouth and kissing him the way lovers kissed. Both men missed each other more than they had known. Kurt was kissing David as if he was trying to eat him whole, and David soon reciprocated. They were hungry for each other, starved.

"Oh, David, it's been a week, an entire week," Kurt said, barely audible as he took his mouth off of David's just long enough to get the words out.

"Tonight is ours, Kurt. Just a few more hours and we will be together again."

Both of them had to force themselves off the other or before long they wouldn't be able to. "I am going to love you like you've never been loved before, David. After doing all this for me, your body will be on fire." David could feel his arousal begin to grow, and with one last embrace forced himself from Kurt, if only for a little while. Both looked at each other with lust and hunger in their eyes. "Let's feed the kids so we can come back here, the sooner the better." Kurt could feel his jeans tighten and had to look away from David before he ripped his clothes off and had David right then and there.

Trey had asked where Kurt's room was, to which David explained that Kurt and he would be sharing a room. David had been prepared to explain their relationship as best he could, but Trey's only concern was Kurt's happiness. "That's nice, Daddy. It's good to share." Trey had hurried off to play, and David had breathed a sigh of relief. Just answer the questions, David, and everything will take care of itself in time, he reminded himself yet again.

Sara had promised the kids an attic sleepover, and had an entire evening of fun prepared. They were going to have a picnic and play games and, as a statement that no dads were allowed, Trey and Cheyenne insisted on closing the drawbridge-like door to the attic. Kurt and David looked at each other after the kids said goodnight to them. They weren't going to have to wait until after supper. They were ready for bed right now.

Kurt told David that he definitely needed a shower first, after the long day and long drive to Denver. David squeezed Kurt's buns and winked at him, waiting until he heard the shower before undressing and waiting in bed for Kurt. His arousal had made itself known at the thought of Kurt naked in the shower, the water from the shower shooting its stimulating streams onto Kurt's completely naked body.

David couldn't wait. He walked into the bathroom and almost came as he watched the silhouette of Kurt's body being massaged everywhere by his own hands. David stood there for a moment, his dick fully erect, unable to move. David opened and closed the shower door without Kurt knowing that he had joined him. David reached around Kurt and squeezed his balls with one hand, while the other hand firmly grasped Kurt's dick. "I have something for you," David said into Kurt's ear. Kurt dropped the soap at David's touch and David's seductive words. He could feel David's erection forcing its way between his buttocks, causing Kurt's knees to nearly buckle. David repositioned one hand on Kurt's chest, while enjoying the feel of Kurt's balls and Kurt's arousal with the other. "Mm," David sighed beside Kurt's ear, and then ran his tongue along Kurt's neck. Kurt reached his hands behind David and firmly cupped and squeezed his firm ass, forcing David's erection more firmly against the innermost place between Kurt's spread buttocks. David's gasp was audible in Kurt's ear, causing him to become even more aroused than he already was. Kurt leaned forward bracing himself with his hands on the shower wall. David eased his erection out from its snug home between Kurt's clenched buttocks and replaced it with probing fingers sliding along the well-defined track that led to the place that Kurt was making very available by spreading his legs wide. David's fingers lingered there for a moment, and then slid between Kurt's legs to stimulate that area that caused Kurt to gasp. David forced Kurt's buttocks apart with his forearm as his hand reached even further between Kurt's legs to squeeze his balls hard.

Kurt's head was against the shower wall now, as he surrendered his entire being to his lover. "Ohhh," moaned Kurt, as his body slid along the shower wall to settle where two walls came together. David continued his motions as he found Kurt's parted lips with his own and kissed him with kisses only a lover knows, while the shower jets teased their bodies with each new pulsation. The sensations that David was providing between Kurt's legs were making it difficult for Kurt to breathe, much less kiss David with the same intensity that David was kissing him. Just as David had full control of all that he found between Kurt's legs, he now had full control of Kurt's mouth as well. Kurt could only lean against the wall, his lips parted, as David enjoyed his mouth in its entirety. He ran his tongue along Kurt's lips, and then explored the inner pleasures of Kurt's mouth until he slowly sucked Kurt's tongue into his mouth fully until their lips met. Kurt pulled his mouth off David's and forced David against the shower wall. Then his mouth found David's nipples and nibbled them until they were fully erect. Kurt's mouth on David's nipples along with the stimulation from the jets beating down on them caused David to lose control of the situation. Kurt forced David's legs apart and probed and massaged in between. As Kurt continued to massage that most sensitive area between David's legs, he kneeled before him and slowly and seductively welcomed David's erection into his mouth.

David's heart was beating wildly and he moaned and writhed uncontrollably. "Oh, yes, Kurt, that's what I like." Kurt did know what David liked. "I think I know what you like better, don't I?" David liked sucking Kurt, and Kurt knew it. He also knew that David liked being deep inside of Kurt and Kurt loved it when he was there. Kurt opened the shower door and led David by his dick to the bed where he opened himself wide to David. "Fuck me, David. Go deep, baby. I've missed you so much." David reached between Kurt's legs and squeezed his balls. Then he squeezed Kurt's buns, separating them wide, and entered him slowly, while he made moaning sounds that caused Kurt to once again surrender himself wholly to David's will. "Ohhh," was all that Kurt could get out as David entered him again and again, while holding Kurt's engorged penis firmly with one hand.

As Kurt neared climax, his breathing came fast, and he begged David to go faster. "You want it bad, don't you baby?" David's words almost caused Kurt to climax. "Yes, bad," Kurt gasped out the words. David withdrew almost entirely, and then entered Kurt so fast and so deep that Kurt's entire body moved forward. David's thrusts were more forceful and deeper than Kurt remembered and he nearly screamed with ecstasy. David was quickly losing control and with a last hard thrust he came with such force that he and Kurt gasped and moaned over and over until they fell limp on the bed.

Just as David's once erect penis slipped out of Kurt, he turned Kurt onto his back and straddled him. With his spread buttocks looking extremely inviting so close to Kurt's face, David did what he had been looking forward to all week. He engulfed Kurt's erect penis all the way to the base as he once again squeezed Kurt's balls, then pulled them up and massaged deeply underneath. David was certain that he had full control of the situation as he intensified his sucking and massaging, until he felt Kurt's hands on his ass. While his hands were on David's ass,

Kurt's fingers soon discovered that very special space between David's buttocks that was open and eagerly awaiting their touch. When Kurt's fingers outlined this inviting space, and then entered this space stopping just long enough to slightly enter that emptiness that only Kurt could fill, David squeezed Kurt's thighs to keep from screaming. He bent down further so that his buttocks were spread even further apart, the empty space more open now, begging for Kurt. David couldn't move. Kurt's erection was deep within his mouth. He was once again able to focus on Kurt's pleasure and intensified his sucking. He was determined to bring Kurt to an explosive climax.

As Kurt's climax neared, he allowed his probing fingers to go where they had been begging to go. He entered David slowly with just one finger, just as David was pulling on Kurt's cock with his mouth so forcefully that Kurt cried out. Kurt went deeper into David and he wanted that part of Kurt that was filling his mouth to be filling him the way he knew Kurt wanted to. David stopped his sucking and sat straight up, enjoying the feel of a part of Kurt inside him. "Take as much as you want, David," Kurt said behind him. "Kiss me David," Kurt commanded. David forced himself off of Kurt just long enough to turn and face him. "It's yours for the taking, baby," Kurt said seductively. David kissed Kurt, and Kurt eased David's spread buttocks onto his awaiting erection. Kurt moaned into David's mouth as he entered David. David loved the feel of Kurt inside him. He filled him completely, and knew exactly how to please him. David was squeezing Kurt's dick hard as he raised himself up and Kurt hurriedly pushed him back down. Kurt's dick had found a place it never wanted to leave. David raised himself up on Kurt, and moaned loudly as Kurt maneuvered his skillful erection into the deepness of David. David's eyes were closed and he was moaning freely, lost in his own pleasure. Kurt was looking at David, and loved the look of complete abandon on his face. Kurt's climax was as much a surprise to him as it was to David. David gasped as he felt the impact of Kurt's orgasm filling his most intimate recesses. Kurt pulled David down on him as he thrust his pelvis upward, entering David until he had been satisfied completely.

They lay together just as they were, holding each other as they slept until morning. Neither had slept as well as they did that night in an entire week. With David in Denver and Kurt closing on his house in Colorado Springs, this past week seemed to last forever. This is the way they were meant to be, meshed one to one as they slept following passionate explosive lovemaking.

The following week David returned to work and Kurt continued his business just as he had restructured it in Colorado Springs. Trey had returned to school and was so proud to hold Cheyenne's hand as she began preschool. He felt like he was really a big brother now. Working at home and not traveling nearly as much as he had, Kurt was able to pick up the kids from school every afternoon. Kurt could see right away that David had been right in moving them to Denver.

The diversity of the students in both Trey's and Cheyenne's classes was great. The entire school was a tribute to the great melting pot that America had promised to be. Trey had friends whose origins represented many cultures. Cheyenne fit right in. There were children of almost every race in her class. It was not uncommon to see white parents with black children, or vice versa, and it was also not uncommon to see a couple that represented two entirely different cultures. Kurt had wondered if there were any gay parents, but didn't know yet. He thought that there were a few kids with two mommies, but couldn't be certain. He was, however, very pleased with Cheyenne's school.

Once home, the big brother in Trey in no way went into hiding. He explained to Cheyenne how important it was to do their homework before they played, and he also took charge of snack preparation. Sometimes Sara was already upstairs studying when Trey and Cheyenne came home from school, and sometimes she came home a little later. If she were already home, Trey and Cheyenne knew they were always welcome to do their homework in her apartment while Sara did hers.

Kurt was happy. He didn't know how he had gotten through the days, much less the nights, without David in his life. David's days were long, but he didn't seem as tired as he was before he and Trey had taken their vacation cruise. He loved Kurt and thought about him much of the day, looking forward to the nights when he never tired of the feel of Kurt's body next to his. He could become aroused just thinking of Kurt touching him. Kurt was a stay-at-home dad now and he loved it. He hoped he never had to work outside the home again.

Although Trey loved being in charge of Cheyenne, a self-designated role, he eagerly awaited David's return home from work and would follow him to his bedroom that he shared with Kurt, shut the door behind the two of them, sit on the bed while David changed his clothes, and recount the day's events in great detail.

At the end of their first full week as a family, Trey followed David into his bedroom as he had every day that week, and shut the door behind them. Today, however, David sensed that Trey had something on his mind other than the day's events. David changed his clothes, and then asked Trey what was on his mind.

"Daddy, why is there only one bed in here?"

David tried not to show the panic that was forming inside him. "Well, Trey, there isn't room for more than one bed in here."

One simplification wasn't going to satisfy Trey, not this time. "Who sleeps in the bed, then? Do you have to sleep on the couch since this is Kurt's bed?"

Blessed child, this one, thought David. He's concerned that I'm okay. "No, buddy, Kurt and I share this bed." There, he had said it. Now all he had to do was await Trey's reaction. David craved Trey's approval just as much as Trey craved his.

Trey looked up at David with the sweetest eyes, the eyes of a child. "Why?"

Of all the responses David could have imagined at this moment, this wasn't one of them. How could such a small word hold so much?

David pulled Trey close and put his arm around him. Then he held both of Trey's small hands in his free one. "I care a lot about Kurt, Trey, and he cares a lot about me. We realized how much we had in common when we were together on the cruise. We also saw what a great family the four of us would make."

David's heart was beating so fast and so hard that he was sure Trey could hear it too. Expecting judgment, David was shocked when Trey turned to him and hugged him so hard he could barely breathe.

Trey kissed him and said sweetly, "I'm glad you're happy, Daddy. I have two daddies now, and so does Cheyenne. Tony and Megan have two mommies." Trey just looked at David and smiled.

David pulled Trey to him and hugged him tight. He didn't want Trey to think he was sad if he saw the tears welling up in his eyes. David was so touched by Trey's innocent sweetness that he couldn't stop the tears.

Trey pulled away. "Daddy, are you sad?"

"No, Trey, I'm very happy. These are happy tears."

Trey shook his head. "Grownups are weird."

David was laughing and crying at the same time. He was curious about Tony and Megan. "Have you met Tony's and Megan's mommies, Trey?"

"Yep, one of them picks Tony and Megan up from school every day, but I know they like each other too because sometimes they come together and hold each other's hand."

Trey said this so nonchalantly that David was almost ashamed of himself that he had doubted Trey's reaction. Trey no doubt knew more than David gave him credit for.

With such diversity in Trey's school, perhaps there is hope for the future, thought David. Maybe it would be Trey's and Cheyenne's generation that would break down the many barriers that separated us as humans. Maybe one day the dreams of all those who had dreamed before him would come true. David hoped that he would be alive to witness this blessed day.

"Daddy, can Tony and Megan come home after school and play sometime? Tony's in my class, and Megan is in Cheyenne's class. We play together at school."

"Of course you can, Trey, anytime you like." David kissed him on the forehead, and Trey headed off to play outside with Cheyenne.

David was sitting on the bed with his head in his hands when Kurt opened the door. When he saw David sitting like this, Kurt closed the door behind him. He sat beside David on the bed and put his arm around him. "What's wrong, love?"

David hadn't heard Kurt come in, so lost was he in his own thoughts. He sat up and looked at Kurt. "Oh, nothing Kurt, nothing at all." David hugged Kurt as tightly as he had Trey. When he recapped his and Trey's conversation, Kurt was as touched as David had been. "Why did I make such a big deal about it, Kurt?"

"Because you care so much, David. We're always afraid of losing that which we most care about." Then David told Kurt about the "two mommies" that the kids knew.

"I guess we're not as much of an anomaly as we thought, buddy." David winked at Kurt as he said this.

David was tired after the first week back at work, and lay back on the bed. Kurt joined him, and the two stared at the ceiling desperately trying to stay awake. Waking up in each other's arms was what each had been missing for a very long time. They could have slept until noon, but Trey and Cheyenne wasted no time in spoiling their plan.

They knocked on the door at 8:00 a.m. wanting to get a head start on the weekend. Kurt and David slipped their jeans on and opened the door. Cheyenne and Trey ran and jumped into the bed and wanted Kurt and David to snuggle with them. Cheyenne curled up next to Kurt, and Trey next to David. Then they informed Kurt and David of all the fun activities they were going to do this weekend. Kurt and David felt tired," but happy, just thinking about doing as many things as the kids had planned.

They did have fun that weekend. Trey led the tour of the city, eager to share every part of his life with his new little sister. Kurt and David followed Trey's lead, knowing now how it felt to be a family. They were a diverse family, as unique as this country. They were two gay fathers with one adopted white child and one adopted African-American child, who had discovered the basis of family, any family, and that was a deep love and respect for its members.

Saturday came and went quickly, with everyone eager to go to bed early. David and Kurt couldn't imagine sleeping alone again. Their entwined bodies rested easily as they held each other throughout the night, though they rarely made it through the entire night without enjoying the pleasures that were known only to those deeply in love.

The Sunday morning following their first very full week as a family was one such time. Kurt awoke to the feel of David's hand between his legs after David had awoken to find Kurt's leg draped over him. David couldn't resist the feel of Kurt's body. He watched a sleeping Kurt moving with his hand as it explored the luscious place between Kurt's legs. David slid his forearm between Kurt's legs, opening them further, as he reached up and caressed Kurt's gorgeous ass. Kurt was as hard as David was. Still sleeping, Kurt moaned as he positioned his body for maximum pleasure. He mumbled while he slept, and this combined with his body begging for greater attention from David's probing hand was a turn-on for David.

It was when David kissed his open mouth and entered him slightly with just a finger that Kurt opened his eyes. "Oh, David, I thought I was dreaming," Kurt said as he separated David's buttock with his hand. David draped his leg over Kurt, just as Kurt had over David. He entered David just as David had entered him. Kurt had been turned on for awhile now, and wanted more. He was on top of David before David knew what happened, and eased himself onto David penis.

David gasped both from surprise as well as from pleasure. "Oh, Kurt," David said with a sigh. "I know, baby." He teased David's nipples as long as he could before he lost all sense of anything except for the feeling of ecstasy that also accompanied David entering him. Kurt closed his eyes and took all of David deep inside him. David filled him completely, entering so deeply that every pleasure spot was discovered and satisfied.

Lost in ecstasy, Kurt began to masturbate himself after the feel of his hardened entity had been enjoying the feel of David's body as it moved up and back with Kurt's up and down movements on David's hardened entity. Watching Kurt masturbate with total abandon was making it difficult for David to stave off his own climax. Kurt squeezed his own balls and stroked his dick while David watched, desperately trying to control his own climax. He desperately wanted to remove Kurt's hands and replace them with his own, but he was too engrossed watching Kurt and too close to his own climax to do anything. Instead, he held onto Kurt's buttocks as his dick continued to enter Kurt over and over. "David," Kurt said as he pulled hard on his dick, and then added a long "ohhh," as he came right in front of David's eyes which caused his own explosion deep inside Kurt. David pulled down hard on Kurt's buttocks, holding them in place as he found the innermost part of Kurt as he experienced a climax like no other. This feeling caused Kurt's body to shudder, and he steadied himself until he knew that David's climax was complete. Then Kurt moaned as he lowered himself onto David and kissed him hard, forcing his mouth open as far as he could, and holding David's head, stroking his cheeks. Then as he continued to hold David's head, he laid his head on David's shoulder.

Breathily, he spoke with his mouth on David's ear. "David, I love you as I have loved no other man. I can never thank you enough or repay you for all you have done for me. I couldn't go on without you if you were ever to leave me."

David was not expecting these words, not now or ever. How did he respond to this? Holding Kurt tightly, he said aloud so that Kurt would be sure to hear, "You will never know what life is like without me because I could never live my life without you, Kurt. I can't even imagine what my life would be like without you, and I have forgotten what it was like before you." Kurt kissed David on the neck and they held each other, enjoying the essence of the other.

They spent a leisurely Sunday together as a family. David and Kurt made an old fashioned Sunday brunch for the four of them. Sara was spending the weekend at her parents' house, the first weekend she had been away from Kurt and Cheyenne in at least six months. Trey and Cheyenne had invited their friends Tony and Megan to play this afternoon in the one of a kind playhouse that Kurt and David had put together in the basement. It looked like a miniature house and the kids loved it.

Tony and Megan arrived with both their mommies, and David and Kurt were thrilled to talk to another couple who shared a very similar love as they. What was more exciting, especially to Kurt, was that they had started their own business and welcomed his expertise. They welcomed the opportunity to be clients of such a good businessman, and they made a list of other lesbian couples for him to contact. David was happy for Kurt. He's going to be okay, thought David.

Six

All of You

Monday morning came and they all had a very difficult time waking up. Sara had arrived back sometime during the night and as soon as the kids heard her moving around, they hurried up to her apartment to tell her all about their weekend.

As soon as everyone had gone, Kurt began working on his new account and looked at the list that their new friends had provided him. As he was reading, the words on the page became blurry. He felt lightheaded, and his face became hot. He became dizzy. He tried to take a deep breath but couldn't. This was not an unfamiliar feeling to him. He stumbled to the bedroom and barely made it to the bathroom where he ripped his clothes off and turned the shower to cold. Then he sat on the shower floor leaning against the side of the shower. He hadn't had a panic attack for awhile now, and had stopped taking his medication. What brought this one on? Everything is great for me.

He must have been out of it because he jumped when Sara knocked lightly on the shower door. "Kurt, I've been calling for you. Are you okay? I'm going to call David." Kurt couldn't answer. He couldn't move. Sara knew what was happening, and knew that Kurt needed David.

It was a relatively slow Monday for David, so he took a personal day and was home within minutes. He thanked Sara for staying until he arrived. She told David what she thought had happened, though she didn't actually see what had happened. Sara left, and David hurried to be with Kurt.

He opened the shower door and turned off the water. Kurt was shivering from the cold water, and was now lying on the floor of the shower in the fetal position. David removed his shoes and scrubs bottoms and knelt on the floor beside Kurt. Oh, this was a bad one, he thought. He grabbed his fleece robe and wrapped it around Kurt. Then he spoke slowly and softly. "Kurt, it's David. It's okay, baby. It's okay." Kurt's heart was beating fast, and David was afraid that Kurt was out of his medication. "Let me help you to the bed, okay? We can do this together." Kurt couldn't look at him. He knew what had happened, and was ashamed. David turned Kurt toward him and held him close. Kurt was exhausted, as he always was after his attacks. "Lean on me, Kurt, and we'll do this together." Kurt's legs were wobbly, but somehow they made it to the bed.

David removed Kurt's web robe and replaced it with a dry one, and covered him with as many blankets as he could find. That, along with the heated mattress pad and David's arms around him, was enough to at least stop Kurt's shivering. David held Kurt's huddled body close to him. "I love you, baby. We'll get through this, I promise. You've been through a lot, Kurt, more than most experience in a lifetime, and you've come through beautifully."

Kurt stretched his legs out and moved closer to David. David held him as close as he could. David felt Kurt's heart begin to race again, and knew he needed his medication. "I'm here, baby. I love you. It's okay." I've got to get Kurt's medicine, thought David. "Kurt, can you tell me where you medication is?" David whispered in Kurt's ear. Kurt did not answer. "You know you can trust me, baby. Let me help you." Kurt's heart beat faster. David moved down underneath the covers and held Kurt's face in his hands. "Baby, do you remember where they are?"

Kurt was scared and it showed in his wide open eyes. "Gone. I stopped taking them because I'm fine now." These words came out very slowly through Kurt's chattering teeth. "It's okay, baby. Hold on." David had gotten a prescription in his own name just in case of an event such as this. In his practice he saw people every day try to convince themselves that they no longer needed their medication.

David rolled onto his back to reach the bottom drawer of the nightstand where he had kept this medication hidden. He had barely moved when Kurt grabbed him around the waist, fearing he was leaving. "I'm not going anywhere, baby. I'm right here." He reached the tiny dissolvable tablets and once again held Kurt as tightly as he could. He spoke evenly and softly into his ear. "Baby, I have the same medication as you, but mine is a stronger strength. I'm going to place it under your tongue just like the others. I doubt that it will make you sleep, but you may feel drowsy and I don't want you to fight it, not this time."

Kurt's shaking was intensifying, and David struggled to steady him enough to give him the pill. Kurt was trying to help, but was hindering more than helping. David kissed him on the cheek, and spoke softly once again. "Let me do it, baby. Close your eyes, and let me do it all." David could feel Kurt's head nod as it lay against his chest.

Working by feel alone, David opened Kurt's mouth with a single finger and quickly slid the tiny tablet under his tongue. He held his finger on Kurt's tongue to keep the tablet in place until it dissolved. With Kurt's shaking, the pill could have easily been swallowed, and Kurt needed relief as quickly as it could be delivered. Kurt was holding onto David's side with all his might. Kurt was scared. He had never had an attack this bad. "It's all done, baby. You'll feel better very soon, I promise." David held him close, and as Kurt began to relax, David gently massaged his back, and said over and over, "I love you, baby. It's okay now."

Kurt's body finally relaxed and after the extensive amount of energy he had expended during the attack, he was soon asleep. David stayed with Kurt as he slept. Kurt's body began to warm as he slept. David continued to speak gently to Kurt, though he didn't think Kurt could hear him. David was tired enough from the long weekend that he too dozed off and on.

Kurt awoke after about an hour and his body was relaxed now. He snuggled close to David once again, which awakened him. "I'm here, baby. You never have to worry about that," David assured.

"David," Kurt began.

"Yes, Kurt, I'm here for you. You can tell me anything, you know that."

"I'm sorry," he said.

"Oh, Kurt, no apology is ever needed. This is a part of you, but it in no way defines you. Having panic attacks is no different than having diabetes, or any other condition. But, like a diabetic, it is important that you take you medication on a regular, steady basis. There is no need to feel ashamed, though, no reason at all."

Kurt didn't say anything, but David knew he was listening. Kurt was fortunate that David was a P.A. He had seen just about every illness there was.

"I'm going to call your physician and have your prescription transferred here, and then we'll get you established with a local physician. Are you okay with that, baby? Do you understand everything I just said?"

Kurt nodded his head against David's chest. He was very drowsy and almost asleep. "How long until awake?" Kurt was falling asleep fast.

"You may doze for a few hours off and on, but please don't fight it, baby." Kurt couldn't fight it even if he wanted to. "I'll be here the entire time. Go ahead and sleep, baby." Kurt slept well in David's snug embrace. It was just 10:00 a.m., so they had plenty of time before the kids would be home.

A day of rest was just what Kurt needed. His life had changed so much in the past month. David should have been more aware that this might happen. He had seen it in many patients. Maybe this was why physicians were discouraged from treating family members. It was too easy to overlook symptoms when we are with someone every day. David slept too, with Kurt in his arms until noon.

Kurt awoke in the arms of a sleeping David. David awoke immediately when Kurt moved. Kurt looked up at him. "How are you, buddy?" David asked, and then kissed Kurt lightly on the top of his head.

"I'm a lot better, David. Thank you."

David just smiled. "Do you remember what happened today, Kurt?"

Kurt admitted that he had.

"You'll take your medication on a regular basis from now on, right?"

"I promise, David."

David called right then to have Kurt's prescription transferred. David could pick it up at the pharmacy this afternoon. "All done, baby. I'll pick it up later today."

Kurt started to get out of bed, but had trouble standing. David was soon by his side. "Whoa, you're not used to this strength of your medication, Kurt. Where do you need to go?"

Kurt was really embarrassed now. "I have to go to the bathroom, David."

"I can help with that, buddy. No problem." David helped a wobbly Kurt to the bathroom. "You'd better sit down this time, Kurt." David helped him, and then waited outside the door. "Don't try to walk without my help. I mean that." Kurt swallowed his pride and called for David who helped him back to bed. "You should be standing on your own two feet in a couple of hours."

Kurt was feeling better already. He was thinking clearly now. David continued to lie beside him, holding him as they lay on their sides facing each other. "Why did it happen now, David? Everything is great."

"That's why, Kurt. You feel you have a lot to lose now, and without your medication the fear that you could lose your newfound happiness was given the opportunity to override the intellectual part of your brain. We know we really care about something or someone when we realize we could lose that something or someone."

"Will it happen again? How can I stop it?"

"I think you know the answer to that, Kurt. Take your medication regularly, as prescribed." David winked at him, but Kurt knew that David was very serious. "Because of your condition, you feel some things more acutely than others might." David kissed Kurt on the lips and hugged him tightly. "I love you, baby. I will always love you." David had Kurt's prescription delivered, so he didn't have to leave Kurt alone.

When Sara returned, David explained to her what had happened while Kurt slept. She offered to take Trey and Cheyenne to her apartment, and hurried off to create a great after school snack.

Sara knocked on the door with Kurt's prescription in hand and gave it to David. David placed it in the nightstand drawer after explaining to Kurt exactly how it would be taken, no exceptions. He was serious, and Kurt knew it. He had seen that "doctor look" on David's face too many times to misinterpret it. "You will take it, Kurt, as prescribed," David stated, looking Kurt directly in the eyes.

Kurt knew now that when David spoke sternly it was because he cared. "I promise, David," he replied. David planned to keep a very close count of Kurt's pills for awhile. These attacks scared David as much, if not more, than they did Kurt.

Kurt drifted off to sleep again, and David propped himself up on two pillows while he took care of his patient orders with the use of his laptop and the Internet. Kurt mumbled something in his sleep, and then wrapped his arms around one of David's legs. David finished his work quickly, then scooted back down underneath the covers and repositioned Kurt's arms around his waist as he wrapped his arms around Kurt. Kurt's security is more important than work, thought David. Kurt mumbled again, and buried his face in David's chest. David knew that the medication would make Kurt drowsy, with on and off sleeping all day, and then he could begin his normal regimen after dinner which would provide him a good night's sleep.

David knew that moving to Denver as quickly as he had would be good for Kurt long-term, but the rush to get the house ready for its new owners had been exhausting for Kurt. I should have been watching more closely, thought David. I shouldn't have left him alone, either. David knew he was being hard on himself. He had been taking care of the children and trying to make his own home welcoming for Kurt.

When the kids came home from school, Sara met them at the door and explained that Kurt was feeling well but assured Cheyenne that he would be all better tomorrow. She allowed Trey to go in and see David. Kurt was asleep, so Trey sat beside David and told him about his day. Then he kissed him on the cheek, and hurried to join the fun with Cheyenne and Sara.

David knew that Kurt would be fine, but wanted to do something special for him. What Kurt needed most of all was sleep. He would love for the two of them to be alone for a couple of days. That might be good for both of them. Their time alone had been amazing, but limited. They needed time to do nothing but talk, eat and sleep, and of course make love. The physician David worked for had a cabin just ten miles out of the city. That would be the perfect getaway for Kurt and him. Kurt wouldn't feel as though he were too far away from Cheyenne or his work, and knowing that he could go to her if she needed him would make it much easier for Kurt to relax.

When the medication finally wore off, David brought Kurt dinner in bed and after he had eaten, watched as he took his medication. "But David, I'll sleep all night," Kurt protested.

"Yes, Kurt, you will," David stated, anticipating a bit of protestation.

When Kurt saw the all familiar look on David's face, he took his medication and was soon sleeping soundly.

Kurt awoke at 4:00 a.m. He felt good, but he was thirsty. He pulled on his shorts and walked to the door of the bedroom, but couldn't open it. It was dark, so he couldn't see what was wrong. The knob turned and it would open just barely, but Kurt couldn't get it to open. David awoke from the noise and was immediately at the door. He put his arm around Kurt. "Where are you going, buddy?"

David startled him. "Oh, I'm just going for some water, but the door is stuck. I'm sorry I woke you."

David kissed him on the cheek. "That's what I'm here for, baby. And the door isn't stuck, it's locked." David reached up on tiptoe and unlatched the hook at the very top of the door. "I locked the door only for your safety, Kurt. I didn't want you to sleepwalk and I not know about it. You were quite medicated yesterday, and sometimes that can lead to sleepwalking as it wears off."

Kurt didn't say anything. He knew that David cared about him. David went with Kurt to the kitchen and poured himself a glass of water as well. They took their glasses and returned to the bedroom. David closed the door and locked it again. "Just for a few more hours, okay?"

Kurt was okay with it. The two of them propped up their pillows and lay side by side, their bodies next to each other. "You've been through a lot, Kurt. Be proud of all you've done. You're quite an inspiration."

Kurt laughed. "I'm a mess, David, haven't you noticed?"

"No, Kurt, you're not a mess. You are the most loving man I've known." David recounted all that Kurt had done, how he adopted his sister's child and became an instant father, how he had juggled business and family beautifully, how he had reinvented his business for the betterment of the gay community, how he had relocated for his new love and his son, and also for Cheyenne, how he loved with his entire body and soul, and so much more.

Kurt laughed again. "You make me sound like a superhero, David."

David leaned over and kissed him on the mouth. "To me, you are a superhero."

They lay back down and held each other again, dozing off and on for another hour or two. David needed to get the kids ready for school, but wasn't sure about leaving Kurt alone. Kurt assured him that he would be a good boy and stay in bed while he was gone. David winked at him, and left to wake the kids.

David assured Cheyenne that Kurt was fine. She was used to Kurt being away on business and was too young to know what was really happening. David waved goodbye to the kids as they headed out the door, and then he sat down with Sara to explain what he thought might be good for him and Kurt. She thought it was a wonderful idea, and would be more than happy to take care of the kids for a couple of days. She and David both agreed that it would be best to do this during the week so that the kids would be busy with school, and not missing their dads as much as they might on the weekend. He thanked her and she left for class.

Then he returned to the bedroom to discuss his proposed plan with Kurt. At first, Kurt wasn't at all sure about going to the cabin. He craved the familiar. David explained that the cabin was only about ten miles out of the city, was a very quiet place, very secluded, and would give the two of them the opportunity to have the alone time that they needed. "We're no different than newlyweds, Kurt. Let me do this for us."

Kurt agreed, knowing that David had his best interests at heart, and also knowing that the two of them were going to have a very relaxed and loving two days alone. "We're doing things backward, David. We made sure the kids were well adjusted before doing what was necessary to ensure our own adjustment to our own new relationship."

"Yes, we did, Kurt, and that's because we love our kids, which is good, but we need each other as two men, not just two fathers," David said, with a smile.

The cabin was just as David had described it. It was a short drive from the city, secluded, and beautiful. It really wasn't what Kurt would have referred to as a cabin, but rather a small house. It contained all the features of a home. It had a soothing décor, a cheery kitchen, a small living room with a breathtaking view of the Rocky Mountains, one bedroom and one bath. It was cozy, and Kurt was glad he came.

David brought their bags in and placed them in the bedroom. Kurt didn't hear him come in. Kurt was standing at the living room window mesmerized by the magnificent view of the Rocky Mountains. David walked up behind him and put his arm around him. "Beautiful, isn't it?"

Kurt put his arm around David. "Yes, David, the mountains are beautiful. I've never really taken the time to "see" the mountains. I've always been too busy. They are truly majestic."

David knew what Kurt meant by not "seeing" the mountains. He, too, had been consumed by work, until he adopted Trey. Seeing life's beauty through the eyes of a child was magical. David appreciated the simple things now. He noticed the beauty of not only the mountains, but of the people he came to know every day, and was no longer too busy to share a kind word with someone.

David kissed Kurt on the cheek. "We've been very blessed, buddy," he said to Kurt.

"Yes, we have," Kurt agreed as he reached for David's hand, who gave it freely.

"Come with me," David said, as he walked hand in hand with Kurt to the kitchen. "How about some hot chocolate?" David asked.

"I'd love some," Kurt answered. The two of them made hot chocolate the old fashioned way, as there was no microwave here. David's boss had bought this place to provide its guests a slower pace than their busy work lives allowed. Kurt and David sat snuggled together as they drank their hot chocolate and enjoyed the beautiful picture that nature had painted just for their pleasure. By the time the delicious hot treat was gone, the sun was disappearing behind the mountains.

Kurt laid his head on David's shoulder. "I love you, David."

David wrapped his arms around Kurt. He gently rested his lips on Kurt's, and the two shared slow unhurried kisses, taking the time to let the love of the other fill them.

It was getting cold inside the little cabin, and the night very soon would be upon them. David suggested they start a fire in the fireplace, and they were soon warmed by the flames. There was the most beautiful rug in front of the fire that was softer than anything either had felt. They lay in front of the fire on the rug watching the flames.

"I've made many fires, David, and never noticed the beauty of the flames, how the various shades of red and yellow blend to become something so warm."

"I know what you mean, Kurt."

Kurt's life had changed so much since he had met David, and David knew that Kurt's life would be enriched even more than he could imagine now that he would be home a lot more. Cheyenne's recounts of her days would bring him joy unimaginable.

As the fire warmed them into a sleepy haziness, they were both eager to make love. Kurt leaned over and gently pushed David's chest down onto the rug. Kurt looked into David's eyes as he unbuttoned David's shirt. Laying David's shirt open, Kurt caressed David's chest. As he caressed, his eyes never left David's. He was arousing David with his steady gaze. Kurt leaned down and kissed David's slightly parted lips. When his lips left David's, Kurt couldn't mistake the look of lust in David's barely open eyes. The discovery of David's firm nipples underneath Kurt's fingers caused David's mouth to open in desperate wanting of a second kiss. Kurt continued to tease David's nipples, and kissed him ever so lightly on his open lips.

David placed his arm around Kurt and pulled him closer, forcing the kiss to last. Kurt kissed him hard and full, but only for a little while. Then he held David's hands on the rug above David's head while he enjoyed the feel of David's nipples on his tongue and inside his mouth.

David's body was on fire. He raised his chest for greater satisfaction which Kurt provided with more intense sucking. "Mmm," David said. Kurt leaned up again and looked at David. He loved David so much. He eased the zipper down its track on David's jeans and spread the denim material. David wanted Kurt. That was clear. David's hardness welcomed the release from its tight enclave. Kurt outlined David's erection with his hand. Even through his shorts, Kurt's touch was almost too much for David. He thrust his pelvis upward, begging for Kurt to deliver his erection from all that kept it from its anticipated stimulation. Kurt slid David's jeans down and off, tossing them aside. David bent his legs, and spread them wide. Kurt touched David just like he wanted, but through his shorts, making David beg for Kurt to take him. Not realizing that Kurt's hands were no longer holding his to the floor, David kept them there now knowing he had the power to pull Kurt to him.

Kurt watched David with satisfaction, knowing that he was bringing him this much pleasure. David meant so much to him, and he would do absolutely anything for him. Kurt slid his fingers inside David's shorts just underneath his balls, and David almost came. He moaned. Kurt wanted to touch David everywhere. He wanted to kiss David everywhere. David was moving his body every way he could to encourage more touching. Kurt was too busy exploring the beauty that David's shorts held within to notice the intensity in David's face. "Oh, Kurt, put your mouth on me," David commanded, realizing that his hands were free to remove his shorts entirely. Once off, David leaned up and held Kurt's head, kissing him lovingly with an open mouth. Then he looked at Kurt. "I love you, Kurt." Kurt touched David's face and ran his hand along David's chest, downward to where his erection was begging for attention. David lay back down as Kurt gently lay David's legs apart until his knees were almost resting on the rug. Kurt massaged David's upper thighs as his mouth enjoyed all that had just a few minutes earlier been confined by clothing. Kurt's tongue found that area hiding shyly underneath David's balls and as it pressed firmly against it and slid upward, David gasped. The slow intensity of Kurt's tongue was overpowering. David fought hard to control his climax.

When Kurt's mouth found David's balls and took one and then the other inside its warm wetness, David moaned aloud. Kurt began making "Mm" sounds as he enjoyed his new snack, which only added to David's not-to-distant explosion. Kurt slid his tongue along David's penis, massaging with his fingers that area that had just before enjoyed the intensity of Kurt's tongue. David's breathing was coming in short quick breaths as Kurt's mouth slowly engulfed David's quivering hardness in its entirety, slowly sucking its way downward until Kurt's lips met David's balls. Oh, hold on David, he thought to himself. It felt too good to come to an end now. With each trip that Kurt's mouth made along David's penis, the more Kurt's body wanted David's penis deep inside it. Kurt let his mouth slide up and off of David's throbbing hardness, and kissed David's mouth. David threw his arms around Kurt and pulled him down. David's dick was on fire. "David, I want you deep inside me." David wasn't at all expecting these words, and could feel himself nearing orgasm. "Yes," was all that David could say. David helped Kurt out of his clothes, stripping his jeans down and off, and spreading Kurt's legs wide and sucking on his dick and balls with an intensity so great that it caught Kurt off guard. Kurt tried to turn over so that David could enter him, but David stopped him. "No," David commanded. He slid his hands under Kurt's buttocks and spread them apart. Then he teased the opening that Kurt so desperately wanted to be filled by entering with just the head of his penis, and enjoying the feel of Kurt's skin as he gently caressed Kurt's body. Kurt was trying to force David in deeper, moaning with ecstasy. David eased his pulsating member deep within Kurt's awaiting emptiness as he slid upward along Kurt's body until Kurt was filled completely and David's lips were on Kurt's. David kept his open mouth on Kurt's as he continued to enter him again and again.

As he neared orgasm, David kissed Kurt with a hunger that he didn't know was his. His passion for Kurt was so strong it was overpowering him. Kurt was holding onto David, his passion equaling that of his lover. David lifted Kurt's buttocks, entering him so deeply that Kurt gasped and moaned into David's mouth on his. These deep thrusts were bringing an orgasm all their own, and when David climaxed, both men held the other, never wanting this feeling to end.

When David's climax was complete, he lay upon Kurt, both men trying to catch their breath. Once breathing evenly again, David could feel Kurt's erection hard underneath him. Before Kurt could object, David turned around and straddled him, lifting his perfect ass high as David enjoyed the pleasure of Kurt's dick as it entered his mouth with every squeeze of Kurt's beautiful ass. Kurt's legs were dangling in midair, his buttocks facing the ceiling, and David's mouth was eagerly awaiting every gentle push of Kurt's buttocks that would provide it the pleasure of Kurt's throbbing erection. Kurt was taken by surprise by all of this, but so damned turned on he knew he wouldn't last long. "David,

I'm...", Kurt said, as he exploded. David knew what he was trying to say, and David wasn't going to let Kurt's dick free of its imprisonment until it had completed its entire sentence. Then he let this flaccid entity slip away as he placed Kurt's legs back down on the rug.

David and Kurt lay naked, their chests together as David lay over Kurt. They could feel the other's heart beating as if trying to reassure the other. David turned his head and whispered into Kurt's ear, "I love you, Kurt. I love you more than I can ever tell or show you." David wrapped his arm around Kurt's head.

"I love you, too, David. I owe you so much." Kurt's voice was shaky as he spoke.

David ran his fingers through Kurt's hair. David leaned up on one arm and looked at Kurt. His eyes were full and he knew that if he closed them, the tears would slide out of the corners, but close them he did. "Oh, baby, I love the way you love, with your entire being. I certainly don't feel that you owe me. You and I were meant for each other, baby. We are perfect complements."

As the sun rose over the mountains the next morning, its warming rays streamed in through the glass window landing on David's raised buttocks as if forming a spotlight for their debut. The contrast between David's white skin and the golden color of his sun kissed buttocks was beautiful to Kurt. He loved every part of David, inside and out, and his sleeping body across Kurt forcing David's supple round buttocks to demand their much deserved illumination provided by the sun, awakened parts of Kurt that had been enjoying a much deserved night's sleep. Kurt continued to enjoy the roundness of David's buttocks. Stroking them gently with smooth strokes, Kurt found their beauty to match that of the mountains. David's legs were spread just enough to cause his buttocks to part, allowing Kurt to discover the crevice between them.

Just as the mountains hid their secret valleys, so too did David's buttocks. Although hidden, it was this crevice which brought so much pleasure to one when provided by another. Kurt knew the hidden pleasure of this crevice, and wanted David to know how well he could please him the same way that David pleased him. Sliding his fingers down this crevice, Kurt stopped at the area which Kurt was eager to fill. He wanted to bring David to a climax he had yet to know. Kurt separated David's buttocks further, allowing a finger to enter David. David, in his dreamy state, spread his legs apart to allow that very pleasing feeling to continue. Kurt was so turned on knowing that he was in David's dreams. David was still sleeping, and definitely dreaming. He was dreaming of his lover entering him over and over, but his lover was teasing him into submission, forcing him to wait for the pleasure his body was aching to feel. He raised his buttocks high so that the object of his pleasure could enter him deeply and completely.

Kurt was hard now, his own pleasure soon to be realized. He couldn't believe David was sleeping through this stimulation. Kurt was certain that he wouldn't have been able to sleep through this if David were doing the same to him. David was up on his knees now making it easy for Kurt's finger to enter him as far as he could. Even though sleeping, David wanted more. He wanted this unknown pleasure to enter him more deeply and fill him more completely. Kurt slid out from underneath David and kneeled behind him. He spread David's buttocks wide and placed his hard penis at the entrance of that opening that would bring David the pleasure he deserved. Kurt entered him slowly as he continued to hold David's buttocks wide apart. David moaned, and pushed his body back against Kurt, forcing Kurt's erect penis to enter him. David's backward movement was so forceful that Kurt lost control of his own penis and he had to hold onto David for support. With a loud "ohhh", David awoke from his dreaming state. "Oh, Kurt, I thought I was dreaming." "Oh, no, baby, you aren't dreaming. This is real."

The two of them were each enjoying the other's forceful movements, not denying their own pleasure. Kurt knew exactly what he was doing. He rolled David onto his side, placed his leg on his shoulder, and entered him, filling him in a way that was new to David. Kurt stroked David's penis and squeezed his balls as he continued to enter him again and again. David looked at Kurt with lust filled eyes, moaning louder and louder, and trying to utter the word, "Kurt", as his pleasure intensified. He gave Kurt full control as he could barely breathe from the intensity of the feeling that was his. Kurt thrust deeper and stroked harder until David was completely and totally lost in physical pleasure provided by his lover, a lover like no other. David moaned and called Kurt's name until he could do nothing but try to breathe. Kurt lifted David's leg high, and thrust his erect penis deep until both Kurt and David could feel Kurt's balls firmly against that most sensitive area between David's legs. Their moans echoed the other as Kurt and David came together, each steadying himself as the intensity of their orgasms was nothing short of explosive. Kurt leaned against David's leg as his quivering member emptied all of its contents deep within David. David grasped the soft rug underneath his naked body as Kurt provided the final masturbatory thrusts that caused David's entire body to shudder.

When both men had returned to their pre-orgasmic state, they lay on their sides and held each other, neither willing to release his embrace of the other. When their breathing had returned to normal, they kissed each other, and whispered, "I love you" in the other's ear.

Their two days together at the cabin were spent telling each other of their past loves, their past loves lost, and their hopes for the future. Their maturity provided the perfect foundation for their love. They had played the games, had won and lost, and now were ready to experience a mature love, a love that went far beyond the physical, a higher love, a love that included children, a love between two dads.

Along Came You

Matthew had fallen for Greg Stevens and Matthew had fallen hard. Before Greg, Matthew had thought that finding true happiness was not meant to be, for him. When a mutual friend fixes him up with Greg, Matthew continues to doubt his chances for true love. Greg is much younger than he and just beginning his career. When he shows Greg the carvings above the fireplaces that his grandfather had built years ago, Greg sees in them the same "sign" that Matthew had seen ten years earlier. When a baby girl is abandoned at the hospital where Greg works, he and Matthew wonder if the fireplace carvings could have been designed from a premonition of Matthew's grandfather and that perhaps this wise man years ago had known what lay ahead for his grandson.

Greg quickly briefed his chief resident who would be finishing his rounds for him this morning, and then hurried to the school to pick up his daughter. What could possibly have happened? The school nurse had said that Nichole wasn't feeling well, but hadn't gone into detail. Fearing the worst as always, Greg hurried as fast as he could to be with Nicky.

Out of breath after running from the parking lot to the school, Greg could barely speak when he walked into the nurse's office. "What's wrong? Is she sick? Did she fall?"

"We're not sure, Dr. Stevens. She said that her stomach hurt and that she wanted her daddy."

"Okay. Where is she?"

The nurse led Greg to where Nichole was lying down on a cot. "What is it, baby? Does your tummy hurt?"

Nicky nodded her head.

"Do you want to go home?"

Nicky nodded again.

"Let's go. I've got someone to cover for me at work."

Nichole took Greg's hand and the two of them walked to the car. Once inside the car, Greg pulled Nicky onto his lap and held her like a baby. "What's wrong, Nicky? Can you tell Daddy?"

"Um, we were playing at recess and my friend Tommy said that he was dopted like me. Am I dopted? What is dopted?"

"Oh, Nicky. The word is adopted, honey, and yes, you are adopted. Adopted is a good thing, baby. It's a wonderful, beautiful thing. That is how you became my little girl and how I became your daddy. Let's go home, Nicky, and I will tell you all about it."

Greg buckled Nichole into her seat, and drove his precious little girl home.

"Let's pop some popcorn and have a carpet picnic. You pick the room."

"Let's have a picnic in my room, daddy."

They took their popcorn and headed to Nichole's room. They made themselves comfortable on the floor leaning against the bed, and Greg began to tell Nicky the story of how the two of them came to be father and daughter.

******

Dr. Greg Stevens had just completed his residency in neonatology when he met Matthew Balderson through a mutual friend.

Matthew was ten years older than Greg, but it didn't seem to matter to either of them.

Matthew picked Greg up for their first date together and took him to a very nice French restaurant. "I'm glad you agreed to go out with me, Greg. I thought maybe you would think of me as an old man."

"Not at all, Matthew. Anyway, if what I've heard about being a doctor is true, I'll be your age very soon."

Matthew had thought Greg's comment was sweet, and he also thought that Greg was sweet.

"You know what I do, Matthew. What is it that you do?"

"Have you heard of the Balderson Brothers Bakeries?"

"No, sorry, but I'm new to the Pacific Northwest, and I didn't see much of Seattle as a resident."

"Well, I'm one of the Balderson Brothers. Actually, the brothers were my father and his brother, and now I am *the* Balderson. We have several bakeries along the West Coast, but our home has always been Seattle. I'll take you to the main bakery downtown some day."

"Sounds yummy," Greg said. "How do you stay so fit spending so much time around such deliciously decadent sweets?" Greg asked. Matthew *was* fit. He was tall and lean, and gorgeous.

"Well, I run a lot, and the rest is genetics, because I do love the goodies at the bakery. Fortunately, now I work only around fifty hours a week instead of sixty plus that I worked ten, twenty years ago."

When Greg laughed and said, "You aren't that old, Matthew", he told him that he was forty now.

"Well, I'm thirty-two, so I'm not that far away." Greg marveled at Matthew's fitness, and hoped that he, too, didn't let himself go like so many in his field did as their lives became busier and the demands on their time greater.

Matthew had been the perfect gentleman on their first date. He picked up the check, left the tip, and walked Greg to the door of his apartment when the date ended. He took Greg's hands in his and said, "Thank you for the date, Greg. May I call you?"

Greg was touched by Matthew's sweet words and gentlemanliness and said, "I would like that, and thank you."

Matthew kissed him on the cheek, and then looked into his eyes. "Goodnight," he said, and walked back to his car.

Greg watched him walk away, and then unlocked the door to his apartment.

True to his word, Matthew called Greg just two days later and asked if he had been to the Space Needle yet. "No, I must confess. Residency kept me locked away from the outside world."

"If you're not busy on Saturday, Greg, I would love to take you. We can take the monorail from downtown and spend the day at the Seattle Center," Matthew had offered.

"I am free Saturday, on call on Sunday, but not Saturday."

"I will pick you up at eleven then," Matthew had said.

It was only Wednesday, and for the rest of the week Greg found himself thinking of Matthew and wishing that it were Saturday already. Matthew was unlike the guys that Greg was used to seeing, though he hadn't really been out with anyone since early in his medical school days. Matthew was mature, and didn't waste time playing manipulative games. He seemed confident, and was definitely a hard worker. Matthew worked more hours a week than Greg.

Greg woke up early and was out of bed at eight on Saturday, anxious to see Matthew again. He showered and spritzed his clean body with a very light cologne, then searched his closet for the perfect shirt and pants. He assumed the attire was casual, but he really wanted to impress Matthew. He wanted Matthew to think that he was with someone mature, and not just a kid.

It was ten by the time Greg was finally satisfied with his attire and was ready to go. He read the paper, but couldn't seem to focus on the words. He was nervous about going out with Matthew. Matthew knocked on the door just before eleven, and Greg invited him in.

"It's not much, but it's home."

"You've decorated it to perfection, Greg. I'm impressed."

"Thank you. That's the perfectionist in me, I'm afraid."

Seeing Matthew in the daytime did not diminish his good looks. If anything, Greg thought that he looked even more distinguished in the daylight. He was tall, like Greg, with black slightly curly hair and bright blue eyes. He had just a hint of gray in his hair that only added to his good looks. He was fit, and obviously worked out. Greg knew that he was not nearly as gorgeous as Matthew, although he had been told that he was handsome. Greg's hair was brown and straight, his eyes brown, and still had the leanness that comes with too much work and too little time to eat.

"I've promised myself more than once that I would see the wonders of Seattle, but never allowed myself the luxury," Greg admitted, as Matthew opened the car door for him.

"Well, we'll see them together," he said.

They drove to downtown Seattle, and took the monorail out to the Space Needle. "This is nice, Matthew. I love it."

Greg had worked so much over the past six years that he appreciated every minute of free time that he now had. It was around two by the time they had grabbed a quick bite to eat. They walked around the Center taking in all the shops, and talked about everything. They sat by a fountain and talked for hours.

"So, tell me, Greg, what did you really think when I told you I was a baker?"

Taken aback by the question but admiring the honesty of Matthew's question, Greg looked at him. I guess no one is completely confident about themselves, Greg thought.

"I admire your business intelligence, Matthew. There are a lot of physicians who could use some of that."

"Thank you," Matthew said, with honesty. "I guess a lot of people just see the baker when they look at me, and not the businessman. You've just won a lifetime supply of anything you like at Balderson Bakeries," he added, with a smile.

"Well, I do love doughnuts, the cake kind, dipped in powdered sugar," Greg confessed.

"What do you think of me taking care of the teeny tiny babies?" Greg asked.

"When I heard that about you, I think I started to fall for you before we had even met," he said in almost a whisper. He continued to look into Greg's eyes, and Greg knew he was blushing. He could feel his cheeks growing hot.

Matthew touched Greg's hand. "Let's take that ride to the sky now," he said, and the two of them walked to where the line had formed. The ride to the top was breathtaking.

"Look at the mountains, Matthew," Greg said in awe of the majestic peaks.

"They are beautiful, and even more beautiful up close. We'll go sometime."

Matthew watched as Greg looked out at the city and the Pacific.

"I should have gotten out more, Matthew," he said, and laughed. "I could stay up here all night," he added.

"I'm glad to hear that, Greg. We have a reservation right here in the dining room in the sky." Matthew's surprise left Greg without words.

They walked inside and were seated in a primo spot. Greg stared out the window. "Matthew, this is too much. You are too much."

Matthew held his hand. "I wanted to experience this with you, Greg, and only you," he said, and once again his shining blue eyes sparkled.

Greg looked at Matthew, and was mesmerized once again by the brilliance he saw in his eyes. "There is an entire world view up here, you know," Greg said, as he watched the world go around.

"Yes, there is," Matthew agreed.

The two of them enjoyed a very leisurely dinner in the sky, complete with a shared very high caloric dessert.

"I will have to run twice as many miles as usual after eating this delicious thing," Matthew lamented, but continued to spoon the sweet treat into his mouth.

"So that's how you do it," Greg said.

"Yes, I run, and with every birthday I'm forced to add another mile."

Greg smiled, and the two of them finished the dessert and their coffee.

It was late by the time they left the Space Needle, and Greg didn't know where the day had gone. The week had seemed so long without Matthew, and the day with him had flown by. Matthew once again opened the car door for Greg and they drove back to Greg's apartment. Greg put his hand on the door handle of the car, and Matthew said, "Wait, Greg", and placed his hand on Greg's arm. "I would love for you to see my house. It's just twenty minutes out of the city. Let me make us dinner next Saturday night."

Greg thought about his schedule. "Absolutely, I'm not on call until the following Saturday."

Matthew walked Greg to his door, and this time Greg invited him in.

Greg poured them a glass of wine, and they talked for awhile longer. "That was the best surprise, Matthew, the entire day with you, and especially the dinner in the sky."

Matthew set his glass down and then took Greg's from him and set it down too. He held Greg's hands and then moved his hands up along Greg's arms. He held Greg's arms and leaned toward him. Greg's heart was beating hard and fast when he felt Matthew's lips on his own. Matthew's kisses were gentle and sweet, yet very passionate. Matthew put his arms around Greg, and Greg held Matthew in his. Matthew kissed Greg for several minutes, and then kissed him on the cheek. "I'd better go now," he said.

Greg hugged him after they stood up, before letting him go. "I had the best day, Matthew, and thank you for next Saturday."

"I will e-mail the directions to my house. I can pick you up if you like, though I am planning the most spectacular dinner for the two of us."

"Oh, I'm sure I can find it, but thanks," Greg responded, so taken with Matthew he could barely speak.

Matthew left, and Greg plopped down on the sofa. Greg was in love, or at the very least, smitten.

The next week started off with yet another surprise from Matthew. On Monday, Greg received a basket of cake doughnuts dipped in powdered sugar fresh from the Balderson Bakeries at his office. The card was very discreetly written, but Greg knew they were from Matthew. The entire office enjoyed Matthew's gift. The week went by fairly quickly, surprisingly.

On Wednesday, Matthew sent the directions to his house, and in his e-mail he also thanked Greg for the kiss. Greg blushed when he read it. If this is what it was like being with a mature man, Greg would never date anyone under forty again. He really hoped to not date anyone other than Matthew ever again.

Greg slept in on Saturday, having been at the hospital very late on Friday night. He finally rolled out of bed around noon, and quickly made himself some freshly brewed coffee. He loved his days off. He took his time reading the paper and drinking his coffee, but this morning he stared out the window and thought about how wonderful it would be to wake up next to Matthew. He could still feel Matthew's lips on his and how he had felt when Michael kissed him.

Greg made sure the shower water was hot before stepping inside. The pulsating jets of hot water felt good on his stiff back. He had been on his feet for too many hours yesterday. He turned around and let the water hit the front of his body, and thought about how great a whirlpool tub would feel right now. He looked down at his soft dick and fantasized about how good Matthew's hand would feel around it, loving it, loving him. Greg could only imagine how gentle and giving a lover Matthew would be. Oh, it has been a long time, he thought.

He finished his shower and then dressed and as he was putting on his shirt, he thought about tonight. I wonder if Matthew is expecting me to stay the night. He hadn't said or hinted that he did. I'll pack a bag just in case, and leave it in the car. That way I'll be ready just in case he asks. Greg hadn't had sex in so long that he didn't even have any condoms. Should he stop and buy some? Greg, you are just nervous, he thought out loud.

Greg waited until almost five before heading to Matthew's. The directions were easy to follow and the traffic wasn't too bad. He enjoyed getting out of the city, and realized once again just how little of this beautiful area he had seen in the six years he had lived here.

Matthew didn't live too far out of the city, and his driveway was clearly marked with a huge overhanging sign that read, "Balderson."

Greg drove down the long lane through the most beautiful trees he had ever seen. They were huge, but very well kept. The lane led to a house that Greg was not expecting. This was a mansion, a paradise of nature. With the mountains in the background, Greg thought this would be a great inspiration for an artist. Damn, the man's a billionaire. Greg felt smaller and smaller the closer he got to the huge home which seemed to overshadow him, and his car seemed small when he pulled up to the front entrance. Matthew must think I live in a box, Greg thought, when he thought about his apartment.

There was a camera at the entrance of Matthew's grand palace, and a buzzer. Greg pressed the buzzer and immediately heard Matthew's voice.

"Greg, is that you?"

"Yes," he said.

"Come on in," Matthew welcomed, and Greg heard a click and then the front door opened automatically.

Greg walked in and the door closed and locked behind him. Matthew walked into the foyer, his chef's apron on. "All I need is the funny hat now," he said. "Come on into the kitchen, my favorite room in the house."

Greg felt comfortable again. Matthew wasn't about all the glitz and glitter. Matthew was real. I just have to remember that, Greg told himself.

"Well, you didn't turn around when you saw the house. That's a good sign." Matthew kissed Greg on the cheek, and then went back to his cooking.

"I guess I was a bit surprised at the size of this place," Greg admitted.

"Well, it didn't scare you away and besides, my grandfather built it many years ago when things were a lot cheaper. I'm just the lucky beneficiary."

Matthew wiped his hands on his apron and sat down at the table across from Greg. "We're not a pretentious people, Greg. Grandfather got into the bakery business when there was not much competition."

"I don't think of you as the snobbish kind, Matthew. I didn't think that for a minute."

Greg's words were reassuring to Matthew. "I'm glad, Greg. I like you a lot." Matthew's sparkling blue eyes once again left Greg speechless. "Dinner is served. Would you like some wine?"

"Sure," Greg said, and got up to pour a glass for both of them.

Matthew really was a chef. The dinner was delicious. The wine was the perfect touch. "This is great, Matthew."

"Thanks, Greg. I don't get the chance to do as much cooking as I would like, but I love having someone to cook for. And, for dessert, homemade éclairs."

Greg poured them another glass of wine, and devoured the sweet dessert. "Oh, this is good, Matthew. The entire meal was delicious. It has been a long time since I had a home cooked meal." Matthew just smiled at the compliment. "And, thank you for the doughnut bouquet," Greg said, blushing at his own comment.

"The best for the best," Matthew replied, as he reached for Greg's hand.

Greg felt his nerves again. The wine helped calm him a bit, but always made him horny too.

"Would you like to see the house, Greg?"

"Sure," he said.

As Matthew led him through the massive estate, Greg was surprised at how simply it was decorated. It was very classy, yet simple, and not at all showy. The furniture was old, but very well maintained. Antiques filled the home from top to bottom.

Matthew explained to Greg that his grandfather and father had taught him two very important things. One was how to run a respectful and profitable business, and the other was not to waste, but to maintain.

"Grandfather lived through the Great Depression, and Father was a product of the life's lessons that were learned from Grandfather's experiences."

Many of the paintings had been drawn by Matthew's grandmother, and Greg stopped to admire each one. Matthew loved that

Greg loved what he did, or at least was taking an interest. There was a beautiful pool in the back lawn, but Matthew hadn't used it in years.

"How long have you lived here alone, Matthew?" Greg asked, and then wanted to take the question back the minute he asked it. "I'm sorry, Matthew. That is none of my business."

"No, I don't mind, Greg. My father is gone and my mother lives in assisted living in Seattle, and I have lived here alone for about five years."

Greg had hoped he would continue and mention former lovers, but was not going to ask that quite yet.

"I don't use much of the house, just the kitchen, family room, and I've transformed the den off of the foyer into a bedroom."

When the tour was over and they were on their way back to the kitchen, Matthew stopped just short of the kitchen. He opened the door across from the kitchen, and turned on the light.

"Here it is, Greg. This was a den, but is now my bedroom. It feels like a cozy little house living in it this way."

"It's nice, Matthew. It really is."

Greg started to leave the room, but Matthew took his hand. "Greg, I would love it if you stayed with me tonight, but please don't feel pressured to do so. I won't hold it against you if you don't feel comfortable with staying, and I certainly will not stop seeing you. I like you a lot, Greg." There, he had said it, and now the ball was in Greg's court.

Greg looked at Matthew with his endearing smile, his bright blue eyes sparkling. He kissed Matthew lightly on the lips. "I would love to spend the night with you, Matthew," he whispered, as he moved closer. "I've thought about what it would be like waking up next to you."

Matthew pulled him closer and put his arms around him. They held each other for a long time, and then Matthew kissed Greg on his neck and then his cheek, and finally their lips met. It had been a long week without each other, and their lips seemed to know it too. They kissed more passionately tonight, more hungrily.

Matthew led Greg to his bed, and the two of them unbuttoned the other's shirts and took them off. Matthew pulled the covers back and invited Greg into his bed. The room was dark, but they undressed separately before getting into bed and moving toward each other. They embraced again, holding each other, kissing each other.

Matthew was a passionate lover and took his time, two things that Greg was not accustomed to. Matthew stroked Greg's face as he kissed his lips and when his hands caressed his chest, Greg was completely at his mercy. Greg caressed Matthew's back, his perfectly toned back. Matthew kissed Greg's chest, licking his nipples.

The covers had slipped off of Matthew so that his butt was now in full view of Greg. Damn, I hope I look that good when I'm forty, he thought.

Matthew looked at Greg, leaned up and kissed him on the lips again. "Greg, look at me." Greg half opened his eyes. "Greg, I love you. I know that our relationship is very young, but I know that I love you." Matthew was not expecting a response from Greg, and went back to kissing his chest. Greg was too stunned to speak, and too turned on by Matthew's kisses to even try.

Matthew pushed back the covers from Greg's body and ran his hands along his legs. "You're beautiful, Greg," he said, and looked at Greg's closed eyes.

Greg was definitely ready for sex which could not have been missed by Matthew and yet, he continued to take his time. Matthew massaged Greg's inner thighs and Greg slowly parted his legs in response. Matthew looked at Greg's aroused body and was eager to please this man he loved.

With his hand on Greg's inner thigh, Matthew licked around Greg's navel and just below, tasting the part of his lover that had recently escaped from the organ of his arousal. He ran his tongue along Greg's erection several times and then placed his lips on the spongy head. He stroked Greg's chest as he slowly took his cock into his mouth. He held Greg's balls, playing with them, enjoying the feel of them in his hands.

Greg moaned, and ran his fingers in Matthew's hair. It wasn't long before Greg said, "Matthew", in a voice filled with passion. Matthew moved back up and kissed Greg on the mouth as he brought him to orgasm.

Greg thrust upward to Matthew's movements, unashamed, uninhibited, feeling the rightness of their lovemaking. He held Matthew and kissed him on the top of his head. "Matthew, I love you, too."

Matthew looked at Greg, and smiled. "How can I give you what you just gave me?" Greg asked.

"The same way, baby, the same way."

Greg did not want to disappoint Matthew with his lack of experience, but Matthew was far from disappointed. He had never felt as sexually satisfied with a former lover as he had tonight with Greg.

They slept huddled together soundly until late Sunday morning. Matthew kissed Greg, and said that he had never slept this well for as long as he could remember.

Matthew prepared a light brunch and neither took his eyes off the other. Mid afternoon came, and Greg knew he should be going back to his apartment.

"You've been quiet today, Matthew," Greg said.

"I don't mean to be, Greg, but there is something I want to ask you."

"I'm all ears, Matthew."

"Greg, move in with me. You won't regret it, I promise."

Greg was surprised, but pleased.

"I know it's soon, Greg, but I know what I want, and I want you."

"I would love to, Matthew. Let's go get my stuff."

Matthew kissed Greg for a long time before they went to Greg's apartment to get his stuff.

Very soon, they had Greg all moved in at the mansion. "It's a little longer drive for you now, but I hope you don't mind."

"No, Matthew, I don't mind at all. I love you."

Their days were long and their schedules did not always allow them to be together as much as they would have liked, but they respected and understood the other's passion for his work which was more than a job to each of them. They realized it was this passion that lay inside them that had attracted them to each other. They had a passion for their work, a passion for life, and a passion for each other.

When they both finally had an entire weekend off at the same time, Matthew had decided to open the house up more and to enjoy all that his grandfather had brought to his beloved home. They had planned to transform the entire main level into the main living part of the house. The very top level of the house had been designed to be a library and Greg brought all of his medical books which filled an entire wall of the built-in bookshelves.

"These shelves are beautiful, Matthew," he said, as he lined up his books.

"Grandfather had wanted them to be, Greg. He built them himself. They are solid cherry wood."

Matthew painted what little of the room was not bookshelf while Greg made the shelves shine with an oil perfect for cherry wood.

"What was the second floor supposed to be, Matthew?"

"Let me show you," he said.

They stopped what they were doing and Greg followed Matthew to the second floor. "It's open like the top floor, with a fireplace on either end."

Greg looked at the huge room that was cozy despite its size. The fireplaces were made of ivory and were gorgeous. They had carved faces set in the beauty of the ivory. "They are beautiful," Greg said, as he looked at the fireplaces.

Matthew watched and waited for Greg to notice what he hoped he would notice within the carvings.

"These are unique, Matthew."

"What do you mean, Greg?"

"It appears that in each there is a carving of a man with a child, and in this one there are two men with a child, but no woman. That is interesting."

"I thought so, too, Greg, when I finally took the time to really see them," Matthew remarked, as he walked up behind Greg and put his arms around his waist. He kissed him on the back of his neck. "I rarely came up here, and didn't study these until probably ten years ago. I've often wondered what Grandfather was thinking when he had these put in. It's a bit of a mystery, or perhaps Grandfather had some sort of premonition about his grandson." Greg looked at Matthew. "Spooky, isn't it?"

"A little," Matthew agreed.

"I don't come up here much, but it is a very cozy room despite its grandeur. The view is spectacular."

Matthew led Greg to the wall of windows from which they could see far into the distance. Matthew walked to the far end of the windows. "It would make a great room to sit in, in a comfy chair and dream while looking out the windows," he said to Greg.

Greg looked at Matthew who appeared to already be dreaming. "Let's do it then, Matthew. We'll make this a fun, warm, cozy room."

Matthew walked over to Greg and surprised him with a kiss.

"We'll put a fluffy carpet in and get these fireplaces working," Greg said.

It was much easier for Matthew to get away from work than it was for Greg, so he took care of meeting the carpet layers and getting the fireplaces working.

As Greg became more and more established in his practice, he was able to be home more on the weekends. One Friday night, Greg came home later than usual and seemed distraught to Matthew. "What is it, Greg?"

Greg had tried to hide his mood, but quickly learned that he couldn't do that with Matthew. Matthew was much too intuitive. "Oh, nothing," he lied. He poured himself a glass of wine and handed one to Matthew.

Matthew looked at him. "I've known you for almost a year now. You know you can't hide from me, Greg."

"I know," he said, and put his arm around Matthew. "There was a little girl who was dropped off at the emergency room today, Matthew. She has been in foster care since she was born and has had good care, but the foster mother said she just cannot do it anymore. I'm happy that she admitted it at least, instead of maybe harming the child or neglecting her. I was called to examine her."

"Was she okay?" Matthew asked.

"Physically, she's fine. I guess her birth mother was not able to keep her for whatever reason I don't know. She was just so precious, Matthew, and sweet and loving. I held her and she put her little arms around my neck." Greg stopped then and wiped a tear from his eye.

Matthew took Greg's glass and set it down along with his own. Then he took Greg's hands in his. "What is it, Greg? What are you holding back that is coming out in these tears?" Matthew wiped a tear from Greg's face as he spoke.

Greg blinked his eyes. He tried to hide his eyes, but Matthew refused to let go of his hands.

Matthew put his hands on Greg's upper arms. "Tell me," he said.

Greg's eyes were full as he looked at Matthew. "Her name is Nichole and I've never felt this way about a baby before, but I want her. I know I could be a good father to her. We could be good fathers to her."

Matthew pulled him close and held him. Greg held onto Matthew. He had no idea how Matthew felt about kids and had assumed that at age forty-one now, he hadn't wanted to be a father.

Matthew's voice was soothing and comforting to Greg. "Let's do it, Greg. You and I would be terrific fathers."

Greg pulled away. "Are you sure?" He could see by the wetness in Matthew's eyes that he was sure.

"I thought it was too late for me, Greg, and I've never felt like a part of a family until you."

Greg kissed him, their tears mingling. "I'm going to try desperately to get it fast tracked. But, I guess the legal guardian would be just one of us," Greg said sadly.

"I know, Greg, and I don't mind. You are younger, and your reputation in the medical community here is solid. I will know that I'm her father. That's all I need."

Greg thought he was the luckiest man alive to have found Matthew, or to have been found by him. "I love you, Matthew. Come with me." Greg took Matthew by the hand and led him to the second floor.

The carpet was soft and fluffy, the fireplaces shiny and clean, the windows glistening, and the moonlight streaming in cast a romantic glow on them both. "Make love to me, Matthew. It's been too long."

Greg undressed Matthew and then undressed himself, and the two stood naked by the windows in the moonlight.

"Greg, I've missed your touch," Matthew said, as Greg ran his hands along Matthew's back and over his well toned butt.

He kissed Matthew's parted lips and chin, and then kissed on down to his chest. He knelt before Matthew and ran his hands along the hair on his legs. He held Matthew's butt, pulling his balls to him and licking them, holding each one in his mouth, enjoying their fullness. Matthew played with Greg's hair, and opened his legs for Greg's exploration.

Greg slid his tongue along the shaft of Matthew's penis and around its hardness until he reached the top. He licked the top and played with the spongy head with his lips.

Matthew was holding onto Greg's hair now as Greg slid his mouth over Matthew's very ready cock and downward until he had taken it all. He kneaded Matthew's butt with his hands while he enjoyed bringing pleasure to him in the light of the moon.

"Greg, I'd better sit down," Matthew said, panting and weak with desire.

Greg helped Matthew to the floor and laid him down in the softness of the plush carpet.

"Oh, my sweet lover," Matthew said, as Greg devoured his luscious beautiful cock.

Matthew was close, and Greg wanted all of him tonight. He drank in all of Matthew's warm cum, emptying his heavy balls, until Matthew lay in the soft carpet complete in his release. He sat up and kissed Greg lightly on the lips. "Lie down, my love," he said, and Greg obediently lay flat on the beautiful carpet.

Matthew kissed his way along Greg's cock until he reached the top where he watched the first drop escape as if it had been waiting for this very moment to greet his awaiting lips. Greg wanted Matthew more and more with every passing day, and wanted more of him every time they made love. He stroked Matthew's hair. "Matthew," he said, as he stroked his arms.

Greg pulled him up to where they were face to face. Then he held Matthew's butt, gently opening the two gorgeous cheeks and sliding his dick in between. Matthew looked at Greg. "Are you sure?" he asked. Greg was sure. "Yes," he said.

Matthew was more than eager and very willing to have Greg inside him. He lowered himself onto Greg and closed his eyes. His lover for life was now very intimately inside him. "Matthew," Greg said, at this new orgasmic sensation. Matthew ran his hands in Greg's chest hair, enjoying the feel of his skin under his fingers with the hair teasing their way between them. "Greg, oh Greg," he moaned.

Greg reached for Matthew's soft penis that was moving along his stomach with Matthew's movements. It began to become erect again within Greg's grasp, and as Matthew moved toward orgasm his own cock was again hard and begging for Greg's attention. Matthew squeezed Greg deep inside him and watched as Greg experienced his first orgasm of this kind. Matthew was equally turned on just watching Greg's reaction. Greg held onto Matthew's arm and looked at him as he came deep inside him. "Matthew," he said, and Matthew leaned down and kissed him. "I know, baby," he said. He lay on top of Greg while the two of them enjoyed their physical closeness.

Greg squinted when the sun's bright rays streamed in through the clear glass windows. Then he looked at Matthew sleeping on top of him. He stroked Matthew's back and thought about what an amazing man he was, and how very fortunate he was that Matthew was in his life. Matthew *was* his life. He was so thoughtful, so compassionate, and so very passionate. "I love you," Greg said, louder than he had planned.

Matthew looked up, and squinted from the sunlight too. "Oh my gosh, have we been here all night?"

"Yes we have, just like this," Greg admitted.

"Oh, I slept hard," Matthew said, and lifted himself up and off of Greg and onto his back next to Greg. "We did pick good carpet, didn't we?" Matthew said, and stretched out on the soft blanket that stretched from wall to wall.

"Yes we did, and we christened it last night," Greg said, and winked at Matthew.

Matthew took his hand. "Look up, Greg, over the fireplace. It must have been a sign."

Greg looked up at the carved faces of two men and one girl. Then he looked at Matthew. "I believe so," he said.

Greg left for work earlier than usual on Monday, eager to get the adoption process started. He was granted emergency foster care of Nichole while the process was initiated, but the adoption looked very promising.

Greg was given a few days leave from work to get Nichole settled, and he couldn't wait to tell Matthew. A woman from his office let him borrow her car seat and showed Greg how to place the baby in it, and then he headed for home.

Matthew arrived at the house at the same time Greg did, and hurried to open the door for his baby daughter. "She's beautiful, Greg, absolutely gorgeous."

Greg unbuckled the car seat and Matthew picked her up and held her to him. "Oh, you beautiful sweet little thing," he said, and kissed her on the cheek.

Greg was impressed with Matthew's instantaneous fatherly love. Greg walked around the car and put his arm around Matthew. "We did it, Matthew. She's really ours." Greg kissed Matthew on the cheek, and the three of them walked into the house.

Greg set down the bag. "Oh, how nice, Greg. You've got diapers and clothes."

"Oh, Matthew, one of the ladies from the office went out and had this bag fully stocked while the paperwork was being processed."

The three of them went into the family room and Greg sat with Nichole in his lap. Matthew filled the tippy cup with milk, and they watched as their wide-eyed Nichole drank happily while she looked around. They took turns holding Nichole for the rest of the day, even while she napped, neither wanting to let her go.

"We're a family, Matthew. We're a family." Greg still could not believe it.

"You've made my life so much more than I ever thought it could be, Greg."

"I'm so happy, Matthew. Life is rich."

Once the adoption was finalized, Matthew and Greg felt that their lives had become even richer. Not wanting to miss a day in the life of their little girl, they rearranged their work schedules so that they worked only four days a week, hiring a nanny to care for Nichole while they worked.

Before they knew it, Nichole was in school. Matthew and Greg continued to work four days a week, taking one day a week to be together as a couple. "I love you more each day, Matthew," Greg said on one of their days off, while they were making love. Matthew was too busy kissing Greg's beautiful body to do anything but look up quickly and smile at him. Greg loved the touch of Matthew, the kiss of Matthew, the scent of Matthew, everything of Matthew. Greg turned to his side and motioned for Matthew to do the same.

They were eager to give themselves to each other. Greg loved the taste and feel of Matthew's erect penis as it passed through his lips and slid into his mouth. He took his time with Matthew just as Matthew always took his time with him. They both loved to please each other. They stroked each other between their butt cheeks, lingering at the entrance to that hidden pleasure that was made for lovers to discover.

They were always ready for each other, and today was no exception. Matthew loved the feel of Greg's hard balls and never tired of playing with them, and when they were firmly in his hands Greg always moaned. Matthew knew exactly how to touch him inside and out. Matthew couldn't wait for Greg to firmly plant his hands on his butt, kneading it, as he brought his cock into his ever pleasing mouth. Their pace intensified until they both came at the same time.

They held each other afterward for as long as they could. "I love you, Greg."

Greg kissed Matthew' shoulder, and whispered, "I love you, too, Matthew." He sighed with content.

On Fridays, their day off each week, they would plan their weekend with Nichole. Now that she was in school, they would plan something that she could invite a friend to join them in doing or seeing on Saturdays, and Sundays were always reserved for just the three of them.

"Let's take Nichole to the Space Needle next Saturday. She's almost six now. She will have a great time," Greg suggested one Friday.

"Sounds great, Greg."

******

The popcorn was gone now, and Nicky was sitting in Greg's lap, listening intently and looking at him through her big beautiful eyes. He had loved telling the story of how he had become her daddy, leaving out the lovemaking parts of course.

Nicky hugged Greg with the biggest hug she could manage, and kissed him on the cheek. "I love you, Daddy."

Greg adored Nichole and cherished those four little words. "I love you too, baby."

She looked at Greg with a questioning look.

"What is it, baby?"

"If you are my daddy, then Matthew is my daddy, too?"

"That's right, Nichole. Matthew and I love each other very much, and we both love you."

Still a little puzzled, she paused, and then asked another question. "So, some kids have just one mommy or one daddy, and some kids have one mommy *and* one daddy, and some kids have *two* daddies?"

"That's right, baby, and some kids have two mommies and no daddies," Greg added. "What is important is not *who* we love. What is important is *that* we love."

"Hmm," she said. Satisfied, she changed the subject and asked if her friend, Tommy, could play this weekend.

"Of course, honey. We were planning on a trip to the Space Needle. Do you think Tommy would like to come?"

Nichole's eyes were wide with excitement. "Oh, boy. Can we call his mommy?"

Greg hugged her. "Let's wait a little while. He may not be home from school yet."

The turn of the key in the lock brought Nichole up and off of Greg's lap. She ran to the front door, meeting Matthew with a commentary on her day. Greg was listening and smiling as she recounted every detail to Matthew.

"I was dopted, and I have two daddies. Some kids have one daddy *and* one mommy, some kids have one daddy *or* one mommy, and some kids have two daddies or two mommies."

Leading Matthew by the hand, they joined Greg in the family room. "Quite a day I see," he said.

Greg ran his hand through his hair, looking tired. "Yes it was. Yes it was."

The phone rang then, and Nichole hurried to answer it.

"Are you okay, love?" Matthew asked Greg.

"I'm great. We have quite a young lady now, Matthew."

Matthew kissed Greg. "Yes we do, and she is growing up very fast."

Nicky ran back in and said that it was Tommy's mom wanting to talk to Greg.

"Dr. Stevens, I am so sorry. Tommy told me what he had said to Nichole and that it made her feel bad."

"It's fine. Nicky and I had a long talk today. I guess we should have had this talk a little sooner," Greg lamented.

"Well, it shouldn't have come from Tommy, and I am very sorry."

"No apology needed. And, Nicky would love for Tommy to go with us to the Space Needle on Saturday."

"Oh, he would love that. I'll drop him off at your house, okay?"

Greg said that would be great, and that they would leave around eleven in the morning. Nicky was thrilled. She loved to play mini-golf and ride the rides at the Fun Forest. The Children's Museum neither she nor Tommy had visited yet. Matthew had been there years ago, but Greg had not yet. Matthew explained to Greg that the Children's Museum was fantastic and that it was an interactive museum.

"Children learn so much more in a hands-on environment," Matthew said. "Sometimes we have school groups tour the bakery and let the kids design their own doughnut or whatever they like, and they have a wonderful time."

Being a doctor, Greg certainly could appreciate the concept of hands-on learning.

On Saturday morning Nicky was up early. Greg could hear the cartoons on the television, and looked at the clock. Seven o'clock. "Matthew, guess it's time to get up."

Matthew rolled over. "Oh, I guess so. I'll start the coffee."

Greg went into the family room and kissed Nichole on the head. "Good morning, princess."

Nicky giggled like she always did when he called her princess. "Ready for a fun day?"

"Yep," she said, and then turned her attention back to her cartoons.

Matthew handed Greg a cup of strong hot coffee. "Mm, smells great. Thanks." They drank their coffee and watched the Saturday morning cartoons with the love of their lives, their little princess, their beautiful Nichole.

Their day at the Space Needle was very tiring, but very fun. Tommy and Nicky rode the rides over and over, played mini-golf for as long as they could which Matthew and Greg also enjoyed playing, and then they all had a great time exploring everything in the Children's Museum.

Nicky loved sharing her day with her two daddies, and her two daddies wouldn't trade a minute with her for anything in the world. When it was time to leave, both Nicky and Tommy protested for a minute, until Greg told them that they were going to eat at the very top of the Space Needle. Neither of them had ever done that. It would be the first time back there for Greg and Matthew since the night that Matthew had surprised Greg with a romantic dinner.

When they walked into the restaurant, Greg looked at Matthew and Matthew looked at Greg. "This was our beginning," Greg said.

Matthew put his arm around Greg for a brief minute. "I loved you then, and I love you even more today," he whispered.

Greg smiled, and then blushed when they were seated at the very same table as they had been on that very romantic evening, which had been secretly arranged by Matthew.

"How did I get so lucky?" Greg asked.

Matthew just smiled, his brilliant blue eyes sparkling.

Bear Hugs

When Eric spends a day in the park in search of just the right setting for his painting with a romantic flair, he meets a man who is both passionate and charming, and who very quickly wins Eric's heart. Eric soon realizes that he has never known a love like the love he feels for this man. When this man confesses a desire that he has carried with him for almost half a century, Eric wonders if his own desire for true love may not be the same love that this new man in his life seems to desire. A trip to the homeland of this man of Eric's desire reveals much more than Eric had expected. Eric now wonders if he may have gotten himself into something he may one day regret.

One
The Artist

Eric awoke early today. It was Saturday, a day when many people may have chosen to sleep in, but not Eric. Eric worked for a thriving telecommunications firm during the week, but after work and on the weekends he painted. Eric lived in the perfect house and in the perfect city for the inspiration the artist in him needed. Portland, Oregon, had distinguished itself as an eclectic city where sophisticated and alternative styles coexisted peacefully.

Known as the City of Roses, with the most perfect of climates for growing the most perfect of roses, Portland had never failed to provide Eric with a new shade or splash of color that made his paintings practically jump off of the canvass. Eric had found Portland to be rich in culture and very friendly. Eric had moved to Portland from Chicago, thinking that the weather would be much the same, cold and humid in the winter and hot and humid in the summer. But Eric had been wrong.

Portland's climate was quite temperate and with the Pacific Ocean and the Cascade Mountains, this wonderful city offered Eric what he considered to be the best of both worlds. He loved the beach, but had developed a deep appreciation for hiking and skiing in the mountains, which was something that he could not do in Chicago.

Eric had chosen to live in the Pearl District of Portland, which was once home to Portland's industrial center. The Pearl District had given itself a complete makeover, converting its old buildings into contemporary urban living spaces. Like the other houses in the Pearl District, Eric's house sat on top of a retail business, making it seem very cozy, yet in no way secluded.

Eric's house sat on top of a bakery, which Eric didn't even try to resist. Eric was a slender man with a slight frame, and had been born with a metabolism that allowed him to eat as many of the yummy baked goodies that he desired. Every morning he would indulge in more than one of the delicious treats that were baked just below him, and he loved the way his house smelled all of the time as the savory aromas wafted up from just one story below him. Eric had been complimented often on the wonderful aromas of fresh baked breads and sweet treats that his guests enjoyed during their visits. He would humbly thank them, but gave credit where credit was due.

Eric got out of bed and stretched. He walked down the hall to his formal dining room which he had transformed into his art studio, and looked out of the window and down at the street below him. Not much was happening yet, but soon the street would be bustling with tourists and residents of this beautiful city.

Living alone, Eric had had little need for a formal dining room, and its location within his house was perfect for painting. Eric looked at the various pieces he had painted. "I am quite the artist," he said aloud. He gathered up his supplies and carried them down the stairs and into his car.

Every Thursday, the many galleries in Eric's little corner of the world were open to the public, and this Thursday would be Eric's very first Thursday to display his personal works. The only thing he needed to complete his collection was a nature painting with a romantic flair.

There was only one place to find this picture perfect setting for Eric's romantic painting, and that place was Laurelhurst Park. If Eric hadn't chosen to live in the Pearl District, his second choice had been the Hawthorne District from where the breathtaking Laurelhurst Park was a short distance. He visited the Hawthorne District quite often, to partake of the latest vegan dishes that were created there, though Eric was not a vegan. That didn't mean that he couldn't enjoy some of the wonderful dishes that could be found there. It was healthy for him, anyway. Today, though, two delicious fresh baked muffins and a steaming cup of his favorite brewed coffee accompanied Eric to the park.

Eric found a bench where the sunlight was perfect, and set up his easel. He relaxed and enjoyed his muffins and coffee while he looked around. "Well, time to work," he said, but to him this wasn't work. Painting was Eric's passion. "One day I will make it big. Who knows, I could be the next Picaso," he said, with a laugh.

From Eric's vantage point, he had a perfect view of a crystal clear lake, a beautiful expansion of green grass, beautiful roses of course, and a mostly clear blue sky. In the distance was a forest of old growth trees which Eric planned to paint at the very edge of his canvass to add just a hint of mystery to his romantic painting. "This is going to be the perfect day," he said. The setting was just right for the perfect painting of nature's finest.

Eric looked out at the lake. There were two beautiful white swans swimming, and the slight ripple in the water behind them was breathtaking. "That's it," Eric said aloud. "That's the money shot." Eric often used that phrase, though he didn't paint for money. Eric painted for pleasure. Still, he wouldn't mind being "discovered."

Eric had painted for almost three hours, concentrating on the two white swans and the romantic ripple of water behind them, completely oblivious to all other activity in the park, when he suddenly realized that he was being watched. He wouldn't have noticed, except that the sun had moved and the intruder's shadow was now blocking his light. Eric turned around.

"You're quite the artist," the man said.

"Oh, thanks," Eric said.

"I don't mean to stare, but for the last hour you have had me completely mesmerized."

Eric was flattered, and could feel the heat in his cheeks begin to rise.

"You have captured the detail of the swans and their movements exquisitely."

Eric shrugged. "Oh, it's just a hobby. Well, I guess it's really more of a passion of mine," Eric added. He leaned down to pick up the brush that had fallen and when he looked up again, the man had taken a seat next to Eric on the bench.

"I hope you don't mind if I watch for awhile."

Eric looked at the man. "No, I don't mind," he said, a little uneasily.

The man looked to be in his middle to late forties, or so Eric guessed, though he knew he could have been off by at least ten years. Eric had turned thirty-five this year, but had always had somewhat of a baby face. He had hated that about himself until the last five years or so when he realized that looking younger definitely had its benefits.

The man sitting beside Eric was nice, very friendly and easy-going. He extended his hand and said, "I'm Aiden, Aiden Nelson."

Eric quickly placed the end of his paintbrush in his mouth and shook the man's hand. Then holding the brush in his hand, he said, "I'm Eric Kovach."

Aiden stretched his arms across the back of the bench, which brought him even closer to Eric. "Kovach, huh? Is that Polish? I don't mean anything by that. I have always been interested in name origins. I majored in cultural studies in college many, many years ago."

Eric smiled. "It's Croatian."

Aiden loved the way Eric's dark hair against his white skin seemed to make his entire being stand out, as if he were in one of his magnificent paintings. "Well, you may have guessed that I am of British descent. In fact, I lived in London until I was twenty. Over the years, though, I have lost much of my English accent, but if you listen closely you will hear remnants of it."

Eric smiled, and glanced over at Aiden.

"I hope that I am not bothering you with my idle chitchat."

"Not at all, Aiden. I'm putting the finishing touches on my painting right now. I have a small collection that I hope to show at one of the galleries this week."

"Oh, yes, in the Pearl District. Well, I shall make it a point to stop by."

Eric smiled, and glanced at Aiden once again. Eric had never been as easy with people as Aiden seemed to be. "What line of work are you in, Aiden?" Painting while he talked made the conversation a lot easier for Eric. He could avoid direct eye contact that way.

"As for myself, I don't live far from here at all. I own a vintage clothing store," Aiden offered.

Eric looked at Aiden. "I'll bet I've been to your store. I love everything vintage, vintage clothes, furniture. Antiques I can't get enough of." Continuing to look at this nice man, Eric wanted to know more about his store.

Aiden continued. "I design some, that is, when I can find the time. My mother designed wedding dresses in London, so I learned to sew at a very young age, and she must have given me my creative side as well as my eye for design." Aiden smiled, and Eric smiled back.

"Well, I'm finished with my painting," Eric announced proudly.

"Magnificent, Eric."

Eric felt Aiden's hand on his shoulder. Aiden squeezed Eric's shoulder and then put his arm back on the bench. Eric knew that his face had probably turned a few shades of red, but he didn't mind Aiden's touch. He didn't mind it at all.

Eric packed up his things, and then turned to Aiden. "It was nice meeting you, Aiden, and thank you for the generous compliments."

"All well deserved, I can assure you," he said. "I would love to show you my store sometime, Eric. I will be back there today at around two. Just taking a little breather here."

Eric knew that he should say something now, but what?

"If you are not doing anything tonight, stop by and I will show you around, maybe get something to eat?"

Eric was glad that Aiden had spoken, but now he was even more nervous by the invitation.

"Sure. I'll come by," Eric said.

"Around six then?"

Eric nodded. He picked up his easel and other paint supplies that he kept in an oversized backpack and walked away. He wanted to look behind him to see if Aiden was watching him, but had a feeling that he was.

As soon as Eric arrived home, he set up his new painting in his dining room/studio and stood back and admired it. "Well done, Eric," he said. Then he fixed himself some lunch and lay down with his favorite book.

Two
Date of a Different Kind

At five, Eric took a quick shower, and then nervously drove to Aiden's store. "I have *definitely* been here before," he said. Eric walked inside the vintage clothing store, and Aiden was checking out the last customer.

The customer left, and Aiden locked the front door. "Well, this is it, Vintage Aiden," he said.

"I *have* been here and more than once," Eric said. "I love your store. I have actually made a few purchases, but I don't remember seeing you," Eric said.

"Well, I was probably in the back at the time. Come with me, Eric. My studio awaits."

Eric followed Aiden into the back part of his store. "Ooh, it's a bit eerie," Eric commented.

"That's just the mannequins. They do look lifelike, though, especially at night," Aiden agreed.

The room was filled with creations by Aiden, all vintage of course, and all beautiful.

"These are beautiful, Aiden, and very unique." Eric was impressed with Aiden's artistic eye.

"I love to design, and fortunately I can still sew. If I am not out front, then I am back here creating."

Eric looked around. "You seem to have put a somewhat modern spin on vintage designs."

"I must say that even I am impressed with how my passion has grown into a business, Eric."

Eric would love to paint all day every day, and not work, but he knew that running a business was not all fun and games. "Have you always done this, I mean, created vintage designs?"

Aiden looked at Eric's youthful face, wondering how young he actually was. He seemed to look younger here than he had in the park. "No, I taught a literature course at the university for ten years after I earned my Ph.D., and now I have had the store here for the last ten years." Aiden noticed Eric's hesitancy to ask more, and so Aiden freely offered. "I tired of the university politics, but I loved teaching literature. I am a voracious reader. And then one day I wandered into this terrific neighborhood, and I have been here since. I realized the day I walked into this store that I had repressed my true passion, and I also realized that I was not getting any younger."

Eric smiled, and then looked down. He tried to put the timeline together to figure out how old Aiden was, and guessed him to be in his mid forties.

"Well, I'm not a vegan, Eric, but I do know where to find mouthwatering vegan dishes. Sound good to you?"

Eric, of course, loved vegan food. "Sure. I'm not a vegan, either, but I do like some of the tasty dishes I have found here in Portland," he said in agreement.

Aiden locked his store, and offered to take his car. He drove Eric to a very intimate little place that Eric had never been.

"This is nice, Aiden."

"Thank you, kind sir," Aiden said, and opened the door to the restaurant. He had made reservations, and the two of them were given the V.I.P treatment. Eric was impressed with the restaurant, and was even more impressed with Aiden. Aiden was the perfect gentleman. Eric had never been treated this well.

"Well, Eric, would you care to share a bottle of wine while we watch the sunset over the Pacific?"

Eric nodded, unaccustomed to such formality. Aiden's British origin combined with his extensive studies in literature had formed the perfect gentleman's manner of speaking. Eric felt as if he had stepped back in time to a time of old English aristocracy.

Aiden drove them to the beach. It was breezy and a bit chilly so close to the water, so they sat in Aiden's car drinking their wine and looking out at the ocean. Eric didn't say much. He didn't think he had anything to add to this perfect evening. He quietly sipped his wine. Before he knew it, his glass was empty. He looked over at Aiden. It was almost completely dark now, and Eric thought Aiden looked very distinguished and dignified in the moonlight.

Aiden took Eric's empty glass and set it with his own on the top of the dashboard. He put his arm on the back of the seat and turned toward Eric. "Well, Eric, before we head back, I want to thank you for a lovely evening," he said.

Eric felt like a schoolboy. He wanted Aiden to kiss him out here in the moonlight. "I should be thanking you, Aiden. You did all this for me." Eric looked down.

Aiden moved closer to him and put one hand on Eric's knee. He put his arm around Eric. "Eric, may I?"

Eric looked up and Aiden's very distinguished looking face was right in front of him. The look in his eyes, the wine glistening on his lips, and the heat of his breath were making Eric dizzy with lust. Eric leaned his head on the back of the seat, closed his eyes, parted his lips, and waited. Aiden moved closer to Eric until his pelvis was pressed against him, held him tighter with one arm over his shoulder and the other arm holding his body close to him. Then Aiden looked at Eric's closed eyes and parted lips. He lightly touched his lips to Eric's lips, and then pulled away, just slightly. Eric leaned forward slightly, asking for more.

Aiden touched his lips to Eric's lips again, this time pressing them firmly to Eric's. Eric slowly raised his arms and placed them around Aiden's thick chest and broad shoulders, sliding them downward along his back. Aiden put his arms around Eric, pulling him forward, holding him in a big bear hug embrace. Eric opened his mouth to Aiden's kiss. Aiden lightly ran his tongue along Eric's lips and then kissed his lips again, lovingly, slowly, yet fully and passionately. Aiden felt the warmth of Eric's embrace and held him longer than he had planned this first night together. Aiden didn't want to stop, but he didn't want Eric to think he was taking advantage, either. He liked Eric a lot, and he would have loved to make passionate love to him tonight, but he would wait until the time was right and the two of them could wake up in each other's arms.

Aiden slowly withdrew his lips from Eric's, and touched Eric's face very gently. Eric laid his head against the back of the seat, his breaths coming quickly. Aiden leaned back and rested his hand on Eric's leg. Eric looked at Aiden, who was completely lost in Eric's eyes. For the first time that day, Aiden was without words. There were no words to describe his feelings right now.

Aiden cleared his throat nervously. "I...I guess we should be getting back," he said.

"Yes," Eric agreed, barely able to say that one word.

Aiden felt Eric's arms leave his body. Aiden took Eric's hands in his and one at a time he held them to his lips and kissed them lightly. Then he gently placed Eric's hands down onto his lap, and slid back over to the driver's side. He picked up the wine glasses from on top of the dashboard and set them in the backseat.

Aiden and Eric said nothing on the way back to Eric's car. They were both thinking similar thoughts, however. When they stopped in front of Aiden's store, Aiden couldn't let the silence last any longer. He turned to Eric.

"Eric, may I see you again?"

Eric was fighting the heated blush rising to his cheeks. He looked at Aiden, and in the darkness he could see only his eyes and the outline of his gorgeous face. "Yes," he said, and then quickly looked away.

"Name the day, and I am all yours, Eric," he said, sounding more like his usual self again.

"Well, is Monday night good for you?" Eric asked.

"Monday is perfect, Eric. Let me bring dinner to you."

Eric felt nervous and excited at the same time. He looked up at Aiden, and said, "thank you."

Aiden squeezed Eric's hand and said, "I look forward to Monday."

Eric smiled at Aiden, and opened the car door. Aiden sat in his car and waited for Eric to drive away before he went into his own house just above his store. He had no idea that a trip to the park would end in such a sweet way.

What a day! Eric thought, as he looked at his paintings, and especially the painting that had been admired by the man who Eric now admired. He had no idea that his quest for a painting set in nature's romantic movements would have taken such a sweet and unexpected turn.

Eric was exhausted after his very eventful day the day before, and slept soundly until the next morning. He awoke late that Sunday. It was nearly noon when Eric looked at the clock. "I never sleep this late," he said. He thought about last night while he prepared his paintings for Thursday's gallery showing.

Eric liked Aiden, maybe more than he should. He had just met the man yesterday, yet he had wanted him last night in a way that he hadn't wanted a man in a very long time. In fact, Eric hadn't really felt anything with any of the guys he had met since college. In college, his relationships had been relatively brief, but there had always been fire and passion in them. Eric had attributed some of the passion to teen angst or simply, a growing up period, but after last night Eric knew that his passion for Aiden had been very real. It was the passion that he had missed, and desperately needed, and there was no doubt in his mind that there had been passion last night with Aiden.

"If there is that much passion in just a kiss, I can only imagine what it would be like to make love with Aiden." Eric stared out of the window. He then closed his eyes. He could almost feel Aiden's lips on his again. He began to imagine what a passionate lover Aiden would be. If Aiden's kiss was any indication of his complete lovemaking, Eric couldn't wait to find out. He opened his eyes and looked at the painting in front of him. He tried to see the swans and the water through Aiden's eyes. It was beautiful. Meeting Aiden had been exactly what Eric had needed.

Eric prepared his brushes to add his signature to each of his paintings. He practiced on plain canvass a few times, experimenting with different styles and various flairs. Toward the end of the day, Eric had finally perfected each of his paintings and had set them in a semicircle for the paint to finish drying. Tomorrow was Monday, and Eric couldn't wait to see Aiden again.

Fortunately for Eric, his Monday was a busy one. He had hoped that the day would go by quickly. Eric had hoped that Aiden would have called him yesterday, but he was no doubt very busy with his store. Eric hurried home from work, showered, and thought about Aiden touching his naked body. It had been a long time since Eric had made love with anyone.

Three
Dinner at Six

Aiden arrived promptly that night at six. He set the promised dinner down in Eric's kitchen, and then pulled Eric to him. He put his arms around Eric and held him tightly. "I missed you," he whispered, his mouth over Eric's ear, his hot breath making Eric's entire body quiver. He slowly drew his mouth off of Eric's ear, kissing the lobe and holding it in his mouth for just a second before letting Eric go.

Aiden began to open the delicious smelling dishes that he had brought, while Eric grabbed onto the kitchen counter to keep from falling over. Aiden's effect on Eric was incredible. Eric would somehow gather the courage to ask Aiden to spend the night. He knew that he would regret it if he didn't.

"How was your day, Eric?"

"Good," he said, the strength in his legs coming back finally after Aiden's passionate embrace.

Aiden continued preparing the already mostly prepared buffet that he had brought, insisting that he needed no assistance. "Think of me as your very own gentleman's gentleman tonight," Aiden said, turning to look at Eric.

Eric melted at Aiden's words. He thought again of making love to him. He couldn't help but think about it.

Aiden opened a bottle of wine, and poured two glasses. "What shall we toast to, Eric?" he asked, his eyes looking longingly into Eric's. Eric felt that same quivering feeling once again. Aiden spoke for him. "To us?" he asked. Eric smiled.

"To us," he said, and raised his glass.

"Dinner is served, my good man," Aiden announced. He formally escorted Eric to the seat of honor. The touch of Aiden's large hands just brushing Eric's thighs as he seated him at the table was electrifying to Eric. Aiden served Eric and then he served himself. It was not yet dark outside, but Aiden lit a single candle. The flame of the candle and the beautiful paintings of Eric provided the perfect ambience for what Eric and Aiden had both hoped would be their first night together.

"This is delicious, Aiden."

"I cannot take credit for the cuisine, Eric. There is a wonderful little deli not far from the store that I must give the credit to for tonight's cuisine."

Aiden poured them a second glass of wine. "There are a number of eateries very near the store and as you can see, I do not pass them by easily." Aiden laughed after he said this, which Eric thought was charming. Aiden's body was thicker than Eric's, but Eric loved Aiden's body, and Eric wanted Aiden's body to make love to his. "Well, Eric, are you ready for Thursday?" Aiden asked, as he looked at the paintings in the dining room. "Your signature is perfect," he added.

"I think I'm ready. I've taken some time off, Thursday and Friday, so that I can meet some of the other artists." Eric wanted to know more about Aiden, but never wanted to pry into another's personal business. Still, Aiden wasn't just another person. Aiden was very quickly becoming someone very special to Eric. "What are your days like, Aiden?"

Aiden turned to Eric. "My days are a surprise, every one of them, Eric. I plan to design every day, but if I am needed to work in the store, which is quite often, then my designs are put on hold."

Eric was unaccustomed to someone like Aiden, someone so formal in manner and speech, but thought that it was probably because Aiden was British.

"Well, Eric, I did make my specialty dessert, cheesecake topped with strawberries, another of my weaknesses," Aiden announced, patting his stomach. Eric smiled. "Shall we wait awhile?" Aiden asked.

"Probably," Eric agreed. Eric felt that he was failing miserably in his attempt to get closer to Aiden. I'm scaring him off. I just know it. He stared out of the window, not realizing that Aiden had been talking to him. "I'm sorry, Aiden."

Aiden motioned for Eric to sit with him in the living room. Eric went with him. Aiden turned to Eric as they sat together on the sofa. It was almost dark in the room, the only light the slowly fading flame of the single candle. The darkness made it much easier for Eric to relax. Aiden took Eric's hands in his after he had moved very close to Eric.

"The flame is flickering its last," Aiden commented. He kissed Eric on the cheek. Eric could feel shivers throughout his entire body. If he could just say it. If he could just tell Aiden not to go tonight.

"Stay," Eric heard his own voice say. He was sure that it had only been a whisper. Aiden surely couldn't have heard the single word.

"I had every intention of staying," Aiden said, his warm breath next to Eric's ear.

Eric felt as if he were melting. Eric wanted to melt into Aiden. Eric closed his eyes, but turned his lips to Aiden. Aiden's big strong arms went easily around Eric, and he lightly touched his lips to Eric's lips. Eric's body wanted Aiden, and Eric's shyness only intensified Aiden's arousal. Eric's body was not shy, however. Aiden's arm brushed against Eric's arousal, and Aiden kissed Eric's lips passionately, opening his mouth and running his tongue along the inner edge of those lips. Eric slowly reached out and put his arms around Aiden's thick body, and Aiden pressed his body to Eric's much slighter one.

Aiden was not just kissing Eric. Aiden was making love to Eric, slowly, passionately. Aiden took his time enjoying the taste and feel of Eric's lips. This kind of love was new to Eric. His other lovers had never kissed him for this long. Lovemaking had been very rushed, until now, until Aiden. Aiden slowly moved his lips from Eric's, and Eric gasped for air as Aiden kissed his chin. Eric tilted his head back so that Aiden's lips could continue their downward trail. Aiden held Eric with one arm around his waist and the other arm resting on his hip. Eric knew that Aiden could feel his erection with his arm resting across his pelvis, but he didn't care. Aiden had aroused erotic feelings in Eric tonight that hadn't been aroused in a very long time, and Eric wanted Aiden to touch him, to kiss every inch of his naked body, and Eric wanted to feel Aiden's sensual lips around his cock. Eric's body ached as he thought of Aiden and him naked together in his bed.

Aiden kissed along Eric's neck and when he reached the top button of Eric's shirt, Eric let his arms slowly slide down from Aiden's back. He thrust his chest forward for Aiden. He wanted to feel Aiden's lips on his nipples that were pressing their hardness against his shirt. Aiden unbuttoned Eric's shirt with his mouth, and then separated the two sides by sliding his tongue along Eric's chest. Eric heard himself moan, but kept his eyes closed. Aiden unbuttoned every button on Eric's shirt down to his belly button which he swirled his tongue around and in. He opened Eric's shirt, and his hand on Eric's naked flesh caused Eric's body to jerk. Eric sighed.

Aiden slid his tongue upward in a straight line on Eric's chest until he had reached the level of his nipples. Aiden then slowly kissed his way to Eric's left nipple. He opened his mouth and pressed his lips to Eric's chest surrounding the nipple. He breathed out forcefully and his hot breath on and around Eric's nipple caused Eric to push his chest toward Aiden's lips.

"Aiden," he said softly.

Aiden slid his tongue across Eric's nipple, back and forth, several times, and then nibbled it lightly. Eric placed his hand on Aiden's back. He wanted more, much more.

"Harder, Aiden," he murmured.

Aiden took bigger and sharper bites on Eric's nipple. Eric slid his hand down Aiden's back and onto the suppleness of his butt. Aiden helped himself to Eric's right nipple, giving it the same passionate stimulation as he had the left one.

Aiden kissed his way back up to Eric's open mouth and licked the tiny specks of wetness that glistened at the corners. Aiden kissed Eric passionately on his mouth, but not for long this time. Aiden looked at Eric's body in its complete surrender to him, eased back until his feet touched the floor, and then lifted Eric and stood up. Eric struggled to lift his head, but Aiden helped himself to one of Eric's nipples, and Eric moaned and gave all control to Aiden.

Aiden looked at Eric's sweet face. "Where to?" Aiden asked.

"Last door," Eric said. Eric could feel the wetness on his skin, on his chest from Aiden's kisses, and deep inside his pants from his own eager arousal.

Aiden very carefully carried his lover to the room at the end of the hallway. The room was beautiful, as was its inhabitant, and Aiden placed Eric on the downy comforter. Eric looked at Aiden, not knowing exactly what role was expected of him. Aiden leaned over Eric and placed his hands on Eric's chest. Eric's eyes began to drift shut, and Aiden removed Eric's shirt. He placed his hands on Eric's hands which were laid above his head on the bed, and he kissed Eric unexpectedly on the lips. He slid his fingers downward along Eric's arms, stopping to play with the hair that lay nestled in a place of their own where his arms met his chest.

Eric moaned at the erotic touches, many of which he had never felt until now. Aiden's fingertips found Eric's erect nipples, and Aiden allowed each finger a single touch while he kissed and licked Eric's stomach. Eric could feel his leaking cock, and Aiden had gotten him so aroused that he thought he might explode at any moment. Eric opened his legs to Aiden. He wanted him to free his aching cock. Aiden undid Eric's pants and slowly ran the zipper down its track. He, too, could see how aroused Eric had become, and smiled. He wanted Eric to be aroused, and he wanted to be the one who had aroused him. Eric waited as Aiden removed his pants. His body ached for Aiden's touch. He opened his legs for Aiden again, and felt one of his balls slide out of his shorts.

Aiden wrapped his arms around Eric's parted thighs, and placed his mouth over the escapee from Eric's shorts. Aiden's hot breath forced Eric's ball into Aiden's mouth by the sudden jerking of Eric's body. Aiden rolled it around in his mouth, pulling it upward with his tongue and then pushing it back down again. Aiden knew that Eric's body was ready for him now.

Aiden uncovered Eric's cock, and removed the thin cloth that had kept it hidden from him. Already soaked with pre-cum, Eric's cock was a mouthwatering sight to Aiden.

Before going any further, Aiden removed his own clothes, first his shirt, then his pants, continuing until he was standing naked. His own erect cock lay on the bed as he stood next to the edge. Aiden held Eric's thighs and pulled Eric to him. Aiden's cock head was nestled between Eric's butt cheeks and was pressed against his entrance.

"Ohhh," Eric moaned, breaking the silence. Eric could feel the heat of Aiden's breath on his cum soaked cock, and then he felt those luscious lips form around the head of his cock, and finally, his entire cock slid quickly into Aiden's welcoming mouth.

Eric bent his legs and dug his heels into the edge of the bed. He thrust his pelvis upward, giving Aiden what he had wanted. Eric's body was on fire. "Aiden, Aiden," he called, and he looked at Aiden.

Aiden's eyes were closed. He looked content as he eagerly accepted Eric's offering as it was given to him. "Mmmm," he hummed, causing Eric's pelvis to rock back and forth. Aiden's mouth made slow and steady trips up and down along Eric's cock, and Eric's body thrust harder and faster to urge Aiden to quicken his movements.

Eric grabbed onto Aiden's hair as he tried to steady himself for the explosive orgasm that was to come. "Oh, Aiden, I think it's…" Eric stopped and thrust harder. Aiden hummed continually with his movement up and down Eric's cock. "Now," Eric screamed, and pulled at the bed as his explosion was even more forceful than he had anticipated.

Aiden strengthened his movements, squeezing Eric's cock with his lips, as Eric's cock drained itself into Aiden's awaiting mouth. Eric's body was still while Aiden squeezed any remaining drops from Eric's cock.

Eric closed his eyes. He had never felt anything nearly as good as this. Aiden slowly laid Eric's softening penis onto his warm skin using only his tongue. Aiden continued to hold Eric's legs and he lightly kissed his inner thighs. Eric's skin flinched. He opened his eyes to Aiden's smile.

"You are wonderful, my love," he said.

Eric was surprised at Aiden's comment. "But I didn't do anything," he said, somewhat sheepishly.

"Oh, but you did, my love," Aiden assured him. "You gave me your body completely."

Eric closed his eyes and moaned softly. "How could I not, Aiden? Ohhh."

Eric opened his eyes again and looked at his naked body and his soft penis. Then he looked down at what had been shamelessly pressing against his entrance, as if begging to be invited inside. After what Aiden had just done for him, Eric wasn't all that shy any longer. "Mmm, what are we going to do about that?" he teased.

Aiden noticed the glint of mischief in Eric's eyes, and he said, "We should probably put it away." Aiden slid the head of his penis along Eric's inner path just once, and then allowed its heaviness to pull it down onto the bed. Eric made a sound like a whimper, and Aiden flipped him over like a pancake. "Uh," Eric grunted, as he landed on his stomach.

Aiden bent Eric's legs underneath him, and determined to hear Eric's moan of surprise at least one more time, he slid his hot thick tongue along Eric's crack. Eric scooted backward on the bed to lift his butt up to Aiden. "My love likes that, does he?" Aiden teased.

Eric moaned, and Aiden entered him with the full thickness of his hot tongue. Eric gasped with this sensation that was new to him. Aiden had an amazing tongue. Aiden was determined to find what he was looking for and when he did, Eric grabbed the bed again. His body stilled. Aiden made long strokes with his tongue, and Eric's breaths came in short gasps. Eric could feel the first stirrings in his penis as his erection began to grow once again.

Aiden forcefully withdrew his tongue, and positioned the head of his cock at Eric's hole. "Mmm," Eric moaned, opening himself to

Aiden. Aiden's thick cock entered Eric, and Eric pushed back against it, to welcome its long awaited arrival. Aiden's cock slid all the way into Eric's tightness, and Aiden wondered if this was his first time.

Aiden had to stop for a second to adjust to Eric's tightness. "You okay, my love?"

Eric responded with a moan and another push backward.

Aiden joined Eric on the bed and leaned over him, holding him as he stroked him deep. Aiden slid his hands along Eric's chest and on downward until he reached Eric's hardening cock. "Mmm," he moaned. Eric closed his eyes to the combined sensations. Aiden stroked Eric both inside and out, and Eric laid his arms out flat on the bed, giving himself completely to Aiden again.

Aiden felt his own orgasm nearing quickly as he looked at this man accepting his lovemaking so eagerly. "Eric, my love, I'm nearing," he warned.

"Ohhh," Eric muttered, but thrust his body as forcefully as he could against Aiden.

Aiden stroked Eric's cock with strong quick strokes, and thrust deep inside him with long strokes. He felt Eric nearing his climax, and could hear his quick breaths. "Oh, my Eric, I'm giving it to you now," Aiden said loudly. "That's my man. Eric, my love, you are so good to me," he said.

Eric wasn't used to such a talkative lover, but found it very erotic. Eric moaned softly as he came for a second time that night. Aiden's climax seemed neverending and Eric loved every minute of it. Aiden was in full control of Eric's much slighter body, and pulled and pushed it to his desire. "Oh, that's it, Eric, that's good," Aiden said finally, and pulled Eric's legs flat onto the bed and lay down over his body.

The feel of Aiden's large sweaty body over his own made Eric feel more manly than he had ever felt. He could stay like this forever. Aiden kissed and licked the back of Eric's neck. Eric reached his hand back and grabbed one side of Aiden's supple butt and squeezed it.

Eric murmured something, but Aiden couldn't hear it. He kissed Eric's earlobe, and asked, "What was that, my love?"

"Stay like that, Aiden, all night. Sleep on me."

Aiden licked along the top of Eric's ear and then made himself comfortable for a good night's sleep.

Eric awoke to the sound of the alarm. Aiden rolled over and off of his lover and turned off the alarm. He then lay on his back. "Oh, Eric, last night was the best," he said.

Eric rolled over and put his leg over Aiden. "It was perfect, Aiden. I've never had a lover like you."

"I'll bet you say that to all of your sweeties, don't you, my love?" Eric circled Aiden's large nipples with his finger.

"No, I don't," he said, seriously.

"Oh, my love, if you keep that up, something else is surely to come up, too," Aiden teased.

"I know. And I also know that I have got to go to work. Just two more days until my big debut."

"You know that I will be there," Aiden assured him. Eric looked up at Aiden. He could feel his shyness slowly returning. "What is it, Eric? What is on your mind?"

Eric looked away. "You'll think I'm crazy," he said.

"No, I won't. Tell me your thoughts, my love."

"I've never lived with anyone, you know, like that, and I've never wanted to, Aiden, until now, until you. I don't want you to leave."

Aiden rolled Eric onto his back and then spread his large body over his slender lover. He held Eric's face in his hands. "I will move in tonight, my love. I have everything I need right here." He kissed Eric passionately, like last night, and then forced himself to stop. "Work is a demanding mistress, or master in our case, I am afraid," Aiden remarked.

Eric loved the supple body of Aiden, and he watched him as he put his clothes on. Eric didn't move until Aiden was fully dressed.

Aiden lightly kissed the top of Eric's dick. Eric moaned. "I will see both of you tonight," he said.

Eric lay exactly where he was until he heard the door close behind Aiden.

Eric slowly made his way to the shower. He missed Aiden already. Aiden surprised Eric that day when one single red rose was delivered to him at his office. Eric blushed, but it made his day much brighter.

Four
Moving In

Aiden arrived at Eric's house shortly after Eric returned home from work. He had borrowed a friend's pickup truck, and Eric had cleared out a room for Aiden to use as his very own design studio. "My goodness, Eric. This is fabulous. I just assumed I would be designing and sewing in my office at the back of my store."

Eric felt his shyness returning, but just a little. "I guess I'm a little selfish. I want us to be here together as much as we can be," he said.

"And that is how it should be," Aiden announced, in complete agreement. He walked over to Eric and pulled him to him in a big bear hug, his large body swallowing Eric's much smaller one. Then he kissed Eric with the passion of last night, and Eric felt his body melting once again. Aiden left Eric breathless when he pulled his mouth off of his to bring in more of his belongings.

Eric had plenty of room in his big house. They reserved one bedroom just for sleeping and for lovemaking, made one bedroom into a dressing room, and then there was one for Aiden's very own to create his designs. "Well, my love, what shall we do with the last bedroom?" Aiden asked.

"I'm sure we'll find something to do with it," Eric said, knowing that Aiden was teasing. Eric loved having Aiden in his house. He was good natured, outgoing, and very talkative. He brought out the best in Eric, and Eric was just what Aiden had needed in his life to encourage him to continue with his designs.

On Wednesday night, the night before Eric's gallery debut, Aiden helped calm Eric's nerves about his debut as an artist by making sure that every one of his paintings was perfect in its arrangement with the other paintings.

B.K. Wright   133

On Thursday, Aiden enjoyed spending the entire day with Eric and his paintings.

"Do you think they'll like my paintings?"

"Yes, my love," Aiden said, and he meant it.

Eric was surprised and relieved when his paintings were well liked by many who visited the gallery that day. He sold them all, except the one that he didn't bring to the gallery. Eric just couldn't part with the painting that had first been admired by his new love, the one that Eric had been painting in the park the day the two of them had first met. Aiden had left the gallery for only a short while the entire day to check on things at his store.

When the two of them were alone that evening, Aiden opened a bottle of champagne. "To the artist," he proclaimed, and Eric smiled. After one glass, Aiden took Eric's glass from him and set both of them down. "Eric, my love, I have something to discuss with you," Aiden said, taking Eric's hands in his.

"Is there something wrong?" Eric asked, a look of fear in his eyes.

Aiden kissed him tenderly on the lips. "Not at all, my love," he assured. Then he spoke softly to Eric. "I had received a telephone call today while I was at the gallery. Eric, my love, I should have discussed this with you prior to settling in with you." Eric could feel his eyes filling with tears. Aiden pulled him close. "Eric, it has nothing to do with you and me as a couple. I love you, and I am not leaving you."

Eric remained with his head against Aiden's chest. He did not want to move from Aiden's loving embrace.

Aiden kissed Eric on the top of his head. "Eric, my love, I am forty-two years of age," he said.

Thinking that their age difference was worrying Aiden, Eric quickly spoke up. "I'm thirty-five, Aiden. That's not much of a difference."

Aiden held Eric against his thick chest. "It's not that, Eric. A few years ago I wanted a child, and I wanted a child badly. I felt certain that I would be a good parent. I went to an agency and inquired. With the many upsets remaining in the countries of the former Soviet Union, I was asked about foreign adoption. There are so many children, Eric, with no one to love them. I, of course, could not say no. I waited and waited, and called the agency many times. There is always so much work involved with this sort of thing, and time passes. After two years, I gave up on becoming a parent. I could hope no longer."

Eric had never heard Aiden's tone so mournful, so sad, and it made him feel even closer to Aiden, but it also frightened him a little.

Eric started to lift his head and look at Aiden, but Aiden held Eric's head to his chest and began to stroke his hair. "The call today, Eric, was from the agency. There are two Romanian children, a brother and a sister, who are in very dire straits. They have been living with an agency manager, but will be forced to go to an orphanage if not adopted soon. They were not born yet when I had first inquired about adoption. The boy is four years of age now, Eric, and the little girl not quite a year." Aiden stopped talking, but continued to hold Eric to him. Aiden had longed to be a parent, but did Eric? Aiden couldn't bear to think of life without Eric. He had lived for too many years and had had too many empty relationships to live without him now.

Eric wondered what Aiden was thinking. Did he want the kids and not him? He snuggled into Aiden even more. He couldn't think of life without Aiden's strong arms around him. He had never felt about anyone the way he felt about Aiden. Neither said a word for a few minutes. Then Eric slowly lifted his head to look at Aiden.

Eric was shocked to see Aiden's eyes as full as his. "Oh, my love," Aiden said, and kissed Eric's lips.

"What are you really telling me, Aiden?"

"Eric, I could never live without you. It has taken me forty-two years to get here, my love, almost half a century." Aiden kissed the single tear that fell slowly from each of Eric's eyes. "What are these tears for, my love?" "I guess I thought that maybe you wanted the kids instead of me," he admitted.

Aiden held Eric's sweet face in his hands. "What I want, my love, is you *and* the kids, but I would never ask anyone to be a parent if he did not want to be one. But without you, my life is empty, and I could not ask children into an empty life."

"But, what about before?"

"Yes, before you, I wanted children, and I would have been content to raise them alone, but at forty-two I had given up on finding a true love such as ours." Aiden paused for just a second. "Am I talking in circles, my love?"

Eric smiled. "I understand," he said.

Aiden held Eric close to him again.

Eric spoke into Aiden's chest. "Aiden, I would love to be a parent with you," he said quietly.

Aiden continued to stroke Eric's hair until he could gather enough strength to talk again. He held Eric away from him and looked into his sweet eyes. Aiden's eyes were as full as his heart. "Eric, you do not have to do this. It is not a requirement for my love," Aiden assured him.

"I know," Eric said, quietly.

"But have you thought about children, my love?" Aiden asked.

"No, not really, but I assumed that children were not meant to be a part of my life, and so had not considered a life with children. When I would see them in the park with their daddies, I would often wonder what was wrong with me, though. I would think that somehow I was not quite right, you know, and that being gay was perhaps a punishment." Aiden began to speak, but Eric stopped him. "I know that being gay is not a punishment, but sometimes when I'm alone I can't seem to keep these thoughts from entering my mind."

Aiden knew exactly what thoughts Eric was referring to. He had had them himself. It was what society had programmed them to think. "You are not alone any longer, my love."

Eric nodded against Aiden's chest. "Are they coming here?" Eric asked, referring to the children.

Aiden held Eric's face in his hands, and kissed his lips. "Oh, my goodness. In my concern for your feelings, I forgot to mention the details. We must go to them and bring them home." Aiden smiled. "That sounds nice, doesn't it? Bring them home?" But Eric, my love, can you get the time off from work?"

"Oh, that's no problem at all, Aiden. I have a lot of vacation time. I rarely take time off from work."

"Well, then, I guess that I have work to do," Aiden announced. "I can get my assistant, Shelley, to run the store. She is very dependable, and very knowledgeable. I trust her, yet it is hard to leave a business that I have built from the ground up in someone else's hands."

"When do we go?" Eric asked, having no knowledge about these kinds of things.

"As soon as we can. I cannot bear the thought of two young children without a home any longer than they absolutely must be without one." Aiden sighed. "Eric, my love, let me call the consulate and make the arrangements," Aiden offered.

"Sounds good to me," Eric replied. He loved the way Aiden said, "my love", after his name, and he was growing to love Aiden's

British manner of speaking. Some may have thought it "stuffy", but Eric found it endearing.

Aiden made all of the necessary arrangements, and Eric scheduled time off from work immediately. Packing for two weeks was not easy, and they joked while they packed.

"I can't remember when I had two weeks off from work, Aiden."

"This will be good for both of us, my love," Aiden replied.

Five
Trip to the Homeland

Before they knew it, Aiden and Eric were landing at Heathrow Airport in London. Eric looked around. "I have never been out of the United States, Aiden, except to go to Canada, but that's not very far from Portland. Guess my passport came in handy, after all."

"Eric, my love, I am very happy that you had that. I could not have left you behind." Aiden took Eric's hand as the plane neared the terminal. "There is no one I would rather share my homeland with than you." Eric smiled at Aiden.

They hailed a taxi and were on their way to a surprise destination that Aiden had arranged. Eric watched from the window as they passed the many sites of London.

Aiden patted Eric's leg. "Quite a city, eh?"

"It sure is. It's beautiful, Aiden." Eric marveled at the size of Big Ben and Parliament. "You must think I'm acting like a starstruck teen," he said to Aiden.

"Not at all, my love."

When they reached the hotel, Aiden and Eric were escorted to the very top floor. "Aiden, what have you done?"

Aiden just smiled. He opened the door to their suite, and said, "After you, my love."

Eric walked into the room, and dropped his bag. The remainder of their bags was soon brought in. Aiden tipped the man, and then the man left them alone. Eric walked around the massive room. "This is beautiful, Aiden. I was expecting a room, a bed and a bath, but this is like a mini house. But then, we can bring the children back here maybe before we make them take a long plane ride."

Aiden walked up behind Eric and put his arms around him. "Thank you, Eric."

Eric turned around. "For what?"

Aiden pulled him close in his usual big bear hug. "Thank you for giving me a family."

Eric wrapped his arms around Aiden. They stood for a few minutes, holding each other.

Aiden kissed the top of Eric's head. "You must be hungry, my love. As for myself, I am starving. Come on. I've lunch arranged for us." Eric looked at Aiden with wide eyes. Aiden winked at him, and took him by the hand. "This way, Eric, my love, your chariot awaits."

The taxi took the two of them to Aiden's surprise lunch. The taxi approached the London Eye, and it became bigger and bigger as they came closer and closer. Eric peered out of the window at the gigantic wheel. Aiden smiled as he watched Eric's reaction to this magnificent marvel. When the taxi stopped, Eric looked at Aiden questioningly.

"Lunch in the sky, my love?"

"You did this?" Eric asked, stunned.

"It has all been arranged. This is the perfect way to see London in all of its glory. We have a private capsule, my love, the London Eye Afternoon Tea Capsule."

Eric walked with Aiden, hand in hand, to their awaiting capsule. "How long does it take to go all the way around?"

"Thirty minutes, my love, but for you, it will go around twice, for a leisurely hour lunch," Aiden announced proudly.

Their host brought them each a glass of champagne. Aiden toasted to discovering the love of his life at a time and in a place he never would have expected to find it, and to the very different and very full life that awaited them. Then he kissed Eric with the passion that Eric had known only with Aiden.

As they ascended into the sky, Eric walked around the capsule looking out at Aiden's homeland. "The views are spectacular, Aiden."

"They certainly are, my love. I have been in the Eye only one time before today, five years ago." Eric took Aiden's hand so that they could share each and every sight together.

When they reached the very top, their host brought them a tray of London's finest. "Maybe it's not a bad idea to sit down," Eric commented, as he realized how high in the sky they were now.

"You are okay, right? My goodness, I did not even consider that my love may have had a problem with heights."

Eric sat down. "No, I'm fine, and hungry."

Aiden sat beside Eric, not letting go of his hand, and presented him with the beloved foods of his homeland. "We have smoked salmon which is scrumptious." Eric agreed. "Mother used to make scones, Eric. It is a classic English treat." Aiden lifted a bite of a freshly baked scone to Eric's lips, and Eric devoured it. "It's good, Aiden, and my first taste of scone."

Aiden helped himself to the delicious tastes from his homeland. "Mmm. I must keep our home stocked with these from now on," he added. Aiden shared with Eric two of his favorite desserts. "We have lemon drizzle cake, my grandmother's specialty, and these delectable mini chocolate éclairs which are partly responsible for my physique."

"Aiden, you are definitely not fat, and I love your physique," Eric added, blushing a little. "I do come from sturdy stock," Aiden added.

Eric smiled, and helped himself to an éclair. "This is perfect, Aiden. The food is delicious, and the views are breathtaking."

"All for you, my love."

Eric felt even closer to Aiden here than he had in Portland, and felt honored that Aiden chose to share all of this with him. They ate and talked for the entire hour, and then Aiden tipped their host very generously, and a taxi took them back to their hotel room.

"I think I ate too much, Aiden."

"As did I," Aiden agreed. "Well, if we are going to have little ones, we should probably get used to naps," Aiden said, half jokingly, but took Eric's hand and led him to the bedroom. They got out of their tight clothing and slipped underneath the covers in just their underwear. Eric curled up next to Aiden, and the two of them were soon sleeping soundly. Eric awoke in the middle of the night and felt Aiden's big warm arms around him. He snuggled closer to Aiden and threw one leg across him. He was soon sleeping again to the steady sound of Aiden's soft snoring.

Aiden awoke the next morning and looked down to see the top of Eric's head. Sometime during the night Eric had climbed completely on top of Aiden and was sleeping soundly sprawled across him. Eric had slid down to where the head of Aiden's cock was nestled snugly between the cheeks of his lover's butt, with only the thin layer of cloth of Eric's underwear between where it now was and where it wanted to be. Aiden felt his cock give a little twitch. He looked down at the sleeping Eric, his beautiful body spread over him, his legs open to him, and Aiden wanted him. He stroked Eric's hair and then began to massage his back. He loved the feel of Eric's body both on him and underneath his fingers. He could feel his cock pushing harder now against his lover, as it continued to grow just thinking about making love to Eric again.

Aiden shifted a little, and Eric stirred. Then he lifted his head and looked around. "Good morning, my love," Aiden said, continuing to stroke Eric's hair.

Eric looked up at Aiden and then at himself. "I didn't know I had climbed on top of you, Aiden."

"Oh, my love, I wouldn't want it any other way."

Eric looked down at his legs spread across Aiden. "Mmm," he said, wiggling his butt to accommodate Aiden's growing cock. "How did I get here?"

"I don't know, my love. Perhaps your cute little butt found the perfect place to call home." Aiden reached down and gave Eric's butt a firm squeeze, parting the two halves a little more.

Eric slid up and down, enjoying the feel of Aiden's cock between the two halves of his butt. Even with the thin layer of cloth keeping their bodies apart, Eric liked the feeling and began to feel the rise of his own cock between their bodies.

"Mmm," Aiden moaned, as Eric's hardening cock pressed into his stomach. Eric stretched his arms up and ran his fingers through the hair on Aiden's chest. His head lay on Aiden's stomach and his eyes were closed, as he bathed in the love of Aiden. Aiden's big hands were the perfect massagers for Eric's tight muscles. Aiden's eyes were closed.

With every pass of Eric's fingers across his nipples, Aiden became more and more aroused. The longer they lay together, the more Aiden thought about sex with Eric. He could make love to Eric anytime day or night, but wasn't sure that Eric felt the same way. Maybe Eric didn't like sex in the morning. Aiden suddenly felt a little insecure, which wasn't like him at all. The longer they lay together, however, the hornier Aiden became.

Aiden, never one to hide his feelings, was just about to say something to Eric, when Eric lifted his head and rested his chin on Aiden's stomach. "So, my sexy Briton, you planning to do me in your homeland, or what?" Then he wiggled his sexy little butt a little more, teasing the head of Aiden's cock.

Aiden lifted Eric up to him and kissed his sexy mouth. He slid his hands inside Eric's underwear and lightly ran his fingers along Eric's crack. Eric reached around and pushed his underwear down and off. Then he broke from Aiden's hold and forced Aiden's underwear off, too.

Aiden was a little surprised at Eric's boldness and at his urgency. Eric took Aiden's cock into his mouth, not wasting any time. He took Aiden's cock in one motion, sliding his hot wet mouth all the way down until his nose was tickled by Aiden's nest of hair. "Oh, my Eric," Aiden moaned.

Eric sat up and straddled his lover again. He forcefully pushed Aiden's cock inside him and then slowly lowered himself down. He looked at Aiden's eyes. "Oh, my Eric," he moaned again.

When Eric's body had completely devoured Aiden's cock, Eric ran his hands through the hair on Aiden's chest again. "Aiden, I love you," he said, not knowing what to expect in return.

Aiden opened his eyes and placed his hands over Eric's hands. "Eric, my love, I love you more than simple words could possibly say." Then he lifted Eric's hands, one by one, and kissed them gently.

Eric said, "Lie back, Aiden, and enjoy." Eric took full control of Aiden at that moment, and Aiden felt as if his body were floating away. He felt his body tense, and Eric felt it too. He squeezed Aiden's cock with his body. He wanted Aiden to remain inside him as long as possible. Aiden moaned and thrust hard into Eric. He filled Eric with his love. Eric placed his own cock inside Aiden's hands. He didn't want to move. He wanted to keep Aiden and his cock right where they were.

Aiden's hands were as good as the rest of him. Aiden's hands made love to Eric's cock, and Eric looked at Aiden and then at his cock as it unleashed its contents on Aiden's chest and stomach.

"Oh, Aiden," he moaned.

"Looks like we found something to do the first thing in the morning," Aiden said.

"Anytime, Aiden, anytime," Eric agreed.

They lay next to each other for a long while their first morning in the land of Aiden's home. "Well, Eric, my love, what do you think of my merry olde England?"

Eric turned to Aiden, wondering if he was serious. "I love it, Aiden, but, of course, I've seen the very best of it." He took Aiden's hand.

"Well, yes, the London Eye is quite spectacular," Aiden teased.

Eric rolled over and kissed Aiden's cheek. "Yes, it is," he teased back. "Do you miss London?"

Aiden looked up at the ceiling. "Perhaps I miss being younger, my love. You know, I haven't lived here since I was a boy."

After one more day of sightseeing and enjoying the very best of London, it was time for Eric and Aiden to become parents. "We've an early plane to catch tomorrow," Aiden commented, as they lay in bed together. "Eric, my love?"

Eric looked at Aiden. "Yes?"

"Are you sure this is what you want? You wouldn't do this just for me, would you?"

Eric snuggled next to his lover. "Yes, and yes," he said, looking into Aiden's eyes.

"I am afraid that I do not understand."

"Well, yes, this is what I want, and yes, I would do this for you. I would do anything for you, Aiden. We're not kids, Aiden. We've done the bar scenes, the single hooking up scenes, and now I would like to think that we have grown from our experiences. Those experiences made us who we are, and for some reason, who we are attracted us to each other." Eric laughed as he finished his thought.

"For some reason, huh?" Aiden said.

"For some odd, strange, weird reason, it's you and me," Eric teased.

Aiden pulled Eric over and onto him, and kissed the top of his head. He lifted Eric up so that Eric's head was pressed against his chest, and then separated Eric's legs to straddle his body. He pulled the covers over then both. "There, that's better," Aiden said, and was soon snoring that comforting snore that made Eric feel safe and loved.

The alarm sounded in what seemed like only a few seconds after they had said goodnight. Eric looked up at Aiden. "Oh, dear," Aiden said, as he reached over to stop the irritating sound.

"Well, it is early," Eric said, forcing his tired body to leave its safe haven. "I'll shower first, Aiden. You can rest for a few more minutes."

Eric leaned up and kissed the love of his life, and then forced his tired body to walk to the shower.

Aiden had the flight to Romania all taken care of. "Let's see now. We arrive in Bucharest where a member of the government will take us to the orphanage. The children are not yet a part of the orphanage, but I suppose the meeting was scheduled there in the event that we had changed our minds about the adoption. We don't have to stay long, and then we will be on our way back here."

Eric nodded, and rested his head against the seat of the plane. They made themselves comfortable in their plane seats, but both of them were more nervous than they wanted their partner to know.

Aiden placed his hand over Eric's. "Would you think less of me if you knew that I was scared to death?"

Eric turned his head toward Aiden. "I would probably wonder about you if you were not at least a little scared. The few first time parents that I have known have all voiced at least some fear as parenthood approached."

Aiden sighed. "I guess we are no different than they, my love."

"I know of two very lucky children though, Aiden."

Once in the air, Eric looked at Aiden. "Aiden, I have never asked you the names of these two precious babies."

"Well, I should have told you, Eric, my love. The little boy is Hayden and the little girl is Hannah."

"Those are beautiful names, Aiden, and the pictures of them are perfect."

Aiden looked at the pictures. "They are not all that clear, but I have worn them out looking at them so much."

Eric laughed.

"What is it?"

"You know, Aiden, we have no things for the children, at home."

Aiden thought about that. "Well, my love, we have the most important item ready for them."

"Room, we have room for them," Eric said.

"We have love for them, Eric, my love."

Eric folded his fingers with Aiden's for the remainder of the flight.

When the plane touched down in Romania's capital city, Aiden and Eric were two huge bundles of nerves. It was rainy and dreary, but Eric and Aiden didn't notice. They were met by a woman named Greta and taken directly to the orphanage. Eric hoped that they didn't see a lot of children who seemed sad. He knew that they couldn't take them all home, but wished that they could.

Eric said little on the drive to the orphanage, but offered moral support to Aiden. Aiden was the adoptive parent, and Eric didn't want to jeopardize the adoption in any way. He knew that some didn't consider gay men appropriate parents. Eric hoped that one day he would be a "true" parent to Aiden's children, but in his heart he already was a true parent to them. Being a parent on paper isn't nearly as important as being a parent in person, he told himself. Eric had known too many parents who spent little time with their biological children to think that biology was the basis of parenting.

Six

Two to Four

Greta said little to either of them when they arrived at the orphanage. Aiden signed and signed and signed. Then they waited in a small room for the children.

"Oh, Eric, my love, I'm afraid my fear is getting the better of me," Aiden admitted, when they were alone in the little room. "It all seems so clinical."

"It will be so much different when we are back home, Aiden. We will be a family."

Greta opened the door with a little boy holding her hand, and a baby in her arms. "Hayden, this is Mr…"

Aiden quickly interrupted the woman. "I'm Aiden, honey. Our names rhyme. Isn't that wonderful?"

Eric took the sleeping Hannah and held her in his arms. Greta left them alone for awhile. They had only thirty minutes to talk before heading back to London.

The little boy stood in the middle of the room and began to cry. Immediately, Aiden took control of the situation. He was on his knees instantly, and he pulled the little boy to him, holding him as tightly as he had held Eric. Eric knew exactly how loved Aiden's hugs had made him feel, and hoped that they did the same for the scared little Hayden. Aiden's big bear hug swallowed Hayden's little body completely, and Aiden talked to him nonstop.

"I love you, Hayden. I look at your picture every day. I have been waiting a very long time for you. I have a home, a big home, and you will have lots and lots of toys. We will make up games to play, and have a wonderful time. How does that sound?"

A very muffled, "okay", could be heard, and then Aiden picked the little boy up and sat beside Eric and Hannah, with Hayden on his lap.

Hayden mumbled something into Aiden's chest that Aiden couldn't quite hear. Not loosening his hold on the scared little boy, Aiden lowered his head. "Tell me in my ear, okay, Hayden?"

"Can we take Hannah? She's my sister."

Then Aiden held the little boy away from his body, and looked directly into his tear filled eyes. "Yes, Hayden. You and Hannah are both going home with me, and Eric, too. Honey, were you worried about your sister?"

Hayden looked down, and nodded.

"I am so sorry, honey. You needn't worry any longer. We are all going to live together."

The little boy scooted as close to Aiden as he could possibly get, and buried his face in Aiden's thick chest. Aiden looked at Eric, his eyes full. "Oh, sweetie. I love you, Hayden. I love you and I love Hannah. Eric loves you, too."

Hayden looked over at Eric, but kept himself safe within Hayden's loving hold. "You do?"

"I sure do," Eric whispered, so that he wouldn't wake the sleeping Hannah.

"Where do you live?" Hayden asked, keeping his face meshed with Aiden's chest.

Aiden held the little boy and rubbed his back. "We live in the United States, Hayden. Do you know where that is?"

"No. Is it close to America?"

Aiden's eyes were full as he continued to console the sweet child. "Yes, my love, they are the same place. We live in America."

"Oh," he said.

Hannah woke up and began to cry. Hayden quickly climbed down off of Aiden's lap and went to his little sister. "It's okay, Hannah."

Eric's heart melted at the sight of the little boy trying to console his baby sister. Eric helped Hannah to sit and lean against him. "Will you show me how to make your sister feel better?" he asked Hayden.

"She likes to hold your fingers."

Eric held his hands so that the little Hannah could hold a finger from each hand. "Oh, look, it worked. You helped me a lot, Hayden."

Hannah looked around at the strange surroundings. It wasn't long before she began to whimper again. Eric held her, and then he stood up and began to sway back and forth. "I've seen people at work do this when they spouses brought their babies to show us." Aiden smiled at Eric.

The door to the room opened, and Greta gave Aiden a bag for each of the children. Then she handed Aiden a carry-on bag with a few games and diapers and bottles. "Have a nice trip," she said, and quickly left the room.

Eric and Aiden felt kind of bad for the woman. "It must be rather difficult for her," Aiden said.

"Hannah usually has a binky," Hayden said.

Eric looked at Aiden. They had no idea what a binky was. "Honey, can you describe that to us?"

"What?"

"A binky," Aiden said.

"Oh, she sucks on it."

"Oh, a pacifier," Eric exclaimed, as if he had just solved a puzzle. "Sure, Hayden, we can get one of those."

Aiden picked up the bags. "I'm sure they will have a binky at the airport," he said.

"I can help," Hayden said.

"Thank you," Aiden said, very graciously to the sweet young boy. Aiden handed Hayden the lighter of the two bags, and the four of them left for the airport.

Hannah was very happy when she got her new binky. They waited for their flight to be called, and Hayden looked sad.

"What's wrong, sweetie?"

"Are we coming back?"

Aiden scooped the child up and onto his lap. "We sure will. I will not let you forget your home country, Hayden. My home country is England, and my parents did not want me to forget. I know a little bit about Romania, and the rest we can learn together, okay?"

"Okay," he said eagerly.

"I must say, Aiden, that I don't know much about history at all," Eric added.

"Well, Eric, my love, I had little interest in history myself until I left my homeland. It became much more important to me then." Aiden thought about Romania. He tried to think of just one thing, one very positive thing that he could tell this young yet precocious child about his homeland. "Do you know the name of the biggest city in your country?"

Hayden shook his head.

"It is Bucharest," Aiden announced, with great emphasis, making the name sound very big.

"Is it really big?"

"It is really, really big. That is why it has such a big name. Bucharest is the biggest and it is also the capital, and that makes it the most important," Aiden assured the young child.

"Wow," Hayden exclaimed, his eyes big.

Then Hayden looked at Eric and his sleeping sister. "Did you know that, Eric?"

"I can honestly say that I did not know that, Hayden."

Their flight was soon called, and the four of them were in the sky on their way back to England.

Heathrow Airport was very busy when the four of them arrived, and Hayden held tightly to Aiden's hand. When little Hayden saw the massive crowd, he stopped and placed both of his arms firmly around one of Aiden's legs. "Oh, honey, I'm so sorry. Here. Up you go." Aiden lifted the little boy and carried him on his hip. "How's that?"

Hayden held tightly to Aiden, and leaned against him. Eric smiled. He knew the comfort that could be found in Aiden's arms.

"You're a natural, Dad," Eric said, with a wink.

Aiden smiled. He felt as though he had been little Hayden's dad for the four years of the young boy's life instead of just a little over two hours. They tried to spend as little time as possible in the crowded airport, and went as quickly as they could to find a cab.

They walked into the hotel room and set their things down. "Is this America?" "No, my love, this is London. Eric and I stayed here when we first arrived from America."

Hayden looked down. "When will we be home?"

Eric looked at Aiden. They had planned to stay another week in London, but now realized that it was best to get Hayden settled. "We will leave tomorrow, and we will be home tomorrow," Aiden announced.

Eric took Hayden into the bedroom to help him change into his pajamas and also to help with Hannah, and Aiden quickly tried to change their flight plans. Eric closed the door partway. He didn't want Hayden to worry if Aiden wasn't able to change their flight.

"Good news," Aiden announced, in his comforting yet boisterous voice. "We leave at six in the morning. We will be up very early tomorrow."

Eric and Aiden knew that they wouldn't get much sleep that night, but the smile on little Hayden's face when he knew he would be home soon made it all worthwhile. "My pajamas are small," Hayden said, struggling to get into them.

"Well, Hayden, we will have to do some shopping as soon as we get home. How about we sleep in just our skivvies tonight?"

Hayden looked puzzled.

"We will sleep in our underwear," he added.

"You mean, like a tent sleep?"

Aiden agreed with the excited little boy, though he wasn't sure what a tent sleep was at all.

"Oh, Aiden, do you think I got this diaper on right?" Eric asked.

"Well, it looks okay to me," he said. "We will just have to learn as we go, like any parent, my love." Aiden didn't censor his words of love toward Eric for Hayden. Hiding one's true self rarely helped anyone, but it could certainly do harm. Aiden had seen this all around him. Eric tried to seem as comfortable as he could about him and Aiden, but was not nearly as sure of himself as Aiden seemed to be. Eric was sure of his love for Aiden, though, and loved him more each day.

Aiden put Hayden to bed in the room next to the one he shared with Eric, and they had a crib brought up for Hannah. It was quiet in the room, and Aiden took Eric's hand. "You are doing a wonderful job with little Hannah. Are you feeling overwhelmed, my love?"

Eric looked at him and smiled. "A little."

Aiden pulled him over and held him. "Well, I guess that makes us true parents."

Eric moved up and kissed Aiden tenderly, yet passionately. "I love you, Aiden."

"Eric, my love, you are my world, you and our children."

"That sounds nice, Aiden, our children."

Aiden squeezed Eric tightly, and they fell asleep quickly together.

Eric had moved to the far side of the bed sometime during the night, and didn't hear the sound from the next room at first, over Aiden's low snores. He lifted his head to listen, and then jumped out of bed and ran into the room where Hayden was sleeping. "Hayden, it's Eric. Honey, are you okay?"

"No. I'm scared."

"Do you want me to sleep in here with you?"

Hayden continued to whimper and sniffle. "Can I sleep with you?" he asked, between sobs.

"Of course you can. Come on."

Hayden held Eric's hand tightly and walked into the room where Aiden and Hannah were sound asleep. Hayden climbed up onto the bed and scooted over to Aiden's big warm body.

"What, what's going on?" Aiden asked.

"Eric said I can sleep with you," Hayden said, looking up into this big man's face.

Aiden turned onto his side and pulled the little body to him, wrapping his big loving arms around the boy. "Well, of course you can," he said. Aiden winked at Eric, who smiled back at him. Hayden, feeling loved and secure snuggled next to Aiden, fell asleep instantly.

The alarm sounded, and Hannah began to wail. "Oh, Aiden, I didn't think about the alarm. She must be scared to death." Eric picked Hannah up and out of her crib, got her a bottle, and then held her in bed as he fed her.

"Looks like I've got myself a little buddy," Aiden commented, looking at the sleeping child snuggled against his body.

"You have a way of making people feel secure and loved, Aiden."

Aiden laughed his big deep laugh, and Hayden began to wake up. "How's my little buddy?"

Hayden looked up at the big man who was holding his little body in just one arm. "Is it time to go home now?"

Aiden pulled the little guy up onto his stomach and chest. He hugged Hayden and kissed the top of his head. "You bet it is, and I cannot wait. Let's dress your sister."

Eric took a quick shower while Aiden changed Hannah's diaper and changed her clothes, with Hayden's good instruction of course.

"Well, I think she looks good," Aiden proclaimed.

Hayden giggled as he watched the big Aiden make funny faces at his baby sister, making her laugh and drool. Eric and Aiden were both surprised at how few clothes the children had with them, and wished now that they had brought some with them.

"Well, young Hayden, how about a shower?" Hayden looked at Eric, and then back at Aiden. Eric could see the little boy's face begin to change. He looks like he is going to cry, Eric thought.

Aiden picked him up and squeezed him again. "What is it, buddy?"

Hayden buried his head in Aiden's chest.

"How about this, Hayden. If I promise to tell you when I am afraid of something or do not understand something, will you promise to tell me when you get afraid or do not understand?"

Aiden could feel the child's head move up and down against his chest, in agreement.

Aiden rubbed the little boy's back. "Tell me, Hayden," he urged.

"I can't do it myself," the young boy admitted.

"Oh, sweetie, I did not mean by yourself. We will help you. That is my fault, Hayden. I should have told you that. I will try to be much clearer with my words from now on. How about that?"

Aiden felt the little boy's head move up and down against his chest again. Eric smiled at Aiden's worried expression. They knew that they both had a lot to learn about being parents. "Let's go," Aiden said, carrying the child to the shower.

Aiden didn't really feel comfortable being completely naked in front of the child, so he got into the shower with his boxers on. He and Hayden had fun splashing the water as it came down.

Aiden soaped the little boy, and Hayden splashed water on Aiden until he was completely soaked. "Your shorts are all wet now," he said, laughing.

"They sure are. Let me wrap this towel around you, and then go ask Eric to help you get dressed. I will be out in a few minutes."

"Okay," Hayden said, still giggling and still splashing Aiden.

Aiden showered and dressed, and soon the four of them were ready to leave London.

"We're going home," Hayden announced proudly to the lady in the hotel lobby. She smiled, and after a short taxicab ride, they once again found themselves at Heathrow. "I'm not scared today," Hayden announced proudly.

"That's great, Hayden, but let's hold hands anyway," Aiden suggested.

"Why does Hannah sleep so much?" he asked. Eric held the sleeping baby, whose eyes were open now. "She's awake, but she's quiet. I think that's good, don't you?" Hayden agreed that it was good.

The four of them settled in for a very long flight, but Aiden had been able to get them bumped to first class with his last minute change and Hayden was thrilled. "This seat swallows me up," he said.

"Yes it does, Hayden, and it reclines, too."

Aiden showed Hayden the magic of his first class seat, and then he took Hannah and set her onto his lap. "You need a break, Eric, my love."

"I think holding that sweet little girl is a break, Aiden, and just the break I needed."

Aiden knew that little Hayden was tired, and hoped that he would be able to sleep on the plane. When he began to whine and fidget, Aiden tried to console him but what the little boy really needed was sleep. "Here, buddy, let's do this." He picked Hayden up and held him against his chest. Aiden reclined the seat so that Hayden was on his chest and stomach. "No, let me up," he squealed. Aiden held him and began to hum quietly in his ear. "You're a bad singer," he said. Aiden continued with his bad singing, and after approximately fifteen minutes, Hayden was silent.

Eric sat beside Aiden so that Hayden could see his little sister. Aiden rocked Hayden the little bit that he could in the seat of the airplane, and waited for Hayden to close his eyes. "Little sister is watching us, Hayden," he said.

Eric soon signaled that Hayden's eyes had closed. "He gave it a good fight, but sleep won out," Eric whispered. "How's mine doing here?"

"She looks like she's in a trance, watching her big brother sleep," Aiden told Eric. Aiden closed his eyes, too.

Eric waited for Hannah to drift off and go limp in his arms. Then he slowly reclined his seat, and the four of them slept together as a family.

Seven
Home in Portland

When the plane landed in Portland, Hayden awoke immediately and pushed up against Aiden's chest. He looked around and not seeing anyone or anything familiar, he started to cry.

"Hayden, look at me. Hayden."

Hayden turned his head and looked at Aiden.

"We are home now, buddy. The four of us are home now."

Hayden calmed down and rested his tired body on Aiden's chest again.

Once inside Eric's and Aiden's house, Hayden seemed to be doing much better. "We'll stay here now?"

"We will stay here forever, Hayden. The four of us live here now."

Aiden was puzzled by Hayden's tears now. He picked the little guy up and carried him to his room. "This is your room, Hayden. We will fix it up any way you like. We can paint it, and get some toys, and whatever you like."

Hayden wiped his eyes. "When can I come back out?"

"Oh, sweetie, this is not your only room. The entire house is yours, it is all of ours, but this is your very special place." Aiden's stomach was in knots as he thought about all that this sweet child had probably experienced in his four years, although he did not know the details. "Let's go see Hannah," Aiden said, and lifted Hayden up again. What he needs most is someone who cares. The little guy just wants to be loved. Aiden was the one who felt like crying now.

When the doorbell sounded, Aiden explained to Hayden what it was, and the little boy couldn't wait to go see who was waiting on the other side of the door. Aiden took him down the stairs and opened the door to a delivery of toys, and clothes from Aiden's store.

"Well, honey, you didn't need to do this," he exclaimed to the woman who had worked for him for years.

"Aiden, we made most of the clothes while you were gone. We had it all planned. You taught us how to sew very well. We all went together and bought a few toys, too."

Aiden led the woman up the stairs, and Hayden couldn't wait to see what she had brought. "Oh, give me that baby," she said.

"Eric, just make me a list and I will go shopping for baby supplies."

"I'm afraid that's where my problem lies. I have no idea what to put on the list," he admitted.

"Well, then, I will make your list for you. Be back in a jiffy."

Aiden gave the woman more than enough money to cover baby supplies, and then sat on the floor with Hayden and his new toys.

"You have a store?" Hayden asked.

"I sure do, a store of clothes. I will take you there tomorrow."

Aiden was happy now that Eric had insisted that he redo one of the bedrooms into a designing and sewing room. He could work from home now and not miss one minute of his time with his son and daughter.

Within the hour, the woman was back with more than enough baby supplies for one little girl, and a few more things for Hayden. "What are these?" Hayden asked, when he noticed Eric's paintings.

"They are good, don't you think?" Aiden boasted of his lover's passion.

"Uh, huh," Hayden agreed.

"Eric is an artist, Hayden. He paints pictures and sells them in fancy galleries."

Eric laughed at the word fancy. "You can help me if you like," Eric suggested. Eric set up an easel just for Hayden and let him explore his talents as much as he liked.

That night, their very first night at home as a family, Hayden was excited about his new home and wanted to sleep in his new room by himself. "Okay, buddy, but if you get scared, come on down the hall, okay?"

"I won't get scared," he said, proudly.

Hannah was comfortable in the little crib that was set up in the hallway just outside of Eric's and Aiden's bedroom. Hayden and Eric were exhausted. They lay together in bed, alone for the first time in what seemed like weeks. Hayden took Eric's hand in his. "We did it, my love. We made a family."

Eric turned toward him. "Yes, we did." Eric continued to look into Aiden's eyes, and Aiden looked into Eric's eyes. Eric wanted Aiden just as much as Aiden wanted Eric.

"We make a good team, Eric, my love."

"Yes, we do, Aiden." Eric moved closer to Aiden, and Aiden turned onto his side and pulled Eric into his arms. Eric had missed the comfort and warmth of Aiden's embrace, and the low steady snoring lulled Eric to sleep.

Aiden and Eric slept so well that first night back in their own bed and back in each other's arms that they hadn't realized that Hayden had joined them until the next morning. Eric was awake at the first light streaming through the window, and he rolled over to kiss Aiden good morning.

"Oh, how sweet," he said aloud, and Aiden opened his eyes.

"When did this happen?" he asked Eric, when he turned to see Hayden sprawled out between them.

"I have no idea, but I love it." Eric kissed the sleeping child, and he rolled over in his sleep. "I think we're doing great, Aiden. He knew he could join us when and if he wanted, and he did. You made him feel secure, Aiden." Aiden held Eric's hand across their sleeping son.

"I'd better check on Hannah," Eric said, and hurried to the baby's side. She woke up as Eric approached the crib and held out her little arms. "Oh, how's my sweetheart this morning?" He picked her up and changed her diaper. "I'll bet you're hungry, aren't you?" Eric brought Hannah and her bottle back to bed with him. "I love it when we're all together like this, Aiden."

"I do, too, Eric, my love," Aiden whispered.

Hayden woke up and looked around. He looked at Aiden, but this time there were no screams or tears.

"How was your first night, little buddy?"

He turned onto his back. Then he looked at Eric and his baby sister sucking happily on her bottle. "It was good, but I didn't stay in my bed. I wasn't scared, though. I just thought you and Eric might be lonely."

Eric smiled at Aiden. "And you were right, Hayden. We were very happy that you joined us."

Aiden turned onto his side and pulled the warm little body of his son to his chest. He squeezed Hayden tightly, and the little boy laughed. Aiden rubbed his back.

Hayden sat up between Eric and Hayden, and began talking about his future plans. "I'm going to paint with Eric, and I'm going to go to your store, Aiden." He looked at Aiden. "Tell me more things about my homeland," Hayden demanded. Eric looked at Aiden, hoping that he could answer the little boy's demands.

"Well, let me think. There was once a king named King Michael." Eric watched as little Hayden became completely entranced as Aiden talked about Romania. Aiden told a story as he talked, instead of merely stating facts to such a young child.

"Did everybody like him?"

"I think most people liked him, but you know, not everyone likes everyone."

Aiden did not want to sugarcoat his words, but he did want to paint a positive picture for this child. Little Hayden would have years to learn that no one and no country is all good or all bad.

"What did the king do?"

"Well, a long time ago there was a very big war that involved the whole world," Aiden said, spreading his arms to emphasize the bigness of the war.

Hayden's eyes were wide. "Really?"

"Really, and they called it World War II."

"Wow," Hayden exclaimed.

"King Michael was given a medal, like a trophy, by one of the presidents from right here in the United States," Aiden continued.

"Which president?" Eric asked.

Hayden then looked at Eric, having forgotten that he and Hannah were still in the room. His attention had been completely focused on Aiden and his story. "It was President Harry S. Truman," Aiden pronounced proudly. "He was from Missouri. Let me show you where Missouri is." Aiden popped open his notebook computer and pulled up a map of the United States. "This is Missouri, in the middle here, and we live all the way over here, in Oregon." Hayden squealed with delight when he saw what he thought was the word Portland. "That's right, Hayden. We live here." Aiden put his arm around his son. "You are very smart," Aiden added. Aiden looked at Eric, and Eric smiled. They wanted these two young children to be curious about their world, and Aiden and Eric wanted to be the ones to share the world with them.

The rest of their first week home as a family went by in a flash. Hayden loved seeing all the people at Aiden's store, and the employees treated the little guy like royalty.

"You can work at home and you can work here," he said to Aiden one day.

"That's right. I can work at home when you are at home, and I can work at the store when you go to preschool.

Hayden looked worried. "What's that?"

"That is where boys and girls go to learn and play. It is three days a week in the mornings." Aiden wanted to sound as upbeat as he possibly could. He knew that Hayden had not known a lot of stability in his young life, but he also knew that curiosity like his deserved to be nourished.

Eight
Storm Clouds

When Eric returned to his full-time job, it was hard on all of them. Eric was exhausted, and Aiden was working a double shift as he juggled his designing business and store with caring for Hannah and Hayden. They had many offers to baby-sit from Eric's coworkers and Aiden's employees, but it didn't make them any less tired. Aiden was worried about Eric. He seemed distant more and more every day, and Aiden was beginning to worry that Eric was going to leave him.

One Wednesday, Eric called to say that he would be working late but didn't give a reason. Aiden's insecurity was growing as he put the children to bed and still Eric had not come home. Aiden poured himself a glass of wine and drank it in the dark, alone.

It was after ten when Aiden heard Eric's key in the lock. He was surprised at the darkness in the room. Eric put his things down and walked toward the kitchen. He hadn't seen Aiden sitting alone in the dark.

Aiden followed Eric into the kitchen. He flipped the light on, and Eric froze in his tracks. "It is late, Eric."

Eric turned and looked at Aiden. Aiden hadn't realized just how much Eric had changed. He had always been a slender man, but he now looked too thin, and he looked old to Aiden. Have I done this? he wondered.

"I know it's late, Aiden. We've been working on a big project, and two men quit a week ago. I'm the only one they've got who can do what needs to be done now."

Aiden moved closer to Eric, and Eric steadied himself by leaning against the counter. "You are tired," Aiden said.

"Yes," Eric agreed.

Eric didn't have the energy to argue, if that was what Aiden was planning.

"Come here, Eric."

Eric followed Aiden into the dining room, wondering what he was so upset about. "Remember these?"

Eric looked at the paintings that were gathering dust. "Yeah, I'll put them away this weekend. We need to get a nice table in here, anyway."

Aiden stood directly in front of Eric and put his big hands around Eric's slender upper arms, and to Eric, Aiden's huge body was rather intimidating after such an exhausting day. "No, Eric, you will not put them away. What you will do, however, is paint. What happened to that passionate artist I met in the park and fell in love with?"

"I have a job, Aiden."

Aiden still needed to know how Eric felt about him and how he now felt about having a family. Had it all changed?

"Aiden, I'm tired. I have to be back at work at five."

"No, Eric, not tomorrow," Aiden stated.

Eric wanted badly to sit down, but Aiden was holding him up. "Aiden, I have to work."

"Eric, I love you. You do know that, don't you?"

Aiden's tone softened as he spoke, and Eric leaned his head against Aiden's chest. Aiden grabbed him and held him. "Yes, I know that. I love you, too, Aiden."

Aiden pulled him close and rubbed his back. "I have missed you, Eric. I have missed your beautiful body next to mine. I need to make love to you."

Eric was almost too tired to make love tonight, but knew that he had been neglecting Aiden. "Oh, Aiden, I'm so tired." Eric began to slide down Aiden's body, and Aiden picked him up and carried him into the living room.

"Tonight we will sleep, Eric, my love. Tomorrow you will quit your job and paint here at home or in the park or on the street, but paint you will."

"Aiden, those paintings didn't bring in that much money," Eric weakly protested.

"Eric, my love, we have plenty of money. What we do not have is a lot of time. I have waited a lifetime for you, and I am not willing to live what remains of my lifetime without you."

Eric was so tired that Aiden's words were not making much sense to him. "I'm not going anywhere, Aiden."

"Eric, you have been leaving me for quite some time now, and you are working yourself too hard. I have seen a lot in my almost half century of life, Eric, and you are not living. What you are doing is existing." Eric looked at Aiden. "Our children miss you, Eric. Please tell me this is what you still want, that you still want the children, and that you still want me."

Eric looked into Aiden's pleading eyes. "Aiden, I've never stopped wanting you, and the kids are great."

"Then, Eric, my love, do not miss it. Do not miss these young years. Think of how our lives could be if you were painting right here at home. When Hayden begins preschool and Hannah takes her morning nap, I will make love to you all morning. Your body will be satiated with my love."

Eric's cock gave a little twitch at Aiden's erotic words, its signal that it was in complete agreement with Aiden's plan. "I do miss us, Aiden, and I miss painting. I have saved quite a bit of money over the years."

"As have I, Eric, my love." Aiden kissed Eric gently on the lips. "Come to bed, Eric. No alarm will wake you tomorrow."

Eric took Aiden's hand and followed him down the hallway to their bedroom where he fell into the bed that the two of them shared.

Nine

Clear Skies

After Eric had quit his job and began painting again, he wondered how he had lost sight of life so easily. He stared out of the window and watched the passersby. Hayden had begun his preschool and wished it was every day instead of every other day. Hannah was beginning to crawl, and Eric loved having her with him while he painted. Hannah would sit and play with her toys until she wore herself out and went down for her morning nap.

This was the morning that Eric had been waiting for. Hannah was sleeping soundly when Aiden returned from taking Hayden to preschool. Eric looked up from his painting to see Aiden watching him from the doorway. Eric wasn't certain if he saw love or lust in Aiden's eyes, and he didn't care. Either would do today. He abandoned his art and went to his lover. He reached up and put his arms around Aiden. The lips that he had missed met his, and Eric moaned. He pressed his body against Aiden's. "Make love to me," he whispered.

Aiden lifted Eric into his arms and carried him to the bed. He forced Eric's pants down and off, revealing his cock that had been hard and throbbing since much earlier that morning. "I have missed you, Eric."

Eric closed his eyes. His body quivered with every touch from Aiden. Eric stripped off his shirt, and reached out for his lover. "Aiden," he said.

Aiden stood by the side of the bed and unburdened his aching body of its confining clothing. Eric looked at Aiden's cock that was as hard as his own. He sat up and placed his hands firmly on Aiden's butt. Once Aiden's shirt was off, he gave himself freely to Eric. His hands were in Eric's hair, his body being pulled to its lover. Eric circled

Aiden's cock with his tongue. He sucked on the swollen head. "Oh, my Eric," he moaned.

Eric pulled Aiden's body forcefully down onto his own. Aiden's lips met Eric's, and they kissed like they had kissed the very first time that they made love. Aiden's tongue leisurely enjoyed Eric's lips, and Eric's body begged for Aiden's every touch. "Touch me, Aiden," he begged.

Aiden's hands on Eric's chest were erotic to both of them. "Aiden, my nipples are on fire," Eric said. Aiden's tongue lapped at each of Eric's hard nipples, and Eric thrust his chest upward and into Aiden's mouth. "Mmm," Aiden moaned, turned on even more by Eric's aggressiveness. Eric pulled away from Aiden and scooted onto the bed even more. He held the base of his cock for Aiden to take. "It's been too long, Aiden." Aiden devoured Eric's cock, kneeling between his parted legs. Eric reached for Aiden's butt. "Aiden," he said, pulling at one side of his lover's butt.

Aiden opened himself to Eric, straddling him, and watching as drops of pre-cum slowly dripped out and off of his cock head and into Eric's awaiting mouth. Aiden watched with envy as Eric waited for gravity to bring each new drop to his open mouth. Watching this made Aiden even hungrier for Eric's swollen hot cock that was begging for its lover. Aiden pulled Eric's legs apart and kneaded his inner thighs. He slid his tongue along Eric's cock and then slowly let it slide into his mouth. Eric tried to force his cock into Aiden's mouth, but couldn't move against Aiden's tight hold. "Oh, Aiden, that's it," he moaned.

Eric grabbed firmly to Aiden's supple butt, the butt that he loved, and pulled it down. When his lips met the head of Aiden's cock, both men gasped. Aiden fed Eric all of his swollen cock and Eric pulled on Aiden's balls. He rolled them in his hands, milking them of their juices. Aiden forced Eric's butt upward and stroked between the two half moons. He entered Eric, stroking him deep, and Eric rolled his butt forward for his lover to please him. Eric couldn't resist the temptation of Aiden's supple butt that was teasing him with its manliness.

With one hand firmly on Aiden's balls, Eric entered Aiden and stroked him hard and deep. Aiden rocked his body back and forth as Eric brought him closer and closer to the edge. His moans were loud, yet muffled by Eric's cock which he held in his mouth. Aiden moved faster and pulled harder on Eric's cock while feeding his own cock to Eric. An urgency filled them both, and their breaths came in short quick breaths.

There was no turning back now, and their climaxes were full and forceful after weeks of unintentional abstinence. "Mmm," Eric moaned, as he pulled Aiden's cock hard with his lips. "Oh, damn, Eric," Aiden moaned. "Oh, my love," Aiden moaned again.

Eric and Aiden were then silent. Aiden pulled Eric's body out from underneath him and lifted him up and onto him. Eric straddled his lover and laid his head on Aiden's chest. Aiden rubbed Eric's back. "Oh, Aiden," he said. "Yes, my love, yes," was Aiden's response.

Aiden knew that Eric would never deny him anything, and Aiden would never deny the love of his life, the love that he had waited almost half a century to find, anything.

BunBun

As the only child of two very industrious entrepreneurs who started businesses during the early dot-com years, Trent Johnson is a lucky man. He owns his own apartment, his own business, and is surrounded by very loyal and trustworthy employees. When his parents move to Mumbai, India, to expand their businesses, Trent feels more alone than he ever has. Dating is fun, but Trent is no longer a man in his twenties. He wouldn't mind settling down with that special someone. Where he will find that special someone remains a mystery to Trent, until one very special and unexpected night.

One

A Single Man

The sun streaming in through his bedroom window woke Trent from a sound sleep. He thought he was dreaming. Sun was a rare sight this time of day in this beautiful city that Trent called home. He forced himself to get out of bed. He walked to the window and looked out. The view was magnificent from his vantage point in a luxury apartment twenty floors up. He was already close to the top of the section of San Francisco called Nob Hill, and today he could see the Pacific Ocean. The fog was usually too thick to see very far, which made clear days like today all the more special.

"Come on, guys. Let's go make coffee," Trent said to his two white Persian cats. He had named them Marshmallow and Tootle, and they were his babies. Trent had inherited the two cats when his parents had moved to India last year, and now he didn't know what he would do without the two furry little creatures. They were two years old now, and had slowly but surely taken over Trent's apartment and Trent's heart. "Well, guys, it's Saturday, so you've got me all day, and all weekend, for that matter."

Trent poured a cup of coffee for himself and sat down in the living room. Trent was in no way a snob, even though his apartment was paid for and he owned his own business. He was simply the only offspring of two parents who had made it big in the early dot-com years and had managed to invest their money wisely. Now they owned companies all over the world, and had recently moved to India to open one in Mumbai.

Trent was only in his early thirties, and was living a pretty sweet life for a man of his years, in a very nice, very expensive, very spacious apartment in this affluent section of San Francisco. He couldn't fault his parents any for all they had given him. They had been very good to him.

It was their entrepreneurial spirit and hard work that had allowed him to attend Stanford University, and because of their never ending belief in what others considered the impossible, Trent's parents had made the American dream a reality for more people than Trent could remember.

Trent's father had loved games and had taken that love into the evolving computer age when Trent was a young boy, and now Trent's father was owner of the San Francisco based TJ Enterprises, with companies worldwide. Trent stared out the window as he thought of his parents. TJ stood for Thomas Johnson, which was his father's name, but his dad had thought TJ sounded younger and would attract younger talent to his businesses. "TJ sounds much more marketable, don't you think, son?" he had asked Trent. Thomas Johnson was always thinking ahead. That was for sure. Trent's mother, Jane, was a fashion designer, who had the curiosity and ingenuity that equaled her husband's, and together the two of them had created an interactive way to design that was slowly revolutionizing the entire fashion industry.

Trent had both Marshmallow and Tootle on his lap now and was petting them. "Wasn't Dad silly, guys?" Trent's father had told his mother that TJ was short for Thomas Johnson, but Trent knew that it was really short for Thomas and Jane to include her. The two sleepy cats looked up at Trent for a second, and then laid their heads back down in his lap.

Trent had carved out his own little niche in the high tech world, although the world his parents had built was a big part of that niche. Trent owned a small software development company that specialized in interactive medicine. San Francisco was a leader in the field of healthcare, having the first universal healthcare system in the country, and Trent never lacked for something to do.

Trent walked over to the window again. "I love this city," he said to no one. "It has so much energy, so much drive."

Two
Blind Date

Trent jumped when the phone rang. "Hello," he said, not expecting a call today. "Oh, dear. Okay, I'm on my way."

He turned to his two cats. "Well, guys, there's a problem with one of the software programs, so Daddy has to go to work for awhile."

Marshmallow and Tootle barely opened their eyes. They were already settled in for their morning naps. Trent locked the door behind him, and headed for the office. He loved not having to get into his car to go to work. San Francisco was considered the most walkable city in America. Between the walking and the cable cars, Trent could go an entire week without using his car. And, the exercise was good for him, he had to admit.

Trent opened the door to the office and found Troy sitting there, looking frantic. "Hey, there's my good friend. What's the problem?"

"Trent, this is awful. There is some kind of glitch in this one program and I cannot figure out what the problem is."

"Well, let's take it from the start, Troy. We'll figure it out."

"I've got to get out for awhile, Trent."

"Okay, no problem. Go get yourself some lunch. How long you been here, anyway?"

"Since very early," he said.

Trent knew he couldn't change Troy. He was a workaholic and a worrier, but the two of them worked well together. They had just seemed to mesh well from the first day they had started working together. Troy had helped him get the business off to a good start, and Troy now had partial ownership in the business. Trent didn't know what he would do without him. Trent did wish that Troy would slow down just a little, or let Trent hire some help for him, but Troy insisted on doing it all himself. Trent had just recently gotten Troy to take a day off.

Trent sat down and looked over the program. "Oh, here it is," he said. Trent was good at solving computer glitches, but Troy was just as good. "Poor guy just overlooked it. It's no wonder, with the number of hours he has been working." Trent left his friend and business partner a note about what he had discovered with the program, and then walked back home.

When he walked into his apartment, Marshmallow and Tootle were still sleeping soundly. He plopped his keys down and noticed that there was a message waiting for him. "Hmm," he said.

"Wonder who that could be?"

Trent pressed the button on the machine and waited for the message. "Uh, Trent, I, uh, something's come up. I'm afraid I can't get back to the office this weekend. Call me when you get this."

That doesn't seem like Troy, he thought. Troy was usually pretty calm and sure of himself. "Well, let's call him," he said to Marshmallow and Tootle.

Trent dialed Troy's number. It rang for quite a few times before he heard Troy's voice. "Hello," he said, in an out of breath voice.

"Troy, it's Trent. What's up?"

"Oh, I think I may need a few days off, but I can make it up at night," he said, with a worried tone in his voice.

"Don't worry about making it up, Troy. You put in too much time as it is. Take as many days as you need."

"Thanks, Trent," he said, and hung up the phone. That was odd. Trent was curious now. Troy sounded upset, or something was different. "Oh, well, Trent couldn't think about that right now. Trent had a date tonight.

Trent had met Charlie through his parents, of all people. They had met for dinner a week ago, but tonight was their first real date. Charlie was a medical technologist and analyzed blood specimens for a local physicians group. Trent and his partner, Troy, had developed a software program for the clinic where Charlie worked, and Trent's parents had set up the dinner as a way to get the two of them together. "We'll just have to see how things go, won't we, guys?"

The two cats barely lifted their heads as Trent spoke to them. Trent took a shower and got ready to meet Charlie at the same restaurant where they had met last week. "Well, see you later, guys," Trent said, as he kissed the top of Marshmallow's and Tootle's heads. "Wish me luck."

Tonight was one of the few times that Trent drove in San Francisco. He had it made, with everything he needed well within walking distance of his apartment. Trent pulled into the parking lot of the restaurant. He didn't know what kind of vehicle Charlie drove or he would have tried to find it and park beside it.

Trent walked into the restaurant, and Charlie was waiting for him. "Have you been here long? I hope I haven't kept you waiting."

"Oh, no, I haven't been here long, Trent. Got us a table in the back."

Trent followed Charlie to an intimate corner of the restaurant. He knew that he was on a date now, if he hadn't known it before.

"How was your week, Trent? Any major catastrophes?"

"Just a small one this morning, but nothing that couldn't be fixed."

"And how is the 'blood' business?" Trent asked, with a grin.

"It's bloody," Charlie answered. "But it's a living."

The two of them made easy conversation over dinner and drinks, and Trent had expected Charlie to ask him back to his place afterward. "Well, guess it's time we should be going," Charlie said, picking up the check.

Trent left the tip, and the two of them left the restaurant.

"Where did you park, Trent?"

"Over there," he said, and discovered that Charlie was parked beside him.

Trent was uncomfortably confused now. Charlie had asked him to go out, and yet Trent felt as if he were somehow in charge of the situation. Trent stopped for a moment at Charlie's car since it was the nearer of the two vehicles. Charlie stood next to Trent, not knowing what to do or say really, which further confused Trent.

"Well, thanks for coming tonight, Trent. I had a good time," Charlie said, nervously.

Trent could see Charlie's nervousness now, which made him feel a little better about the situation. He couldn't fault a guy for being nervous. "I did too, Charlie," he returned, and put his arm lightly around Charlie, just for a second, and then withdrew it.

"Um, would you like to do it again?"

Trent nodded as he walked to his car. "Sure, Charlie. Call me anytime."

Charlie smiled as he got into his car. Trent sat in his car and waited to leave until Charlie had driven away. That must have been the oddest date I've ever had, Trent thought. Oh, well, time to go home. At least I still have my cats, he thought.

Three
Surprises

Trent walked into his apartment to the sound of the telephone ringing. He hurried to answer it, thinking that everyone he knew would call him on his cell phone. "Hello," he said, in a hurried tone.

"Is this Mr. Johnson?" a very young girl's voice asked.

"Yes, this is Trent Johnson," he said slowly.

"Um, my daddy is sick, and he said to call you," the sweet voice said.

Trent thought that the girl must have dialed his number by mistake. "Are you sure you have the right Mr. Johnson?"

"Um, I think so. Can you help my daddy?"

Wanting to do whatever he could for such a sweet sounding girl, Trent replied, "I will certainly try. What is your daddy's name?"

"Troy Landis," she said.

Trent almost dropped the phone. He had known Troy for awhile now and he had never mentioned a daughter. Trent knew he had to say something, anything. He could hear the little girl breathing on the other end. "Yes, honey, I can help your daddy. Is he there with you, at home?"

"Uh, huh," she said.

"What is your name, sweetheart?"

"Victoria," she said, with all the sweetness of a young girl.

"I'll be right there. Tell your daddy I'm on my way."

"Okay," she said, and hung up the phone.

Trent rushed to get himself ready. He quickly fed Marshmallow and Tootle, and then hurried out the door. Troy lived well within walking distance, and Trent jogged most of the way.

He knocked on the door of Troy's house. "Victoria, it's Trent Johnson," he said.

The door opened, and Trent saw a little girl with the face of an angel. Victoria's eyes were almost as big as the rest of her. "Hi, Victoria," Trent said, squatting down so that he was at eye level with the young girl. He held out his hand. "Can you take me to your daddy?"

She said nothing, but took Trent's hand in hers. Trent closed and locked the door behind him.

Victoria silently led Trent into Troy's bedroom. "Daddy?" she said, as she walked up to Troy. She climbed onto the bed and sat next to Troy. Troy was shivering.

"Troy, it's Trent. You don't look so good, buddy."

"Trent?"

Trent pulled the covers up and formed them to Troy's body. "It's me, buddy. We need to get you some help."

"I'm so cold. Where's Victoria?"

"I'm right here, Daddy."

Troy's teeth were chattering.

"Troy, how long have you been like this?"

"T..t..today," he said.

"You're burning up. I'm taking you to the hospital."

"I c..c…can't. Victoria."

"She can stay with me, Troy. She will love my cats. Don't worry about anything, Troy. I will take care of everything." Then he turned to Victoria. "Let's get your daddy some help, honey."

"Okay. But, when will we be back?"

"Honey, you will stay with me, okay?"

Trent looked into Victoria's sweet frightened eyes.

"Okay," she whispered, fighting back tears.

"You can help me get your daddy some help, how 'bout that?"

The little girl nodded.

"Troy, let's sit up, buddy."

Trent stood up and then lifted Troy to him. He was so weak that his head fell against Trent. Trent kept the blankets wrapped around him and held him, Troy's face pressing against his jeans. "Buddy, do you think you can walk to the car? Let's try it, okay? I'll hold you up the entire way, and if you need to stop, we will."

Troy weakly lifted his arms to put them around Trent.

"That's it, buddy. I've got you." Trent held Troy's arms around his waist and tried to lift him up. The two men were about the same size, and Trent knew it would be difficult to help Troy to the car.

"Will Daddy be okay?" Victoria asked, and one lone tear fell onto her cheek.

"We're going to get him the help he needs, aren't we, sweetie?"

She nodded.

"Okay, Troy, up we go." Trent lifted Troy to his feet, and his entire body began to shake. "Okay, buddy. Let's lie back down." Trent eased him back down onto the bed where he continued to shiver. "Let's get everything ready, Victoria. I'm going to carry your daddy to the car, and then you can lock the door behind us."

The little girl nodded.

Trent left Troy just long enough to make sure the front door was locked, so that all Victoria had to do was shut it. He had seen Troy's car outside, found his keys, and now wished he had driven over here instead of walked.

"We'll take your daddy's car, sweetie. Can you be brave for me?"

Victoria nodded, and then wiped a few more tears from her face.

"Okay, sweetie, you go ahead of me and open the door."

Victoria ran to the front door and opened it for Trent.

"Okay, buddy, here we go," Trent said, and painstakingly lifted Troy.

Somehow he made it to the car. Victoria surprised Trent when she was able to open the back door of the car all by herself.

"We did it, sweetie," Trent said, as he laid Troy down in the back seat.

She looked at her shivering father, and then looked at Trent. "I'll go close the door. Can I bring BunBun?"

Trent said yes to little Victoria's request, not knowing who or what BunBun was. He tucked the blankets around Troy and talked to him. "We're on our way, buddy. You still with me?"

Troy half opened his eyes.

Trent touched his warm cheek. "It's okay, Troy. We're almost there."

Trent watched as Victoria closed the door to the house and then ran to the car. "Ready," she said, holding a stuffed bunny.

Trent smiled at Victoria as she clutched the stuffed bunny tightly to her little body. Then he buckled her in the seat, closed the car door, and hurried around to the driver's side. He started the car and then looked at Victoria. "This must be BunBun," he said, with a smile and a pat to the top of the stuffed bunny's head. Victoria nodded, holding her little friend as tightly as she could.

It didn't take long to get to the hospital. Trent pulled into the Emergency Entrance. He shut the car off, and he and Victoria hurried inside, with Trent calling, "I need help out here," in a firm and demanding voice. He led a couple of young men to the car where they retrieved a very ill appearing Troy. Trent parked the car, and then he and Victoria went inside to be with Troy.

Trent had no idea how to answer the many questions that were asked, though he tried as best he could. Victoria confirmed that they had not been out of the country or around sick people as far as she knew. Troy was being given intravenous fluids and an antibiotic which they hoped would help, at least until they were able to get more information.

"We'll need to draw some blood," a young man said, and looked at Victoria.

"I'm okay," she said.

Trent put his arm around her. "Victoria is a hero," Trent said. She called me today all by herself.

"Help me hold him still, okay?" the man asked.

Trent walked over to Troy. "Troy, this man is going to take some blood from your arm now," he said, and lifted Troy's shivering arm out of the blankets. He held it still until the man had gotten the blood he needed, and then tucked it back inside the blanket. "All done, Troy. You did good, buddy."

Trent sat back down next to Victoria, and they waited for the doctor to return. A nurse came in periodically, and with her last check she told them that Troy's fever was down a little.

"Looks good, guys. Troy's fever is down, and he isn't shivering nearly as much."

Trent looked at the nurse and then at Troy. "What should we do for him?"

"Let's put these heated blankets on him. He may begin to sweat, but try not to let him take the blankets off. I'll be back in a few minutes." She smiled at Victoria, and then left the room.

"Daddy?" Victoria said, having noticed that Troy's eyes were open now. Trent stood up next to the bed.

"Where am I?" Troy asked, beginning to try to sit up.

"Lie back down, buddy. You are in the hospital. You got sick, remember?"

Troy did not remember, but as they talked, bits and pieces began to come back to him. "Victoria?"

"I'm okay, Daddy. I have BunBun. Your friend is nice, too." She smiled at Trent.

"Victoria is the real hero, Troy. She called me today all by herself."

"I'm so tired," Troy said.

"Your body is fighting something, Troy. That's why you're tired. They will know what it is pretty soon."

The doctor walked in then. "Troy, I'm Dr. Walker." He took Troy's hand in his for a moment and then laid it back down on the bed. He turned to Trent and Victoria. "Could you excuse us for a few minutes?"

Troy looked at Trent with a very worried expression. "Can they stay? He's my boss, and that's my daughter, Victoria."

The doctor shook Trent's hand. "I'm so sorry. I didn't realize. Of course you can stay."

"What's wrong with me?" Troy asked, with a shaky voice.

"It wasn't an obvious discovery for us, but we kept digging until we found an answer. You have, or have had, rather, streptococcus A. Your titer was positive, and we will be changing your antibiotic momentarily."

Troy looked confused. "You mean strep throat? I don't have a sore throat."

"It is the same bacteria, Troy, but it does not always manifest as a sore throat. Your fever and shakes is common, and you probably had trouble walking today, didn't you?"

Trent answered for Troy. "Yes, he did. I carried him to the car."

The doctor laughed a little at that. "I admire your strength, Trent. I need your workout secrets."

Turning his attention back to Troy, Dr. Walker continued. "Not to worry, Troy. Your joint stiffness is a sort of residue, or leftover, of strep A. Have you noticed any red bumps anywhere on your body?"

Dr. Walker uncovered Troy's feet and noticed two small red nodules.

"What is that?" Troy asked, with obvious alarm in his voice.

"Those will be gone very soon, Troy. But, what you have is erythema nodosum, which is a sequela, or residual, of streptococcus A. We will be giving you a week's worth of a pretty high dose of steroids, if you have no problem with that."

Troy shook his head. He just wanted to feel better.

The nurse came in then and changed Troy's antibiotic. "Can you swallow, honey?" she asked sweetly.

Troy nodded.

"It's prednisone," she said, and handed the little white paper cup to Troy. He took the little pill and chased it with water.

After she had left, Dr. Walker finished giving Troy his instructions. "We'll let you go home in about an hour. Your fever should have broken by then. I'll be back in about an hour to check on you." He walked to the door, stopping to talk to Victoria. "They tell me you were a hero today, little lady. You keep your daddy company until I get back, okay?" He shook her hand, and Victoria smiled and nodded.

Dr. Walker left the room, and Victoria put her head in her hands and started to cry. Troy tried to sit up, but Trent had already pulled the little girl into his arms.

"It's okay, sweetie." He held her in a big bear hug while she sobbed into his chest. "You were so brave for so long, honey. It's okay. Here, sweetie."

Trent lifted Victoria onto his lap, and held her to his chest. He began to gently rock from side to side. "Daddy's going to be okay. Daddy's going to get well really fast." Trent could hear her trying to speak between her sobs, but didn't understand what she was saying. He lifted her head away from his chest just a little. "I'm sorry, honey. I didn't understand what you said."

Keeping her head down, she said, "I...th...thought...that...my daddy was...going to die." Then she buried her head in Trent's chest again.

"Oh, no, sweetie. He's better already. See?"

Victoria slowly lifted her head and looked over at Troy. Then she whispered to Trent. "Is he asleep?"

"Yes, he is. But he isn't shaking any longer, and he has pushed the blankets back. He isn't feeling cold any longer, and that means his fever is going away."

Victoria studied her dad as if she were trying to memorize him. Trent rubbed her back as she sat on his lap. He said nothing for a long while, allowing her the time she needed.

"You okay, sweetie?" Trent asked.

Victoria looked at him. Then she whispered to Trent once again. "Can I talk to him?"

Trent didn't know how to answer Victoria's sweet question, but he knew he had to come up with an answer soon. He knew very little about children. Cats he knew about. Talking to children was an entirely new experience for Trent. How could he say no to a child whose only request was to talk to her father? Trent had no idea where Victoria's mother was, or if she even had a mother. "Sure, Victoria."

Trent held Victoria's soft little hand and they walked to the head of the bed. Then he lifted her up so that she could sit beside her father. Trent leaned forward on his knees on the floor. "Daddy?"

Trent was touched by the way this sweet little girl was comforting her father. She patted his back. Then she looked at Trent. "His back is wet," she said, with a worried look on her sweet little face.

"That's okay, honey. When his fever broke, he began to sweat some as his body temperature returned to normal." Trent smiled, and Victoria tried to talk to her daddy again.

"Daddy?"

Troy opened his eyes and looked at her. "Honey, are you okay?" He didn't see Trent.

"It's okay, Troy. I'm here." Trent leaned up so that Troy could see him.

"I'm okay, sweetie. Guess I fell asleep."

"It's okay, Daddy." Troy wiped his forehead.

"I feel better now," he said.

Dr. Walker and his nurse came back into the room. "Well, looks like you're ready to go home," he announced. The nurse reported that Troy's vital signs were all normal.

"Well, Victoria, are you ready to take your daddy home?"

She nodded shyly at the man.

"The nurse will get everything ready, and then you'll be out of here."

Dr. Walker left the room, and the three of them waited for the nurse.

Four

Changes

When they returned to Troy's house, Victoria picked up BunBun and ran to unlock the front door. "Here we are, Daddy." She held the door for her father, and Trent helped him to the door.

"I'm doing better, don't you think?" he joked.

"Definitely," Trent agreed.

"I think I'll stay up awhile," Troy said, and headed to the sofa.

"I don't think so, buddy boy. Not quite yet."

Trent steered Troy to his bedroom. "Now, get into bed, at least for the rest of today. Doctor's orders." Trent smiled at his friend and employee, and helped him into bed.

"Sweetie, do you have water in the refrigerator?"

Victoria nodded at Trent, and ran to the kitchen to get water for her daddy. Trent turned away from Troy, and Troy grabbed his arm. "What is it, Troy?" He took Trent's hand, and Trent sat beside him on the bed.

"Thank you, Trent. I don't know what would have happened if you hadn't been here."

Trent held Troy's hand between both of his own. "You've got a very brave little girl, Troy. She did a very grownup thing today."

Troy lowered his eyes. "I know. She has had to grow up much too fast. Guess I owe her. She has been so understanding about my work hours. I promised her that we would do something together this weekend."

Trent was beginning to understand now why Troy worked so hard. He didn't know that he was a single father. "We can hire more help, Troy. I had no idea you were under so much stress. You don't have to push yourself for me. I know you're the best. You deserve to have time with your daughter."

Troy sighed.

"Here you go, Daddy," Victoria said, running into the room and handing the bottle of water to Troy.

Trent offered Victoria a knee to sit on and she climbed up into his lap.

"Looks like you've made a new friend, Trent."

"I sure have," he said, giving Victoria a hug. "I do need to go home and check on my cats, Marshmallow and Tootle. You can come with me if you want to, Victoria, and if it's okay with your daddy."

"Okay," Victoria said quietly.

Trent let go of Troy's hand, and Troy looked at him. Trent patted Troy's arm, and he and Victoria made sure that Troy had everything he needed before they left.

As they left the bedroom, Trent turned around as they were leaving and smiled at Troy. Troy looked at Trent, and although neither spoke a word, each was wondering if there was something in the look they had just shared. I'm probably imagining things, Trent thought. Troy was thinking the same thing as he watched his little girl leave with the man he admired more than Trent knew.

When they got to Trent's apartment, Victoria was thrilled to see Marshmallow and Tootle. "Can I touch them?"

"Sure. You can help me feed them."

The two cats loved all the attention from this new little person.

"They like you, Victoria."

"They are very soft," she said, trying to pet them both at the same time.

Trent put their food in a bowl and handed it to Victoria. "You want to feed them?" They had already begun to eat before Victoria had a chance to put the bowl down.

"I can pet them while they eat," she said, surprised.

"Yeah, they love attention any time."

"What else do they eat?"

"They eat their dry food whenever they want throughout the day and night," Trent told her, pointing to their food and water bowls. "They take lots of naps during the day, short ones, and eat small meals often."

Trent continued to talk to Victoria while he changed clothes and straightened up. When he noticed that she had stopped talking, Trent hurried to the living room, afraid that she may have left the apartment without telling him. "Oh, how precious," he said aloud. Victoria had fallen asleep on the sofa by the window, and both Marshmallow and

Tootle had jumped up to join her. Trent got a small blanket and covered her. Then he stretched out on the other sofa and fell asleep.

Trent hadn't realized that he had fallen asleep until something woke him up suddenly. Trent looked around. He had been asleep for two hours. Victoria was sleeping soundly, protected by the two cats that had just adopted her as their own. For a guy who knows precious little about children, I think I'm doing pretty good here, Trent thought. Then he jumped to his feet. Troy must be crazy with worry, he said to himself.

Not thinking, he dialed Troy's number, and then hoped there was a phone near his bed.

"Hello," Troy said.

"Hey, buddy, I'm sorry we've been gone so long."

"Oh, I guess I fell asleep, Trent. Is it late?"

"No, no, it's not late. You go ahead and sleep. Victoria fell asleep on the sofa and I guess I did, too. Should I stay here, or bring her home?"

Troy was touched by Trent's offer to keep his daughter. "Oh, that's up to you. You can bring her home if you like."

"No, I love having her, Troy. Let's let her sleep awhile, and then when she wakes up, we'll come back. How does that sound?"

"Sounds good, Trent, and thanks," Troy said.

They both hung up the phone, but continued to stare at it, both wondering if they had heard something from the other that hadn't really been said. Troy finally rolled over and went back to sleep. Trent lay back down on the sofa, but couldn't get his mind off of Troy.

Trent dozed off and on until almost noon when he was awakened by the sound of Victoria's sweet little voice. "Daddy?"

Trent was on his feet instantly. "No, honey, you're at Trent's house. We both fell asleep after feeding Marshmallow and Tootle."

She looked down and noticed the two cats curled up around her legs, and then she giggled. What a sweet little laugh, Trent thought. "They were watching over me," she said.

"Yes they were, sweetie. Shall we go see your daddy now?"

"Okay," she said.

Trent went to his bedroom to get something and when he came back, Victoria was petting his sleeping cats. "Ready to go?"

"Um, Trent?"

Oh, no, he thought. She looks like she could cry again. Trent hurried over to where Victoria was sitting. "What's wrong, honey?"

Continuing to stroke the cats, Victoria said, "Can you stay with Daddy and me, and Marshmallow and Tootle, too?"

Trent had no idea where this had come from, or why she wanted this. He had no idea how to answer the little girl, but said the first thing that popped into his head. "Of course I can, Victoria. We'll need to get it approved by your daddy first, okay?"

She turned around and looked at Trent, a broad smile across her face.

"Okay. Let's go. Then we can come back and get Marshmallow and Tootle after their nap."

She took Trent's hand and pulled on his arm to hurry him to the door.

Fresh from her nap, Victoria ran into her house, calling "Daddy, Daddy", and Trent hurried to catch up with her.

"What is it, Victoria?" Troy asked, just waking up.

"Trent can come stay with us, Daddy, and Marshmallow and Tootle are coming, too."

Trent walked into the room, hoping that Troy wouldn't be upset with his daughter for asking that he stay with them.

"What?"

"I asked Trent if he would stay with us and bring his cats. They are soft, Daddy, and they like to sleep."

"Honey, I could use another bottle of water. Could you get it for me?"

"Sure, Daddy," she said, and scampered off.

Trent sat on the bed beside Troy. "Don't be upset with her, Troy. I think she feels a little overwhelmed right now. If it makes her feel better, I really don't mind. I would love to help out. And she is right about Marshmallow and Tootle. They will love this big house, not to mention a yard to roam in for the first time in their lives."

Troy sat up and leaned against the back of the bed. "Thanks, Trent. I guess we could use the help right now."

"Consider it done. Victoria and I will bring the cats over a little later." He patted Troy's leg and then began to gently massage it. He looked at Troy, and Troy was watching him. Troy held out his hand for Trent. Trent took his hand and held it. He looked at his hand in Troy's, and then looked at Troy.

"Here you go, Daddy," sang an excited Victoria, carrying a fresh bottle of water to Troy.

"Well, sweetie, shall we go get Marshmallow and Tootle and bring them to their new home?"

"Really, can we, Daddy?"

"I think that sounds like a great idea, honey."

Holding her stuffed bunny tightly against her small body, Victoria said, "Will you take care of BunBun for me?"

Troy opened the blanket and patted the bed. "I've got a warm spot right here just for BunBun."

Victoria kissed the top of the stuffed bunny's head and laid it gently beside Troy. She took Trent's other hand and blew a kiss to her daddy. Troy looked down at his and Trent's hands as Trent slowly slid his hand out of Troy's. They looked at each other once again. "We'll be right back," Trent assured his friend. He left the room holding the hand of Troy's little girl, once again confused about what he was not only thinking, but was now feeling. He turned to look at Troy who had already closed his eyes.

"Daddy knows how to take care of BunBun," Victoria announced proudly as she and Trent walked to the car.

"I'm sure he does, Victoria. He takes wonderful care of you."

Trent was thrilled that the little girl he had met just one day ago felt comfortable with him already. She chattered almost nonstop on the way back to Trent's apartment.

"They didn't move at all, Trent," Victoria said, as she went immediately to the sleeping cats. "Remember me? We had a nap together."

Trent couldn't help but smile. He only wished that Troy had said something earlier about having a daughter. "I'll pack some things, honey, while you wake up Marshmallow and Tootle."

Victoria just smiled, and Trent hurried to pack his things. With two suitcases in his hands, Trent hurried to the door. "I'll put these in the car and be right back," he said to Victoria. Then he stopped at the door. Shit, he said to himself. What am I thinking? "Come with me, okay, Victoria? I'll need help with the car door."

Trent noticed the slight fear in the little girl's eyes begin to fade when he said this. How stupid of me, he thought. Children her age can't be left alone, or shouldn't be left alone, anyway.

After the two of them had put Trent's things in the car, Trent and Victoria went back for the cats. "We have to put them in their carry case for the trip, Victoria. But it won't be for long." She helped Trent put the sleepy soft cats into their case, and then helped him with their stuff.

Victoria talked to Marshmallow and Tootle all the way back to Troy's.

"They like you a lot, Victoria. You may find them in your bed when you wake up every morning."

"You really think so?"

"I really do," he said.

When they arrived back at Troy's, Victoria was helpful even more as she helped get the cats settled in their new home. "Can I put their bed in my room, Daddy?"

"Sure, sweetie," Troy said.

With one cat in each arm, Victoria showed them the sun room at the back of the house. "You want to see our whole house, Trent?"

"I would love to, Victoria."

Trent stopped briefly to talk to Troy before Victoria treated him to a tour of the house. Her room was at the opposite end of the hall from Troy's, and Trent was amazed when he walked in. "Honey, this looks like Barbie's Dream House." Then he whispered to her. "I've seen Barbie's Dream House in stores."

The little girl giggled. Trent loved her sweet laugh. She deserved to laugh. Somehow, Trent felt that Victoria had been through a lot in her young life.

Victoria showed Trent the sunroom last, which was just as spectacular as the rest of the house. "Look at Marshmallow and Tootle," he said. The two cats had made themselves at home already. They looked very comfortable on the back of the long sofa against the window. The back yard was mesmerizing to them as they watched the birds come and go from the bird feeder.

Victoria ran across the room and jumped up onto the couch. "You like your new home, don't you?" She petted the two very content cats, and then looked back at Trent. "They're purring," she said, with a giggle.

"You talk to them for awhile, honey, and I'll go see if your daddy needs anything."

"Okay, Trent."

Trent walked back to Troy's room, with a smile on his face.

Troy was sitting up when Trent walked in. "Well, buddy, where do you want me?" Trent picked up his suitcases, and waited for instructions.

"Oh, I'm sorry," he said, starting to get up.

"No, you stay right there, and tell me what to do."

"Through the bathroom is another room a lot like this one. It seems odd, but there is a lot about the layout of this house that seems odd. I love it, though. Guess that makes me odd, too," he added, with a laugh.

"This is nice, Troy. You've done a lot with the house." Trent set his stuff down and looked around. Then he walked back through the bathroom and into Troy's room.

Trent sat on the bed next to Troy. "You look good, Troy."

"Thanks, Trent. I'm glad you're here. Victoria has a part-time nanny during the week, but I don't know what I would have done this weekend, without you."

Trent took Troy's hand in his again. "You could, and can, count on me anytime, Troy. All you have to do is ask."

Troy closed his eyes. "I know," he said, and then opened his eyes again. "Are you wondering how I got Victoria?"

"I think I can figure that out, Troy," he said, with a smile.

"You know what I mean," he said.

"It doesn't matter, Troy. But I think you're very lucky to have her."

Troy nodded in agreement. "I was married once, Trent, but for a very short time, a year to be exact. She got pregnant right away, but I was hiding something from her and from me."

Trent looked puzzled. "What was that, Troy?"

"I was secretly involved with someone else. We were together before the marriage, but you know, I thought marriage was expected of me somehow."

Trent was confused. "So then, this other woman didn't want to get married, or what?"

"I wasn't involved with another woman, Trent. What I hate most is that Beth came home one day and caught us."

"Did I miss something?" Trent asked.

"Yes, you did. His name was Dan. The person I was involved with was Dan. Beth knew about him, but I guess she thought I could change or something."

Was Troy gay? Trent wondered.

Trent held Troy's hand a little tighter. "If you're telling me you're gay, Troy, it's okay. It's not a disease. It's not something you need to get over."

Troy couldn't look at Trent yet. "I know," he said, with a shaky voice. "It's just that I didn't mean to hurt her, you know. But there we were, my lover and me, bare assed naked, with a dick in both of our mouths, having a gay old time."

Trent couldn't help but laugh.

Troy glared at him. "What's so funny?"

"I'm sorry, Troy. I just got a mental image."

Troy closed his eyes and then opened them. "And it was a humorous image?"

"No, actually, the image that popped into my mind was rather hot," Trent admitted, fixing his gaze on Troy's eyes.

Troy looked at Trent and saw that same look that he thought was there before. He started to pull his hand out of Trent's hand, but Trent stopped him. "No," Trent commanded. He moved closer to Troy, and kissed him lightly on the forehead. Then he moved back and looked at Troy.

"What happened to Dan?"

"Oh, he moved away after Beth caught us together. He said he didn't need the drama in his life. I don't think he ever really forgave me for giving in to societal expectations."

Trent kissed Troy's hand. "Do you still love him?"

"No, Trent, I don't. It took a long time to get over him, but that was a long time ago."

Troy bent his legs. He didn't want Trent to know that his touch aroused him. He had always been attracted to his boss, but he didn't think he needed to see it, not yet, anyway. The two of them looked at each other for a long time, both seeing desire in the other, and neither wanting to admit it.

Troy continued with his story. "Then, in an odd twist, Beth was killed in an automobile accident about six months after Victoria was born. There is a picture of her in Victoria's room, but she has no recollection of her mother, of course. I tell her often, though, how much her mother loved her."

Trent felt a lump in his throat. "Damn, Troy, I had no idea."

"I know you didn't. I guess I've avoided getting close to someone, until now at least."

Troy swallowed hard as he continued to figure out what exactly it was that he was seeing in Trent's eyes.

"Daddy, you should see Marshmallow and Tootle. I think they like it here a lot."

"That's nice, honey."

She jumped onto Trent's lap, needing no invitation this time, and picked up her stuffed bunny. "BunBun, our family is a lot bigger now." She squeezed the stuffed animal and kissed it on the top of its head.

"That poor bunny has been through a lot," Troy said.

"Daddy, can I still go to Chelsea's house tonight?"

Troy's eyes opened wide. "Oh, honey, I forgot all about that. Chelsea invited you to spend the night, didn't she?"

Victoria nodded.

"I can take her, Troy. Just give me Chelsea's address and I will get you there," he said to a giggling Victoria.

"I can't ask you to do that," Troy protested.

"Troy, remember what I said?"

Troy sighed. "Yes. Show Trent where Chelsea's address is, honey, and maybe he can help get your suitcase."

"Sure, I can. Let's go." He patted Troy's hand and left with Victoria. Once she was ready to go, Trent stopped in to talk to Troy.

"I'll be back in a little while, Troy."

Troy was out of bed. "Okay. I think I'll take a shower while you're gone."

Trent let go of Victoria's little hand just long enough to stop Troy. "I think you will wait until I get back home to help you," he said, helping Troy back to the bed.

"Yes, boss," Troy teased.

"Take care of BunBun, Daddy," Victoria said, and kissed the worn out stuffed bunny again.

Five

A Special Friend

When Trent returned from taking Victoria to her friend's house, Troy was sitting up in bed holding the tattered bunny.

"You know, Trent, BunBun has been a lifesaver. Whenever Victoria was scared, I told her that BunBun was brave and would keep her safe. Whenever Victoria was sad, I told her that she could always talk to BunBun and he or she, whatever this thing is, would understand." Troy laughed in spite of himself. "I had no idea how to raise a child."

Trent walked over to Troy and hugged him. "There isn't a parent in this world who hasn't felt that way at some time, Troy. But from what I've seen in the last two days, I'd say you've done a damned good job. The kid is loved, and that goes a long way in this life."

"Thanks," he said into Trent's chest as Trent continued to hug him. "You still want that shower?"

Troy nodded, but not really wanting to leave the warmth of Trent's body. Trent made sure that Troy had made it to the shower okay before leaving the bathroom. Through the steam of the shower, Trent could barely make out the naked silhouette of his friend and employee. He and Troy had known each other for a long time, but Trent hadn't realized his own feelings for Troy until now.

Trent walked back into Troy's bedroom and sat on the bed, thinking. He thought about the time the two of them had spent together, the late nights, the early mornings. They had become friends, yet neither realized the strength of their friendship. The care and concern they had for each other Trent now realized was love, but was it a compassionate love or a companionate love? He wasn't sure.

"Trent?"

Trent hurried to the bathroom. "I'm here, Troy. You need help?"

"I think I might," he said.

Trent didn't hesitate to open the shower door and step inside fully clothed. Troy leaned against the wall. Trent immediately put his arms around his wet friend. "Do you feel weak? Just lean on me and I'll help you to the bed."

"Just a minute, Trent," he said.

Trent stepped back, his arms still around Troy, and waited for whatever Troy wanted him to do next. Troy looked at him. His heart was beating fast, just as it always had under Trent's touch. He couldn't be sure if Trent felt anything for him, though, in that way.

"I don't think I can wash myself," he said, with pleading eyes.

"I can wash you. Can you lean against the wall?"

Troy nodded, not really feeling weak at all, but wanting to feel Trent's hands on his body. He craved Trent's touch on his naked skin.

Trent didn't see a washcloth nearby and didn't want to leave Troy alone in the shower, so he made a thick lather with his hands and began to wash his friend. He washed Troy's neck and then his arms. He looked down at Troy's nipples that had become hard from the water, and he closed his eyes. Trent's wet clothes clung to him, and he could feel his pulsating cock against the tight denim of his jeans. When his hands moved down along Troy's chest and his fingers met Troy's nipples, Troy gasped. Trent looked up at him.

There was no mistaking the look in Troy's eyes, and Trent knew the same look was in his own eyes. The look of desire could not be missed now by either man. Trent looked down at Troy's nipples again and the droplets of water that slid lazily over them. As his soapy hands moved downward along Troy's tight stomach, Trent saw for the first time what he had wanted for a long time. He wanted Troy. He wanted all of Troy. The perfectly shaped head of Troy's fully erect cock was just inches from his mouth and Trent fought the urge to take his friend right here as the water from the shower beat down over them.

Troy knew that the fluid that was now on the head of his cock was not only water, and he, too, was fighting an urge. He was fighting the urge to rip Trent's clothes off of him and take him right here on the shower floor. As Trent's hands moved down along Troy's stomach, he gasped again. "Trent," he sighed. Trent looked up. Troy took Trent's head in his hands. Their lips were so close now that even through the water they could feel the hot breath of the other.

Troy could wait no longer. "Kiss me," Troy demanded, and pulled Trent to him.

Trent's body pressed against Troy's, pinning him firmly against the wall. He forced Troy's mouth open with his lips and kissed him with a hunger that only now was fully realized. Trent slid one hand down along Troy's back until it rested firmly on his butt.

Troy pulled Trent's water drenched shirt up, forcing it open and off of Trent's body. He pressed his hand against Trent's soaked jeans, discovering his manhood for the very first time. Trent moaned with his new lover's touch, but his lips did not leave his new lover's lips.

"Let it out," he mumbled into Troy's open mouth.

Troy quickly unzipped Trent's jeans, pushing them and his drenched underwear down. Trent stepped out of them and pushed them aside. Troy didn't wait to help himself to Trent's aching body. He firmly grasped Trent's hardness and slid his hand upward along the shaft. Trent's mouth came off of Troy's, and Trent held his new lover now with both hands on his ass.

Trent pressed the tips of his fingers firmly between Troy's butt cheeks, separating them, and sliding his fingers downward along the path of their separation. Troy continued to stroke Trent's cock and he grasped Trent's balls firmly, causing another, even louder gasp from Trent. When Trent's hand made its way around to Troy's erection, Troy moaned. "Trent," he said again.

Trent looked at Troy, and then kissed him again. Troy could barely move, but he somehow found the shower down and forced it open.

The two men slowly made their way to the bed, not letting go of the other, sandwiched together by the heat of their passion. Trent lifted Troy onto the bed, and lay on top of him. They continued to kiss each other. They could not stop. They fought each other for dominance, demanding from the other what they both had needed and wanted for a long time. Troy's hand was firmly around Trent's cock, and Trent forced his lover's legs apart to please him.

Trent stopped kissing Troy and looked hungrily at his manhood now firmly in his grasp. He looked at Troy, and said, "I want you."

Troy's eyes were half shut, his body lost in passion. Trent lowered his mouth to taste his new lover for the first time, and Troy pulled Trent's butt around, forcing his legs apart so that he could be fed what he had been holding firmly in his hands. Trent squeezed Troy's inner thighs as his lips held the swollen head of Troy's throbbing organ. He lowered his own engorged throbbing member to his lover's lips. Troy was hungry for Trent. He held the two firm halves of Trent's ass and brought Trent's cock to his lips. Trent devoured Troy's cock as if he hadn't eaten in days, tasting every inch of him.

Troy began making love to Trent's cock as Trent lowered himself to please his lover. The two men made love to the other's organ of desire, taking their time, feeding each other's passion. Both men felt as if they could explode at any moment, but both wanted this, their first time together, to last as long as it possibly could. They both slowed their lovemaking just a little, but their hunger for each other was too strong.

Troy forced Trent to feed him all of his hardness, not willing to be denied any longer. Moaning loudly now, their climaxes were closer than their minds were willing to admit. They came fast and hard, both satisfying their own and their lover's needs.

Six

The Real Thing

They lay together afterward, holding each other in the afterglow of their lovemaking. It seemed an eternity had passed before either man dared to speak. Trent kissed Troy's neck with one gentle brush of his lips and then leaned up on his elbows. Troy's eyes were closed.

"Troy," he said, softly.

Troy slowly opened his eyes.

Trent was hoping that what he saw in those eyes was love. "Tell me this is real," Trent pleaded.

"Yes," Troy answered, a little confused.

"I'm not a substitute, am I, for what you felt for Dan, or for Dan himself?"

Troy opened his eyes fully now. He put his arms around Trent. "No, Trent, no. I wanted you. I've wanted you for awhile, but I guess it took this, this incident, and everything that has happened in the last two days for me to realize it."

Trent fell onto Troy, covering his body with his own, and covering his mouth with kisses once again.

"I know, Troy, I know," Trent said, with his head over Troy's shoulder.

They slept awhile longer, and woke around sunrise. Trent had rolled to the other side of the bed sometime during the night and he lay watching Troy sleeping peacefully beside him. Troy woke a few minutes after Trent. He looked over at Trent and smiled.

"Oh, man, what is underneath me?"

Troy pulled a flattened BunBun out from underneath him and fluffed the worn stuffed bunny back into shape. "This old thing must have a hundred lives."

Trent laughed and took the stuffed bunny from Troy. "I like him," he said, and gave BunBun a hug.

"He's a big part of our little family, Trent. That's for sure."

Troy watched as Trent played with the stuffed animal, dancing the bunny across his stomach.

Troy rolled onto his side. "Thanks, Trent, for being so good to my little girl."

Trent turned onto his side, facing Troy, and laid the stuffed bunny between them. "I have no idea what I'm doing when I'm with her, but you're welcome."

Troy laughed. "I guess no one is one hundred percent sure of himself when it comes to relating to children," he said to his new love.

"What time do I pick her up, Troy?"

"Oh, I almost forgot. Chelsea's mom said she would bring her back around ten."

"You think for now we should sleep in separate beds?"

Troy reached for Trent's hand. "I think that's best, but it doesn't mean we can't spend part of the night together, if you know what I mean."

Trent knew what he meant. He smiled. "I know," he said.

Trent and Troy were sitting in the sunroom with Marshmallow and Tootle when Victoria came home. She ran to see them, focusing her attention on the cats first. "Daddy, you're up," she said.

"I feel much better, honey."

"Did you sleep good in your new home, Trent?"

"Yes, Victoria, I did. Thank you."

Trent was impressed at the little girl's politeness. Troy was doing a better job with her than he gave himself credit for doing.

"Um, Daddy?"

"Yes, honey," he said.

"Chelsea's mommy and Chelsea's aunt are going to take Chelsea to the zoo today. Can we go, too?"

Trent looked at Troy.

"I think that would be great, sweetie," he said.

"Are you sure you're up to it, Troy?" Trent asked, knowing how the man pushed himself.

"I think getting out would be good for me, and we won't stay all day," he replied.

Victoria squealed with delight, and ran to call Chelsea to tell her the good news.

The three of them got ready to go to the zoo, and Victoria was thrilled when she met up with Chelsea. The two little girls walked hand in hand, with Chelsea's mom and aunt not far behind. "I think we're lucky the girls are tired, Trent," Troy said. "They don't seem to be moving too fast."

"Daddy, come on. Trent will love this."

Victoria had heard the train whistle and knew that "Little Puffer" was on its way.

"She loves this little steam train," Troy said.

"I'm ashamed to admit it, Troy, but I haven't been to the zoo in a very long time."

"Well, the train is great. We get to rest."

"Here we go, Daddy," Victoria announced, as they boarded the miniature steam train.

"This train takes Victoria past her favorite animals, the bears," Troy quietly told Trent.

They went around twice on the train, and on the second trip they departed at the Hearst Grizzly Gulch. "I love the bears, Trent," Victoria said enthusiastically.

Trent nodded and smiled at the excited little girl and her friend. "The bears are beautiful, but I wouldn't want to meet one in the wild," Trent admitted.

"They look like teddy bears, don't they, Daddy?" Victoria asked.

"Really big teddy bears," Troy added.

The polar bears were swimming and looked like they were having a good time. "You know, Troy, I had never noticed until today that the polar bears have partially webbed feet. No wonder they can swim so well."

Troy nodded in agreement, and watched the bears.

"Did you know that the grizzly bear is on our flag, Trent?" Victoria asked, proud in her knowledge of her home state.

"I did know that, Victoria," he said.

After a couple of hours, the girls were tired, and so was Troy. "This is why we have season tickets," Chelsea's mother whispered to Troy and Trent. They both smiled. The two little girls said goodbye at the front entrance to the zoo, and they all left for home.

Victoria was rubbing her eyes on the way home and had to admit that she was tired. "Here, sweetie, you and BunBun go take a nap," Troy suggested, handing the stuffed bunny to Victoria. She carried the little bunny down the hall and climbed into bed.

Trent and Troy lounged in the sunroom with the still sleeping cats while Victoria took her nap. "Trent, I have a lot to do at work, but I don't know if I can do it all. I'm not as well as I thought," Troy admitted to Trent.

Trent walked over to where Troy was stretched out on the sofa. He held Troy's hand. "You are not to work all week, Troy. Give yourself time to heal."

"But I could work some," he protested.

"No, Troy. If you work some, then you will stay longer and longer each day, working ten hour days before you know it. No more of that. I'm selfish. I want you to be here with me in the evenings, and in the mornings, too. We can get you help. But this week you will be right here."

Troy looked down at Trent's hands around his, and smiled. He looked up at Trent, and whispered, "Okay, boss."

The next morning Trent was up early. He had people to hire, and a long day ahead of him. Troy was in the kitchen when Trent walked up to him. "Shall I give Victoria's nanny the week off, with pay of course?" he asked Trent.

"If you like. I'll be home around six. What time does Victoria go to school?"

"Mrs. Walker takes her to school at eight and brings her back home around four, but I can take her and pick her up this week. It will be fun, Trent. I rarely get the privilege."

Trent gave Troy a quick kiss on the lips. "Victoria will love it," he said. "If you don't feel up to it, call me, and I can pick her up, okay?"

"Deal," Troy agreed.

"Tell Victoria good morning for me. I'll see her tonight."

Trent left quietly around seven. He hadn't planned to stop by his apartment until later in the day, but it was so close to the office that he decided to see if he had any messages. He had left in such a hurry that he hadn't told his parents where he could be reached. I'll just stop by and have my calls forwarded, he thought.

He opened his apartment door and walked over to the phone. I'll just forward all these to my cell phone, he told himself. There was only one message. It was from Charlie. "Oh no, I forgot all about Charlie," he said to no one. He listened to Charlie's soft spoken message. "Oh, hey, Trent. I had a great time, but I um, I guess I just don't want to see anybody right now. Well, thanks again." That was odd, Trent thought.

Short and to the point. Oh, well. Guess it's better this way. No one gets hurt.

Trent walked to the sofa underneath the window and sat down. Staring out of the window, he thought about this past weekend. I guess I had been attracted to Troy all along. Why didn't I see it? We worked together and were good together at the office. Maybe I should have taken more time and gotten to know him on a more personal level. The man has a daughter and I didn't even know it. Trent smiled when he thought of the bright-eyed Victoria. Do I really know what I'm doing? What will happen to the little girl if Troy and I don't work out? What will happen to me if that happens and Victoria is no longer in my life?

Trent shook his head, trying to shake the doubts from his mind. He picked up his briefcase to check today's schedule. When he opened it up, there on top of everything squished almost to flatness was BunBun, along with a card from Victoria.

"Dear Trent, BunBun wants to be with you today. Bring him back home with you tonight. Love, Victoria."

Trent picked up the worn and flattened stuffed bunny and held it to his face. The sweet smell of Victoria filled him, and it was at that moment that Trent knew for certain that he was exactly where he was meant to be.

He Came With a Rose

Ethan has a wonderful life, filled with his two dogs, horses, and many other animals which have wandered onto his land over the years. He has the best friend that any man could have, a man who has become more than just a friend, if only in Ethan's mind and in his dreams. When his friend asks him to attend a dinner with him one Saturday night, Ethan discovers much more about his good friend, who is also the veterinarian to his many animals, than he had already known. Dr. Holing has a secret which Ethan could not have imagined in even his wildest of dreams. Ethan's Saturday night quickly becomes an adventure, an adventure which will change his life forever.

One

Ethan

It was still dark outside when Ethan drove his trusty old pickup truck into the lot of the College of Veterinary Medicine Clinic on the north end of the beautiful campus. "Just a few more minutes, Princess, and you'll be all better." Ethan loved his Sheltie puppy. She and her brother, Hawker, were the loves of his life on the farm that he owned just a few miles north of the city. Ethan was a wheat farmer, and the land was to him what Tara was to Scarlett O'Hara in <u>Gone with the Wind</u>. It was his strength.

Dr. Bryce Holing met Ethan at the back door of the clinic. One of the best of the best veterinarians in the country, Dr. Holing knew Ethan well. He came out to Ethan's farm whenever Ethan needed him, to tend to the larger animals that could not be brought to the city.

"How's our little Princess?"

"Not so good, Bryce. She swallowed something, but I don't know what. I just hope it's not something harmful."

Bryce knew how much Ethan genuinely loved his animals, especially his two Shelties, and he picked the sleepy dog up into his arms and carried her into the hospital. Ethan was right behind him, afraid for his precious Princess.

Dr. Holing laid the pretty dog on the table and looked her over. "She'll be fine, right?"

Bryce placed his hand on Ethan's arm. "I'm sure she will be, Ethan," he said, in his always comforting, always reassuring voice. He petted the sleepy dog and drew some blood. "We'll get this back in just a few minutes, Ethan. Then we'll know what to do."

Bryce continued to pet Princess and talk to her as if she were a young child. He spoke this sweetly to all of his patients, and Ethan had never met a man with as much compassion as Dr. Holing. He watched as the kind doctor made his Princess feel better with the stroke of his hand on her soft fur.

Bryce's assistant came back in with the lab results and handed them to the doctor. Bryce turned his back to Ethan as he studied the results. Ethan petted his sweet baby and waited for Bryce to turn back around. "Looks good, Ethan. I'm going to give her an injection which will kill the toxin. It will probably make her sleep most of the day. Just keep her safe and inside the house for the rest of the day, which I know that you will."

He was stroking Ethan's arm as he spoke, and Ethan knew exactly why Dr. Holing's patients loved him. Bryce's touch was comforting to him, too, maybe a little too comforting. Bryce was not only nice, he was also very sexy, at least that was what Ethan thought.

The doctor was about six feet tall, or so Ethan guessed from his own height of just an inch shy of that. Bryce was broad shouldered, slender, with black hair that had just enough silver to give him that distinguished look, and he had the voice of an angel. His voice was deep but soft, and Ethan could listen to it for hours. He looked forward to seeing Bryce when he came out to the farm, and the two of them often talked for hours about the animals and the crops.

Ethan realized now just how little he knew of Bryce's personal life. He was in awe of Dr. Holing, and felt like a tongue tied teenager in his presence. Ethan smiled at Bryce and thanked him for doing what he did best, picked up his sleepy Princess, and carried her to his truck.

Bryce walked outside with them and opened the door for Ethan. Ethan laid the now sleeping dog on the seat beside him and when he stood up, Bryce was right behind him, his hand on the door. Ethan felt awkward being so close to Bryce that he could smell the musky scent of his cologne, though he didn't know why.

Mistaking his nervousness for concern for his dog, Dr. Holing rubbed Ethan's back. "She's going to be just fine. I can come out later and see her if you like."

Ethan glanced quickly at Bryce, who in the darkness looked more handsome than he did in the sunlight, and said a quick "thanks." He got into the truck and turned the ignition.

Bryce closed the truck door and patted the side of the truck. Ethan watched as he walked back to the hospital.

The sun was just beginning to peek its head over the horizon as Ethan pulled out of the parking lot and headed back to the main road that would lead him out of the university. College students off to early morning classes could be seen here and there, and Ethan looked fondly at his alma mater.

Ten years ago he was one of them, and had spent many hours in Waters Hall, graduating with a degree in Agricultural Economics from this great university. Ethan was proud of his alma mater, and proud to give his time and money to his beloved Kansas State University.

Born and raised right here in Manhattan, Kansas, five miles outside of the city was as far away as Ethan ever wanted to live. He loved his farm and country living. He loved planting the winter wheat in the fall that lay dormant over the winter and sprang to life in the spring as if awakening from a deep sleep, eager to be harvested in late June or early July, and ready to be made into the best bread Ethan had ever tasted. He always had plenty of help for planting and for harvesting, from students at the university eager to earn next year's tuition.

Dr. Holing was nice enough to recommend Ethan to his veterinary medicine students to intern with, and Ethan loved sharing his knowledge of, and love for, his animals with them. He also loved that Dr. Holing came along with the students whenever he could. The two of them had spent hours together, and Ethan and he had walked across the wheat fields trying to assess the quality of the year's crop.

Ethan also had students who were majoring in Food Science and Industry come out to the farm to witness firsthand the process of wheat planting to wheat harvesting, to baked goods, cereals, grain for farm animals and fuel, and so much more that was reaped from this wondrous wheat.

Ethan was often invited to give lectures to students in the various sectors of the College of Agriculture, and never turned down an opportunity to share his knowledge and love of the land with the next generation.

When Ethan returned home, Princess was sound asleep, and he hated to move her from the front seat of his truck. He gently lifted the sleeping dog and held her like a baby. Carrying her into the house, he laid her in the middle of the queen sized bed that she shared with her brother. "We have to let her rest, okay?" he said to Princess' brother, Hawker.

The curious dog sniffed his sister, and then he followed Ethan into the adjoining bedroom that was his. Ethan smiled when he thought of how lucky and loved his two dogs were. Having no children, these two beautiful Shelties were the next best thing. But how many dogs had his or her own bed and bedroom?

Ethan walked back to the bed and stroked Princess who was sleeping peacefully now, and then went into the kitchen, with Hawker following close behind. "Here you go, boy," he said, filling his food bowl. "I'll bet you were hungry. It's way past your breakfast time." The dog ate his food and wagged his tail.

Ethan made himself a pot of coffee and read the paper. He had a group of students coming tomorrow to start the fall planting, and today was his only day to relax a little.

Ethan was tired, so he took the paper into the living room and lay back on the sofa, and was soon asleep. He had been up most of the night with Princess, and was soon sound asleep.

He heard the deep comforting voice of Dr. Bryce Holing and felt his gorgeous body on his.

"I've wanted you for a long time, Ethan. You know we've been tiptoeing around the truth for a long time now."

Ethan felt Bryce's lips lightly brush his.

"You want me, Ethan?"

Ethan opened his mouth, eager to feel the lips that he had wanted from the first time he had met the kind doctor. Bryce kissed him gently, then firmly, like a lover. Ethan felt Bryce's hands on his chest, speaking softly and seductively to him.

"I want you so much, Ethan. I love you."

Ethan felt Bryce's lips on his again before he could respond. His arms were around Bryce's, eager to touch his warm body. The feel of Bryce's hand on his hard cock was almost too much for Ethan to bear. He heard himself moan as Bryce reached his hand deep inside Ethan's jeans, cupping his balls. He stroked Ethan's pulsating cock, and Ethan could once again taste Bryce's lips on his. "Mm," he moaned. Bryce's lips were just out of reach. Ethan tilted his chin upward. "Kiss me, Bryce," he said.

Ethan could hear a phone ringing. "Let it ring, Bryce. Come back and make love to me." The ringing continued, and Ethan could no longer feel Bryce's body next to his. He probably went to answer it, he thought. Then he felt Bryce's hand on his balls again, and Ethan moaned. Bryce's hand was wrapped firmly around Ethan's cock and was stroking him faster and faster. Ethan heard his own moans, and then he felt his warm cum as Bryce brought him to their first climax together. "Oh, Bryce, why did we wait so long?"

The phone was still ringing, and Ethan opened his eyes. "Oh, shit," he said. He looked down at the sticky substance covering him. "It was just a dream. I must really want that man." Hawker was sleeping on the floor beside the sofa. "You must have gotten quite a show," Ethan said to the sleeping dog.

He got up and wiped himself off. The phone had stopped ringing, but now was ringing again. Ethan zipped up his jeans and stripped off his shirt. "Hello," he said.

"Ethan, how's my baby?"

Stopping himself from answering, "fine", Ethan quickly realized that Bryce was referring to his dog, Princess. "Oh, hi Bryce," he said, feeling embarrassed after his very erotic dream about his gorgeous and very sexy friend. "Princess is fine. She's sleeping on her bed."

"I'm on my way out to see her, Ethan. Hope you don't mind. I'll be there in about ten minutes."

"That's great, Bryce. I'll see you in a few."

Ethan hung up the phone and hurried to check on Princess and then take a very quick shower. He had just gotten dressed when he heard the knock on his door. Hawker barked hello when Ethan told Bryce to come on in. Ethan finished toweling his hair dry, and felt even more embarrassed about his dream now that Bryce was here in person, more embarrassed than he had been when talking to him on the phone.

Ethan looked down at his naked chest, his nipples hard from the water of the shower. "Excuse me a minute, Bryce," he said, and hurried to his room to get a clean shirt. Damn, I can hardly look at him, he said to himself.

When he walked back through the bedroom that his two dogs shared, he noticed that Princess was sitting up on the bed. "Bryce, come in here. Princess is awake and looks great."

Bryce hurried into the room and stroked the waking dog. "You are a beautiful baby. Yes you are."

That voice turned Ethan on. He couldn't help it.

"She's fine, Ethan. Probably hungry."

Ethan picked her up, and they went into the kitchen. Hawker was happy to see his buddy back to her old self, and was anxious to help her eat her food. "Thanks again, Bryce. I owe you big time."

Bryce stroked Ethan on the back and his touch was intoxicating. "Well, there is no need for repayment, but I would like to invite you to a dinner meeting tomorrow night. It's with other veterinarians, so it won't be very exciting. I just hate to go alone." He looked down when he said this.

"Sure, Bryce. We've known each other for awhile now. You know I would do anything for you."

Ethan noticed something different about Bryce today. He seemed shy, and not as sure of himself as he usually seemed.

Bryce glanced quickly at Ethan and then looked at Princess. "She has her appetite back," he said, as he watched the dog eating with her brother.

When Bryce bent over to pet princess, Ethan couldn't help but notice the absolute perfection that was Bryce's butt. It was the perfect shape, not too big and not too small, and Ethan fought the urge to grab it and hold it in both hands.

Bryce stood up and turned around. Ethan looked down at the floor, embarrassed that he had been looking at his friend in a sexual way. "Well, Ethan, I'll be going now," Bryce said, as he held Ethan's arm. He looked up at Ethan and for a moment the two of them were facing each other, their bodies almost touching, their lips seeming to want to feel the others'. Did Bryce feel what Ethan had just felt? Did Ethan feel what Bryce had just felt? Both were wondering the same thing, but no one dared to speak of it. "Let me write down my home address for you, Ethan. I've been out here so much it's hard to believe that you have never been to my home. It's easy to find. Is six okay? The dinner is at seven."

He laid the piece of paper on the table in front of Ethan, and Ethan followed him to the door. "I'll be there, Bryce, and thanks. Thanks for coming all this way to see Princess."

Bryce nodded, and headed toward his car. Ethan watched as Bryce walked away.

Remembering the dream, Ethan felt his face begin to heat up. He went out and fed the horses and looked out across the land. He loved this peaceful corner of the world. There were no mountains to obscure his perfect view of the horizon. Sunset and sunrise were beautiful here in northeast Kansas with its gently rolling hills and fresh air.

As he walked out to the barn, his two dogs playfully running alongside him, Ethan thought about Bryce. He knew so little about him, though they had spent plenty of time together over the past couple of years. He realized that they talked about their work and what was new at the university. He thought about Bryce's somewhat shyness when he had asked him to go with him tomorrow night. "Don't read too much into it, Ethan. You're probably just remembering how you wanted him in your dream." Ethan often talked to his dogs and horses. They couldn't disagree with him.

Ethan went to bed early that night. Princess was still a little tired, and Hawker climbed onto the bed and lay beside her.

Ethan awoke from a dream again with his hand firmly around his dick. Damn, he thought. I cannot get Bryce out of my head. He slept off and on that night until finally the alarm sounded. Ethan felt as if he had just barely gotten to sleep.

He forced himself out of the bed and looked in on his dogs who were sleeping soundly. He took a long hot shower and forced himself to wake up. Students were coming this morning to help with the fall planting, and Ethan was glad that they had helped him last year. He was too tired to train new students today. He only hoped that he didn't fall asleep tonight when he was with Bryce.

It took Ethan only an hour to get the eager students off to a great start. The day went by quickly, and at five in the afternoon Ethan called it quits and went inside to get ready for his evening with Bryce.

He had thought about tonight all day, although he had tried not to. He showered again, and dressed in business casual attire. He took a suit jacket just in case he needed it. With the somewhat uncomfortable exchange he and Bryce had had yesterday, Ethan wasn't sure what Bryce had in mind for *after* the dinner, if anything. Did he expect me to stay the night? Was he wanting me in his life in a more personal way? Was he wanting me in his bed? Ethan was driving himself crazy with his thoughts about Bryce, which no doubt existed only in his mind. He splashed on some cologne, and thought about taking an overnight bag with him, but then decided against it. Bryce knew that Ethan wouldn't leave Hawker and Princess alone that long, and Bryce definitely wouldn't want him to leave Princess alone so soon after her middle of the night trip to the hospital.

At the last minute, Ethan decided to ask one of the students to stay with Hawker and Princess until he returned home. He told him that it might be late, but he didn't mind. All of the students loved Ethan's dogs, and they especially loved Ethan's generosity when it came to paying his dog-sitters. Ethan kissed his two babies on the head, and left the country for an evening in the city of Manhattan.

Two

A Change of Plans

The directions to Bryce's home were very easy to follow, especially since Ethan knew Manhattan so well he could have found his way around the city blindfolded. Bryce lived on the northwest side of the city, almost outside the city limits of Manhattan. Ethan turned onto the street where Bryce lived and drove almost to the end, to a beautiful home on a cul-de-sac.

Ethan pulled into the drive and parked his car. He grabbed his suit jacket and walked along the flower lined sidewalk to the front door. A stone between a group of flowers read "Holing", and Ethan was in awe of the well manicured lawn.

Bryce met him at the door. "Come in, Ethan," he said. Ethan noticed that Bryce wasn't dressed for a formal dinner. In fact, Ethan had never seen his friend this disheveled. "Have a seat, Ethan. I'll get us some iced tea."

Bryce scurried off to the kitchen, but Ethan did not sit down. He followed Bryce into the kitchen. Bryce was just standing in the kitchen, as if he had no idea what to do.

Ethan slowly walked over to him and put his arm around him. "Bryce, you okay, buddy?"

He looked at Ethan. "I guess I forgot what I came in here to do," he said, and looked around frantically.

He started to walk away, but Ethan kept his arm firmly around him. "Let's go back into the living room and sit down. Come on, Bryce."

Ethan led Bryce slowly and carefully into the living room, never taking his eyes off of him. He looked scared and anxious, though Ethan had no idea why. "Here, Bryce, sit with me awhile." Ethan gently forced Bryce to sit beside him, but held him firmly, and also held one of his hands in his.

He rubbed Bryce's arm and talked softly, but firmly. He took Bryce's other hand and held them both. "Talk to me, Bryce. You know you can tell me anything. Is it the dinner? We don't have to go. We'll have a nice evening here together. Are you upset about something?"

Bryce took a deep breath. "Ethan, I need to lie down," he said, with an urgency unlike his usual manner. He tried to break free from Ethan's hold, but Ethan would not let him.

"Okay. Let's lie down here on the sofa."

Bryce tried to stand up, but Ethan forced him to lie down on the sofa. Ethan sat beside him, hoping that he would talk to him. "Oh, I'm sorry, Ethan," he said, and closed his eyes.

"Good, you're back," Ethan said, still holding his friend's hands.

"I don't know...," Bryce stopped to catch his breath.

"Take your time, my friend. We've got all night."

Ethan undid his tie and unbuttoned the top buttons on his shirt. Bryce opened his eyes and tried to focus. Then he started to sit up.

"I was getting you some tea," he said.

"No, Bryce. Let's lie back down now."

Ethan gently forced Bryce's head back down. He leaned over him and looked into his eyes. "What is it, Bryce?"

"Ethan, I can't go tonight."

"Okay. That's fine. Tell me about your day, Bryce," Ethan said, hoping this would jog his memory.

"I had a call from my...," he stopped.

"Who called you, Bryce?"

Bryce wiped sweat from his forehead. Ethan knew he needed a wet cloth, but was not willing to leave him alone yet. "I was married once, Ethan, and it ended badly. She called today."

Ethan couldn't imagine what could have been said to cause Bryce such pain. "Tell me about it, Bryce. I'm all ears."

Bryce looked into Ethan's kind eyes. "Ethan, I have wanted to tell you something about me for a long time, but didn't know how. The reason my marriage ended was because we never should have gotten married in the first place. I wasn't honest with her then, and I haven't been honest with you."

Ethan was hoping that Bryce's secret was that he was gay. "You can tell me anything, Bryce. I will always be your friend. We've known each other too long to let that go." Ethan was trying to keep Bryce talking. He knew what it was like to keep secrets.

Bryce was sweating more now and trying to unbutton his shirt, but his hands were shaking.

"Let me get you a cool cloth, Bryce. Are they in the bathroom?"

"Thanks," he said, and nodded.

"Promise me you will stay right here," Ethan said, and wiped his friend's forehead with his hand. Ethan walked down the hallway until he found a bathroom, found a cloth, and ran it under cool water.

Bryce was still struggling with the buttons on his shirt when Ethan returned. "Here you go," he said, and placed the cloth on Bryce's forehead. Then he gently took Bryce's trembling hands and laid them one on top of the other on his stomach. He unbuttoned a couple of buttons for his friend and placed the cool wet cloth on his neck. Bryce moved his hands to try to unbutton more of the buttons, but was trembling too much. "Here, buddy, let me do it."

Ethan unbuttoned Bryce's shirt and inched it out from inside his pants. He laid the two sides of the shirt on either side of Bryce's chest, and slid the wet cloth along his chest. Bryce had closed his eyes, and Ethan continued to slowly run the cloth along his chest. He watched as the nipples hardened and stood erect, begging to be kissed. Ethan looked at Bryce's chest with hungry eyes. The dark hair glistened from the wetness of the cloth, and the beauty of Bryce's chest was overpowering.

Ethan ran the cloth downward along the center of Bryce's chest, dipping it in and then across his navel, and on down until he reached the top of Bryce's pants. The line of hair that stretched from Bryce's chest to where it met the button of his pants and beyond was so sexy that Ethan thought he heard himself moan.

He looked up quickly and was relieved to see that Bryce's eyes were still closed. He glanced down at Bryce's crotch which was covered by thick corduroy material, and he wanted what he knew was hidden inside. This man was beautiful. Please tell me that you are gay, my good friend, he said to himself. "Is that better?"

Bryce nodded.

"Take your time, Bryce. You haven't done anything to me that can't be repaired. I can assure you that."

"Ethan, my marriage ended because I am not the kind of man she needed to be with," he said, and looked at Ethan, but only for a moment.

Ethan held Bryce's hand. "What kind of man did she need, Bryce?"

"A real man, or at least that is the way she said it."

"You *are* a real man, Bryce. You are a kind and caring man, and *that* is a real man," Ethan said, as he looked at his eyes that were open now.

"Thank you for that, Ethan. I needed to hear that today."

"It is only the truth, my good friend." Ethan rubbed Bryce's hand with long smooth strokes. He waited for Bryce to tell him more.

Bryce looked up at Ethan's eyes which were filled with concern. "Have you ever wondered why you have never seen me with a woman, Ethan?"

"No, I've never really thought anything of it. You don't see me with a woman either."

"I guess you're right," he said, managing a slight smile. "Ethan, I value your friendship more than I can say, more than I probably know myself. I need you in my life, Ethan. We've been through far too much to let that go."

Ethan leaned down to where he was only inches from Bryce's face. "Listen to me, Bryce. You mean more to me than you know. You are not going to lose me. Believe me, that is not in the cards."

Bryce carefully studied Ethan's face. Was he trying to tell me the same thing that I need to tell him? He wasn't sure what he was seeing in Ethan's face right now.

"Tell me what it is you need to say, Bryce."

He looked at Ethan. He was so close to him now. His lips were close enough that Bryce could almost taste them. He wanted to taste them. Ethan's hand on his naked chest felt better than he had imagined, and he had imagined Ethan's hands on his chest often. He smelled so good tonight. His cologne mixed with his natural man scent was more than a little sensual. It was sexual. Bryce looked at his hard nipples and then up at Ethan's lips, wishing they could meet.

Ethan did not miss the lowered eyes of his friend, and was wishing the same thing. Say the word, Bryce, say the word and my lips will be on every inch of you. Bryce moved his free hand up and picked up the cloth, tossing it aside. "Do you need that wetted again?" Ethan began to reach for the cloth, but Bryce stopped him, holding his hand.

"Ethan, I'm not sick, I'm not a pervert, I'm just not the man you think I am," he said in self defeat.

"Since when are you a mind reader? What kind of man do you think I think you are?"

"Well, buddy, how is this for you? I am gay. That's right, Ethan. I am a gay man. I am a man who loves men. I am a man who has sex with men instead of women, though I haven't had sex with either for a very long time."

Bryce's confession did not shock Ethan. If anything, it made him happy. Bryce was his friend. They knew each other intimately. If they were to become lovers, how great would that be? Friends first, lovers second, that was the way good relationships became great ones.

Bryce was watching for Ethan's reaction. He didn't see shock in his friend's eyes. That was a good sign. Ethan hadn't jumped up and headed for the door. That, too, was a good sign. But what was his long time friend really thinking? Bryce closed his eyes, anticipating some type of rejection.

Ethan looked at the kind doctor's face and wondered how he had ever gotten so lucky. Ethan did not use words in his response, not in his first response, that is. He lightly ran the tip of his tongue over his lips, and then lowered his lips to those he had longed to kiss for too long. He lightly touched Bryce's lips with his own, but not too lightly. He wanted Bryce to know that this kiss held the promise of the kisses of a lover. He slid his wetted lips over Bryce's and then kissed his cheek.

Bryce opened his eyes just as Ethan was rising up. "What was that?" Bryce asked.

Ethan laughed. "Has it been that long, my friend?"

"I guess that did sound a little odd. Ethan, are you like me?"

"Yes, my good friend, I am gay, if that is what is meant by 'like you'." He placed his hand flat on Bryce's naked chest and with one finger slid it along the line of hair that separated the two sides, stopping at the top of his pants. Bryce watched the finger all the way down. He was beginning to get aroused and was glad he had chosen to wear corduroys tonight. He didn't want Ethan to think…oh, he didn't know what he wanted Ethan to think or not think.

Ethan rested his hand on Bryce's stomach. "Bryce, you and I have been friends for a long time now and if you have even half the feelings for me that I have for you, we have something that is realized by very few in their lifetime. I think you would agree with that."

"Yes, I do agree, and I have loved you and wanted you for a long time, Ethan. I just didn't know." He closed his eyes, and then opened them.

Ethan kissed his friend's cheek. "Can you tell me what your wife said that upset you so today?" Ethan knew that it had to be something really big to upset him as much as it had. He was definitely "out of it" when he had arrived at his home tonight.

"Oh, I guess now it doesn't seem so bad, after this latest revelation."

Ethan just smiled at his friend, who was now much more than a friend. Bryce placed his hand over Ethan's. "Thank you, Ethan. Thank you for loving me."

Ethan kissed two fingers and then placed his fingers on Bryce's lips. "The rest is easy now, Ethan. My ex is remarrying and moving to Scotland, where her new husband is from. She lives in Chicago now." Bryce swallowed before continuing. Ethan was even more curious now. He couldn't imagine Bryce having any more secrets. He knew him too well.

"Remember, I'm not going anywhere. Tell me your secrets." Ethan tried to keep things light.

"Ethan, we were married for five years and it ended a year ago. I didn't know it at the time, but she was pregnant when we divorced. It's funny, you know, we had sex so infrequently that I didn't think it was possible."

Ethan thought that he had somehow skipped a chapter in a book, or a part of a movie at this point. "You didn't think what was possible, Bryce, sex with a woman?"

"No, not that. I was surprised that she was pregnant. I didn't know until she had the baby three months ago." He looked at Ethan whose eyebrows went up at this news.

Wow, I definitely was not expecting this, he said to himself.

"I guess my ex thinks it will be better if she starts new with her new husband."

Ethan couldn't hide the shock in his eyes. Bryce surely wasn't saying what Ethan thought he was saying. "You don't mean?"

"Yes, I do mean, Ethan. She does not want the baby."

Ethan was silent for a moment, thinking all this through. Was he sure the baby was his? He sure hoped that Bryce knew for sure. "I guess I don't know what to say, Bryce. Tell me the rest of the story."

"I haven't seen her yet, Ethan. She's three months old now, and I had planned to see her when and if Mary, my ex, was going to let me."

Ethan had decided to just come out with it. "Bryce, what is your ex planning to do with your daughter?"

Bryce just looked at Ethan. My daughter, he thought. I have a daughter. "She said if I don't want her, then she will put her up for adoption. She doesn't want her to be a part of her new life in Scotland."

Ethan closed his eyes for a second. How painful. He had no idea that his friend, his love, had a child, a daughter. Ethan smiled at him. He held Bryce's hand. "How can we bring your little girl home, Bryce?"

Bryce was touched by the "we" that Ethan had just used to describe the two of them. "I guess as soon as possible. Everything will be handled by her attorney, and the baby, I mean, my daughter, will be given to me then. I won't have to see my ex. She hates me. We didn't say much on the phone. The last thing she said today before hanging up was that it was my fault that she got pregnant. I had always thought that it takes two."

Ethan loved the thought of being part of the life of a little girl. He had just assumed that being a father wasn't in the cards for him. "I'm going to scoot you down now so that you are flat on the sofa and give you a neck massage, babe. I want you to close your eyes and relax, and listen to the sound of my voice."

Ethan laid Bryce flat on the sofa and placed his arms to his sides. He gently caressed Bryce's face with his thumbs, and with his fingers began to massage the back of Bryce's neck. He could see some of the stress begin to leave Bryce's face. Ethan did not speak for awhile, instead concentrating on relaxing his friend. He moved his fingers to the sides of Bryce's neck and began to massage the very tense muscles. This was not a deep massage. It was a gentle loving massage. He waited for about five minutes before talking again. When he did speak, his voice was soft, almost like a whisper. "Let your mind wander," he said.

Ethan began to massage Bryce's upper chest with his thumbs while continuing the neck massage with his fingers. He stopped speaking after each spoken thought for a few minutes, so that Bryce's mind could better absorb each one.

Bryce started to speak to counter what Ethan had said, but Ethan pressed a finger to his lips. "Not yet, Bryce. Relax, take slow deep breaths, and think about my words and concentrate on my fingers touching you."

Ethan placed a rolled pillow underneath Bryce's relaxed neck to prevent tensing, and moved his hands to Bryce's shoulders and upper arms. He loved doing this for the man he loved and the man who loved him. He also could not deny that he loved the feel of this man's skin underneath his fingers. He tried to concentrate on his thoughts and words, but could not stop looking at his friend's chest. His hands slid lovingly along Bryce's upper arms, gently rubbing the inner part of them with his thumbs. Bryce licked his lips, and Ethan fought hard his urge to kiss them.

"Your daughter can live with you right here, if you like. She will know you over time and will love you, just as I do. I will be with you all the way."

Bryce once again started to speak. "Shh, not yet, babe. Relax and think only about my words and feel only my touch."

The tenseness that Ethan felt return to Bryce's shoulders soon eased under Ethan's touch.

"I'm afraid," he said, and waited for Ethan's response.

Ethan caressed his friend's face, gently running his thumbs along Bryce's lips. "I know you are, Bryce. But it will all work out. You will see. If you give your daughter the chance to know her father, she will love him. That, I can promise you."

He once again lightly touched Bryce's lips with a finger and rested his hands on his friend's chest. He waited for Bryce to say something. The rise and fall of the chest under his hands was slow and steady, and Ethan knew that Bryce would be okay. Bryce licked his lips again, and Ethan fought hard not to kiss them. He needed Bryce to be ready for him first. Bryce opened his eyes and looked at Ethan's hands on his chest. He liked the way they looked there and for a brief time, pictured them lower on his body as Ethan made love to him, pleasuring him for the very first time as a lover.

Bryce looked up to see the kind caring eyes of the man he loved. Ethan smiled. "Thank you, Ethan," he said. He wanted Ethan's lips on his again, but had never been good at making the first move. He felt much more comfortable with animals than he did with people. But Ethan was his now. Ethan loved him.

Bryce closed his eyes again. He placed his hands over Ethan's hands. Bryce opened his eyes, and the two of them looked into each other's eyes for what seemed like hours, but was really only a few minutes. It was as if each was waiting for the other to do or say something.

Ethan has been so kind to me tonight, Bryce thought. He could have walked out on me the moment he saw me. I was so out of it when he first walked in the door. He didn't do that, and I just have to keep reminding myself of that.

Bryce looked directly into Ethan's eyes, and said in a whisper, "Kiss me."

Ethan leaned down and gently placed his lips on Bryce's. Bryce put his arms around Ethan, pulling him to him.

"Mm," Ethan sighed, and put his hands on Bryce's face and kissed him passionately.

They didn't need air. All they needed at this moment was each other. Bryce held Ethan to him, and Ethan devoured him. His hands were in Bryce's hair, on his face, and on his side. Bryce held Ethan firmly with one hand, and with the other hand he pulled at the buttons on Ethan's shirt. Ethan stripped his shirt off and climbed onto the sofa, his legs on either side of Bryce. He pressed his chest to Bryce's and kissed him hard, with a passion that surprised him. Bryce tried to lick his lips, but Ethan caught his tongue and pulled it into his mouth. He held it inside his mouth, never allowing his lips to leave those of his lover. He slid a hand underneath him and onto Bryce's chest. He found the nipple that was waiting for him. He wanted to hold it in his mouth and let his tongue slide across it. He felt Bryce's hardness underneath his own, and he wanted to bring his new lover to a full and complete orgasm. He wanted Bryce to call out his name. He had wanted Bryce for a long time, but the passion he was feeling now was stronger than he had ever known.

Ethan lay on his side as he continued to kiss Bryce, and he slid his fingers just inside the waistband of Bryce's pants. Bryce moaned and tried to speak. Overcome with desire, Ethan was almost unable to stop long enough to hear Bryce's words. He kissed the top of Bryce's shoulder. "What is it, babe?" "I don't...I'm so new to..." Ethan stilled him with a finger to his lips.

Realizing his friend's uneasiness, Ethan struggled to control his own passion for even a few seconds. "Take me to your bed, Bryce. Let me love you tonight."

Ethan helped his friend sit up, remembering his earlier weakness. "Okay?" Ethan asked.

Bryce nodded, and held out his hands for Ethan to hold. Ethan helped him up and held him close, his mouth unable to resist his friend's parted lips. He kissed him quickly, and then walked beside him, their arms around each other, as Bryce led Ethan down the long hallway to his bedroom.

It was dark now, with the only light being the little sliver that could force its way through the nearly closed door that Bryce had pulled after they had entered. He pulled back the covers and when he looked up, Ethan was naked. In the darkness of the room, Bryce could see the silhouette of the man who had declared his love for him, his erection full. He was beautiful, and he had come to his bed with desire and passion in his eyes.

Ethan climbed into bed and covered himself to his waist. He moved to the middle of the bed while Bryce continued to stare. Ethan patted the bed and said, "Join me."

Bryce sat on the edge of the bed, his back to Ethan. He slowly undid his pants and eased them down over his very prominent erection and onto the floor. He sat for a moment, almost afraid to turn and face his lover.

Ethan leaned up on his knees behind his lover. He kissed his neck and slid his hands downward along Bryce's chest. His hands brushed along the back of Bryce's erection, and Bryce gasped a short startled gasp that also indicated that the feeling was one that he found arousing.

Ethan caressed Bryce's chest and kissed his neck up to his earlobe which he held between his lips. "I love you. I have so much love for you. Lie down next to me, Bryce, and let me love you."

Bryce closed his eyes. He shifted back on the bed and lay on his back. He covered his manhood, but drew Ethan to him. Ethan kissed his slightly quivering lips. Bryce kissed him. His body ached for Ethan.

"Love me, Ethan."

Ethan kissed him deeply and passionately. Then he kissed Bryce's neck and chest. He caressed his arms while he played with Bryce's nipples with his warm wet tongue. He sucked in one and then the other, nibbling them just enough to cause Bryce to thrust his chest upward in eager anticipation of the next nip.

Ethan's hands went lower, and then down along the side of Bryce's hips and underneath to the round firmness of his gorgeous butt. He uncovered Bryce and caressed the innermost part of his thighs. He held his lover's hand and kissed his fingers. He looked at his large full balls and the fullness of his erection just begging for his kiss. He looked at Bryce who was watching him. "You are a beautiful man, Bryce. I love you so much."

Bryce relaxed and closed his eyes, opening his legs to Ethan's exploration. Ethan held his lover's full balls up with his hand and leaned down, giving them a gentle kiss. Bryce gasped, and Ethan watched as the first drop of cum eagerly made its debut at the very top of Bryce's cock. Bryce closed his eyes and let Ethan make love to him.

Ethan licked two fingers and stroked that silky smooth area beneath Bryce's heavy cum filled balls. He let his fingers go just low enough to feel the area of gentle separation of the two perfect halves of Bryce's perfect butt.

He looked at Bryce's face. His lips were parted, his breathing steady, as he gave himself to Ethan. Ethan held the two halves of Bryce's butt apart with one finger, and leaned down until his mouth was over Bryce's balls. He exhaled, and the warmth of his breath on Bryce's balls caused a moan to escape his lover's lips.

Ethan straddled Bryce's left leg, his full erection resting on Bryce's muscular thigh, as he lifted one of Bryce's balls onto his tongue and gently pulled it into his mouth. Bryce breathed in and then forced an exhalation. Ethan gave the same loving attention to his lover's other ball. He moved to Bryce's side once again and held both balls in one hand, stroking Bryce's chest with the other hand.

Ethan's erect penis was pressed against Bryce's left buttock. He wanted Bryce to know how very great his arousal was just from being with him. Ethan laid his tongue flat at the base of Bryce's erection and slid it slowly to the top. He slid the very tip of his tongue along the little slit at the very top of the spongy head of his lover's cock and claimed the eager drops that were waiting for him. Just as one was claimed, another made its debut. An endless supply waited to be the chosen ones as Ethan licked the yummy drops from the head of his lover's manliness.

Bryce opened his legs more, begging for Ethan's touch. Ethan looked at Bryce's face, so lost in the pleasure his body was receiving from its lover. Ethan sucked on the head of Bryce's penis, a deep purple it now was, and held it in his mouth. "Ethan," Bryce managed to say.

"Mm," was Ethan's reply. Ethan knew how good it felt. It had been a long time for Ethan, too, but he did remember.

He gently squeezed Bryce's heavy balls as he slowly took his lover's hard heavy cock into his mouth. He held Bryce's butt and lifted it upward, bringing his cock into and then back out of his mouth. Bryce's legs were off the bed now as he thrust upward to give Ethan all of him. Ethan molded Bryce's ass with his hands and thought of how he would love to have his own throbbing penis between the two halves of his lover's beautiful butt. Bryce began to push harder and faster, and Ethan tightened his mouth around Bryce's hardness.

"Ethan, stop. I can't hold it in much longer."

Ethan was determined to bring his lover to the explosive orgasmic release that he deserved, and replied with only, "Mm."

"Ohh, Ethan."

Ethan sucked hard on Bryce's cock after hearing his name called out so passionately.

Bryce ran his hands through Ethan's hair, and warned again of his very near climax, this time with more urgency. "Ethan, I mean it. I can't..."

Bryce came with such force and emptied more than what Ethan had expected, that they both jerked a little.

Ethan savored his lover's load, and was not going to stop until the fullness had completely gone from his lover's balls.

Bryce's legs were on the bed again, and Ethan gently licked his now sensitive penis as it became soft once again. He kissed Bryce's navel and looked up at him.

"Oh, Ethan. I had no idea."

"I know, baby."

Bryce took Ethan's very hard cock into his hand and then let it slowly slide back out. Ethan lay on his back and opened his legs, welcoming Bryce's exploring hand. He kissed Ethan's nipples and licked them, feeling their hardness on his tongue. "I might not be as good..."

Ethan pulled Bryce's head up and held his face with his hands. "There is no good or bad here, Bryce. We are making love to each other."

Bryce still could not believe his luck in having a man such as Ethan. He wanted him in so many ways. He kissed the top of his penis and Ethan could not believe how arousing that would be. "Ohhh," he moaned.

Bryce felt more confident in his skills as a lover with Ethan's moan of obvious pleasure. It had been awhile for Bryce, but not *that* long. Bryce wanted his mouth on every part of Ethan. He had admired him and longed for him, his body so close to him so many times. He put his hands underneath Ethan's ass and caressed it, sliding his fingertips along that erotic place where the two halves parted. Ethan begged for Bryce's touch, and encouraged him with his movements. "Oh, Bryce, I've waited for so long."

Bryce pulled Ethan's balls one at a time into his mouth, squeezing them with just the right amount of pressure to make Ethan call out his name. "Oh, oh, baby, kiss me," Ethan begged. Bryce moved up and kissed his mouth with deep passionate kisses, and Ethan groaned when their lips parted.

Bryce couldn't wait any longer. He had to taste what he had desired for two years now. He slid his mouth over Ethan's cock head and let it slide along his tongue as it went in all the way. "Oh, man, Bryce. I'm going to explode." Bryce slowed his pace and Ethan groaned. He wanted to know the climax that he knew was well on its way, but he didn't want Bryce to stop touching his body. Bryce knew Ethan was close already, and that his body was aching for release.

After several slow strokes, Bryce quickened his pace, and with his mouth he formed a tight hold on his lover's aching hardness.

Ethan's moans were loud now as he called out Bryce's name. "This is it, baby. Right now."

Bryce had no idea how good this would be, taking in his lover's seed and taking in the manly aroma of his lover's scent.

Ethan moaned and writhed until he had been drained by his lover of the very last of his release.

Bryce moved up and lay on Ethan's spent body. He held Ethan, and Ethan held him. They lay together until they were almost asleep.

"Bryce, you know I don't want to leave, but I hired a sitter for the dogs because I didn't want to leave Princess alone yet."

Bryce looked at him. "I forgot, Ethan. I forgot everything for awhile," he said, with a slight chuckle.

"Come out to the farm tonight, Bryce. The dogs love you, and we weren't exactly finished with our discussion. We just couldn't keep our hands off of each other." "And our bodies," added Bryce.

"I'll be okay here. I can come out tomorrow," Bryce assured him.

Ethan looked into his lover's eyes. He didn't think that Bryce should be alone tonight. He had been through quite a shock, and Ethan didn't want him to get himself all worked up over things that were definitely solvable. Ethan stroked his back. "You know you want to sleep naked with me tonight. You can have me again. You can have me all night long." Ethan's seduction was working.

"You know I'll be hard again very soon if you keep talking like that," Bryce said.

"Mm," Ethan moaned and licked his lips.

"Okay. You talked me into it. I'll pack some things, and drive behind you."

Bryce got up off the bed and bent over to put his pants on. Ethan reached over and slid a finger lightly all the way up Bryce's crack that was too enticing to pass up.

"Hey," Bryce admonished, and pulled his pants on.

"I couldn't resist. I thought you were offering."

Ethan smiled that sweet smile of his, and Bryce knew that he would want his lover again very soon.

Bryce packed a bag while Ethan picked up his own clothes from where he had stripped his body of them, piece by piece, and helped Bryce lock up his house. "Ready to go?" he asked, and in the light of the living room they looked different to each other, more connected, like a couple, a couple in love. Bryce looked at Ethan, and all doubt was gone from his mind. He knew he loved Ethan, and he now knew without a doubt that Ethan loved him. He nodded, and then followed Ethan in his car out to the sweet country home that he loved.

Three
Chicago and Back

As Bryce parked his car at the farm, he realized that this was where he felt most alive, here in this house with Ethan. He followed Ethan inside and was greeted by Princess and Hawker with barks and begs for kisses. He dropped his bag and sat on the floor of the kitchen and let the dogs jump on him all they wanted. Ethan thanked the "babysitter" and watched as she pulled out of the drive. Then he turned the outside light off and took Ethan's bag into his bedroom.

He returned to the kitchen and joined Bryce on the floor. "Well, it looks like you have the seal of approval," he said, and winked at Bryce.

"I have asked myself many times why I have never had pets, but I'm just not home enough. I wouldn't feel good about leaving such a sweet thing like these little guys at home alone."

After the dogs had given Bryce the official welcome, they had worn themselves out, and lay down in the living room.

"Come on in, Bryce. It's Saturday night. Let's have some wine."

Ethan brought the wine and poured them each a glass.

"Mm, just the thing I needed," Bryce agreed, and helped himself to a second glass. "So, tell me more about this little girl of yours."

Bryce turned toward Ethan on the sofa and Ethan set down his glass to give him his full attention. "Her name is Rose. That's all I know. I haven't seen her. I know nothing about raising a daughter, Ethan."

Ethan waited to speak until he was sure that Bryce had finished each thought. "You know, Bryce, I don't think there is a man or woman in the world who really knew how to raise kids before they actually raised one. You learn as you go. Now, what do we need to do to bring her to this wonderful place we call home?" Ethan took Bryce's hands in his. "I'll bet you knew nothing about caring for sick animals before you went to vet school, and didn't really know how until you actually cared for the animals. Caring for a child and raising a child is a process, Bryce. It grows and changes throughout a lifetime. You can do this. We can do this."

Bryce looked down. The wine was beginning to take effect. "Can we do this tomorrow," Bryce said, beginning to slur his words.

"Sure. Let's go to bed."

Bryce was tired, and fell asleep almost immediately after snuggling into Ethan's cozy bed.

Ethan snuggled up next to him and put his arm around him. "I love you," he said, and fell asleep holding the man he loved.

Ethan awoke to the sound of his usual alarm clock. Hawker and Princess jumped on the bed and playfully pulled the covers off of Ethan and Bryce. This woke Bryce and as he tried to pull the covers back up, Princess held them firmly in her mouth and growled. She loved this game. Ethan laughed at the sight.

Once Bryce was fully awake, he looked at the sweet dog. "What a way to wake up."

"I don't ever have to worry about being late, for anything," Ethan said, and continued to play with his two babies. "Guess I should let them out. They won't let me get back to sleep."

Bryce lay back on the bed.

Ethan got up and let the dogs out. They loved the morning, and raced each other to the fence. Ethan started the coffee and lay back down beside Bryce.

"No wonder those dogs are so fit. They get plenty of exercise."

"They sure do, Bryce. We all do out here."

Sunday was the one day of the week that Ethan took it easy. He was happy to let some of the kids from the college do the chores, and they needed the money as well as the experience.

Ethan got up again, poured two cups of coffee, and brought them back to bed. "Breakfast in bed?" Bryce teased.

"Anything for you, darlin'," Ethan teased back. "So, tell me, Bryce, when do you get your Rose?"

Bryce smiled. "I like the way you say it. I'm not sure. I guess I should call my ex. Oh, no, you don't think she's already gone and left little Rose who knows where?"

"No, Bryce, I don't. Let's not let our imaginations get the best of us. Call her from here. You'll feel better."

Bryce kissed Ethan on the cheek. "Thanks."

Bryce went to the kitchen and called his ex from Ethan's phone. It rang several times before Bryce heard a man's voice on the other end.

"Yeah," he said.

"Is Mary around? This is Bryce."

There was silence on the other end, and then he heard his ex-wife's voice. "We're on our way out, Bryce. What do you want?"

"I want my daughter."

Ethan stayed in bed, but could hear everything that Bryce had said.

"Mary, I will pick Rose up tomorrow at your attorney's office in downtown Chicago. Name the time."

Bryce could barely hear as his ex-wife spoke to her fiancée with her hand over the mouthpiece.

"Whatever, Bryce. I don't care."

"I'll call you back with the time of my flight," Bryce said, ending the conversation.

Bryce hung up the phone and returned to Ethan. He looked worried, and Ethan was not at all surprised, given what he had just heard. "I have to go to Chicago, Ethan. I won't feel good about this until my baby is here with me. I just don't trust my ex."

"Okay, okay. Let's work on getting a flight."

"You mean you'll come with me?"

"You bet, that is, if you want me to. I can get one of the students to watch the dogs."

Bryce picked up his coffee, but his hands were shaking.

Ethan took the cup from him and set it down. "Take it easy, buddy. We can do this."

Bryce lay down on the bed and closed his eyes.

"Let's look on-line," Ethan offered, and opened his laptop.

They would have to drive to Kansas City and fly out from there. "There's a flight out of K.C. later today that would put us in Chicago around eight or nine tonight. That looks like the best option, Bryce." Ethan knew that the longer they waited, the more anxious and upset Bryce would become. Getting him to Chicago as quickly as possible would be the best thing for him.

"Let's do it, Ethan. Can you get someone to watch Hawker and Princess?"

"Oh, sure, no problem." Ethan made a call and then packed his bag.

As soon as the student arrived to take care of his dogs, Ethan and Bryce drove into Manhattan and packed a bag for Bryce.

They pulled into the parking lot of Kansas City International Airport with only thirty minutes to spare. "I had no idea the traffic on I-70 would be so bad. We'll have to hurry, Ethan."

"We'll make it," Ethan replied, but wasn't too sure.

They practically ran through the airport to the terminal. The passengers were just beginning to board the plane when Ethan and Bryce walked up.

"Hey, no waiting," Ethan said, thankful that they had made it. "Shouldn't take long now," he said, as they took their seats.

The traffic through the city had been heavy, and Ethan was tired. He sat down in his seat and leaned back. He never would have dreamed that his Saturday night would have ended up with great sex, a friend becoming a lover, and now a trip to Chicago. What a weekend!

They arrived in Chicago a few minutes after eight in the evening. "We're here," Ethan announced. Bryce looked at him and smiled.

While they were waiting for their bags, Ethan remembered that they had made no plans for tonight. He laughed, and Bryce looked at him.

"What?"

"We have no place to go. We didn't make any hotel reservations."

"Oh, man," Bryce said, laughing with Ethan.

"Well, there must be something in this city."

They picked up their bags and hailed a cab. Neither of them got away from their jobs very often, so they decided to splurge and stay in one of the more expensive hotels along Chicago's well known Magnificent Mile. They booked a room high enough to have a good view, and walked into a beautiful suite. "Looks like a honeymoon suite," Ethan said, as he looked out the window.

Bryce walked up behind him and put his arms around him. "Sure does." He kissed Ethan on the neck, and Ethan felt his body tingle. He turned around and kissed his long time friend and now lover, holding his body close to his.

"Thank you for coming here with me, Ethan. I don't think I could do this alone."

"You will never be alone again, if I have anything to say about it," Ethan promised. They held each other where they stood, in front of the window.

After several minutes had gone by, Ethan whispered in Bryce's ear. "Let's take a shower, and go to bed."

Bryce said nothing, but took Ethan's hand and followed him to the bedroom. Ethan started the shower, and then returned to where Bryce was undressing. Bryce's back was to Ethan, and Ethan stood still.

Ethan waited until Bryce was down to his shorts, and then he walked over to him and stood in front of him. He took both of his hands in his. "You're a beautiful man, Dr. Holing. I've loved you for a very long time."

Bryce looked surprised. "You have? I didn't know, Ethan."

"I didn't know it myself fully, until yesterday."

"I suddenly feel very naked," Bryce admitted, looking at Ethan fully clothed.

"I can take care of that," Ethan said, and undressed down to his shorts. "Your shower awaits," Ethan said to Bryce, and took his hand and led him to the steaming water.

Ethan opened the shower door, and led Bryce inside. They could barely see each other through the thick steam, but they could definitely feel each other. They looked at the wet shorts that clung to their bodies. They reached for the other's shorts and pulled them down and off. "Ethan," Bryce said, as he reached up and held his face in his hands. He kissed Ethan, tasting his lips and the water between them. Ethan held him and kissed him, his body wanting this man who had been his close friend for so long.

Bryce slid his hands down along Ethan's back until they rested on his butt. He waited to see if Ethan would pull away, but Ethan pulled him closer and kissed him deeper. Ethan draped his leg around Bryce's leg, and planted his hands firmly on his ass. Through the steam and the water, Bryce forced his mouth off of Ethan's just long enough to say,

"So many years…"

Ethan knew. "It's just the beginning."

Ethan's words made Bryce want him even more. His mouth found Ethan's again, and he held Ethan's mouth while he searched for his tongue. Ethan welcomed Bryce's hunger and the warm tightness of his mouth as it pulled his tongue all the way inside and then let it out just a little before pulling it back in again. Their hands were in each other's hair, on each other's face, and their lips parted only enough to allow a breath.

Each looked at the other through the steam. They touched each other's chest, stroking the hair made wet by the pulsating jets of the shower. Bryce rested his hands on Ethan's back and touched the erect nipple with the tip of his tongue. Ethan arched his back, forcing his nipple into his lover's mouth.

Even in the warm water, Ethan felt a shiver up and down his body when Bryce's lips met his nipples. "Ohhh," Ethan moaned, and offered his other nipple to Bryce. He leaned back and put his hands behind his head. "Oh, Bryce."

Their cocks were hard and were hitting each other's body wherever they could, but neither of them minded. They hadn't even noticed until their desire for each other became stronger than the rest of their bodies could satisfy. Ethan reached for Bryce's cock just as Bryce reached for Ethan's.

Bryce looked at Ethan through the steam of the shower. "I need you, Ethan," he said, and Ethan opened the shower door and the two of them made their way to the bed, rolling on top of each other, Ethan on top of Bryce as he kissed him passionately, thrusting his cock upward against Bryce's body, and then Bryce on Ethan's body, their lips never leaving the other's, their cocks ready for the other's love.

Ethan forced his mouth off of Bryce's, and moved down to take his cock into his mouth. He opened Bryce's legs as he devoured his cock. Bryce opened his legs for Ethan, and Ethan stroked the smooth area beneath his lover's full heavy balls that were eager to surrender their contents to Ethan, and Bryce moaned, a loud, "Ohhh," and an even louder, "Uhh," gasping sound.

Bryce lifted his bent legs, urging Ethan enter him with his probing fingers. "Ethan," he moaned, when the first finger entered him. "Oh, Ethan," he almost screamed, when the second one joined the first finger and found his inner pleasure.

Bryce pulled Ethan's leg over his head and grabbed his cock, pulling it down to his lips. Ethan lowered himself for his lover and welcomed the warm wetness of Bryce's mouth. Ethan stopped for a second as the sensation his lover was giving him took all of his concentration. He moaned, and with Bryce's cock down his throat, it caused a vibrating sensation. Bryce squeezed Ethan's balls, and the tips of his fingers slid along the crevice between the half moons of his ass.

Ethan and Bryce were both stilled by the intensity of the sensations. "Mmm," and "Ohh," were all that was heard in the hotel suite.

Bryce entered Ethan with a finger, searching for the place that Ethan had so readily found hidden deep inside of him, and Ethan's body spasmed. "Bryce, I can't hold on, buddy," he said, and Bryce sucked harder on Ethan's hardness. Ethan sucked Bryce just as hard, and stroked him deep inside with long smooth strokes, as they both neared climax. Bryce thrust hard against Ethan's hold on his cock, and pulled even harder on Ethan's cock with his mouth. Within seconds, they both climaxed. They continued to make love to each other's cocks until they were soft and sensitive and exhausted.

Ethan rested for less than a minute, and then moved up and lay on his lover, wrapping his arms around his chest, and his legs around his legs. He kissed Bryce on his shoulder, and said, "I love you, Bryce, and I always will."

Bryce kissed the top of Ethan's ear. "I will always love you, Ethan," he said.

They realized they had fallen asleep when they awoke in the night and Ethan was still lying on Bryce's warm body. "What time is it?" Bryce was worried that they may have overslept. Ethan looked over at the clock on the nightstand.

"It's 3:00 a.m.," Ethan told him. "Let me scoot off of you so we can get some sleep."

"Don't go too far," Bryce teased, with a pat on Ethan's butt.

Ethan moved over and the two of them got underneath the covers, and snuggled. They were asleep again within minutes.

The alarm sounded at 8:00 a.m. Bryce turned it off, and then woke Ethan. "Better get up, buddy. Got an hour before our appointment."

Ethan rolled over and snuggled up next to Bryce. He looked up at him and then licked his left nipple. "Mm, I wish we had time for that, but we really don't."

Ethan started laughing.

"What's so funny?" Bryce asked.

"Remember that shower we took last night?" Bryce smiled. "Yes?"

"I just remembered that we didn't use soap. We didn't really take a shower."

Bryce laughed with him, and then they realized that they really did need to get going. Bryce scooted out from underneath Ethan, but not before Ethan got the chance to run his hand over Bryce's morning erection.

Bryce winked at Ethan, and walked into the bathroom to start the shower. Ethan watched him as he walked away, and he more than liked what he saw. Bryce and Ethan were no longer in their twenties. Their bodies had seen more than a few years. But for a man nearing middle age, Bryce's body was just right, in Ethan's eyes. He loved the two supple halves of his butt, and the toned enough, but not too toned, body of a real down-to-earth man. He loved everything about Bryce. He loved Bryce.

Ethan waited until he heard the water running, and then he quietly walked into the bathroom. He opened the shower door and shocked the hell out of Bryce who had closed his eyes. He didn't notice Ethan until he felt his lips on the spongy head of his very erect cock. Bryce gasped with surprise. Ethan was watching for Bryce's reaction.

"Oh, shit, Ethan," he said, and held onto Ethan's hair.

Ethan looked at him devilishly. He opened his mouth, and said, "Feed me."

"You asked for it, babe," he warned. Bryce moved closer to Ethan, and Ethan wrapped his arms around his thighs, and waited to be fed. Bryce watched as his cock disappeared inside his lover's mouth.

Ethan devoured what he called his "morning glory", and then pushed it back out with his tongue until the spongy head was resting firmly between his lips. He sucked the head for awhile, and then pulled the hard rod back inside, forcing Bryce to hold onto Ethan's hair, as he moaned. "Oh, Ethan. Damn, I'm close. Watching this is too much." He tried to look up, but couldn't stop watching. He had dreamed of Ethan for years, and now here he was, just like in his dreams.

"Ethan, it's now," he barely got out before his balls unloaded. He held even tighter to Ethan now, steadying himself with his morning explosion. "Oh, man, what a way to start the day," he said.

Ethan stood up. Bryce kissed him. "Can I return the favor?" Ethan took Bryce's hand and wrapped it around his cock. "Too late," he said. He held onto Bryce, and after just a few quick pumps, Ethan unloaded more than he thought he had stored up overnight. "Ohh," he moaned, and leaned against Bryce.

"Wow, Ethan, what caused all this?"

"Watching your sweet ass as it left my bed."

He looked up at Bryce. "I've got it bad, buddy."

They took turns soaping each other and rinsing each other, and then they towel dried each other. "Think we can dress ourselves?"

"I don't know, Ethan. I may need your help."

After they had dressed, they had just enough time to grab a very quick breakfast before they had to catch a cab.

Waiting in the attorney's office for the attorney and the social worker to show up, Bryce couldn't stop fidgeting.

Ethan put his hand on Bryce's leg. "It's okay. You're driving yourself crazy there."

"I know, I know." He looked around the room. "Oh, no, Ethan."

"What?"

"We don't have anything for a baby, no car seat, no diapers, nothing."

"I'm sure she will have some with her, Bryce. We'll stock up once we get back home."

Just then, the door to the office opened, and the attorney and the social worker walked into the room. "Bryce, I'm Ken Madden, and this is Janine Walker. They shook hands, and Janine sat down next to Bryce.

"This is Rose," she said, and began to hand the baby to Bryce.

"I'm not used to…"

"Don't worry," she interrupted. "Just support her head. That's it."

Bryce looked down at the tiny little creature, and then he looked at Ethan. Ethan had to blink to keep from crying. He loved babies, animal babies, human babies, it didn't matter.

"She's beautiful, Bryce."

Bryce looked up. "You think?"

"Yes, I do," he said.

Mr. Madden was finishing the paperwork, and Janine continued to talk to Bryce and Ethan. "I've got a bag here filled with diapers, formula, and everything else I thought you might need." She handed Ethan a small notebook. "I wrote down some of my own little tips that might help. I've raised two daughters, and now they're in college, so I must have done something right." She laughed a little, and Bryce seemed to calm down a little.

"Thank you," Ethan said, and took the notebook from her.

The attorney looked up and spoke to Bryce. "Okay, Bryce. I've got several forms for you to sign, standard documents, not nearly as many since you are the biological father."

Janine took the baby from Bryce.

Ethan patted Bryce on the back, and walked out with Janine.

Janine sat down next to Ethan, and handed him the baby. "Would you like to hold her?"

"Oh, absolutely." Ethan couldn't wait to hold this sweet little girl.

"You're a natural," she said.

Ethan was pretty sure the lady knew that he and Bryce were "together", but she didn't say anything or even hint that she thought they were. "Have you done this before, Ethan?" she asked. "You seem much more comfortable than the new moms and dads that I've known."

Ethan held Rose close to his body. "Well, I have two dogs that I consider my babies. They have their own human bed."

Janine laughed at Ethan's remark. "Well, it makes me happy knowing that this little girl is going to a home with as much love as yours. Do you have any questions, Ethan?"

"I'm sure I do. I just don't know what they are."

"Well, in the front cover of that notebook I have written my home telephone number and my work number. Call me anytime."

"Thank you."

Ethan continued to hold Rose while they talked. When the little girl opened her eyes and looked at Ethan, she started to cry. Ethan stood up and walked around the room, talking quietly to her. She calmed down almost immediately.

Janine handed him a bottle. "I think she's hungry. I've packed several readymade bottles for you."

Ethan sat back down, and Janine showed him how to feed Rose. "There you go," she said.

Ethan couldn't believe his own feelings for this sweet little girl. "She's looking at me."

"Yes, she is. She's watching every move you make."

The little hands were around the top of the bottle, and she made little noises while she sucked on the nipple. "How much do we feed her?"

"As much as she wants, honey. She'll let you know when she's full."

A few seconds later, little Rose pushed the nipple out with her tongue. "You're right. Guess she's done."

Janine smiled. Then she showed Ethan how to burp the baby.

"Wow, she's a natural," he said.

"In a few more months, she will be burping on her own."

Ethan stood up, and held Rose with her head over his shoulder. Then he began to sway back and forth. "Perfect. You know the 'baby sway'." Ethan just laughed, loving the compliments, and loving this little girl.

Bryce walked out of the attorney's office and watched Ethan holding his baby. He had never wanted Ethan more than at that moment. He had never looked sexier than he did right now rocking his baby, looking at her, and humming as he swayed. "Ready to go?" Bryce asked in almost a whisper. Ethan nodded.

Janine walked out with them. "I'm your personal chauffer back to the hotel," she announced. "I have a car seat and some gifts for Rose. Don't open them until you get home now."

Bryce was surprised that this lady they had just met had gifts for them. She helped them carry the things up to their room. "Well, I'll be leaving you now," she said, outside the door of their room. They thanked her, and she told them again to call whenever they needed to.

Bryce carried the things inside the room. He kissed Ethan on the cheek. "I'm so glad you're here. You know what to do."

"Oh, Bryce, it's nothing. Just love her. That's all she needs."

Ethan very gently gave the sleeping Rose to Bryce. She started to wake up, but quickly went back to sleep when Bryce held her close to him the way Ethan had.

"See, you're a great dad already," Ethan told him.

"She's a sweetie, isn't she?"

"She's beautiful, Bryce, just beautiful. Princess and Hawker will go nuts. We won't be able to get near her, they'll be so protective of her."

Bryce took a deep breath and let it out. "Just gotta take it as it comes, moment to moment."

Ethan knew exactly what to say to make Bryce feel better.

"What would I do without you, Ethan?"

"I don't know, and you will never know either, because I am here to stay, my man."

"Your man, I like that."

"Well, Bryce, as much as I would love to stay here, we have a plane to catch."

"Oh, my, we're not late, are we?"

"Not yet, but we will be if we don't get going."

Fortunately, the plane trip back was a smooth one, and Rose slept the entire time. Bryce and Ethan took turns sitting in the backseat with her while the other one drove, so that Rose wouldn't be alone.

"I hate that she has to be in this car seat, Ethan."

"I know, buddy, but it's the safest way. We'll be home in no time."

When they exited Interstate 70, Bryce asked, "You want me to take over the driving?"

"No, no, we're about there."

Bryce had hoped to be living at Ethan's now, permanently. He didn't want to go to his house alone. He wanted them to be a family now, the three of them.

Ethan tapped the back of his seat lightly. "Where are you, Bryce?"

"Oh, what?" He had been so lost in his own little world that he hadn't heard a word Ethan had said.

"I asked if you had remembered what we talked about, you know, the three of us on the farm. You haven't changed your mind, have you?"

Bryce didn't remember having had that conversation. "Oh, never, Ethan. I love the farm. Why do you think I kept coming out even when I really had no reason?" Ethan smiled, and Bryce was relieved. He had waited too long for Ethan to let him go now.

Four
Home

It was almost dark when they were finally home at Ethan's farm. He turned around and said, "Welcome home, little girl." Bryce picked her up and walked with Ethan into the house. Princess and Hawker barked and ran toward them, and Rose began to wail.

"Oh, my," Ethan said.

"Come on, guys, let's go outside."

Ethan took the dogs outside, and Bryce showed off his prize to the dog-sitter who was getting ready to leave. "Oh, she's cute, Bryce. I'll baby-sit anytime."

"Thanks, Molly."

"Well, gotta go," she said, and walked out the door.

Bryce had calmed Rose, and was rocking her when Ethan came back inside. He stood in the doorway and looked at Bryce. "You've never looked sexier."

"You can't be serious. I'm covered in spit-up."

Ethan walked over and kissed him on the lips. "I'm serious."

"Ethan, you don't need to make Hawker and Princess stay outside. That's not fair."

"Molly is throwing their ball with them. That way they'll be calmer when they come back in. Rose will get used to them. Before long, they will be her biggest fans, and best protectors."

Ethan put everything away, and made a list of what he thought a baby might need.

"Well, guys, I think these fellas want to meet Rose now."

"Okay, Molly, thanks again."

Ethan spoke very softly to Hawker and Princess, and they followed him into the living room. "They're just curious, Bryce. Once they see her and pick up her scent, they will love and protect her."

Bryce knew it was true. After all, he was a veterinarian. But still, when it came to his own little girl, he was a little reluctant to share her.

Ethan whispered to the dogs. "This is Rose. She's a baby, like you two, but she's a human baby."

They sniffed her arm, and didn't bark.

"Ethan, how did you know?"

"Oh, I have a couple of nieces. It's been awhile since I've seen them, though, but I remember when they were babies."

Hawker and Princess soon lost interest in the new arrival, and played together in the house, but were unusually quiet, and Ethan rewarded them with treats. "Good babies," he said. They sniffed Rose once again, and then exhausted from all the excitement, they fell asleep together in their favorite chair.

"I guess they just don't want to be excluded."

"That's right, Bryce. Their family has gotten bigger and better, and so has mine." Ethan winked at Bryce.

"It's late, buddy. You hungry?"

"I didn't think I was, Ethan, until just now when you mentioned it. I'm starved."

Ethan made some roast beef sandwiches and soup, and they took turns holding the sleeping Rose while they ate.

"I just can't put her down, Ethan."

"I know, Bryce. It's hard to have her even a few inches away."

Ethan took their things into his bedroom. "Oh, my gosh," he said, when he walked into the room.

"What is it, Ethan?"

Bryce walked into the room with his sleeping daughter in his arms. There was a beautiful crib by the bed with a bow and a card. Ethan opened the card. "Congratulations, it's a girl. All the best."

"It's from our friends at the College of Veterinary Medicine," Ethan read.

"Oh, how nice, Ethan."

"It's a beautiful crib, Bryce, with all the latest bells and whistles."

"You know I'm going to have it right beside the bed," Bryce warned.

"You'd better, or I'll have her in bed next to me," Ethan warned back. They both knew how much the little girl would be loved.

Bryce laid Rose down in the crib and covered her with one of the new blankets that they had unwrapped. "I can't believe so many gifts were sent, from so many people."

"Well, you are well loved, Bryce."

"You've always been the one whose love I've craved, Ethan. Why didn't I have the guts to tell you sooner?"

Ethan put his arms around Bryce. "We've got forever, Bryce. Think of it this way. We had a lot of years to be friends and get to know each other before we became lovers. Those were not wasted years."

He looked at Ethan. "I don't deserve you," he said.

"I know it," Ethan teased.

Bryce pulled his mouth to his. "It's been a long day," he whispered.

"I think so, too," Ethan whispered back.

"What should we do about it?"

"This," Bryce responded, kissing Ethan, holding him, then running his hands down Ethan's back.

Bryce continued to kiss Ethan passionately as he unzipped Ethan's jeans and forced them to the floor. Ethan held him while he undressed him. When Ethan's clothes had all been removed, Bryce pushed him toward the bed. "Wait for me," he said, and Ethan watched as Bryce's own clothes fell to the floor. Then he climbed onto the bed with Ethan, pressing his body against Ethan's. "Ohh," Ethan moaned.

They were more than ready for each other once again. "I love you, Ethan." Bryce's lips were on Ethan's, not giving him a chance to respond. "I want you tonight, Ethan." "Mmm," Ethan responded. They both wanted each other tonight, even more than they had before. Bryce wanted all of Ethan, and was not afraid to help himself to what he wanted, to what he craved.

Ethan's body was on fire. Bryce held Ethan's hands down on the bed and kissed his way down Ethan's body. His lips left Ethan's lips and kissed his neck. Ethan tilted his head back, surrendering to his lover's lips. Bryce kissed Ethan's chest down the middle, and then helped himself to his right nipple, pulling it up and holding it between his lips, and very gently teasing the left one with his fingertips. Ethan opened his legs for Bryce, and Bryce's body moved down even more. He licked the never ending stream that waited for him on Ethan's stomach. He ran his hands underneath Ethan's back and down onto his butt. He claimed the drops that hadn't yet made it to Ethan's stomach, but were waiting for him at the very top of Ethan's throbbing cock.

Ethan couldn't speak. He could barely move. His body was completely overcome with passion and ecstasy from this lover he had wanted for years. Bryce's tongue was making its way around Ethan's cock as it disappeared into his mouth. "Ohhh," Ethan moaned. Bryce couldn't get enough of Ethan. He pulled up on Ethan's cock until the very tip was between his lips, and then he moved all the way down again.

Ethan's hands were in Bryce's hair, as he neared climax. He moved his legs apart and bent his knees. "Bryce," he moaned, and Bryce continued, and held one of Ethan's heavy balls at a time, rolling each one with his fingers. When he touched Ethan beneath his balls and slid a finger as far back as he could until he just barely entered him, Ethan knew he was more than just close. "Bryce, come here, hurry," he said in an urgent whisper.

Bryce turned around and fed Ethan what he was starving for, and fed himself what he had not yet finished. Ethan had taken all of Bryce, and Bryce lost it just as Ethan did. "Oh, man, Bryce. What was that?"

Bryce lay beside Ethan with his arm around him. He whispered beside his ear. "When I saw you holding my baby in the attorney's office, I wanted to take you then and there." Ethan smiled.

"Whaaa, whaaa."

"I think our sweetie is up," Ethan said quietly.

Bryce threw on his clothes, and hurried to pick up baby Rose. "Daddy's here."

Ethan went to get a bottle. "Is little Rose hungry?"

"Looks like it."

She happily took the bottle and fixed her eyes on Bryce. "I love the way she looks at me, Ethan."

Ethan put his arm around Bryce. "I think she likes her daddy."

"I think she likes her two daddies," Bryce corrected. Ethan just smiled.

"I don't remember hearing about your nieces, Ethan. Do they live close by?"

"They live in Missouri, Bryce. My brother's girls. He either was told, or somehow decided that I was gay, and because I am gay, he does not feel that I am the 'proper' uncle for his girls."

"Ethan, I didn't know. I'm sorry."

"That was several years ago. At least I got to see them for a couple of years. That's where my baby knowledge comes from."

Rose had finished eating, and Bryce set the bottle down. He handed her to Ethan. "Care to burp?"

"Sure," he said, holding the sleepy baby against his upper chest.

"I hope this doesn't bother you, being with Rose, since you, well, your nieces."

"Oh, no, Bryce. I'm just glad that you are letting me be a part of your daughter's life."

"I don't know what I would do without you, Ethan. Rose has two daddies, or at least, that's what I want her to have. We're a family, Ethan. We are, right?"

"Yes," Ethan whispered. "We are."

Rose had fallen asleep after a few good burps, but Ethan continued to hold her and sway gently.

Bryce took the bottle back to the kitchen. He stood in the doorway and watched Ethan. "Looks good from where I'm standing," he teased.

With his back to him, Ethan said, "I'm sure it does." He laid Rose down in her crib. "We'd better get a few hours of sleep, buddy," he whispered to Bryce.

They undressed again, and fell asleep within seconds. Four hours later the alarm sounded, and so did Rose. "I'll get her, Bryce. You have to get to work." He kissed Ethan quickly, and Ethan took care of Rose while Bryce got ready for work.

He came out of the shower, dressed, and went into the kitchen. He stopped in the doorway. "I don't know which one of you I want more right now," he said.

Ethan was sitting in just his underwear feeding Rose, his hair going every which way, and in bad need of a shave. "Well, here we are, in our most natural state."

Bryce kissed him. "I love you," he said. Then he kissed his daughter, happily drinking her breakfast. "I love you, Rose."

"We love you, too," Ethan returned.

Bryce made coffee and sat down next to Ethan and Rose. "Look, Ethan. This weekend has been unreal. What was supposed to be a romantic evening with you turned into a whirlwind, complete with a baby."

Ethan listened intently to Bryce's words, knowing that they were coming straight from the heart.

"I had planned to take you to the dinner with me, and then invite you back to my house afterward for drinks. Honestly, I had no plans for seducing you." He joked at this last comment.

"Sure, you didn't," Ethan winked at him.

"I did plan to tell you how much I love you, and how our friendship had grown into something too big for us not to be together."

"You know I've felt the same way, Bryce. You okay, buddy?"

"I'm fine, Ethan. I guess I just wanted you to know that I didn't say I love you just so that I could have help with Rose."

Ethan took his hand. "Bryce, I didn't think that for a minute. What we had together began long before this weekend, and long before you were a father. This little girl, this wonderful little person, is just icing on the cake. She and Princess and Hawker are our babies, all of them."

Bryce was quiet for a few minutes. "I'm beginning to realize what a good decision teaching was, Ethan. I'll be home in the afternoons, most days anyway. What are you going to do while I'm gone, Ethan?"

Ethan continued to hold his hand. "We'll be fine, Bryce. I've got plenty of help, and the students love coming here. I'm happy to help them earn money and learn about the farm. They are going to go crazy over this baby."

"You don't mind, then?"

"Mind? I'm her daddy, right?"

Bryce looked down. "Right."

Ethan lifted Bryce's hand to his mouth and kissed it. "We're lucky, Bryce. We had *us* long before we were blessed with this little cutie pie. We may not have known what we had before this weekend, but we had it."

Ethan smiled his reassuring smile, and Bryce breathed a sigh of relief. "I'm going to miss you guys."

"We're going to have a great life here on the farm, on this beautiful land."

"I know, Ethan, I know. This is our place. This is our home."

After Bryce had gone to work, Ethan dressed, and then made a list of what he thought Rose needed, after he had gone through all the wonderful gifts she had received. "Looks like they thought of everything, sweetie," he said to her. She watched Ethan's every move.

Princess and Hawker were still curious about the new little creature that had come into their home, and they stayed close beside Ethan whenever Rose was in his arms.

When Bryce returned shortly after noon, the farm was buzzing with activity, and when he opened the gait that opened to the big yard made just for the dogs, Princess and Hawker rushed to meet him. "Hi, guys," he said, and let them jump on him and knock him down. They ran off to join in the activity, and Bryce went inside the house.

"Ethan?" he whispered.

"In here," Ethan whispered back.

Despite the noise and chaos outside, Ethan had transformed the house into a quiet sanctuary just for Rose. He kept the door closed, and opened the windows only on the front side of the house. Bryce walked quietly into the bedroom.

"Naptime," Ethan whispered. He was lying on the bed with baby Rose, who was sleeping soundly.

"How did it go?" Bryce asked him.

Ethan placed Rose in her crib and joined Bryce in the living room. "It was great, Bryce. As you can see, I've rearranged things a little. Guess I rearranged things a lot."

"I can see that, Ethan. I love it."

"Thanks, Bryce. There is so much going on out here on the farm, I thought that it would be good for her to have a space that is always calm and quiet. When she is in our room and this other small room attached which I've cleared out and made into a 'baby play room', her world will be calm."

"Everyone needs a place like that, Ethan. For me, that place is right here, with you."

Ethan led Bryce into the small room that Ethan had roughly redone, and he loved it.

He turned to Ethan. "I love you, Ethan."

Ethan pulled him close and held him, their two bodies meshed as one.

Trey's Daddies

After suffering a minor concussion in the postseason games, Derek decides that it is time to end his career as a running back for the National Football League before his career ends his life. Derek and his best buddy, Sandy, a golden retriever, take a much deserved vacation to visit Derek's parents at the old homestead in eastern Colorado. While there Derek meets a very intriguing young man named Craig. There seems to be a secret about Craig, though, that Derek's parents do not want their son to know, but for some reason they do not want Derek to become involved with this young man who Derek cannot seem to resist.

B.K. Wright   249

One

After the Playoffs

Sandy ran as fast as he could, faster and faster, but he just could not catch it. He couldn't catch the rabbit that seemed to always be just out of his reach. "Rrruff, rrruf," Sandy barked, in his sleep. He awoke suddenly, and rolled over.

"Good boy," Derek said, rubbing Sandy's belly. "Today's the big day. Are you ready to go see Grandma and Grandpa?" He patted Sandy on the head. Derek O'Neil was taking Sandy with him to visit his parents in eastern Colorado. "They will love you, boy," he said to the sleepy dog. Derek hadn't been back home for three years.

Derek had been drafted into the National Football League (NFL) right after college and had been on the road much of the time. Being hurt in the playoff games last year had turned out to be a blessing in disguise. Derek loved football, but after spending years on the road and after taking a lot of hits, he was ready to settle down somewhere.

Now he had Sandy, and the sweet golden brown puppy was his best buddy. Derek's parents had joked that Derek thought of Sandy as his child and not as a dog. "Who's my good boy, huh? Are you my good boy?" Sandy rolled over onto his side, and then he rolled back the other way a few times. "Well, let's go. I've got us all packed."

Derek locked his house and picked up his sweet Sandy. "Pretty soon, you will be a big boy and be able to carry me," Derek said to the eager dog. Sandy loved riding in Derek's big truck. It sat up high, and Sandy could stick his head out of the window and let his ears flap in the breeze. "Look at you. You're Bat Dog." Derek said the same thing to Sandy every time they went somewhere together, which was often. Sandy would turn to Derek and give him a quick bark, as if he understood what Derek had said.

Derek and Sandy had at least a full day's drive ahead of them. Derek had been a running back for the Tennessee Titans until he had suffered a mild concussion last year, courtesy of a defensive end from an opposing team. Derek had made a speedy recovery, but wasn't willing to tempt fate. Derek had made a promise to himself years ago that if he got hurt, he got out. After ten years of professional football, Derek's body had taken all the hits that Derek was going to demand of it. Still, the preseason games were right around the corner and Derek knew that when the season started, he would miss being part of the big game.

Football was America's game, and the roar of the crowd could be intoxicating to guys like Derek. "Oh, Sandy, what will we do, just the two of us?" The dog turned to look at Derek for a second, but then quickly returned to the feel of the wind flapping his ears.

After a very long day's drive, Derek yawned as he looked at his watch. "Just a couple more hours, Sandy boy, and you will meet your Grandma and Grandpa for the very first time." "Rrruff," Sandy said to his owner. When Derek saw the "Welcome to Colorado" sign, he knew that in just twenty minutes he would be home.

Derek's father was outside working on his old truck when Derek pulled into the drive.

"Look at you and that fancy new truck," his father said, jokingly. "And look at me with my old jalopy," he added.

Derek knew that his dad was joking. Derek's father was proud of all that his son had accomplished. Derek had done what his father had wanted to do. He had gone to college on a football scholarship and had been drafted into what his father considered to be the finest institution in the country, the National Football League. Derek hadn't played for his father's beloved Denver Broncos, but he had still played football.

"There's my big football star," he said, as Derek walked toward him, and he gave Derek a big welcome hug.

"Dad, this is my best bud, Sandy," he said.

At the sound of his name, Sandy jumped out of the truck, almost knocking Derek's dad to the ground.

"He likes you, Dad."

"Well, of course he does," the older gentleman joked. Derek's dad, Tom, roughhoused with Sandy, and Sandy loved the extra attention from this playful, older version of Derek. "Well, take your buddy here and go see your mother. She's in the house. I should have this old truck up and running in just a few more minutes."

Derek smiled at his dad, and said to Sandy, "Let's go see Grandma", and patted his leg.

Sandy left his playful new friend and followed Derek into the house.

"My baby," Derek's mom said, and hurried to hug her son. "We sure have missed you, honey."

"Me too, Mom," Derek said, and hugged his mother. "And who are you, pretty puppy?" Sandy licked her hand.

"Sandy, this is Grandma," Derek said, and winked devilishly at his mother.

"Well, I guess I am Grandma now," she laughed, and petted the pretty dog. Derek's parents had been quite young when Derek was born, and definitely did not seem old enough to be grandparents, at least not to Derek. "Well, go on upstairs and unpack, honey. Your room is all aired out."

Derek and Sandy walked upstairs in the old Victorian style country house to the room that Derek had grown up in. Derek walked into the room, and Sandy bounded in and jumped up onto his bed.

Derek's home outside of Nashville was three times the size of his parents' country home here in eastern Colorado, but Derek still felt most at home when he was right here in this room he had grown up in.

"Well, Sandy, this is the old homestead," he said, snuggling the soft pretty dog. Sandy was still a puppy, but a big puppy. "You're going to be a big dog real soon," Derek said to the attentive dog. "Come on, Sandy, let's go see what Grandma is up to," Derek said, and Sandy hurried to be the first one down the stairs.

Derek's mother, Mary, had set out a water dish and some food for Sandy. "Is my new grandson hungry?" she asked.

Sandy made himself at home at his very own buffet.

"Well, what has Dad been up to lately, Mom?"

"Oh, just taking care of the land here. It keeps him busy."

Derek's father, Tom, loved ranching, and he loved Colorado.

"Of course, he never misses watching his favorite team. He plans to go to all of the preseason games this year, and definitely all of the regular season games at Mile High Stadium, or, INVESCO Field at Mile High, rather," she corrected herself.

Derek laughed. "Oh, yes, I know. The Denver Broncos can do no wrong."

Mary laughed with him. "Well, this year, your father has gone overboard, I'm afraid. He has leased part of the land at the west edge of

Let It Be

the property to his beloved team for the Broncos to 'get away from it all', as he puts it. It was supposed to be a surprise, Derek. He's going to take you there tomorrow."

Derek nodded in agreement to keeping his mother's secret. After a very welcome home cooked meal, Derek and Sandy went up to Derek's room and slept soundly with the window open, carrying a fresh cool breeze over their tired bodies.

Sandy woke Derek early the next morning the way he woke him every morning. He nuzzled Derek's neck and then licked his face. "Okay, okay," Derek said, hugging his furry friend. He took Sandy outside and watched him run as fast as he could to the far end of the yard. This is a great place for a dog that likes to run, he thought. Derek's father was already outside.

"Well, son, I have a big surprise for you," Tom O'Neil said to his son. "Let's take the old truck," he said.

Derek got into the old truck that his father insisted on keeping, and Sandy planted himself on the seat of the truck between the two men. "Where to, Dad?"

"You'll see. It's not far from here."

Tom whistled happily as the old truck sputtered and dragged itself to the far end of the property.

Two

Broncos on the Range

"What are these?" Derek asked.

"Welcome to 'Broncos on the Range'," Tom announced proudly.

Derek laughed. "What did you say?" he asked.

"Broncos on the Range," his dad repeated. "You know, like 'Home on the Range', but 'Broncos'," he repeated.

"I got it, Dad, but why?"

"Well, son, the Broncos were looking for a place to get away when they needed to, and I offered a portion of my land. Now the team members get to relax right here with me, and I get the inside scoop on my favorite team," he said proudly.

"How many of these houses, or whatever you call them, are out here?"

"Just these two houses so far. Come on, I'll show you inside of one. They are completely furnished, and very Bronco-like." Tom winked at his son when he said this.

Derek followed his dad into one of the houses. Derek was more than just a little impressed. The house was much better than nice inside. "This is beautiful, Dad."

"Well, I can't take credit for that. I just leased the land. I didn't do the decorating."

Derek looked around. "Has Mom seen these?"

"Oh, yes. She put her two cents in about the color schemes and what not."

Sandy had toured the entire place by himself already, and was running back down the stairs, followed by a Denver Bronco.

"Oh, I didn't know anyone was here. Sorry to barge in on you like this." Tom felt a little embarrassed now.

"Oh, no problem. Nice dog."

Derek thanked the man.

"So, are you a preseason hopeful, or in the game for certain?" Tom asked, feeling and looking very uneasy.

"Preseason hopeful, I'm afraid. First game is tomorrow night."

Tom assured the young man that he would be at the game, and that he was looking forward to a winning season.

"I'm Craig," the man said.

Tom introduced himself and his son, and when Derek had turned to shake Craig's hand, Tom winked at Craig knowingly, a wink which Derek did not see. Derek shook Craig's hand.

"Nice kid," Derek said, after Craig had gone back upstairs.

"Looks determined, too, promising," Tom added. "Well, come on, son, let's let Craig get himself ready for his big debut at Mile High Stadium."

The following night, Sandy stayed at home with Mary, and Derek and his father headed to Denver for the Broncos first preseason game. They arrived very early. Tom didn't want to miss one minute of watching his beloved team in action. Craig saw them from a distance and walked over to them.

"You really did come," he said.

"Oh, you bet," Tom said.

"Well, wish me luck," Craig said, and left to join the team.

"The team looks pretty good this year, don't you think?"

"Yeah, Dad, you might actually win a few games this year." Derek had agreed with his dad, but he would always be a Titans fan.

Three

Secret Inhabitant

It was late when Derek and his father returned home, and Sandy had already made himself at home in the middle of Derek's bed. It was just after midnight when Sandy reminded Derek that he hadn't been outside to do his business before going to sleep.

"Okay, Sandy, okay," Derek said, and quietly walked down the stairs and out the back door with Sandy. "You are full of energy tonight, aren't you, boy?"

Sandy took off at a fast run, and Derek had to run as fast as he possibly could just to catch up with the young dog. "Sandy, where are you going?" Derek yelled. Sandy slowed down, and Derek was finally able to catch up with him. Derek was thankful for the many years of football and football practice now. "Let me catch my breath, boy," he said.

Derek hadn't realized how far they had gone until he saw the "Broncos on the Range" in the distance. One of them was dark, but the other one was well lit. I'm sure the team is required to stay in Denver, he thought. So who could possibly be here? Derek looked at Sandy. Dogs were supposed to have a keen sense about things like this, weren't they? Sandy seemed the same, but he was still a puppy. "Let's go see what's up," he said to the dog.

They walked toward the house, and Derek began to get a weird feeling, but he couldn't explain it. The two houses were big, and the one with the lights on must have had every single light on inside. Derek tried to see inside the house, but the windows were too high for him to see in from a distance. Sandy sniffed the ground, not paying much attention to Derek. Derek walked closer to the house, with Sandy right beside him. Derek had to see if anyone was inside. "Come on, boy. Let's see if anybody is home."

Derek walked around to the front door and knocked lightly. When he knocked, he noticed that the lights began to go off one by one. "Okay, Sandy, someone is definitely in there. Come on." The dog was at his side as Derek knocked again. The house was completely dark, but the door was not locked. Derek slowly opened the door. "Knock, knock," he said. "Anyone home?" There was no answer, but Derek hadn't really expected an answer, given the oddness of the situation.

Derek and Sandy slowly walked inside. Derek flipped the nearest wall switch to turn on at least one light. "Hey, if you're in here, I won't hurt you. I promise. Craig, are you here?"

Derek heard something fall, and it sounded as if it was coming from the kitchen. He and Sandy walked slowly into the kitchen. Derek turned on the kitchen light. Standing silently along the far side of the kitchen was Craig.

"Craig, why are you hiding?" Then he noticed that Craig was holding something. "Craig, what is...oh, is that yours?" Derek realized how stupid this question must have seemed to Craig. Craig said nothing, but waited for Derek to do or say something more. "You remember me and Sandy?"

"Yes," he whispered.

"I just got him to sleep," Craig said, looking down at the bundle he was holding.

"Can I see him or her?"

"It's him. Sure. His name is Trey."

Derek walked over and looked at the tiny baby. "He's beautiful, Craig. But aren't you supposed to be in Denver with the team?"

Sandy stretched up to sniff the bundle in Craig's arms.

"I, um, well, your dad arranged this for me, Craig. This is my house, and the other one is empty right now. I'm not sure what your dad plans to do with it."

Craig was silent, not wanting to say more. "Oh. Why did Dad not tell me?"

Craig didn't answer. "I'm sure he didn't mean to keep things from you," he quickly added.

"Oh, no problem. So then, you live here and not with the team?"

Craig nodded. "Your mom keeps Trey when I'm gone," he added.

"Wow, I had no idea. She must love that."

Derek looked at the sleeping baby. He touched Trey's hand, and the little guy wrapped his hand around one of Derek's finger. "Oh, look at you. You've got a strong grip, little guy."

Craig smiled. "I didn't mean to hide. I didn't know it was you."

"Think nothing of it, Craig. Is there anything you need?"

Craig shook his head. "No. We'll be going back to bed now that Trey has had his bottle."

"Well, don't hesitate to ask for help," Derek said.

Craig watched as Derek and Sandy left the house. Then he waited a few minutes before locking the front door. He took Trey upstairs and back to bed. Sandy took off running once again, forcing Derek to get his exercise. "You're keeping me in shape, Sandy," he called after him.

Derek went back to sleep, with Sandy sharing his bed. Derek had trouble sleeping, though. He woke often, and thought about Craig. He looked young to have a baby, and why were Derek's parents so involved with him and his baby?

Derek tossed and turned most of the night, and was just getting back to a sound sleep when the sun began to shine its morning rays through the open window. Sandy was awake and ready to go, and ran down the stairs without Derek. Derek could hear his mother talking to the dog, and had to laugh. "Do you need to go potty, Sandy? Let Grandma open the door for you." Derek lay in bed for awhile, and then forced himself to put his feet on the floor. He walked slowly down the stairs.

"It's about time, sleepyhead," Mary said teasingly to her grown son.

"I know," he said, sleepily. "Sandy wanted to go out last night around midnight, and decided to take me for a very fast run."

"Where did that sweet puppy run to?"

Derek didn't know if he should say where the two of them had gone, but he did want some answers. "He took me all the way to Dad's 'Broncos on the Range'." Derek looked at his mom, hoping to see surprise in her face. Mary said nothing, but did not meet Derek's eyes. "There were lights on in one of the houses, and so Sandy and I stopped by," Derek continued.

"Hmm," Mary said, continuing to flip through a magazine.

"Craig was there," he said. "That's nice, dear. He's a real nice boy," she said. Derek sat down, facing his mother. "Mom, is there something you would like to tell me about Craig?"

Mary O'Neil set her magazine down and looked at her son. "You saw the baby?"

"Yes, mother, I saw Trey. He's darling." Derek smiled when he thought about the baby's hand firmly holding just one of his fingers. "Whose kid is he, and why is Dad so protective of Craig?"

Mary O'Neil looked into Derek's penetrating eyes. "Oh, honey, your father met Craig just a few months before Trey was born. Craig had been getting ready to train with the Broncos, and I guess he saw something in Craig that touched him."

Derek studied his mother's eyes, not knowing whether to believe her entirely. "And the baby? It usually takes two to make one of those."

Mary sighed. "Well, sometimes things don't work out, you know. Trey's mother and Craig were never married, and I guess she just wasn't cut out to be a mother. Craig has full custody."

Derek looked at his mother. There were some parts of this puzzle that were still missing, though he didn't know what they were.

Sandy barked at the back door just then, and Derek went to let him back inside. "You like it here, don't you, buddy?" Sandy helped himself to the water which was fresh from the well that Mary loved, and then jumped up on the sofa next to Mary. "Hey, boy, you're rejecting me already?"

Mary patted the sweet dog on his head. "We're buddies now, aren't we, Sandy?"

The telephone rang and Mary answered it. "Oh, well, don't worry. We'll work something out."

"Derek, your father has a busy day today, and I'm needed at the library. The regular library lady is sick."

"I'm okay here alone, Mom. I live alone, you know."

"Derek, I wasn't concerned about you. You're a grown man. I stay with Trey most days. I'm due there shortly."

Thinking of Trey's little hand around his one finger again, Derek spoke up. "I'll do it, Mom. I'll watch Trey."

Mary looked surprised. "Honey, are you sure? I mean, well..."

"I know I've never taken care of a baby, but I do know a few things about babies. And, you do realize that I'm in my mid thirties now, not exactly a child."

"Yes, dear, I realize that. If you need me, call my cell phone," Mary said.

"Let's go, boy. Let's go see the baby," Derek said to the already sleepy dog.

They took the truck this time. Derek was still tired from last night's romp. He wasn't ready to run again.

"Oh, hi, Derek. Is you mother coming?" Craig asked, a look of concern on his face.

Derek explained the situation, and Craig went through the list of instructions for Trey. Derek found it a bit odd that this much younger man was giving him baby instructions.

"Well, I'll see you tonight," Craig said, reluctantly handing his baby over to this obviously inexperienced man.

"He's what, about a year old?" Craig laughed.

"No, Derek, he's four months old."

"Oh," Derek said, suddenly feeling very unsure of his baby skills.

Craig put his arm around Derek. "Piece of cake," he said.

Derek watched Craig pull out of the driveway, and then looked down at the sleeping bundle in his arms. "We can do this, can't we, Sandy?" Sandy had already found a soft chair to stretch out in, and was busy chasing rabbits in his dreams.

Derek looked at Trey. He was sleeping soundly. He studied Trey's face. He didn't really look that much like Craig. Must look like his mother, Derek thought.

The day was long, and Derek was happy to see Craig when he walked through the door.

"Hi, Derek. How was Trey?"

"He was a little angel, Craig. I loved taking care of him."

"Mind if I take a quick shower before you go?"

"Not at all," Derek said.

Four
Something About Craig

When Craig came back downstairs without his shirt, Derek couldn't help but stare. Football practice definitely agreed with Craig. His chest was gorgeous. Derek decided then and there that he was not going to let himself get out of shape just because he was no longer playing football. Craig walked over to Derek and leaned down to look at his son. Craig was wearing no cologne, but Derek found his natural scent somewhat arousing. Derek had never really believed the whole "chemistry" thing, but thought that he just might be wrong about that.

"Well, Sandy and I should probably go now," Derek said.

Craig turned to him, and said, "You could stay awhile, if you like. I'm just heating up some of your mom's good home cooking. She keeps me well stocked."

Derek nodded. He was definitely hungry. Derek carried Trey into the kitchen. "Trey must look like...," and then he stopped.

"It's okay, Derek," Craig said, not turning around, and not adding anything more to the conversation.

After they ate, Derek said that he really did have to go. Craig met him at the door and stopped him from leaving. He was so close that Derek could smell that arousing natural scent of his again.

"Thank you," Craig whispered. Then, Craig put his arms around Derek and pulled him to him. Derek's hands were on Craig's naked flesh and he couldn't stop them from moving up and down his back at least twice. When Craig backed up, their lips were so close that Derek fought the urge to kiss him.

"No problem," Derek said, and the two of them reluctantly released the other. "I may be back again tomorrow," Derek said, as he and Sandy walked out the door.

The next day, Mary was asked to work at the library again, and secretly, Derek was thrilled. He loved spending the day with Craig's baby, and he found himself wanting to see Craig again, too. When Derek and Sandy arrived at Craig's, he was hurrying around, and seemed somewhat frantic.

"You'd better get going, Craig. I can take care of things around here."

"It's just that I was up most of the night, Derek. I think Trey has a cold, and I haven't had a chance to do any laundry or get his bottles ready or anything. Look at this place."

Derek walked over to Craig and put his arm around him. "It's okay, Craig, really."

Then Craig looked over to where Trey was sleeping. "Now he sleeps," he said, but with a smile.

"I'll clean up here. I can do laundry, too. I know how."

Craig smiled at Derek's offer, and Derek rubbed Craig's arm before releasing him. "I know you do. Guess I forgot you were a bachelor."

Derek helped Craig get his things ready, and then opened the door for him. "Have a nice day, dear," he teased.

Craig turned around and smiled. "Thank you, Derek, for everything."

When Craig passed him, again Derek felt that animal magnetism between them. There was something about Craig's natural scent that was deliriously arousing to Derek.

After Craig had gone, Derek did the laundry and cleaned the house while Sandy and Trey both slept. Derek loved feeding little Trey, and he loved rocking him and singing to him. "I can sing, but I'm way off key," he said to Trey. Trey's eyes never left Derek's when he was holding him, and Derek was falling in love with the little guy.

Very late in the afternoon, Craig called to tell Derek that he would be home quite late. "Do you want me to call Mary?" he offered to Derek.

"No, no, we're fine. Trey seems to be doing much better. Dad brought over a humidifier and it seems to have helped the little guy's sniffles and cough. My skin feels better because of it, too," Derek added, with a laugh.

"Thanks again, Derek," Craig said, and hung up the phone.

"Well, guess it's just you and me, little baby, for awhile anyway," Derek said to little Trey. Derek fed Sandy, and then he took

Trey outside for just a little while so that Sandy could run around the yard.

It was close to ten when Craig walked in the door. Derek was asleep on the sofa with Trey sprawled out on top of him, sleeping soundly. Craig stopped for a minute to look at Derek and his sleeping child. How sweet, he thought. Sandy barked once, and Derek woke up. "Hey, big day, huh?" Derek asked.

"Big, but good, Derek. I'm on the team for sure. Champagne?" Craig opened the champagne and poured two glasses, not waiting for Derek's answer.

"That's great, Craig. To you," he said, toasting Craig's well deserved achievement. They drank one glass of champagne and Craig poured them another glass. After two glasses, Derek felt a little buzzed.

"You know, I don't usually drink," he admitted.

"I don't either," Craig joked, but poured himself another glass of the bubbly anyway.

Derek laid Trey in his crib, where he continued to sleep soundly.

"Stay awhile, Derek. Tell me about your career with the Titans."

"Well, my career is over now, but if you're asking if it was worth it, I can honestly say that it was. Save your money, Craig. That's where a lot of guys get themselves into trouble. They spend like there will never be an end to the money supply."

Craig set his glass down, and then took Derek's glass from him. "Come here, Derek," he said, taking his hand and pulling him to his feet.

"Whoa. You may have to hold me up. Where are we going?"

He took Derek's hands in his and then placed them around his waist. Then he put his arms around Derek. "You know it's there. You feel it, too, don't you?"

Derek did feel it, but did not want to admit it. Craig's scent was killing him with its intoxicating erotic manliness. "What do you mean?" he asked.

"What do I mean? This." Craig brushed his lips against Derek's very lightly, and then pulled back. Derek's eyes were closed, but his lips were parted with the expectation of more, much more from Craig. Then he opened his eyes. "You want to know why I stopped, don't you?"

Derek knew that he couldn't fight Craig's scent *and* the champagne. It was just too much. "Yes," he said.

Craig whispered, "I stopped because I wanted to see this, your passion, your desire. You didn't want me to stop, did you? You still don't want me to stop, do you?"

Derek couldn't speak. Derek was dizzy. "No," he said.

Craig forcefully pulled Derek's body to him, and kissed him again, this time filling Derek's entire being with his arousing man scent. Derek couldn't stop himself from wanting Craig, from taking from Craig anything and everything he had to offer. Craig was like a drug to Derek. It was the scent of him, and it was him. Craig's hands moved slowly down along Derek's back and onto his firm butt. Derek gasped, opening his mouth even more for his lover. Craig pulled Derek's tongue into his mouth with a hard sucking motion. Derek knew that despite the champagne, his erection was full and hard, and pressing against Craig's equally full and hard erection.

"Craig, I didn't know," Derek slowly got out.

"Mmm," Craig answered.

When they finally stopped for air, Craig did not let Derek go. He held him even tighter. His chest was heaving, and his breath came in short gasps. Derek held Craig just as closely, pressing his aroused body to Craig's.

"I didn't know," Derek said again.

"What, that I'm gay?" Craig asked.

"That, too," Derek admitted.

"What else?" Craig asked, still breathless. He didn't wait for Derek's answer. "You didn't know that I'm aroused by your very presence, your manly scent?"

Derek pulled back and looked at Craig.

"It's the same with you, isn't it, Derek?"

Derek looked at Craig for a long time. The heat between them made the room feel as if it were being heated by a fireplace. "Yes," he said. He couldn't deny it, yet he couldn't explain it, either. Derek closed his eyes. He was drunk, but not on the champagne. He was drunk on Craig.

Craig looked down at the bulging material that separated their physical desire from each other. Then he raised his eyes to look at Derek. Craig kissed the lips that were waiting to be kissed by him and only him. He kissed the neck that he had been dying to kiss. He wanted Derek's shirt off of him, but was unwilling to let his hands leave Derek's body. Derek was still. He waited for Craig's next touch, for Craig's next kiss.

Craig forced his aroused body to leave Derek's equally aroused body, and took him by the hand, leading him to his bed. "In here," he whispered. He glanced down at Trey sleeping soundly in his crib right outside the door, and then turned his full attention to Derek.

They undressed each other, slowly, every touch of the other sensuous and arousing. They took turns touching and tasting the other's nipples with their tongues. Their eyes closed and then opened with each new sensation. Their breathing could be heard throughout the room. The sound of a zipper being forced along its downward path broke the silence, and then the relieved yet aroused moans filled the room as full erections were released. The two men pushed all clothing aside and grasped the other's hardness firmly. A loud moan was heard, and then another.

Craig urged his lover to lie down upon his bed. He forced Derek's legs apart and then kissed him while he held Derek's balls firmly in his hand. Derek's hand was immediately searching for Craig's balls. The two men wrapped their legs around each other, pressing their bodies together, drinking in the other's arousing scent. Their hands reached between each other's legs and continued upward, stroking the sensual area where the two halves of their butts parted.

Derek was the first to allow a gasp to escape his lips. When Craig touched him, his entire body responded like it never had before. Craig pressed a finger against Derek's entrance as if it were waiting to be invited inside. Derek stretched his leg over Craig further, a clear signal that he wanted Craig to enter him. Derek was the first to hear the sound of unexpected pleasure when he discovered what most pleased his new lover. "Oh," Craig added, to his continuous low guttural moans. Derek's pleasure was soon discovered by Craig, and more, even louder sounds of pleasure filled the room. Neither wanted to release the other, but both wanted to taste the other.

Craig kissed Derek again, passionately, and then quickly repositioned himself over his lover. His hard cock hung tauntingly above Derek's parted lips and open mouth. Craig kneaded Derek's inner thighs as he parted his lips over the head of Derek's beautiful cock. He felt Derek's strong hands cup his ass, forcing it downward until his cock was pulled into Derek's awaiting mouth.

Their desire for each other was beyond simple desire. Their desire became a need, a need to be a part of the other, as if their bodies had always been a part of the other. Their voices could be heard throughout the entire house, their heat felt around them, and finally, their orgasmic releases came. They drank in the other's seed as if it were the only nourishment that would satisfy the hunger and need of their bodies.

Craig leaned forward onto Derek, drunk with passion for him. Derek held his lover's softening penis within the warm safe haven where it had just experienced its draining orgasm. Derek was not yet willing to let it go.

After their bodies had been nourished by the seed of the other, Craig forced his flaccid penis to leave its lover, and Derek pulled Craig to him. Craig fell over his lover and held him. They slept, not knowing how much time had passed.

The sweet sounds of baby Trey woke them both immediately. Derek and Craig were off of the bed instantly, both hurrying to fulfill whatever need Trey was being denied.

"Look at us," Craig said, as they stood over Trey.

Derek looked at his own naked body and then at Craig's, and laughed. "Well, I guess we've got our priorities straight," Derek said.

Craig carried Trey into the bedroom and held him while Derek dressed. Derek carried Trey into the kitchen to get his bottle ready while Craig dressed. Craig stood in the kitchen doorway watching Derek, whose back was turned.

"You don't have to go tonight, you know. It's late."

Derek turned around, Trey noisily sucking on the bottle nipple. He smiled at Craig. "I wasn't planning to leave tonight," he said.

Once Trey's little belly was full, Derek placed him back into his crib, and Craig welcomed Derek to his bed once again.

The alarm sounded in what seemed like less than an hour after they had gone to sleep.

"Oh, man," Craig said, as Sandy jumped on the bed and licked his face.

"Yes, Sandy, I love you, too," he said. "My personal wake-up call," Derek said.

"Well, that's mine," Craig said, as he got out of bed to the sounds of baby Trey.

"Well, we don't ever have to worry about oversleeping," Derek said, scratching Sandy behind his ears. He got up and let the loving dog outside. "He loves all the extra space out here to run," Derek said, as he watched his buddy take off running as fast as he could.

"Is your mother coming today, or will you be staying with Trey again?" Derek looked at Craig questioningly, wondering which he preferred.

"I don't know. Mom doesn't know that I didn't come home last night."

The phone rang and Craig looked at it. "She knows now," he said. He picked up the phone and told Mary that he had gotten home so late that Derek had stayed the night. "I guess it's going to be you again," Craig said, and hung up the phone. "Your mom is needed again at the library. Derek smiled when Craig told him this, and Craig smiled too.

Five
Learning the Truth

It was close to noon when Derek's mom stopped by Craig's house. "Hi, dear. How is that sweet baby?" She took little Trey from Derek and rocked him in her arms.

"He's sweet, Mom."

"He is a sweetie," she agreed. She sat down and held Trey in her arms. "Well, honey, how was your night?"

A little surprised at the question, Derek said, "Fine. Trey slept most of the night."

Mary looked at her son. That wasn't what she was really asking, and somehow Derek knew it. "Mom, what are you really asking me?" he said. "You know I'm gay. You've never questioned my relationships before."

"Now, dear, I only want you to be happy."

"Well, is there something about Craig that you don't like? Is there some reason that you wouldn't want us to be together, if for some reason we wanted to be together, if he was gay?"

She sighed. "Craig is a very nice man. He will be on the road a lot, though, you do realize."

"I know professional football inside and out," Derek said.

Anxious to change the subject, Mary said, "Well, honey, I've got to get back to the library." She kissed Trey's forehead and handed the baby back to her son.

Derek was upset for the remainder of the day, though he wasn't sure why. "What are my parents hiding from me?" he asked baby Trey. Trey made his usual baby sounds and looked at Derek. "Rruff, rruff," Sandy barked in his sleep. His feet were moving even though his eyes were closed. "Sandy is a silly little puppy, isn't he?" Derek was surprised that Trey actually appeared to be watching the puppy. "Let's try out this fun swing that Grandma brought," Derek said to Trey. "That's fun, isn't it?" Trey was babbling louder and louder as he enjoyed the swing.

Derek sat back and enjoyed the puppy/baby serenade. He thought about last night. Derek had definitely had his share of relationships, some short, some longer, and last night had shown him that Craig was also definitely no novice in the sexual arena.

Derek smiled as he thought about their lovemaking. Craig was definitely, without a doubt, not a novice as far as sex was concerned. What was the big secret about him, though? Am I being paranoid?

Derek tried to remember everything his mother had said over the past few days. Oh, well. He loved this little guy swinging next to him, and the puppy that was no doubt chasing rabbits in his sleep as he lay next to the swing, and maybe, just maybe, he was falling for Craig, too.

Derek was lost in his thoughts about last night when the telephone rang. "Oh, hey, Craig. Are they working you pretty hard up there in Denver?"

"Definitely. I think I forgot to tell you, though, that I'll be staying overnight in Denver tonight. Tomorrow is the season opener against Kansas City."

"Oh, no problem. I can stay here with Trey."

"You'll be here tomorrow, right, with your dad?"

"Sure," Derek said. He hung up the phone. He hadn't had a chance to talk with his dad, but he knew that his dad would never miss a Broncos season opener.

When Mary stopped by after work, she brought diapers and formula. "Thought you might need a fresh supply."

"Thanks, Mom. Dad's going to the game tomorrow, right?"

"Yes, dear. He usually goes with some of his buddies, but you'll go with him, won't you? He has been telling everyone how he and his big football star son are going to the season opener together."

"Sure, Mom," Derek said, with a laugh.

The next morning, Trey was awake and crying early. "Oh, Sandy boy, it's going to be a long day." Sandy stretched and yawned, and then ran to the front door and barked. "Shh, I'm coming," Derek called to the impatient dog. Trey cried even louder when he heard Sandy bark. After a diaper change and a bottle, though, Trey was happy and smiling again.

Tom and Mary were at Craig's house at noon. "Dad, you silly old fool," Derek teased, when he saw his father dressed from head to toe in his Denver Broncos gear." Tom looked Derek up and down. "And look at you. I knew you wouldn't be prepared. Here you go."

Tom O'Neil handed Derek much the same that he was wearing himself. "Okay, Dad. I will wear the t-shirt, but that's it."

Tom was already playing with Trey. "Well, you'll be my little Bronco, won't you, Trey?"

Derek looked at his mother busily changing Trey into what Tom assured Derek was the little guy's favorite onesie. "You have got to be kidding?" Derek said. The little outfit did look cute, though.

"He's a Bronco, son."

"Honey, your father couldn't wait for this season. He would take Trey to Denver with him if I didn't stop him. There is far too much noise in that stadium for Trey's sensitive little ears."

The tiny little socks with the Bronco on the side of each one were the final touch, or so Tom thought.

"Come on, Dad. Let's go," Derek said. "Who knows what else you'll do to that poor kid if we don't get out of here."

Tom and Derek O'Neil were finally on their way to Denver and to the Broncos season opener. "You know, son, everyone in Colorado is a Bronco when Kansas City comes to play with us," Tom said smugly.

"I know, I know. Denver and Kansas City, forever rivals."

Then Tom was silent for awhile. "So, you and Craig are friends now?"

"He's a good guy, Dad."

Tom said nothing. Derek suddenly felt that same uneasiness that he had felt when talking about Craig with his mother. He decided not to get into anything heavy today. Today was the Broncos season opener, and nothing or nobody interfered with that.

Derek was surprised with the somewhat "star" treatment that he and his father received at Mile High Stadium.

"Damned good seats, Dad. You win some big football lottery, or something?"

"I'm a regular here, son, and now I know people," Tom replied.

Derek didn't even think that he could have gotten his father such choice seats at any of the Titans home games. These weren't just seats, either. Tom O'Neil had somehow managed to get himself a place reserved for only a select few, one of the boxes at the very top of the stadium.

"You'll really appreciate being inside when it gets cold up here a little later on in the season," Tom assured his questioning son.

"Whose box is this, anyway?"

"Hey, I'm the owner of the prestigious 'Broncos on the Range'," Tom joked.

Derek was silent. Another connection of some sort to Craig, he thought.

"Besides, it is one of the smaller boxes, and it looks like it will be just the two of us today. I promised my poker buddies a reserved seat up here when they want to come up to a game, but not today. I've got my son with me today."

Derek just smiled at his father.

The crowd showed its usual disrespect when the Kansas City Chiefs players took the field, but the Broncos players were introduced to the roar of the crowd. Tom stood up.

"There he is, Derek. There's Craig."

Derek looked at Craig. "It says Craig on his jersey. Craig is his first name, right?" Tom nodded, which Derek interpreted as agreement.

"They put last names on the jerseys, Dad. His name is not Craig Craig, is it?"

"No, goofball. They must have gotten it wrong."

Derek was hoping that at some point during the game Craig's full name would be announced, but it didn't happen.

Tom and Derek left immediately following the game, but Derek would see Craig later that night. He had a few questions for Craig that deserved an answer. "Damned good game, son. Like I said, we always kick butt when it comes to the Chiefs." Derek loved his father's enthusiasm, even if it was for the Broncos.

Derek was thrilled to see little Trey again, and of course, Sandy. But most of all, he wanted to talk to Craig. Craig walked in the door later that night, tired but happy.

"Good game," Derek said, and pulled Craig into his arms. Craig held Derek for a long time. They had both missed each other last night.

"I had time for a shower this time," Craig whispered. Derek held onto this man he felt such a close bond to, such love.

"How's my little guy?" he asked.

"See for yourself," Derek said, motioning to the baby with the Broncos onesie.

"Oh, that man," Craig said. "He couldn't wait, could he?"

Derek shook his head. They were both very well aware of Tom's love for his Broncos. "I think Mom must have played with Trey all afternoon. He sure is sleeping now," Derek commented.

"Good. I've missed you," Craig said. Craig led Derek into his bedroom once again. He practically ripped his own shirt off and then he went after Derek's.

"Mmm, can't wait, huh?" Derek teased.

"Nope."

Craig pressed his naked chest against Derek's. Craig's lips quickly found Derek's, and that same arousing scent of the other filled each other's bodies. They kissed passionately. Their tongues wrestled for domination. Derek pressed his hand against Craig's hardness. He unzipped Craig's jeans, tugging and pushing them until Craig was completely naked.

Derek had watched Craig and wanted him at Mile High Stadium with every movement of his manly body. "Ohh," Craig moaned, when Derek's hand found his balls and then formed around Craig's cock.

Craig stood perfectly still, enjoying the pleasurable sensations. Then he forced his way into Derek's jeans, pushing them down, commanding Derek to push them aside and lie on the bed. He opened Derek's legs and helped himself to what he had been thinking about during the entire game.

"Derek, I want you so bad," he said.

Derek felt the same way about Craig. He loved Craig. He wanted him on him and in him.

The sensation of Craig's lips as they sensuously slid upward along and around his cock was more arousing to Derek tonight than it had been their first time together, which had been over-the-top.

Derek opened himself to Craig, begging for his touch. He pulled at Craig's hair, and said in a loud whisper, "Craig, I'm a bottom."

Craig looked up at Derek, and the sight of his dick inside Craig's mouth almost caused Derek to explode. "Yes, it's true. I want you, in that way."

Derek didn't have to make it any plainer than that. In his aroused eagerness, Craig over-prepared himself and his lover for what he had just heard from his lover's lips. Derek lifted his legs, and Craig pulled them up and onto his shoulders. "Uh," Derek moaned, not expecting to be entered quite so forcefully. He immediately relaxed as the pleasurable feeling that his body craved took over. "Oh, baby, that's it," Derek urged.

Craig held onto Derek's legs, pulling him and thrusting into him harder and harder, and very soon, Derek was moaning as burst after burst of his own warm cum covered his body. "Ohh, man," Craig moaned, watching this erotic sight.

"You did that to me, Craig," Derek moaned.

Derek soon felt the warm cum of his lover begin to fill him, and Craig's entire body began to shake. "Fill me up, baby," Derek said, watching the face of his lover as his sweet cum exploded forcefully into him. "Damn, that was good," Derek said, pulling Craig down over him.

"Derek, I love you," Craig said, the words unexpected by Derek.

Derek held him tightly. "Craig, I love you, too," he said, dreading what he had to do next.

"I need to talk to you, Craig."

Craig lifted up and looked at Derek. The expression on his face reminded Derek of a frightened child being confronted by a parent. "What's wrong?"

"Oh, baby, don't worry. I meant it when I said I love you."

Craig rolled onto his back and lay beside Derek on the bed. "Okay, what did I do?"

Derek leaned up on his elbow and turned toward Craig. He ran his hand across Craig's chest. "It's your jersey, Craig. It says Craig on the back, but it should have your last name, right? Your name isn't Craig Craig, is it?"

Craig turned and looked at Derek. "No, it isn't. It's Craig Neil, but your dad somehow arranged for me to be Neil Craig. He thought that it would avoid favoritism, you know, O'Neil is so close to Neil."

Derek pushed his hair back. "Speaking of Dad, what's the deal, anyway?"

Craig looked at him. "What do you mean?"

"Whenever I mention you to Mom or Dad, they clam up. It's like they know some deep dark secret about you that they don't want me to know. They care a lot about you, Craig, but I'm not sure they want us to be involved with each other."

Craig closed his eyes. He had promised Mary and Tom that he wouldn't say a word about his past, and had even agreed to change his name.

Craig opened his eyes, and once again Derek saw a scared little boy in those eyes.

"I'm sorry, Craig. I really don't mean to upset you. I just feel that I'm missing something here."

Trey's sudden crying immediately changed the focus of the conversation. "Oh," Craig said, starting to get up.

"No, no, you rest, Craig. You've had a long day. Let me get him."

Craig nodded, and relaxed on the bed. He could hear Derek singing to Trey, off key, but Craig thought it was sweet nonetheless.

Derek walked in with Trey in his arms, happily sucking formula from his bottle. "Poor kid," Craig said, as Derek walked in the room.

"Why do you say that?"

"Because he couldn't escape the grossly off key music," Craig teased.

"You heard that?"

"Unfortunately."

"I was a Titan, not a musician," Derek said, in his own defense.

Derek sat on the bed with Trey. "I'm glad you're here, Derek. Trey likes you. He deserves someone like you."

"But he has you, Craig."

"I know, but maybe he deserves more than just me."

Derek knew that there was still more to this story, to this connection between Craig and his parents, but didn't know where to start. "How do you know my father, Craig?"

"Oh, Derek, can't you just leave it alone?"

Trey finished his bottle and Derek burped him, and then stood up and rocked him back and forth. "No, Craig, I can't leave it alone," he said.

Craig sat up and looked at Derek. Then he began to laugh.

"What?" Derek said.

"It's really hard to talk seriously when you are rocking or swaying, or whatever you call that little dance that you're doing."

Derek smiled. "Okay, laugh all you want, but keep talking," he said.

"Don't you think your parents should tell you about this?" Craig asked.

Derek spoke quietly to not awaken Trey. "Yes, I do, but they won't. They just get this weird look on their face whenever I bring it up."

Craig turned over onto his stomach.

"Don't think you can distract me with the view of your gorgeous ass," Derek jokingly warned.

Craig clinched and unclenched his very well toned butt several times. "Is it working?" he teased.

"Yes, but I will try to control myself," Derek teased back.

Six

Brother of Mine

"It was a long time ago, Derek. I was a freshman in college."

Craig turned over onto his back and looked at Derek. "I got sick that year. I had some kind of virus that made me extremely dehydrated. My kidneys shut down. I needed a new one. Mom wasn't a compatible donor."

"I'm so sorry, Craig. What about your father?"

"I never had a father. I mean, I had a father, but I never knew my real father. My stepfather left us when I was just a baby."

Derek laid Trey down in his crib, and climbed onto the bed next to Craig. He lay on his side, pulled Craig's arm around him, and ran his hand up and down Craig's chest. "This is nice, Derek."

"I love your chest, Craig." Derek snuggled closer. "I love all of you."

Craig sighed. "Anyway, I was so sick that I didn't know what was going on at the time. I didn't know all of this until just a few months ago, Derek, I swear."

Craig's heart started beating faster. Derek looked up at him. "Hey, it's okay. Whatever it is." Craig continued. "I guess that Mom couldn't get pregnant by her husband, and so they went to a sperm bank. When I got sick, Mom did everything she could to find out who the donor was, but too many years had passed, and they could only get as far as 'possibilities' of who my father could be, based on my kidney parameters. Back then, they didn't have all this technical DNA stuff, you know. And, sperm donors did not want to be identified." Derek thought he heard Craig's voice crack. He continued to look at him. "There were quite a few 'possibilities', but only one came forward."

Derek closed his eyes. "And that 'one' was Tom O'Neil, my father, right?"

B.K. Wright   279

"Yeah. He wasn't a perfect match, but he met four of the six necessary criteria to be a match, according to the surgeon. He saved my life, Derek."

"So that's why they didn't want me to get involved with you, or at least it's why they were a little afraid of us getting involved."

"I'm sorry, Derek," Craig whispered.

Derek crawled on top of Craig. He kissed his mouth. "Sorry for what, being alive?"

"No, don't you get it? We might have the same father, and that means we might be brothers," Craig said, in almost a shout.

Derek continued to stroke the hair on Craig's chest. "But the chance is what, one in twenty?" Derek asked.

"I think that's about right, and you can't deny that we have this chemistry thing between us." Craig paused, and then continued, "My manly scent turns you on," he teased.

"Maybe I just had my nose stuck in your armpit a little too long," Derek said, and kissed him on the chin.

"You know you want me," Craig said, still in a teasing tone.

"I know I do, too," Derek agreed. "And, I'm not ashamed to say that I must be doing something for you, too. There is something hard and hot, and ready to be eaten poking me in the stomach."

Craig rolled Derek off of him, and then rolled himself on top of Derek. He sat up, holding Derek's hands. "You mean this old thing," he teased, thrusting his hard cock forward.

Derek looked at Craig's cock head that seemed to be staring at him. "Yeah, that old thing," he said, licking his lips. "Come and give this old man a little taste of your hot football cock."

Craig leaned forward and scooted up on Derek. He continued to hold Derek's hands out to his sides while he offered the soft mushroom head of his cock to Derek's parted lips. "Mm," Derek said, sucking on the head, and then taking the rest of Craig's cock in little bites as it was fed to him.

Craig came forward even more, leaning over Derek's head, moaning, and rocking back and forth as he moved his cock in and out of Derek's mouth. "Oh, damn, Derek," he moaned. Derek loved having Craig in control. He was most aroused when he was the submissive one. He was a bottom, and not ashamed to admit it. "Damn, Derek. How much do you want?" Derek sucked hard on Craig's cock, forcing Craig down to him even more, almost causing him to fall forward. "Okay. I get it. You want it all."

Craig held onto Derek's head as he thrust his cock into his mouth. Craig was soon holding on more than he was thrusting. Derek was sucking his cock hard. "Oh, no, oh, shit," Craig shouted, and couldn't stop the flow of cum that burst out of his dick. He grabbed Derek's hair, unable to move with Derek's mouth firmly holding his dick, and with the hard force of his own orgasm. He leaned down over Derek, sweat forming on his body, panting like a dog. "I think my knees went numb," he said, looking at his soft dick, drained and limp as it lay on Derek's chest. "Really, then this would be a good time to…"

Before Craig knew what had happened, he was flat on his back with his legs in the air. "Hey, I thought you were a bottom," he weakly protested. "I am, but variety is the spice of life, right?" Craig was soon moaning with the well moistened fingers of Derek deep inside him. He closed his eyes, and then abruptly opened them when he felt the pressure and then pleasure of Derek's cock easing into him. "Oh, man, it's been too long since I've been here," Craig moaned. "Give it to me," he said, opening himself fully to Derek. "You mean like this?"

Derek's cock slid all the way into Craig, and he looked at Derek. "Just like that," he said, and let Derek have his way with him. "Shit, man," he moaned, reaching up and holding onto Derek's arms. "Harder," he urged, not once, but with each thrust of Derek's cock.

Derek held Craig's legs, and gave him the works. Craig's head had been pushed back over the side of the bed by the time Derek gasped, and then grunted. He came full force into Craig. Craig threw his arms over his head and over the side of the bed. "Oh, yeah, man, fill me up." Derek filled him up and more. Derek's cum was on the bed and on him when the last of it was released.

Derek pulled Craig by his legs back onto the bed and covered his body with his own. Craig could just barely breathe when Derek's mouth covered his. Craig's arms held Derek and they kissed for as long as they possibly could, until they both had to break for air. Derek lay with his head on Craig's chest, playing with Craig's nipples. "I love sucking these things," he admitted. "I love sucking other things, too." "Shit, Derek. You can just go and go and go, can't you?" "When I'm with the right person," he teased.

"I guess I interrupted our 'serious' conversation, didn't I?" Craig asked.

"Yes, you did. But don't worry. We can pick up where we left off."

Craig sighed. "That's what I was afraid you would say."

"So, I guess Dad surprised Mom with what he had done," Derek said.

"I didn't ask them that, Derek. I still can't believe how good they have been to me."

"I'm not surprised, Craig. They've always been like that."

"Even so, Derek, I feel extremely fortunate."

Derek continued to run his hand along Craig's chest, separating the hairs with his fingers and gently pulling them between. "I'm feeling pretty fortunate right now, too," Derek said.

"I know what you mean," Craig agreed.

Derek and Craig fell asleep where they lay, Derek's head on Craig's chest, and his fingers separating Craig's chest hairs. Derek and Craig slept soundly until they heard the demanding cries of Trey the next morning.

Derek and Craig sat up and looked around. "Oh, shit. It's morning." Derek sat up, and Craig jumped off of the bed to get Trey. Derek yawned and walked slowly to the kitchen for Trey's bottle. "You home today, Craig?"

"No. What I am is late."

Derek carried the bottle back in to Trey. "I got it, Craig. Do what you have to do. We'll be fine."

Craig made himself and Derek a pot of very strong coffee and got ready to go back to Denver. "Thanks, Derek."

"Don't worry about it. We're fine."

Craig gave Derek a quick kiss goodbye, and walked out the door. Derek sat down, holding Trey, and almost fell asleep. "Rruff, rruff," Sandy barked, reminding Derek that Trey wasn't the only one in the room that needed him.

Derek opened the door for Sandy, just as Mary was coming up the front steps. "Oh, hi, Mom," Derek said, surprised. "Craig just left."

"I know, dear. Are you okay?"

"Oh, sure. I've got this whole baby thing down now."

Mary walked in and sat down. "Derek, your father and I should have told you about Craig. Do you want to know how we know him?"

Derek sat down in the chair opposite his mother. "Craig told me about the kidney, if that's what you mean."

"It is, Derek, and we should have told you. Back then, though, people didn't talk about things like that. Your father and I have never talked about why he 'donated', and I guess that's not important. Sometimes there are things that a wife is better off not knowing about her husband. But, we do feel responsible for Craig. You know how we feel about family."

Derek nodded. He knew how important family was to both of them.

"And, if Craig is your father's son, then Trey is our grandson. But, that would also mean that Craig is your brother."

Mary stopped talking and looked at Derek. "I just wanted you to know. Your father and I both wanted you to know."

"Thanks, Mom, but Craig and I are definitely involved now, and we both love this little guy," he said, looking down at Trey. "Perhaps there are things in this world that were meant to remain unknown," Derek added.

"Well, that little guy is very lucky," Mary said. "I'll be going now, dear. I'll be home today if you need me. I'm not needed at the library today."

Derek thanked his mother, and then watched her leave. Sandy came back in just as Mary was leaving. "Well, buddy, I think we are going to be right here for awhile. How 'bout that?" Sandy was too busy eating and drinking to pay any attention to Derek. His needs were simple. "Shall we try the swing again, baby Trey?"

Derek started Trey happily swinging and babbling his sweet baby talk, and then he lay down on the sofa and rested. What a night! Derek thought about what his mother had said and more importantly, what his father had done. He would love to know what had possessed his father to donate his sperm and why he had not told his mother that he had donated his sperm, but that was a long time ago. Then Derek realized that he didn't even know Craig's age, so he didn't know exactly when his father had donated his sperm.

Derek was almost asleep when he forced himself to get up. I can't fall asleep with Trey here, he reminded himself. He drank a cup of strong coffee and began to come to life.

Seven

Three's a Family

Derek was rocking Trey when Craig walked in the door. "Is he sick?" Craig immediately asked.

"No, he's fine. I just like holding him, I guess," Derek admitted.

"You two look good together," Craig admitted.

"So, big day? Derek asked. Craig plopped down on the sofa.

"Yeah. Coach never lets up." He leaned back on the sofa. "Derek, where are we?"

"What do you mean, Craig?"

"I mean, I need to know. I'm on the road so much, and I've got Trey to worry about. I mean, you can walk out the door any time. I need to know that Trey is safe when I'm not here."

Derek was somewhat offended by Craig's comment. "I would never leave Trey alone, you know," he said, in his own defense.

Craig turned his head to look at Derek. "I know you wouldn't. But Trey is a baby, and babies become attached to people. He loves Mary and Tom, and I know they will be here. He's going to get attached to you, too, Derek, if he hasn't already. It wouldn't be fair to Trey if I had different people coming and going all the time."

Derek looked at him. "By people, you mean lovers, and by lovers, you specifically mean me, right?"

Craig closed his eyes. He was exhausted, which wasn't helping his mood. "I guess it is, Derek. I've just had too much of the 'unknown' in my life."

Derek held Trey close to his chest and kissed the top of his head. Then he moved closer to Craig. "Look, Craig. I love you, and you love me. I'm happy with that. I'm not a one night stand. I think the three of us make a great family. Look at this little guy."

Craig looked at Trey lying happily against his lover's chest. Then Sandy came up to Derek, not wanting to be left out of the attention giving and getting. Craig welcomed Sandy onto his lap. "Well, Derek, I hate to correct you, but I think the four of us make a great family."

When Derek's lips met Craig's, Craig knew for certain that the four of them made a great family.

This print book, as well as additional Beau to Beau Books, is also available in ebook form from the following:

Amazon Kindle Stores
Barnes & Noble
Apple iBookstores
Google Play
Sony Reader Store
Kobo ebooks
Rainbow ebooks
All Romance ebooks
Bookstrand
Coffeetime Romance

* 9 7 8 1 6 1 8 4 5 1 8 9 7 *